AIMEE NICOLE WALKER

GROUND ZERO

ZERO HOUR

AIMEE NICOLE WALKER

Ground zero, noun: the center or origin of rapid, intense, or violent activity or change.

Heat, humidity, and homicide are things veteran detective Sawyer Key expects to encounter on his first day with the Savannah Police Department, but the hostile reception from his new partner catches him by surprise. Sawyer isn't a stranger to heartache and recognizes that Royce Locke is a wounded man who's reeling from a devastating loss. Relentless and patient in all things, Sawyer is determined to make the new partnership work.

Savannah, Georgia is known for her quirky people, oak trees draped in Spanish moss, and antebellum architecture. Beneath the Southern charm and hospitality, festering hatred and violence is soaring with the summer temperatures. Locke and Key find themselves at the epicenter when their first case involves the death of a former shock jock who appears to be the victim of vigilante justice.

Opposites in nearly every way, the two detectives set aside their differences to take back their city and restore law and order. From this reluctant truce, an intense attraction grows that will either tighten or shatter their tenuous bond. Falling for his partner spells inevitable disaster, but Sawyer's always been a sucker for wounded things. Sawyer could be the key to the life Royce has always wanted, if he's brave enough to trust him. The fuse is lit, the clock is running, and the zero hour is upon them. Tick tock.

Ground Zero is the first book in the Zero Hour series, which follows Locke and Key's investigations and evolving relationship. Ground Zero has a happy-for-now ending with no cliffhanger. It contains mature language and sexual content intended for adults 18 and older.

Ground Zero (Zero Hour Book 1)
Copyright © 2019 Aimee Nicole Walker

aimeenicolewalker@blogspot.com

ISBN: 978-1-948273-15-2

This is a work of fiction. Names, characters, places, and incidents either are the product of the author's imagination or are used fictitiously, and any resemblance to the actual person, living or dead, business establishments, events, or locales is entirely coincidental.

Photographer © Wander Aguiar—www.wanderaguiar.com
Cover art © Jay Aheer of Simply Defined Art—www.simplydefinedart.com

Editing provided by Miranda Vescio of V8 Editing and Proofreading—www.facebook.com/V8Editing

Proofreading provided by Judy Zweifel of Judy's Proofreading—www.judysproofreading.com
And Jill Wexler

Interior Design and Formatting provided by Stacey Blake of Champagne Book Design—www.champagnebookdesign.com

Copyright and Trademark Acknowledgments

The author acknowledges the copyrights and trademarked status and trademark owners of the trademarks and copyrights mentioned in this work of fiction.

To Hailey Turner and her Bones kitty

Hailey, you make every day a better one with your wonderful sense of humor, kitty pics, and hilarious memes. Thank you so much for letting Sawyer borrow your precious Bones kitty. He was a king among felines, an expert at snatching bread and hearts. I am blessed to know you and call you a friend. xoxoxo

GROUND ZERO

CHAPTER 1

HEAT, HUMIDITY, AND HOMICIDE.

The story of his life, Sawyer Key silently quipped. What would be the subtitle? *A Typical Summer Day in Savannah, Georgia? One Dumpster Fire to the Next? Navigating Hostile Times While Maintaining Humanity?* Sawyer recalled the pair of smoldering gray eyes that had tracked his every move when he arrived at the Midtown precinct. They were certainly hostile as hell.

"What the fuck?" Sawyer asked out loud when he saw the large crowd gathered at his crime scene. Flipping on his sirens to disburse the throng of people, he pulled up to the barricade patrol had set up. A strong sense of foreboding settled in his gut as he made his way to one of the officers assigned to keep unauthorized personnel from stepping beyond the police tape. This level of attention was never a good sign.

"Well, hello, sugar. I haven't seen you around here before. Are you new?"

The unprofessional greeting caught Sawyer off guard, and he just barely suppressed the urge to cringe. He had approached the female officer at a crime scene, not a bar. *A fresh start, Key. Don't make enemies on day one. Let it slide.* The detective's shield clipped to his belt was shiny, new, and felt as heavy as the dread in his stomach. He wasn't a stranger to law enforcement, but it was his first day on the job as a detective with the Savannah PD.

"That's Detective Sugar," he said, covering his irritation with humor. "Most call me Sawyer or Detective Key though. I'm with the Major Crimes Unit." The woman whose badge identified her as Officer Andrews extended her hand and he shook it. "I'm meeting my partner here."

"Oh," the blonde woman said, raking her eyes over his dove gray linen pants, lavender dress shirt, and amethyst-colored tie before meeting his eyes again. "I've heard of you." *I just bet she has.* "I'm Keeley Andrews. It's nice to meet you. Detective Locke is already inside. Good luck," she said then snorted.

It wasn't the first time Sawyer had been warned that morning about the potential lukewarm greeting he could expect to receive from his new, unwilling partner, Royce Locke. The same guy with the hostile gray eyes. Sawyer had listened to Chief Ellen Rigby speak about Locke for forty-five minutes when he reported for duty, which was why Locke and Key were meeting at a crime scene instead of at the precinct as planned. Chief Rigby couldn't disguise her respect for Locke's performance on the job while, at the same time, she lamented about some of his methods.

"He never breaks the law," she'd been quick to tell Sawyer as she fixed herself a cup of coffee and offered him one of her bear claw pastries. "My wife makes these, knowing I can't resist them." She patted her curvy hips. "It's starting to catch up to me. Everything starts going to hell for a woman once she hits middle age while you men keep getting better."

Sawyer had thought it was an odd pivot from Locke and his borderline unlawful ways to her expanding hips, but he was starting to see there was a method to her madness. Ellen Rigby liked to keep people on their toes and to make sure they were paying attention. Sawyer also thought there was nothing hellish looking about the woman sitting across the desk studying him with hawkish, blue eyes that probably didn't miss anything. Her medium brown curls were devoid of gray hair, either by genetics or from chemicals, and her makeup-free skin was nearly flawless except for a few laugh lines around her mouth and eyes. Sawyer thought they added to her attractiveness instead of aging her. As for her hips, she had an hourglass figure that looked neither too big nor too small for her height.

"I can't resist the pastries just like I couldn't resist her all those years ago, even though I knew it could cost me my family and my career. I played hard, and I fought to win."

"And here you are," Sawyer said.

"And here I am. Now I play for keeps."

Sawyer accepted the pastry with a smile then nearly choked on the powdered sugar that exploded into his mouth on the first bite.

"Sherry is a bit heavy-handed with the powdered sugar," Chief Rigby had said with a wry smile. "I don't think a 'dusting of sugar' is in her vocabulary. She's from New Orleans, so it's in her blood."

Sawyer made the connection right away because he'd choked hard after taking his first bite of a beignet during his only visit to the city. He'd never eaten a bear claw before and thought the flaky, buttery pastry, almond paste, and slivered almonds were a lovely combination.

Ellen Rigby's final words to him after their chat over coffee and a pastry still lingered in his head when he arrived at the crime scene in Riverside.

"I wish you much luck, Detective. Locke's going to do everything in his power to push you away. Don't let him; he needs you."

"Nice meeting you too, Officer Andrews," Sawyer said before striding up the walkway leading to the porch. "Detective Sawyer Key with MCU." He flashed his badge to the officer assigned to the front door tasked with making sure only approved personnel gained access to the house. Too many people in and out of a crime scene not only risked the admissibility of forensic evidence in court, but it wasted time when the lab spent hours testing evidence only to find out the

DNA on sunflower seeds spat out at the scene belonged to one of the officers and not the killer.

"Officer Robert Jones, but everyone calls me Bobby. Booties and gloves on, Detective. Sign in here, please," he said in a monotone.

Accepting the clipboard, Sawyer filled out his name, badge number, and the time he arrived on the scene. He noted his partner had signed in a full twenty minutes earlier, which meant the call came in not long after Sawyer sat down in the chief's office.

"Were you the responding officer?" Sawyer asked Officer Jones, noticing the black powder residue all along the white door casing left behind when a CSI tech dusted for fingerprints.

"No, sir. Officer Diego Fuentes was the first one on the scene. He's inside with Detective Locke, the ME, and the crime scene techs."

"Wow, it didn't take long to get everyone to the scene."

"This crime will make national news, and the media will start showing up within the hour, if not...sooner." Jones's voice trailed off, and Sawyer turned to see what had caught his attention. Four news vans pulled in nearly simultaneously—two came in from the north, and two came from the south, meeting in the middle. Each van jockeyed for the closest spot to the Riverside residence, which Sawyer noted was nice but didn't look like the kind of home belonging to someone important enough to warrant the frenzied feeling in the air when the doors of the vans burst open and cameramen and reporters exploded into action.

"Who lives here?" Sawyer asked Officer Jones as he slid the booties over his Gucci leather loafers.

"Lived," Jones corrected. "Died from blunt force trauma to the head. They didn't tell you who the victim was?" The more they conversed, the more the officer relaxed around Sawyer.

"No," Sawyer said. The ominous feeling from when he arrived intensified as he snapped nitrile gloves in place. He'd hope to settle in to his new job with as little drama as possible, but it appeared he wouldn't be so lucky.

"Ever heard of Roland Putzinski?"

Sawyer's eyebrows lifted toward his hairline. "Who hasn't heard of The Putz?" Roland Putzinski was a disgraced shock-jock of the vilest kind. He hated anyone who wasn't a white, straight, Christian, or male. He'd pushed the limits on his nationally syndicated radio show for decades before he went too far and was fired after his incendiary rhetoric incited a gay-bashing incident in Kissimmee, Florida. "*This* is his house?"

"I would've expected him to live someplace grander too, but he probably couldn't afford it after losing the civil lawsuit filed by Micah Gasaway's family." Sawyer remembered the story well. Micah had been the victim of the hate crime and had spent two months in a coma before passing away in the aftermath of the brutal beating. "Six million dollars is a lot of money to pay in punitive damages." It wasn't enough; it could never be enough to pay for the harm the man had caused Micah's family. "He probably should've found a home in a gated community in one of the less pricey neighborhoods."

"Well, I'm sure he's living in a gated community now," Sawyer said dryly. Jones snorted, catching Sawyer's meaning. *May he forever burn in the hell of his own making.* "Good to meet you, Officer Jones."

"Likewise, Detective." He glanced over his shoulder then returned his cool green eyes to meet Sawyer's. "Good luck to you, sir."

"That's the third time someone has said those words to me in less than an hour."

"You'll probably be hearing it every day for the rest of your career with the SPD."

Sawyer sighed, patted Jones's shoulder, then opened the door and stepped inside the home. The foyer, living room on the right, and dining room on the left were immaculately clean and empty of police personnel. Sawyer heard voices in the rear of the home but took his time looking around the space. A cop could learn a lot about a victim by studying their surroundings and the types of things they held dear in their lives. Were there family photos on the walls, knickknack collections on shelves or behind glass cabinet doors, or books or DVDs lying around offering clues to the victim's relationships, hobbies, intellectual level, and choice of entertainment?

Sawyer noted the furniture, although clean and tidy, looked to be old and well-used. Not what he'd expect from a man who had made millions on his previous show and from book sales. People actually paid nearly thirty bucks a pop to read his hateful musings. Above the nondescript brown sofa hung a large painting showing a white man's fist gripping a lightning bolt next to an ornate cross. Below the image were the words: God's chosen race. On another wall was a poster of a naked, buxom blonde sprawled in the center of a bed. The only thing shielding her vagina from the viewer's eyes was her hand. The words beneath the image read: Real Men Eat Pussy.

It was a miracle you lived this long.

Facing the poster was a worn-out recliner, and beside it was a side table with an open bottle of lotion, a wad of used tissues, and a box of Kleenex. It didn't take a detective to know what The Putz used the tissues and lotion for when kicking back in his recliner.

A shiver of revulsion rippled through Sawyer, compelling him out of the room and down the hall toward the voices. The coppery smell of blood and the unforgettable aroma of death got stronger with each step deeper into the home. The hallway led to a smallish kitchen where a crime scene tech looked up from swabbing blood droplets on the floor. Based on the pattern and spacing of the droplets, Sawyer surmised they'd landed there after falling off the murder weapon.

"Oh, hey. You're Detective Key," she said, appraising him from head to toe. Unlike Officer Andrews, Sawyer only saw curiosity in the tech's eyes. He tried not to be a vain man, but he knew his six-two, broad-shouldered frame, dark hair, and dark eyes appealed to men and women alike.

"I am. And you are?"

"CSI Griffin, but my friends call me Casey."

"Can you tell me where I can find my partner, CSI Griffin?"

She smiled wryly. Did she expect Sawyer to consider her a friend within the first five seconds of meeting her? Griffin raised a hand and pointed over her shoulder. "The hallway leads back to his home office slash recording studio."

"Recording studio?" Sawyer asked. "I thought he lost his radio show."

"He did, but you can't keep a vile man down. Putz started a podcast bitching about the evils of political correctness and how the women's movement has set our country back. There was nothing scarier to him than a woman who demanded equal pay and refused to be sexually harassed in the workplace. Putz didn't like our kind either."

"Our kind?" Sawyer asked with a raised brow. Then he noticed the rainbow lanyard holding her ID badge.

"Oh shit. That was totally inappropriate of me to say. I read about your battle with the sheriff's department. I hope you'll enjoy working for SPD a lot more."

"Thanks. I guess I shouldn't be surprised Putz found a new way to spew his venom," he said, steering them back to a more comfortable topic.

"Someone put a stop to his vitriol once and for all," Griffin said, returning her focus to her task. "Good luck, Key."

Annoyance sparked inside him, but he shoved it aside and headed down the hallway to get the awkward initial introduction out of the way. Maybe Locke would go easy on him with witnesses around.

The office was much bigger than Sawyer had anticipated. The area consisted of a large office space with a soundproof booth at one end. He stood in the doorway taking in the quiet effectiveness of the technicians photographing the room, sketching the scene, and looking for evidence while the ME and Sawyer's new partner squatted on either side of the prone body. Sawyer couldn't help but notice the way the dark denim clung to Locke's firm ass but forced his eyes upward to avoid additional awkwardness should he get caught ogling him. A tall, hulk of a man he presumed to be Officer Fuentes stood behind the ME looking over her shoulder.

"Someone really hated this man," the officer said. "I've never seen such a brutal attack before."

"There's a lot of passion in this slaying," the ME said. "His skull is so battered I don't think I'll be able to pinpoint the murder weapon unless the killer was kind enough to leave it behind."

The officer lifted his head to look around the room and noticed Sawyer standing in the doorway. "Oh, hey," he said. "You must be Detective Key." His Southern drawl sounded more Texan than Georgian.

"I am," Sawyer said, noticing the way Locke's body tensed. Sawyer turned his attention to the officer who approached with an outstretched hand.

"Diego Fuentes. It's good to meet you. I've heard a lot about you."

"Yeah?" Sawyer asked, lifting an inquisitive brow. Diego's handshake was firm and friendly as was the expression on his face. If Sawyer wasn't mistaken, the smile pulling on Fuentes's lips was extra friendly, flirty even. He would've been tempted to find out what kind of things Fuentes had heard about him, but he was distracted by Locke rising to his full height.

He was blond, six feet of muscle, broad shoulders that tested the mettle of the black cotton T-shirt he wore, and enough fury vibrating off him to choke a horse. Sawyer swallowed hard with the realization his job was going to be much more difficult than he'd realized. Suddenly, all the "good luck" wishes he'd taken as jokes made sense.

"All good things," Fuentes said.

Locke turned, and their eyes met for the first time. Sawyer nearly sucked in a breath from the intensity in his partner's gray eyes. Every warning he'd received—wild, rebellious, obstinate—showed in Locke's stormy gaze. Of all the things he'd been warned about, no one had alluded to the emotion that struck Sawyer like a fist to his gut. *Wounded.*

Wounded animals were known to strike out and bite anyone who came near, even the ones who only wanted to help them. Sawyer had seen the same look on the gray kitten he'd found hiding behind his trash can on the worst night of his life. All he wanted to do was pick up the hissing ball of fur and cuddle him against his chest, but sharp teeth and claws met his every attempt. It took weeks of calmly sitting on the stoop while the kitten ate the food Sawyer provided before he trusted him enough to allow a single scratch behind one ear, another week before Sawyer could run a hand over his bony spine, and another two before Sawyer could pick him up and feel him purr against his chest.

Sawyer instinctively knew Royce Locke was the most wounded thing—man or beast—he'd encountered in his life. If he ventured too close, Locke's teeth and claws would cut deeper than anything he'd ever experienced, scarring him, and his venom would poison his soul. Sawyer's brain told him to turn around and walk away before it was too late, but the man who ached to heal wounded things couldn't turn away from the challenge glaring at him.

"It's about fucking time," Locke said tersely, striking the first blow.

CHAPTER 2

STIFLING HIS IRRITATION, SAWYER CALMLY SAID, "SORRY. MY MEETING with Chief Rigby went longer than I expected." Which was especially odd considering she was the one who sought out Sawyer for the position, not the other way around. "So, Roland Putzinski, huh?"

"Most of him anyway," Locke replied, the scowl still marring his handsome face. Then he turned his back on Sawyer and returned to studying the body, leaving him to follow or fuck off. Sawyer chose the former.

Instead of crouching again, Locke remained standing, his body coiled tight with tension, reminding Sawyer of a jungle cat on the verge of pouncing.

Ignoring Locke's brusque non-welcome, Sawyer moved to stand beside him. "Good morning, Dr. Fawkes," Sawyer said to the medical examiner as he approached.

"Good morning, Detective Key. I'd shake your hand, but I'm…" She lifted her bloody, nitrile-gloved hands. "It's always nice to see you."

"Likewise."

Sawyer felt Locke's scrutiny as he looked between Dr. Fawkes and him. He figured Chief Rigby would've at least given Locke the rundown on his background when she informed him he was getting a new partner. Maybe Locke wouldn't be so pissed if he knew Sawyer had seven years of experience as a detective with the Chatham County Sheriff's Department. Dr. Fawkes served as the medical examiner for the entire county, not just the Savannah Police Department, and she'd worked with Sawyer on many homicides during his tenure with CCSD.

Sawyer ignored Locke and focused on the victim before looking at the gore inside the sound booth. Blood and brain matter sprayed the soundproofing material on the walls and ceiling in the booth. Sawyer noted several teeth and bone fragments in the pooled blood on the floor. "Christ. Are you even able to make a positive ID of the body?"

"The disgusting tattoo on his right forearm matches the one seen in all of his publicity photos," Dr. Fawkes said, not bothering to hide her revulsion. Sure enough, the tattoo on the victim's right arm matched the God's Chosen Race symbols in the painting above the couch.

"I wonder if we'll find his other repulsive message tattooed somewhere on his body?" Sawyer asked.

Dr. Fawkes snorted. "I'll be sure to let you know later."

"How do we know this isn't one of his zealous fans with a matching tattoo?"

"Excellent point," Dr. Fawkes said, while Locke silently absorbed the conversation. "Facial recognition is out of the question with open and depressed skull fractures such as these. I can try to match dental records to his remaining teeth, but I'm not hopeful. DNA is our surest bet, but we'll need something to compare it to. The techs will grab his toothbrush and hairbrush, and I'll try to extract a viable sample."

"He's been arrested before, so we can match his fingerprints," Locke said, finally breaking his silence.

"Good to know," Fawkes remarked.

Sawyer turned to his partner, no longer willing to be ignored. "Who called in the homicide?"

"The better question is who *didn't* call it in," Locke replied dryly, his eyes still focused on Dr. Fawkes's activities. He finally turned those turbulent gray eyes to Sawyer, sneer still firmly in place. "The Putz's gruesome death was recorded during his latest podcast, which went live this morning. As soon as his equally vile fans heard his murder, calls started flooding in."

"Any sign of forced entry?" he inquired.

"No." Locke's tone was devoid of any inflection, but Sawyer would take the robotic replies over being ignored any day of the week.

Dr. Fawkes removed a thermometer from the small incision she'd cut in Putz's abdomen to measure his liver temperature. "Based on the liver temperature and stages of rigor and livor mortis, I'm going to estimate his time of death to be twelve hours ago."

Sawyer looked at his watch and saw it was a quarter to ten. "Around twenty-one forty-five then?"

"That's my best guess."

Locke finally turned toward Sawyer, folded his arms across his impressive chest, and addressed him directly. The scowl was still firmly in place, but his tone was less pissed off and more resigned to his fate. "The sound booth was constructed to block outside noises from disturbing his recording, which meant he didn't hear his assailant enter his house or his office."

"This home is immaculately kept. The front rooms aren't disturbed in any way, neither are his kitchen or even his office," Sawyer said, gesturing to the tidy desk where the only thing out of place was the black residue left behind after CSI techs dusted for prints. "As angry as the assailant was, there are no signs they disturbed or removed anything from the victim's home."

"The motive definitely wasn't robbery." An African American tech wearing stylish black-rimmed glasses approached with a wallet in his gloved hands. He extended the black, leather trifold wallet with The Putz's symbols embroidered on the front. "I can't say all the man's credit cards are in the wallet, but there are no empty slots."

Sawyer opened the wallet and noticed all the slots were filled, including the one with a plastic window showing Roland Putzinski's license with his arrogant, smirking face. He turned the wallet upright and whistled when he saw how much money was inside it. Thumbing through the twenties and fifties, he said, "There has to be at least five hundred dollars in here. I've never seen a robbery where the assailant only took part of the money and none of the credit cards, but I guess it's possible."

"Usually it's the reverse," Locke said when he moved closer to peer inside the wallet. "A lot of times assailants stage robberies to make it look like a home invasion gone wrong. Not this guy."

"Or gal," Sawyer added, trying to ignore how good Locke smelled. The dark blond stubble dusting his partner's jaw and accentuating his lush, full lips meant the sandalwood, amber, and vanilla scent didn't come from the man's aftershave. Cologne? Body wash? Not that it mattered—or should matter, anyway. "It doesn't take brute strength to bash someone's skull in with a blunt object."

"True. It's hard to tell which minority group of people hated The Putz more," Locke agreed.

"It looks like our perp got in and out without taking anything and without detection," Sawyer surmised.

"CSI is going over the back yard with a fine-tooth comb, and uniformed officers are canvassing the neighborhood."

"Detectives," an animated voice said from behind them. Locke and Sawyer turned at once to look at the officer in the doorway. "CSI found the murder weapon in the trash cans out back."

Sawyer and Locke started for the door at the same time. Sawyer stopped and gestured for Locke to precede him and fell in step behind him. Sawyer's eyes were drawn to his partner's firm ass once more, but he didn't dare permit them to linger. His gaze traveled the length of Locke's legs and noticed he had excellent taste in footwear. Sawyer had the same pair of black leather Bruno Magli boots in his closet. He also couldn't keep himself from appreciating the way Locke's shoulder holster accentuated the muscles in his back and shoulders.

"Finding anything exciting, Casey?" Locke asked the CSI tech when they walked into the kitchen. He was obviously one of Casey's "friends." CSI Griffin had moved on from swabbing blood droplets to dusting empty beer bottles for prints. It wasn't likely the killer stopped to drink a beer, but stranger things had happened. It was better to leave no stone unturned than end up overlooking a key piece of evidence.

"No, sir," Griffin said. "All the excitement is in the back yard and I hear some guffawing coming from the other side of the house. Techs must've found something juicy that doesn't pertain to the crime. Boys," she said then rolled her eyes.

Sawyer couldn't imagine a situation that would justify crime techs laughing at the scene of a gruesome homicide. If a videographer were on the scene, their laughter could taint the jury's opinion of the investigation if the footage had to be played in court. Sawyer glanced over at Locke who wore a similar perplexed expression on his face.

"I'll check it out," Sawyer told Locke. "You head out and take a look at the murder weapon."

Locke's expression changed from confused to irritated in a blink of an eye. He was either still pissed about Sawyer's presence, irritated he had the gall to take the lead, or both. Sawyer didn't care nor did he back down from the glare Locke gave him. After a few seconds of awkward silence, Locke turned and walked away without saying a word.

Breathe in. Hold. Release.

"Hmmm," Griffin said. "That went better than I predicted."

Sawyer didn't comment. He headed down the short hallway until he reached the master bedroom. The CSI techs had gathered around something that had caught their interest in the nightstand drawer beside the victim's bed.

"So, the big poster with Locke's sister spread-eagled on the bed was just a front," the tech on the right said.

"Wait. Is that really Locke's sister in the poster?" asked the tech on the left.

"Hell if I know, but I thought it would be fun to razz him about it," Righty said.

Lefty snorted. "Ask him to get it autographed for you."

"I wouldn't if I were you," Sawyer said firmly. Both men spun around to face the newcomer, their eyes wide and mouths gaping open. "You are aware of how inappropriate your discussion is, right? Not only was the topic vulgar and offensive, but it could've been picked up by a videographer if one had been present. Can you imagine how the jury would respond to hearing your juvenile conversation in the background?"

"Um...I..." Righty stammered. His face was beet red from embarrassment.

Lefty, on the other hand, shook off his initial mortification and straightened to his full height. "Who the hell are you?" he demanded to know.

"I'm Detective Sawyer Keys."

"You're Locke's new partner," Righty stated. "Um, I'm Ned Givens, and this is Steve Lambros. I promise you we're not usually this unprofessional; we were just caught off guard by what we found." Lambros nodded but didn't contribute anything else. "Come see for yourself," Givens said.

Both men moved away from the bed and nightstand, giving Sawyer a wide berth. Sawyer jerked to a stop when he looked into the drawer. He didn't know why he was so damn surprised to find gay porn DVDs, a vibrating dildo, and lube beside Putz's bed. Hadn't he always known the homophobes who screamed the loudest were usually closeted gays?

"Huh," was the only verbal response he allowed to escape. Later, in the privacy of his own home, he might allow himself a good laugh at the irony, but he refused to lecture the techs one second about their lack of professionalism then burst into laughter the very next. "Make sure we get photos. Lots and lots of photos." The small, petty part of him wished like hell there was a valid reason to expose Putz's true nature to the world. The only thing worse than a racist, misogynist, homophobe was one who was also a hypocrite.

"I hate to see what we find in his closet," Lambros said. Sawyer turned and pinned him with a dark look. "Sorry," the tech said, holding up his hands in surrender. "I think I got it all out of my system now. I'll behave, Detective."

"See that you do. I'll leave you to it," Sawyer told them then went in search of Locke and the murder weapon.

"This is how you know someone wasn't messing around," Locke told a tech. "They didn't bring a wooden bat that might break during their furious beatdown; they brought an aluminum one."

"Ouch," Sawyer said, looking at the bloody object Locke carefully held between his gloved thumb and forefinger.

"It rained all damn night, so it washed away any trace evidence out here."

"Any muddy footprints we can get a mold from?" Sawyer asked hopefully.

"Not that they've discovered so far," Locke replied. "What did the techs find in the master bedroom that made them laugh so hard? A penis extender?"

"A little more exciting than that," Sawyer replied, pausing for effect. "Gay porn DVDs, a dildo, and very expensive lube."

Locke's eyebrows rose at the last bit. Sawyer shrugged. Putz was a horrible human being who happened to have excellent taste in lubricant. Sawyer's mother had taught him a person was rarely all good or bad. From what Sawyer could see, the only good thing about Putz might be his choice of masturbation aid. For a brief moment, the left side of Locke's lip ticked upward, and Sawyer thought he might see a ghost of a smile playing across his gorgeous mouth, but it disappeared as quickly as it appeared.

"I'll bag the bat now," a tech said to Locke. "Hopefully we'll get some fingerprints off it."

"So, our person shows up with an aluminum ball bat, enters the house undetected, surprises Putz while he's recording his podcast episode, bashes his head in, and tosses the murder weapon into his trash can on the way back out. No sign of interference anywhere else in the house and they didn't steal his wad of cash or credit cards from his wallet. That's what we have to work with so far."

"You left off one big clue."

Locke tilted his head to the side and squinted at Sawyer. "Oh, yeah. What did I leave out, smart guy?"

"Someone other than Putz uploaded his podcast for his fans to hear."

The annoyance faded from Locke's face when he realized what Sawyer meant. "Our killer made sure everyone heard his savage death."

"If we can gain access to his domain through the host, we'll be able to see who uploaded the recording and possibly trace their IP address."

"Best lead we have so far."

"Detectives," Officer Fuentes said, capturing their attention. "There's a distraught woman making a scene with Officer Andrews at the perimeter of the property. She's claiming to know who killed Mr. Putzinski."

"Well, maybe we'll have this case solved before noon," Locke said, turning to Sawyer with an appraising look in his eyes. "How good are you with hysterical females?"

Sawyer groaned inwardly but knew it was his chance to step up and prove himself. "Guess you're about to find out."

He followed Locke through the house until his partner stopped suddenly in the living room. Locke eyed the tacky poster of the woman on the wall for a brief second then yelled toward the rear of the house, "Yo, Lambros, do you think your sister has any posters left over? Think you could get her to autograph one for me?"

"Damn it," the tech said. It sounded like he was upstairs processing the second story. "He beat me to it."

Givens's laughter drifted down the staircase. "You owe me twenty dollars," he told McIntosh, aka Lefty.

"Double the bet, Givens?" McIntosh asked. "My money is on the rookie not making it a week."

"I'm standing right here, fellas," Sawyer called up the steps. They laughed but no apology followed.

"I'll easily take that bet," Givens told Lambros. "Key is no rookie."

"No, but I bet he's never had a pain-in-the-ass partner like Locke before either."

"Touché," Givens added.

During the entire conversation between McIntosh and Givens, Sawyer met his partner's impenetrable gaze with one of his own. Sawyer's message conveyed: *I'm not going anywhere. Might as well accept it*, while Locke's said: *We'll just see about that.*

CHAPTER 3

APPARENTLY, SAWYER'S AGREEMENT TO TALK TO THE HYSTERICAL woman also meant he was responsible for transporting her to the police station. Neither he nor Locke wanted to interview her outside Putz's property with so many reporters lurking around, and they couldn't take her inside the house to talk either, because CSI was still processing the scene and the medical examiner hadn't removed Putz's body yet. The station was the only option, especially since Fuentes hadn't been exaggerating when he mentioned the woman's hysterical state.

It took Sawyer ten minutes to learn her name and relationship to the deceased because sobs and intermittent keening wails interrupted her words or made them incomprehensible. Sawyer considered himself a good judge of character, and Putz's agent, Shirley Hanover, wasn't faking her despair. It was obvious she was in no condition to drive to the police station, so either he could drive her or Sawyer could ask an officer to do it. The look in Locke's eyes said he expected Sawyer to pawn the sobbing woman off on a uniform, but Sawyer gently escorted the woman to the Dodge Charger he'd selected from the motor pool after discovering Locke had already left for the crime scene.

Shirley Hanover's tears turned into loud hiccups and sniffling that lasted for the duration of the drive. Sawyer offered her an opportunity to use the restroom to tidy up as soon as they reached the station.

"No, thank you, Detective," she said. "I appreciate your kindness." Shirley's voice only wobbled slightly, so Sawyer thought it would be safe to proceed and escorted her to the interview room.

"Can I get you something to drink?" Sawyer gently asked her. He knew damn well Locke was on the other side of the two-way mirror observing his interactions with Putz's agent. "Coffee, perhaps." Sawyer knew from experience the hot beverage had a soothing effect on people, and the sweetness from the sugar and cream helped to counterbalance the side effects of shock. She shook her head.

Shirley Hanover looked to be in her mid-fifties, but it was hard to tell because shock and grief had a way of aging a person. Her gray curls remained neatly styled, but her sobbing had taken a brutal toll on her makeup. Shirley's mascara had smeared beneath her eyes, and watery, black streaks slid down her face; her lipstick had smeared beyond her lip liner, giving her a Joker-like appearance; and her natural skin was showing through where she'd rubbed big patches of her foundation away. Her floral-print blouse had come untucked from her A-line beige skirt on one side. Putz's agent was a big mess—emotionally and physically. He thought it best to start the interview before another wave of grief rose up and delayed their conversation.

"Ms. Hanover—"

"*Mrs.* Hanover. I'm proud to claim my husband's name."

"Pardon me, ma'am. Mrs. Hanover, you indicated to Officer Andrews that you know who killed Mr. Putzinski."

"I can't believe he's gone. I just talked to Roland yesterday evening before he recorded his podcast episode. He sounded like his usual self—happy." Sawyer deserved an award for not reacting to her statement. How could anyone filled with so much hatred toward other people ever be described as happy?

"Did you talk to Mr. Putzinski often, Mrs. Hanover?"

"Yes, nearly every day. I'm all Roland has—*had*—left in the world.

As you can imagine, someone as bold and honest as Roland didn't have very many friends. I was honored to have him in my life."

Sawyer clenched his fists beneath the desk. *Breathe in. Hold. Release.* "He doesn't have any living relatives? No next of kin?"

"None who are speaking to him. *Were* speaking to him," Mrs. Hanover amended then burst into a fresh round of tears.

Sawyer pushed the tissue box closer to her then focused on his breathing rather than his growing impatience.

Mrs. Hanover wept into a crumpled tissue for a few more minutes then sniffed loudly before wiping her eyes with a fresh tissue. "I'm sorry, Detective. Roland's murder has been the biggest shock of my life. I'm reeling over here."

"I understand, Mrs. Hanover. Take all the time you need."

"And let his killer get away?" she asked irritably. "No, sir. I need to pull myself together so I can help you bring this…*miscreant* to justice."

"Why don't we start off with your conversation with Mr. Putzinski and go from there? You're most likely the last person who spoke to him before he died."

"Roland was irate because he'd just found out from Melody's lawyer she'd decided to reject his settlement offer."

"Who is Melody, and what settlement had she declined?"

"Melody Putzinski—well, Jameson. She refused to take Roland's name after they got married." *Gee, I wonder why?* "She is Roland's estranged wife."

"And his next of kin," Sawyer said.

"Their divorce was almost final, but Miss Greedy, Slutty Pants decided Roland's generous settlement wasn't enough for her, even though she was only entitled to what she entered the marriage with." Mrs. Hanover snorted. "Roland should've repossessed her fake tits." Sawyer raised his brow at her unladylike remark and venomous tone. "He paid for her cheek implants, tummy tuck, Brazilian butt lift, collagen lips, and even her hair and eyelash extensions. Nothing about the woman is real, including her feelings for my friend." Sawyer felt it was possible some agents felt this passionately about their clients, but Mrs. Hanover's reactions felt more…personal.

"So, Mr. Putzinski was upset Melody Jameson had rejected the settlement offer at the last minute…" Sawyer said, leading Mrs. Hanover back on topic.

"Yes, even though the prenuptial agreement protected Roland's assets, he offered her two hundred and fifty thousand dollars. He was still in love with her."

Bullshit. There was no way in hell Roland Putzinski offered money he wasn't obligated to pay. It was hush money, and Melody Jameson had decided her dirt was worth more money. Sawyer decided to continue with the line of questioning to find more answers, and possibly a motive to kill.

"Mr. Putzinski's feelings weren't returned? There was no hope for a reconciliation?"

"She never loved Roland. She only wanted him for his money. Her *affection* for him only lasted until he lost nearly everything in that frivolous lawsuit. Don't we have freedom of speech rights any longer?"

Sawyer's eye twitched from the restraint he imposed on himself. He could debate with her all day long that freedom of speech didn't also mean free from consequences, but he had a homicide to solve. The last thing he wanted was Mrs. Hanover going public with claims that the SPD wasn't taking the case seriously.

"So, the couple was happily married until the lawsuit put a strain on their marriage. Were there any other problems. Infidelity?"

"Roland would never cheat on her. She was his entire world."

"What about Melody?"

"Not that I could prove, but I told Roland she spent way too much time with her yoga instructor if you know what I mean."

"Was their split acrimonious? Are you aware of any threats they made to one another?" Mrs. Hanover shook her head. "Did Mr. Putzinski tell you about any threats he'd received lately or any arguments he had with anyone aside from his wife?" She snorted. "Mrs. Hanover?"

"Roland received threatening emails and letters every day. He was never once intimidated or frightened by them. He seemed to thrive on them." *You don't say.* "He read his favorite ones during a segment each week in his podcast. It was called Wimpy Whiners." Mrs. Hanover smiled fondly. "My Roland had a wonderful sense of humor." It took everything he had not to respond, and even though he'd only worked with Locke briefly, he sensed his partner was laughing his ass off on the other side of the mirror.

"Mrs. Hanover, you don't by chance know if Roland kept the correspondence from his Wimpy Whiners, do you?"

"He sure did. He keeps them in a filing cabinet in the office until the drawer gets too full, then he transfers them to his storage unit. He stored the emails on a file in his computer, but I have access to it as part of my admin permissions."

Sawyer felt his right brow lift. "He has a storage unit just for his hate mail?"

"No, silly," Mrs. Hanover said, "he stores furniture and other personal belongings there too. He had to downsize after the lawsuit, and rather than let Melody have any of the furniture that wouldn't fit in his new home, he rented a storage unit and held on to it. Clever, right?"

Sawyer ignored the question and pushed forward. "Do you happen to have a key to his storage unit?"

"Of course. My name is also on the lease. Even though I think it's a waste of your time and resources since Melody is obviously the killer, I'll grant you permission to search and remove anything from the premises you think is pertinent to the case. You won't need to bother getting a search warrant."

"That's very helpful, and the police department really appreciates it." Mrs. Hanover sat straighter in her chair. She either enjoyed the praise or liked that the department was now indebted to her. "Can you tell me who has access to Mr. Putzinski's website?"

"Just Roland and me. I'm listed as an administrator on his domain. What can I help you with?"

"You're aware Mr. Putzinski was killed while recording his podcast, correct?" Fresh tears welled in her eyes, but she held herself together and only nodded. It had to be a horrible experience for her, so he wanted to tread lightly. "Whoever uploaded the file is my number one suspect. Will you help me look at his domain activity without me having to obtain a warrant?"

"Anything you need, Detective."

"Do you know how an unauthorized user might have accessed Mr. Putzinski's domain?"

"He kept a cheat sheet tucked under his keyboard and stored them in his Notes app on his phone. Anyone familiar with his habits, say a wife, would know where to find his username and passwords."

"Okay." At least they weren't dealing with high-tech hackers who could easily hide their footprints inside The Putz's account. "Will you write down what I need to access the domain?"

"Absolutely."

Sawyer slid a notepad across the table to her, and she wrote down the website, her login credentials, and the steps to navigate the system. He would provide the information to the cyber department to see if they could trace the IP address and pinpoint their suspect.

Mrs. Hanover pulled her phone out of her purse. "I have all the legal documents showing I'm authorized to grant you access to the storage unit and Roland's website on the Big Daddy domain site." Sawyer had to mask the chuckle that slipped out with a fake cough. From his brief glimpse of Putz's porn collection, he was a big fan of daddy kink.

"I hope you're not getting sick, Detective. Summer colds are the *worst*."

"Thank you, ma'am. It was just a slight tickle. I'm sure it's nothing to worry about."

"The file with the hateful emails is a little bit more challenging due to the volume, so I'll download it to a flash drive and send it over by a courier this afternoon. I have the documents proving my legal authority stored on my Google Drive, and I can access them through an app. I'll include written consent for search and seizure. What's your email address, Detective?"

That was a good question. Luckily, Chief Rigby had handed him a box of business cards the department had printed for him as soon as he accepted the position. Sawyer removed one from his shirt pocket and handed it to her.

Mrs. Hanover quietly tapped away on her phone for a few minutes. "There. Sent. Do you want to check your phone to make sure you have everything you need?"

"I just transferred over from the sheriff's department," he confessed. "I haven't made it to the IT department to pick up my phone yet. I'm still getting things set up."

"I appreciate you rushing to Roland's crime scene, Detective. It shows how much you care. You just give me a call if I need to resend the documents or if you have any other questions for me."

"Will do. Are you ready to pick up your car?"

"You don't have to drive me, Detective Key. I'll have my husband pick me up so you can get settled."

"That's very kind of you, Mrs. Hanover. I will have an officer drive you back over to your car if your husband isn't available."

By this time, Sawyer had escorted the woman out of the interview room and down the hallway near the glass-walled area referred to as the bullpen where the detectives from MCU worked their cases. Mrs. Hanover was texting as she walked, presumably to arrange for a ride, so Sawyer slowed his stride to keep pace with her.

"There we go," Mrs. Hanover said, sliding her phone back in her purse. "Carl will be here in about fifteen minutes to pick me up. I'll just—" Mrs. Hanover sucked in a sharp breath and jerked to a sudden stop. "It's your lucky day, Detective. There's your killer."

Assuming Roland's widow had arrived, Sawyer looked over toward reception and was shocked to see the model from the tacky "real men" poster standing inside the station returning Mrs. Hanover's hateful glare with one of her own.

Oh fuck! Sawyer didn't have to be a psychic to know whatever happened next would be bad. Before he had a chance to stop Mrs. Hanover, she propelled herself in Melody Jameson's direction, moving faster than Sawyer thought her age and high heels would allow. *Fuck!*

Unfortunately for Sawyer, and any other innocent bystander, Melody had launched herself toward Mrs. Hanover at the same time. The two women met in the middle, their hands flying up to tangle in one another's hair.

"You faithless slut," Mrs. Hanover screamed. "I'm going to yank these extensions out of your hair." With her free hand, Mrs. Hanover swung her designer handbag and clocked Melody on the side of her head with a loud thump. "How about I bludgeon you to death and see how you like it?"

Sawyer reached Mrs. Hanover before she could take another swing at the same time as Locke appeared out of thin air to pull Melody Jameson out of harm's way.

"I didn't kill anyone, you jealous old hag," she sobbed into Locke's broad chest.

"I know you killed Roland. The police will know it too," the older woman screamed, forcing Sawyer to tighten his grip on Mrs. Hanover's biceps to keep her from charging Melody Jameson again. "If you didn't kill him, then you hired your yoga instructor slash lover to kill him for you."

Melody stiffened and pulled free from Locke's embrace. "Jacque wasn't my lover, you imbecile; Roland was the one fucking another man. I didn't kill Roland, but maybe you got tired of waiting for him to return your affection. He knew you were in love with him, and he used it against you then laughed at how gullible you were, how easily you did his bidding."

Mrs. Hanover's fingers bent to form claws, and she started to lunge toward Melody but wasn't able to pull free from Sawyer's hold. "Liar! Roland would never engage in such sinful behavior." Sawyer noticed Mrs. Hanover dodged the second bomb Melody dropped on her, but maybe she was still reeling from the first allegation.

"Except I have proof," Melody said, pulling a file folder out of her sage green Michael Kors tote bag and holding it up for everyone to see. The smile she aimed at Mrs. Hanover was pure evil, and Melody Jameson wasn't smart enough to know she was brandishing her motive for everyone to see.

Mrs. Hanover began to weep and wail, her words incoherent, sounding like a person who'd had her world turned upside down. Sawyer wasn't impervious to Mrs. Hanover's comment about homosexuality being a sin; he was just able to compartmentalize her remarks to focus on the job.

"Ma'am, maybe you should come with me," Locke said to Melody Jameson, his deep voice pulling her focus away from Mrs. Hanover so Sawyer could safely escort her away from her nemesis before things escalated.

"Of course, Detective," she said in a baby-soft voice reminiscent of Marilyn Monroe while eyeing Locke up and down. It was impossible for anyone to miss the blatant way she pushed her chest out. From Locke's height advantage, there was no doubt in Sawyer's mind his partner had one hell of a view of her rounded mounds jutting above the low-cut top and the valley between them.

Locke tore his eyes away from Melody's bosom and met Sawyer's gaze. An impish smile tilted the corner of his mouth, and for reasons he didn't want to consider, Sawyer's stomach pitched.

"Right this way," Locke said, gesturing for Melody to follow him down the hallway toward the interview rooms.

"Thank you so much, sugar," she simpered. Just walking beside the sexy man wasn't enough for the blonde bombshell though. She slid her dainty hand around his bicep like she couldn't possibly make the long trek down the hallway without his manliness to support her.

"I hate that slut," Mrs. Hanover said. "She'll probably be blowing him the second the door closes to the room."

"Mrs. Hanover," Sawyer said, shocked by the older woman's language. "Detective Locke is a decorated detective in our police department. He would never engage in such deplorable behavior."

"My apologies, Detective. I don't mean to impugn his honor, but men can't seem to resist women like Melody," Mrs. Hanover said, sounding like a bitter woman who'd competed for a man's affection and lost him to the younger woman. "I recognized the gleam in her eyes when she looked at Detective Locke. You make my words; she'll be spreading her legs for him before this investigation is over, especially if it delays her inevitable arrest."

Not if I can help it. The unwanted thought came out of nowhere, catching Sawyer off guard.

Completely unaware of the strife she created inside him, Mrs. Hanover continued her tirade. "She won't care if she destroys his career either. The woman destroys anyone she touches. I don't care what's in her folder; she'll never convince me Roland consented to have sex with another man. If she has photos, they're doctored. If she has testimony, it's coerced. Most likely while she was giving the accuser a hand job under the table."

"Shirley!"

Mrs. Hanover jerked her head up and looked at an older man walking quickly to her. "Carl," she wailed and threw herself into his arms.

"Mrs. Hanover, please feel free to call the number on my card if you think of anything else important to the case. Sometimes a detail feels small, but it turns out to be a critical piece of evidence in solving the case."

"I will, Detective. Thank you for your kindness today."

"My pleasure. I'm sorry for your loss, ma'am."

"I'll take it from here, Detective," Mr. Hanover said, offering a kind smile.

Thank fuck!

Sawyer waited for the couple to exit the station before he turned on his heels and slowly made his way toward the interview room where Locke had taken Melody Jameson. Even though he knew he wouldn't find the blonde woman blowing Locke in the small room, he wasn't eager to see his partner flirting to get answers out of her either.

Sawyer took a deep breath then pushed open the door to the small room where he could observe the interview without Melody Jameson knowing he was there. Locke must've realized it though because he glanced up and it felt like he was staring right into Sawyer's eyes, making butterflies take flight in the pit of his stomach.

No. No. No. This can't be happening.

Locke turned his focus away from where Sawyer stood and leveled a smile at Melody Jameson so devastatingly beautiful she sucked in a stunned breath, which of course, made her breasts jiggle. Sawyer had to give Locke credit; his partner kept his eyes trained on her face.

"Oh my," she whispered shakily.

Indeed.

CHAPTER 4

"**I**'M SORRY FOR MY UNLADYLIKE BEHAVIOR," MELODY JAMESON simpered and peered at Locke from beneath her eyelashes.

"I understand, Ms...."

"Melody Jameson," she said, leaning over the table to extend her hand. "Roland Putzinski was my husband." She didn't shed a tear—fake or otherwise.

"I'm Detective Locke." He shook her hand, but when he attempted to pull back, Melody clung to it. Then she placed her free hand over his, sandwiching his hand between both of hers. Locke kept his eyes locked on her face instead of glancing down at her breasts no matter how much she wiggled or jostled them.

When she realized her ploy wasn't working, she released Locke from her grip and sat back in her chair, re-crossing her long legs. She blew out a long breath, and her entire demeanor changed so fast it gave Sawyer whiplash. Melody recoiled and shrank against the back of the chair as if she was collapsing in on herself, the expression on her face shifting from coy to shame. "Jesus Christ," she said in a much deeper voice than the one she'd used on Locke in the lobby. "I didn't use to be this person."

"Excuse me?" Locke asked, looking and sounding as confused as Sawyer felt. Was this an act? Did she have a multiple personality disorder? What the fuck?

"Where's the dark-haired Adonis?" she asked, avoiding Locke's question.

"I'm sorry, but I don't know who you're referring to?" Locke said, but he glanced toward the two-way mirror. It was so fast Melody wouldn't have noticed, but Sawyer saw it—felt it.

"The sexy man who had to restrain Roland's dried-up agent, Shirley Hanover. I assume he's your partner."

"Why would you assume that?" Locke asked, sounding intrigued that she'd leaped to the conclusion.

Melody shrugged. "It was the way you two moved simultaneously to break us up. It was effortless and without thought. Am I wrong?"

"You're not wrong," Locke said. "Can I ask why you want Detective Key to sit in during our interview?"

Putz's widow tilted her head to the side and grinned. "Locke and Key? No wonder you work so well together." Locke had the gall to snort, but he prompted her to answer his question rather than inform her they'd just met that morning.

"I'm sure Detective Key got an earful from *that woman* who will stop at nothing to impugn my reputation. It's one thing for her to say shitty things about my plastic surgery and the state of my divorce, but no one gets to imply I'm a murderess without me fighting back. I did not want Roland dead, and I would prefer to tell this story just one time to both of you rather than rehash it again and again."

Sawyer had news for Melody Jameson; that wasn't how an investigation went. Cops liked to interview suspects and witnesses multiple times to look for inconsistencies in their statements and recollections.

"Okay," Locke agreed, surprising Sawyer. He rose from his chair and exited the room. Had Sawyer been in a generous mood, he would've met the guy in the hallway to make his job easier, but this was the man who'd chosen to snarl at him instead of introducing himself as a decent partner would. Sawyer wasn't feeling magnanimous. The door to the observation room opened suddenly, and Locke stepped in, shutting the door behind him. "Are going to join me in interviewing our top suspect, or are you going to pout in here like an asshole?"

The room seemed to shrink in on them, or maybe Locke's larger-than-life personality just sucked the oxygen from the room. Either way, Sawyer felt boxed-in and found it hard to breathe. Locke's spicy scent tickled his nostrils, making them flare along with a desire he wanted to squelch before it ruined the second chance Ellen Rigby had given him.

Mentally pulling himself together, Sawyer turned and stared Locke dead in the eyes. Locke stood in front of the door, blocking their exit. Sawyer knew he could stand still and wait out his pissy attitude, which his partner probably expected, or he could challenge Locke. Choosing the latter, Sawyer crossed the small space in a few strides and stopped when he was nearly chest to chest with Locke.

"It's Adonis Asshole to you, Locke."

The reaction on Locke's face was minimal—a slight squinting of his turbulent eyes and the faintest hint of a twitch at the right corner of his mouth—but Sawyer knew he'd landed a good one. Locke opened his mouth to respond but shook his head as if he'd thought better of it. Then he blinked and all traces of humor were gone, leaving only the wild wounded look behind.

"Let's go interview The Putz's wife and work the case." *The case, not our case.* Sawyer thought it was a slight step up from *my case* though.

Melody didn't waste her time trying to seduce Sawyer when he introduced himself. She immediately got down to business. "I'm not a stupid woman, Detective. I'm aware I'm the primary suspect in Roland's murder, but I assure you I have an alibi." *How convenient.*

"Which is?" Sawyer prompted.

"I was staying with my sister and her family this weekend. They live two hours south in Jacksonville, Florida. I learned about Roland's death on the radio during my drive home this morning."

"You must've gotten an early start to arrive home so early."

"I have receipts from a Starbucks in Jacksonville at seven thirty this morning and another when I stopped for gas in Darien, Georgia, about ninety minutes later. And yes, I left my sister's house early this morning because, as much as I love my sister and nieces, I was desperate for some peace. I'm not used to four rowdy little girls and their gaggle of best friends coming over for swim parties that turn into a weekend stay."

Locke slid the yellow legal pad toward her. "Can you please write down your sister's name and contact information so we can verify your alibi? We'd also like copies of your receipts."

"Sure thing," Melody said, picking up the pen and writing down the information Locke requested. When she finished, she pulled receipts from her wallet. "I don't need you to make copies, Detective. They'll show up on my bank statement if I'm ever asked to produce them again."

"Even if we can prove you were out of town, we still need to show you didn't hire someone to kill Roland for you," Locke pointed out.

"I understand, Detectives. I had no motive to kill him. I'll freely give you any information you want." Those were points in her favor.

"Let's talk about the divorce settlement offer you declined," Sawyer said.

She snorted. "You mean Roland's hush money?" Was she aware she only made herself look guiltier by admitting it? "I bet you've already figured out his secret though. Did you find his porn magazines, DVD stash, and fetish wear? He was very good at hiding it when we lived together, but I bet he got bolder once I moved out of our old home."

The techs hadn't discovered the porn magazines and fetish wear while Locke and Sawyer were on the premise, but she didn't need to know that. The DVDs and dildo were a pretty big giveaway. "We're aware of his secret, Ms. Jameson," Locke confirmed.

"There's more," Melody said. "I have voice recordings and

33

handwritten notes from Roland verbally abusing me throughout our marriage. Instead of being honest with himself and with me, Roland said my physical flaws were the reason he couldn't get it up." After Locke and Sawyer sat silently blinking for a few seconds, Melody reached into her oversized tote and removed the same folder she'd waved around in the lobby. She opened it up and pulled out two glossy photos and set them side by side on the table in front of us. "The photo on the right was taken when I was twenty-two years old. I'd just graduated from college and dreamed of a job in radio. Look how healthy and happy I looked compared to the manufactured, plastic doll in the photo on the left. That's what six years of being married to Roland Putzinski looks like."

The difference between pre-Roland and post-Roland Melody was shocking. Pre-Roland Melanie had joy and warmth radiating from her smiling eyes. She looked innocent yet confident in her graduation cap and gown standing beside a couple Sawyer presumed were her parents and another young lady who looked so much like Melody that they had to be sisters. Melody wore a modest, beige dress beneath her open gown. She was slender and trim. Her youthful, round face looked naturally vibrant and dewy without help from cosmetics.

In comparison, everything about Post-Roland Melody looked fake and hard. Plastic surgery gave her chiseled cheekbones with hollows beneath them and a more prominent chin to give her face a heart-shaped appearance. Her nose was thinner, her lips bigger, but the biggest change could be found by looking at Melody's eyes. Where there had once been innocence and joy, all Sawyer could see in the older woman's eyes was cold calculation.

Melody tapped the photo of her younger self with a long, hot pink nail. "I want that girl back, Detectives. Contrary to my outburst to Shirley, I never had any intention of outing Roland to anyone. I just wanted enough money to undo the damage he'd done when he told me my breasts weren't big enough and my face was too fat. I want to eat macaroni and cheese without starving myself the next day as punishment. I will gladly give up my Brazilian butt lift implants to re-claim my 'pancake ass.' For years, this man found one excuse after an-other to explain why I didn't physically appeal to him. I already start-ed seeing a psychologist to get help undoing his brainwashing about my appearance and many other things, but it costs a lot of money. I can't right the ship overnight. That's why it was so easy for me to slip back into my old habits when I saw Shirley's judgmental ass inside the station."

"You decided a quarter of a million wasn't enough to accomplish your goals?" Locke asked, keeping the interview on track.

Melody released a shaky breath and offered a small smile. "Here's where I lose your sympathy." *I wouldn't bet on it,* Sawyer thought. "The money probably was enough to cover all my expenses, but I would also require recovery time after my procedures, which would prevent me from getting a job, *if* I could find work once people found out I was once associated with him. Still, I was going to do my best to make the settlement work until I found out he was a lying sack of shit about more things than just his sexual orientation."

"Such as," Sawyer prompted. Her cloying perfume in a confined space was wreaking havoc on his sinuses. He needed to be out of the room and suck in some fresh air before the headache he felt coming on got the best of him.

"He wasn't as broke as he let on. I learned Roland, with help from Shirley Hanover and his sleazebag attorney, Shepard Wilson, started up a shell company that would allow him to hide some of his assets before the civil case. Shep saw the writing on the wall before the sweet young man succumbed to his injuries. I don't know how they were able to hide it from the forensic accountants assigned to validate his net worth."

"Is it possible they had established the shell company years before the civil case? It would explain why the forensic accountant didn't see money moving in and out," Locke told her.

"It's possible, Detectives. I only know I have proof of Roland admitting he'd set up shell companies to hide assets from greedy parties. He could've been talking about the Gasaway family or me, but it doesn't matter. He was just a miserable, vile man."

"I'm curious when you're going to get to the part where I stop feeling like you're another one of Roland's victims," Locke said. Sawyer had been thinking the same thing.

Melody broke eye contact and looked down at her hands folded on her lap. "I'd discovered Roland's secret and used it against him."

"You set him up?" Locke asked, who sounded more impressed than horrified. Sawyer wasn't sure if it was genuine or part of an act to keep Melody talking freely. It worked. Assured of Locke's sympathy, she lifted her head and met his gaze once more.

"Micah Gasaway's tragic death was an eye-opener for me. Roland didn't even care the kid had died nor would he accept responsibility. That's when I knew I wanted to expose him for the closet homosexual he was, and my yoga instructor, Jacque, agreed to help me."

"So you did plan to out him?" Sawyer asked.

"Initially, yes, but I changed my mind. I was a better person than he was. I just wanted money to get free from him and get my old life back. Besides, exposing Roland would have most likely painted a big bull's-eye on my forehead for his freakish fans to take aim at. Roland didn't know I was bluffing about going to the media though."

"What did Jacque get from the arrangement?"

"Besides sloppy blow jobs and horrible sex?" Melody asked. Locke and Sawyer nodded.

"I did pay him a few thousand dollars, but he mostly wanted to help bring Roland down."

Sawyer could understand the need for payback, but there was no way he could get his dick up for a dude like Roland Putzinski. No amount of gay porn or fantasizing behind closed eyelids could make it work.

"Who else knows about your scheme?"

"Jacque, the private investigator I hired to take the photos and record their conversation, and Roland. He wouldn't have confided this information to anyone, especially not Shirley because she as homophobic as he pretended to be."

"We need the name of your PI and contact information for Jacque."

"Okay," Melody agreed easily. She added the information below her sister's name and address. Then Melody replaced the photos inside the file and slid it across the table. "This is yours to keep, by the way. I have other copies."

"Was Roland aware of Jacque's part in the setup?"

"No," she said adamantly. "I know I haven't painted myself in the best light, but I wouldn't betray my friend." In the heat of the moment, she'd told Mrs. Hanover Roland was having an affair with another man but hadn't said Jacque's name. "Trust me, fellas. Roland was willing to give me anything I asked for to shut me up. I had no motive to kill him."

The interview had gone in a decidedly different direction than Sawyer would've predicted when Melody unleashed her femme fatale persona on Shirley then her charm on Locke. Only time would tell if she'd told them the truth.

"We appreciate you coming in and speaking candidly with us. We'll be in touch if we have additional questions."

"Absolutely." She leaned forward and wrote down a few phone numbers. "That's my home number and my cell phone."

Sawyer offered her a warm smile. "If you think of anything else—"

"I'll be sure to call." Melody Jameson swiftly rose to her feet, prompting the detectives to do the same. "Why aren't you asking me the question that's burning foremost in your mind right now?"

"What would that be?" Locke asked casually.

She tipped her head and met Locke's gaze. "Why I stayed with Roland even though I was miserable. Why would I allow the abuse to continue?"

"There are many reasons why people stay in abusive relationships, Ms. Jameson. I'm guessing many of them could apply to your situation."

"Choose one," she challenged Locke.

Sawyer didn't think Locke was going to engage her for a few seconds until he softly said, "You started to believe his bullshit message. He convinced you that you were undesirable and unworthy. He was the best you could hope for, and you should be grateful for his affection." Melody shivered hard then nodded. "You can and will break the chain. Acknowledging the problem is the first step, so you're already on your way."

Sawyer stared at his partner in silent contemplation. Locke sounded like a person who knew this from experience, and Sawyer's curiosity about the enigmatic man soared. The poorly air-conditioned interview room could've caused Locke's flushed cheeks, but Sawyer knew better. He didn't like Sawyer seeing anything beyond the wall he'd erected, but thanks to Melody Jameson, Sawyer found the first chink in his partner's armor.

"Let me walk you out," Locke said, gesturing to the door. "I doubt Mrs. Hanover is still loitering around the police station, but I think it pays to be cautious."

"Thank you," Melody told him. She said goodbye to Sawyer then walked out the door with Locke following in her wake.

When the door shut, Sawyer took advantage of the quiet to process everything he had learned and shift his focus to what he needed to do next. It seemed unlikely to him that Melody or Mrs. Hanover was responsible for The Putz's homicide, but he wasn't ready to cross them completely off the list. He'd follow the leads until he found his perpetrator. And thanks to Mrs. Hanover, they would have access to the person who uploaded the final podcast episode and the people who hated Putz enough to put their contempt in writing.

But first, Sawyer needed to set up his desk. He headed out to his car in the parking lot behind the station and retrieved the box with the personal items he'd brought with him. When he returned to the bullpen,

Locke still hadn't returned from walking Melody to her car. Sawyer saw the empty desk facing Locke's but continued walking toward an empty one in the far corner of the room. If he ever hoped to get past Locke's reticence, he had to show the man he respected the loss of his partner.

Marcus Wilkes hadn't retired early or decided on a career change. One weekend when his wife and kids were away, Marcus wrote a good-bye note to his family and Locke then started his car inside the closed garage. From everything Sawyer knew about the incident, Locke was the one who found his partner's body when Marcus had failed to return phone calls or texts. Only two months had passed since Marcus's suicide, and while Sawyer hoped Locke warmed up to him someday, he realized he might be relegated to sit in the corner for the duration of his career at SPD.

Rather than dwell on the precariousness of his situation, Sawyer followed the directions Chief Rigby had given him that morning to the IT department where he picked up his phone, credentials to log in to the system, and instructions on accessing his email. Then he got to work setting up his desk and retrieving and printing the legal documents Mrs. Hanover provided him along with her expressed permission to search and seize items pertaining to the homicide case. He forwarded the domain access information to the cyber techs so they could begin tracking the IP address to where the podcast episode was uploaded. When Sawyer finished, he rose from his chair and caught Locke watching him speculatively from his desk chair. Was that a hint of respect Sawyer saw in his partner's eyes?

"Ready to check out the storage unit, asshole?" Locke asked.

Around them, the other detectives in their unit watched the interaction with bated breath.

"It's Adonis Asshole to you," Sawyer reminded him, earning some good-natured chuckles from the bullpen.

Locke shook his head and exited the bullpen without saying another word. Sawyer accepted it as a small victory and followed behind him.

CHAPTER 5

"**T**HIS WAY," LOCKE CALLED OUT OVER HIS SHOULDER ONCE THEY exited the building. He headed toward a charcoal gray Charger like the black one Sawyer had chosen from the motor pool.

The oppressive June heat rose off the concrete and blacktop surrounding the police station. The thick, humid air from the high-pressure storm moving in had trapped the heat low to the ground, preventing it from rising upwards. Everywhere Sawyer looked, heat waves shimmered and danced beneath the scorching sun. Having grown up in Georgia, Sawyer wondered why humid summers still managed to catch him by surprise.

"Loosen the noose around your neck before you choke," Locke said. He'd stopped by the driver's side of his car and turned to watch Sawyer's approach. "Who are you trying to impress anyway?"

"Oh, you know the saying about putting your best foot forward." Sawyer wasn't about to tell Locke he'd worn his lucky tie, which had seemed to lose its powers. "Tomorrow, I'll show up wearing a tank top and shorts."

It was impossible to read Locke's expression through his dark sunglasses, but Sawyer almost felt his partner's gaze traveling over his body, making him impossibly hotter. Sawyer discounted the notion immediately. The heat had fried something in his brain.

"Make sure the shorts have belt loops since you wear a holster on your belt. Kicking it old school, I guess."

"Are we going to have a pissing contest over the type of holster we prefer, or are we going to solve a homicide?"

"We can't do both? Is that the paperwork from Shirley Hanover we need to show to the site manager at Stow-N-Go?" Locked asked, nodding his head toward Sawyer's hand.

"No, it's my grocery list."

"Asshole," Locke said.

"What's up with your outfit?" Sawyer asked. "Did you just come from vice? They must've given me an outdated employee handbook with the wrong dress code."

"I'm special," Locke countered.

"I just bet."

Sawyer stared at Locke over the top of the car. He was glad he'd donned his dark glasses too so Locke couldn't get a read on him either. Bantering with Locke made him feel more alive than he'd felt in…years. His partner shook his head then got behind the wheel of his car. Sawyer released a shaky breath and climbed inside too, grateful Locke had remote-started the car to get the air-conditioning going.

"Look, I'm not trying to be a dickhead on purpose," Locke said.

"It just comes naturally?"

"Something like that," Locke said wryly. Sawyer glanced over in time to catch a glimpse of Locke's smirk before it disappeared. "You know the story about my partner, right?"

"I do, and I'm truly sorry for your loss."

"I appreciate that, Key." It was the first time Locke addressed him by his name instead of using an insult. "I need you to understand something. Marcus wasn't just my partner; he was my best friend. I was the best man at his wedding and was there when his three children were born. Marcus and Candace made me their children's godfather. Marcus Wilkes was the best man I've ever known, and there was no one I loved more than him, not even my own family."

Something in Locke's reverent, heartbroken voice pierced Sawyer's heart like a jagged piece of glass, severing the arteries and veins. The pressure in his chest became unbearably painful because Sawyer recognized the grief and heartbreak Locke was describing.

Breathe in. Hold. Release. The pressure eased a little.

Mixed in with his commiseration was a tingle of awareness. *There was no one I loved more than him.* It didn't feel like Locke was expressing friendly or familial love. It felt more…intimate. A confession of sorts? Not just because of what Locke said, but because of the way he said it. Words both rusty and new as if his emotions had been buried and left to wither and were being unearthed for the first time. Had Locke been *in love* with his partner? Why tell him? A stranger he didn't really know or even like. Was he even aware of the secret he'd exposed?

Sawyer dismissed the line of thinking outright. He'd asked around about Locke before he'd taken the job. He'd wanted to know about his reputation as an officer, but mostly heard about his private conquests instead. According to the gossip, Locke wasn't very discerning about the women he slept with and had a revolving door on his bedroom: one lady went in as the other came out. Was the gossip wrong? Was there more to Locke than he let the world see? Or was Sawyer looking for reasons to justify the ridiculous attraction sizzling beneath his skin. His life would be so much easier if Locke were straight, because he'd get past the attraction.

Locke swallowed hard, and Sawyer thought his partner had said all he planned to until he cleared his throat and spoke again. "I need for you to understand the way I'm treating you has nothing to do with you. I didn't want a new partner; I will never want a different partner than Marcus. I might always resent your presence in my life. I won't invite you over for cookouts, and I won't accept an offer from you if you were to extend one. I don't want to know your favorite food, music, books, or movies. I do not want to be your friend today, tomorrow, or maybe even ever. You don't deserve this, and I'm sorry, Key."

It was so much worse than Sawyer had guessed when he'd

looked into Locke's wounded eyes, and the warnings he'd received that morning weren't nearly enough to protect himself from this evisceration. Words failed him, so he nodded.

"Okay then," Locke said, shifting the car into drive. He leaned forward and turned the fan up as high as it would go. The air rushing through the vents was the only noise inside the car when Locke turned right on Atlantic Ave then right again on E. 41st Street. He drummed his thumbs on the steering wheel while waiting for the red light to change at the intersection of E. 41st and Paulson. He was either keeping up with the rhythm of music only he could hear, or he was nervous. Locke didn't strike Sawyer as the anxious type, so he assumed Locke felt relieved, more relaxed, after his little state-of-the-partnership speech.

Locke turned left onto Paulson when he got the green arrow. "The unit is on Maupas, right?"

"Yeah," Sawyer said casually, refusing to let Locke know how deeply his words impacted him. "I think you need to turn left on Maupas and the storage facility will be on the left."

"Thanks."

A few minutes later, Locke parked in front of a dark brown brick building where the offices for Stow-N-Go were located. A driveway beside the structure led to a locked gate where renters would enter a code into a keypad on a pedestal to gain access to their units. Chain-link fencing and razor-sharp barbwire surrounded the perimeter to keep unwanted visitors away, but the dark brown powder-coating covering the metal gave the fencing a classier appearance.

"Pretty swanky for a storage facility," Sawyer said.

"Nothing but the best for The Putz," Locke said. "Did Shirley give you the access codes for the gate and unit?"

"Yes," Sawyer replied.

"We have written permission and the info to open it, so why don't we just drive on back?"

Sawyer turned his head and lowered his glasses so his partner could read his expression. "Because we want to do things transparently. The last thing we want to do is have the prosecution show a video of us lurking around without making our presence known. We do this right so some asshole doesn't literally get away with murder."

"Fucking Boy Scout," Locke grumbled, pushing open his door.

Sawyer blew out a frustrated breath and followed him. Was this what he could expect from Locke every day? Abrupt remarks and insults followed by swift exits that made him feel like a fool? How badly did Sawyer want a job in law enforcement? The dull headache which had started in the interrogation room was getting stronger and seemed to pulse with Sawyer's heartbeat.

Locke hadn't even waited for him at the door. Sawyer entered the office and saw his partner had already started charming the receptionist behind the desk. The brunette stared into Locke's eyes for a few seconds before the sound of the chime above the door registered, indicating she had another visitor. She tore her gaze away from Locke's and smiled at Sawyer. "Two handsome visitors at the same time." She raked her eyes down to his waist where Sawyer kept his gun and badge secured on his belt. There was no way she missed Locke's shoulder holster and badge dangling from a chain around his neck, identifying him as a law enforcement officer. "Handsome officers I should say."

"I'm Detective Locke, and this is Detective Key," Locke said, gesturing to Sawyer when he stepped up beside him. "We're here to search unit twenty-four sixty-nine as part of a homicide investigation."

"Do you have a search warrant, Detective?" she asked sweetly. The lady knew the law.

"We don't need one. Another party on the lease has granted us permission to search the unit," Sawyer told her, handing over the email from Shirley Hanover and a copy of the lease showing her listed as a person who can access the unit.

"I'm sorry, but I cannot accept this, Detectives. While it's true Shirley Hanover can permit you to enter without a warrant, this email isn't signed. It could've come from a phony email account. I'll need to see a letter with a notarized signature, a signed warrant from a judge, or Mrs. Hanover can personally escort you back to the unit. I want to help you out, but I can't."

"You could call her, darlin.' You could verify her permission over the phone," Locke said.

"I'm not your *darlin'*, and our rules clearly state I'm required to obtain the documents I named before allowing you to enter the premise."

"You're a rule follower, and I can appreciate that," Locke said, quickly changing his tactics since schmoozing didn't work. "Do your rules specifically address verbal permission?"

The brunette's brow formed a deep V and her pert nose scrunched up while she thought about it. "Verbal permission isn't addressed one way or the other."

"If your rules and guidelines don't specifically exclude verbal authorization, then it's permissible," Sawyer told her. "We're not trying to give you a hard time, miss. We're just trying to solve a homicide and put a killer behind bars. Don't you want to do everything within your rights to help us?" Sawyer picked up the phone receiver and handed it to her. "Please call Mrs. Hanover. I'm sure the contact phone numbers she's provided in the email match the ones in your records."

The receptionist looked at the email and compared the phone numbers to information on her screen, then she dialed Shirley Hanover's number. "Good morning, Mrs. Hanover. This is Gretchen calling from Stow-N-Go Storage," the woman said in a professional voice then paused to let Shirley respond. "I'm so sorry to bother you at a difficult time, but I have two detectives here wanting access to Roland Putzinski's unit. I see that you're listed on the account, and you do have permission to grant them entrance, but we usually require a letter with a notarized signature or a warrant before we allow the police to search the facility." Gretchen paused and listened to Mrs. Hanover. "I agree with you, ma'am. I want to see the killer brought to justice also, so I thought of a compromise. I'm willing to allow the nice detectives inside the storage unit based on your verbal authorization as long as you promise to provide me a notarized version of the printed email in front of me." Gretchen listened and nodded. "Yes, I can accept an emailed copy of the notarized statement." The brunette smiled at us. "Oh, that's very convenient, and I'm sure the detectives would like a copy as well."

When it seemed like Gretchen's conversation with Mrs. Hanover was going to last a while, Locke gestured to the door and waited for Gretchen to respond. She covered the phone and whispered, "You guys go on ahead. Mrs. Hanover's neighbor is a notary, and she'll get the notarized document to me this afternoon and to the dark-haired, handsome detective also."

"Perfect," Locke said then rapped his knuckles against her desk. "Thank you for your help."

Gretchen smiled at him and said, "It's my pleasure."

It was Sawyer's turn to exit first and saunter toward the Charger while Locke trailed behind him.

"That was some pretty smooth talking back there," Locke said. "Sounded very lawyer-like."

"I suppose it did," Sawyer replied casually.

"Have you read a bunch of law books or subscribed to magazines or something?"

Sawyer turned when he reached the car and shrugged casually. "Something like that." He had no intention of opening up to a man who might always resent his existence on the police force. If Locke wanted to know more about him, he could do his research. It wouldn't take him long to discover he'd gone to law school and passed the bar. Working in his father's law practice didn't stir his passion, so he'd chosen to uphold the law in a different way.

Locke imperceptibly shook his head. "I'll let you keep your secrets...for now."

You'll let me keep my secrets, Sawyer thought to himself. He wasn't sure if he was irritated by Locke's arrogant assumption that he could and would get the truth from him if he chose to do so or disappointed his partner didn't press for more information. Sawyer wanted to kick himself in the ass for caring one way or the other. Locke's smug smirk said he knew he'd won that round.

Even though they hadn't been inside the office long, the car was stifling hot. Sawyer resisted the urge to shove his face against the vent to cool himself off and hide the flush spreading across his cheeks. He considered himself a calm, rational man who didn't let people push his buttons, but Locke somehow managed to burrow beneath his skin in a matter of hours, making Sawyer a stranger to his own mind and body.

Damn him for being a sucker for wounded eyes and pretty lips. Locke would hate Sawyer viewing him that way, but it didn't make it less true. He'd need to harden his heart and excavate the man before he got too damn comfortable and drained the life out of Sawyer like a fucking tick.

"What do you think about Melody Jameson?" Locke asked, breaking the awkward silence as he reversed out of the parking spot. "Do you think she was truthful?"

"About which part?"

"That she never intended to publicly out Putz?"

"It's hard to say," Sawyer said. "I think Melody Jameson *wants* to believe she'd never do that to someone, but we saw what happened between her and Shirley Hanover. It could've been an isolated, knee-jerk reaction because the older woman brings out the worst in her, or it might be who she truly is. I mean, who is the real Melody Jameson?"

"You think she was bullshitting us?"

Sawyer shrugged. "I think we'll know more once we look through the folder she gave us."

"Fuck. I was so distracted I forgot to get the file from the inter-view room."

"She is beautiful," Sawyer said. "No worries though; I locked the file in my bottom desk drawer."

Locke chuckled. "I was referring to the case distracting me. Besides, she's not my type."

"Prefer a more natural beauty?" Sawyer asked to make conversation.

"Yes. I prefer an athletic build and *brunettes* over blondes."

Even though Sawyer suspected Locke meant brunette ladies, he still nearly choked on his saliva. Even if Locke was bi, pan, or even just curious, it was doubtful he'd want to scratch the itch with a man he saw as an unwanted intrusion into his life. It wouldn't be the first time Sawyer was attracted to a man who would never return his feelings, but he always got over it quickly. He didn't believe in wasting time and energy on things that would never happen. Locke would be no different. As soon as Sawyer accepted he was straight, it would be a breeze to get over his attraction, especially with Locke acting like the ace of dickheads.

Wounded eyes. Pretty lips.

"What's the code to get in?" Locke asked, pulling up to the keypad pedestal.

"Sixty-nine sixty-nine sixty-nine," Sawyer said dryly.

Locke turned toward him and shoved his sunglasses on top of his head. "For real?"

"Doesn't it sound like something Putz would use?"

Locke returned his glasses to his nose, punched in the code, and snorted when the gate slowly began to open. "Classy guy."

"The best," Sawyer agreed. "I can't imagine Shirley Hanover punching in that code."

"It's hard to imagine Shirley coming here unless Putz asked her to drop off the latest batch of hate mail at his storage unit."

"I hope this isn't where he keeps his fetish wear," Sawyer said, not bothering to hide the hard shiver working through him. "I don't ever kink shame, but I won't be able to see the items and *not* picture Putz in them. Just gross."

"Fuck. I hadn't even thought about it until you mentioned it.

48

Thanks a lot, asshole." Locke threw up his hands when the gate finally parted enough to fit the Charger through it. "That's the slowest moving gate I've ever seen."

Sawyer looked at the post with directional wooden arrows showing the way to the blocks of units. "Twenty-four hundred through twenty-six hundred is to the left."

Locke hung a left, and Sawyer looked at the wooden signs at the end of each block. "This one ends with twenty-three hundred, so it's the next group."

The units were larger than Sawyer expected, having both regular and rolling doors with electronic keypads on each. Locke chose the regular door and entered the same six-digit code he used to open the gate. A green light came on the keypad, and Locke turned the deadbolt then opened the door. Cool air greeted them when they stepped inside the dark space.

"Air-conditioned," Sawyer said, reaching for a light switch. "That will make our search more comfortable." He flipped the overhead fluorescent lights on and gasped.

"Holy fuck," Locke muttered.

Sawyer expected to see a lot of furniture, a few boxes of hate letters, and maybe a locked trunk Putz kept his naughty secrets in, but he'd been way off. There were only a few pieces of covered furniture, no trunks, and the rest of the large space was wall-to-wall cardboard boxes stacked three or four rows deep.

"These boxes can't all be filled with hate mail, right?" Locke said, sounding hopeful.

Sawyer walked over to the closest stack and looked at the top box. Someone had taken a black Sharpie and written: Wimpy Whiners. May 2019. "Afraid so," Sawyer told his partner.

"Fuck me."

"It's doubtful Putz's killer sent him a letter years ago and is just now acting on the threat. I say we take the boxes for the previous six months back to the precinct with us. We can have the rest picked up

if we need them. I'm sure our tech team found the most recent letters in the file folder Shirley told us about, if not, I can go back to the
scene and grab them." Sawyer put his hands on his hips and blew out
a breath. "I think I understand why Shirley said she'd have to download the digital hate mail onto a flash drive. There were too many to
send separately."

"Christ. Let's hope we solve this case *before* we spend days digging through these boxes."

Sawyer's cell phone rang on his belt. He unclipped it from his belt
and answered it. "Detective Key," he said into the phone. His greeting
was met with silence. "Hello?"

"Um, sorry, Detective," a soft, feminine voice said. "I didn't expect you to answer so fast, and I'd just taken a bite of my mid-morn-
ing snack."

"No problem. How can I help you?" Sawyer asked, not recognizing the phone number or the voice on the other end of the connection.

"Oh, geez," she said. "I'm making a horrible first impression.
First, I sounded like a perv getting my jollies off on your deep voice,
then I forget it's your first day with our department and you don't
have a clue who I am."

Sawyer didn't have the call on speaker, but Locke must've overheard enough to recognize the voice. "Hi, Kelsey," he said loud
enough for her to hear him because she giggled. "Please tell us you
found something we can use, sugar." *Sugar?* What was with that word
today? He should've been used to it living in Savannah his entire life,
but it was something that has always bothered him. At least no one
had blessed his heart yet, but he knew it was still early. "Put her on
speaker."

Sawyer mentally rolled his eyes but punched the button to engage the speakerphone. "Go ahead," Sawyer told her.

"Hi, I'm Kelsey Hightower," she said, starting over again.

"She's our best cyber tech," Locke added.

"Thank you, Detective Charmer," Kelsey replied. "I looked at

Roland Putzinski's domain account, and I was able to trace the IP address to the location where his last podcast episode was uploaded."

"Hot damn," Locke said, clapping his hands loudly then rubbing them together. "Attagirl, Kels."

"Not so fast, Detective," said Kelsey soberly. "I traced it to one of those internet cafés, so it's a little more complicated."

"Because all the computers located there will use the same IP address?" Locke asked.

"They all use the same external IP address provided to them by their internet service provider, but their router will assign unique internal IP addresses to each computer using their network."

"So you can pinpoint the exact computer our guy used?"

"I can if the internal IP addresses haven't been refreshed since our *person* was there this morning."

"Why would they be refreshed?" Locke asked.

"If the computers at the café connect to the internet via Wi-Fi, there will be a DCHP service running on the router that refreshes the internal IP addresses at specified intervals."

"DCHP?" Locke asked. Sawyer could tell he was trying to figure out the acronym.

"Dynamic Host Configuration Protocol," Sawyer told him.

"So you speak legalese and computer geek too?" Locke asked.

"I'm a man of many talents," Sawyer quipped.

Locke raised a brow but didn't comment. "Kels, can you meet us at the cybercafé and help us locate the computer so we can interview the staff and anyone still lingering around who might've been there."

"Absolutely. It's been a while since I got to work in the field." Kelsey rattled off the name of the café and their address. "I'll head out now."

"We're going to load a few boxes of Putz's hate mail into the trunk of my car. We'll meet you at the café."

"I have something else to tell you, and I'm afraid you won't like it."

"Just spit it out," Locke said. "Rip off the Band-Aid."

"Someone inside the precinct recorded the catfight between Shirley Hanover and Melody Jameson and sent it to an online tabloid. There have been a half a million views already."

Locke's and Sawyer's eyes met and held. "Fuck!" they both said.

"There's no way to force the site to take it down either," Locke groused.

"Not without a warrant," Sawyer added.

Locke released a breath. "I don't see how the video can hinder our investigation unless reporters start making a nuisance of themselves by camping outside the station."

"Too late," Kelsey said sweetly.

"They were going to hound us anyway because of Putz's notoriety," Sawyer told him. "We'll just decline to comment unless the chief or someone above her wants us to make an official statement."

"Let's grab those boxes and head out then," Locke said. "See you there, Kels."

"Looking forward to it."

Sawyer disconnected the call and returned it to the holder on his belt. He'd known nothing about this case or his partner would be easy, but he still wasn't prepared for the reality that punched him in the face.

"Put those big muscles to use and grab a few boxes," Locke said.

Lost in thought, Sawyer hadn't noticed Locke squatting down and picking up two boxes. He tried not to turn Locke's observation into a compliment, but he failed. Sawyer liked that Locke noticed his physique almost as much as he liked keeping him guessing about the various skillsets he brought to the job.

"Sometime today, Asshole," Locke said over his shoulder.

"Adonis Asshole with a deep sexy voice," Sawyer countered.

"She said you have a deep voice. You just added the sexy part."

"She meant sexy too."

"He speaks legalese and computer geek and reads minds," Locke said. "I'm almost looking forward to seeing your other tricks."

Fuck if Sawyer didn't want to show him every trick in his playbook.

CHAPTER 6

"**Y**OU WANT TO TALK ABOUT WHY YOU LEFT THE SHERIFF'S department?" Locke asked when he pulled onto the street. Sawyer thought the question came out of left field.

"You didn't read about it in the papers?"

"I did," Locke said firmly. "Now I want to hear it from you."

"Old sheriff retired. New sheriff elected. The new guy hates gays. The end."

"I think there's a lot more to the story than that," Locke said calmly. "I doubt very much Sheriff Wheeler was your first run-in with homophobia in the sheriff's department."

"The last straw came after my husband died. Things were said that I will never forgive. I won't apologize for standing up for my rights and for other members in the rainbow community. Rest assured that I wasn't responsible for leaking internal issues to Felix Franklin at the Savannah Morning News, if that's your concern." Sawyer worked hard to keep his tone neutral and not get defensive.

"That isn't what I said; I simply stated there had to be a bigger story for Chatham County's Golden Boy to walk away from a career he obviously loved. I think I understand better now."

Golden Boy. Sawyer had always hated the moniker when the press had given it to him, and he disliked it even more with the hint of derision he heard in Locke's voice. "I'm neither golden nor a boy." Sawyer kept his eyes trained forward but felt Locke's perusal.

"Guess you're not."

His partner hadn't wanted to know anything about him, then not even thirty minutes later, he started asking personal questions. "What happened to not wanting to know shit about me, anyway?"

"It's not the same thing, and you know it, Key."

"Oh?" Sawyer asked, his voice rising along with his temper. "How do you figure?"

"Not wanting to hear about your preferred burger toppings or knowing how you spend your free time isn't the same as wanting to be certain I can trust my partner."

"Look, we're both carrying baggage into this new partnership that neither of us wants to dissect or discuss. My abrupt departure from the sheriff's office *is* my baggage, and nothing about your attitude entices me to divulge the story to you. If you have questions, you can talk to Chief Rigby or call the sheriff's department and speak to my former partner. His name is Charlie Sharpe."

"In my experience, dissect and discuss usually mean the same thing," Locke quipped, seemingly trying to lighten the mood. *Too fucking bad.* "We don't have to be best buds, but I need to know my partner is going to have my back. I want to do my job without worrying you'll run to Felix Franklin every time I turn around."

Sawyer's jaw tightened, making his headache throb worse.

Breathe In. Hold. Release.

He felt some of the tension draining as his body relaxed. "So now, I'm a lying asshole Adonis with a sexy deep voice?"

Locke let out a long-suffering sigh like he was dealing with a five-year-old on the cusp of a tantrum. "I didn't mean to imply you're a liar."

"I told you I didn't leak the story about the homophobic prick's behavior to Felix, and you turned right around and expressed concern I'd dial him up every time I didn't like something you did. I was not and am not a rat, even if I had the fucking right to be. Do you really think so little of your chief to think she'd bring someone like that into her precinct?" Sawyer turned to gauge his partner's reaction to the question. What *did* Locke think about Rigby?

Locke shrugged like they were talking about something as mundane as whether the Braves stood a chance at winning their division. "I can see it's a touchy subject, and I shouldn't have brought it up until after lunch."

"There will never be a good time for you to imply I'm a dishonest man, Locke. Never," Sawyer said tersely. The pain in his head intensified, throbbing behind his eyes.

His partner blew out a frustrated breath. "I apologize."

Sawyer knew he should accept his apology, but he couldn't so much as nod. They rode in silence the rest of the way to the cybercafé, Bytes and Brew, on Price Street.

"Key," Locke began when he put the Charger in park outside the café. His phone rang before he could say anything else. He looked at the caller ID and muttered something unintelligible under his breath. "I have to take this call. Do you mind? I should only be a minute."

Sawyer didn't answer. He shoved open the door and headed toward the café; every step causing the pain to reverberate in his skull. Locke could think whatever he pleased about him, and he could take all the private calls he wanted. Sawyer couldn't allow those types of things to matter to him. Solving the case was his sole focus. Nothing else.

There were only a few patrons sipping coffee and using the computers, and none of them looked up when the bell above the door chimed as he entered. Even if they'd been present when the potential killer uploaded the podcast episode, it was unlikely these people noticed anything about them.

At the counter, a tall, lean African American woman turned from speaking to the hipster cutie behind the counter and smiled at Sawyer. Riotous curls framed a face so stunning it should be gracing the covers of magazines and billboards. She wore a navy blue sheath dress, matching stacked heel sandals, gold hoop earrings, and a badge on a lanyard that identified her as an employee of the Savannah Police Department. The smile faded from her face when she noticed Sawyer's thunderous expression.

Sawyer immediately regretted the loss of her sunniness. Pulling himself together, he forced a smile and crossed the room. "Kelsey?"

She graced him with another open, friendly smile. "It's good to meet you, Detective Key. I apologize for our awkward introduction earlier."

"No worries. Have you learned anything interesting yet?"

"Detective Key, this is the owner of Bytes and Brew, Levi Hammonds."

Levi smiled warmly then extended his hand. "Good to meet you, Detective."

"Likewise, Mr. Hammonds."

"Please, call me Levi."

The bells over the door chimed again, and Sawyer knew without looking that his partner had entered. He hated the awareness coursing through his veins with a passion. Rather than acknowledge the dickhead, he kept his gaze locked on Levi's, who blushed charmingly.

"Who pissed in Locke's Cheerios this morning?" Kelsey asked. Sawyer held up his hand, earning a melodic giggle from Kelsey. "I think I'm going to like you a lot."

"Catch me up," Locke brusquely said when he joined them.

After Kelsey made quick introductions, Locke asked, "Were you able to figure out which computer our person used?"

"Slow your roll," Kelsey said. "I just arrived seconds before Dark and Dreamy rolled in here like a thundercloud."

"I have a headache I can't seem to shake," Sawyer told her. Kelsey shifted her gaze to Locke and smiled.

"You know I have that effect on people, Kels."

"That I do," she agreed.

"Ms. Hightower provided me the IP address you're looking for. I'll be able to direct you to the right computer, but I'm afraid I won't be able to give you much of a description. We were slammed this morning."

"You don't have security cameras?" Sawyer asked.

"I do, but I only turn them on when we're closed. We've never had any trouble here, so it never occurred to me to turn the cameras on during the day. I'll need to rethink that decision going forward."

"Maybe the person did some other business around the same time, which could give the detectives a clue about their identity," Kelsey said hopefully.

Levi typed a few things into his computer then said, "Computer twenty-seven. It's the one in the far-right corner." He tilted his head to the side and thought for a second. "What time was it uploaded?"

Kelsey consulted the notes on her phone. "It was uploaded at seven this morning."

"It didn't go live until after nine," Locke said.

"You can upload posts and schedule them to release at a future time," Kelsey told him.

"Do you remember anything about the person who used the computer then?" Locke asked.

"Between the students starting summer classes at the community college today, and the locals who prefer to get their java fix here rather than the overpriced coffee chains, we had a full house until ten o'clock. I honestly can't tell you which person who passed through this morning sat at computer twenty-seven."

"What about payment?" Sawyer asked. "They have to buy internet time, correct?"

"That's our only hope," Levi said, typing away. "None of the patrons here now were present this morning. Oh, it looks like your person was on the computer from six fifty to seven twenty. They used a prepaid debit card to pay for their thirty minutes. No information is coming up, so they didn't register the card before using it." Prepaid debit cards were the monetary equivalent to burner phones.

"Damn it," Locke groused.

"Levi, do you get a lot of regulars here each morning?" Sawyer asked.

"Yes, we have several. Some of the regulars are really particular about the computer they use too. In fact, Becca prefers computer twenty-six, so maybe she can help describe the person."

"Do you know how we can get in touch with Becca?"

"I don't, but she should be back tomorrow around six thirty, and she usually stays until eight."

"I'll stop by and talk to her," Sawyer said, watching Levi's adorable blush return.

"In the meantime, I'll unlock computer twenty-seven so you can take a look at the history."

"Perfect," Kelsey said cheerfully. "Thank you, Levi."

Levi looked at Sawyer and said, "I bet I can help you with your headache." Sawyer's eyebrow rose, making the hipster stutter. "I... um...m-meant a cup of coffee on the house. Caffeine helps."

Sawyer looked up at the menu. "I'll take a salted caramel with an extra shot of espresso." Levi shook his head when he reached for his wallet, and Sawyer decided accepting a cup of coffee from the man was harmless. He wasn't a suspect or even a witness.

"I have some ibuprofen tablets in my purse too," Kelsey said. "Want some?"

"Sure. You're a saint."

"Kels," Locke said abruptly, pulling their attention to him. "Would you be able to give Key a ride back to the station? I received an important call right before I came in, and I need to take care of something." His voice was toneless and devoid of emotion and he refuse to meet Sawyer's gaze. Was he telling the truth or just trying to unload Sawyer after their argument in the car?

Kelsey looked back and forth between the two men. "Of course."

"Thanks, honey. I owe you lunch." Sawyer tried his best not to be insulted by Locke's remark. "I won't be long, but call me if something comes up." Since his partner had decided to talk about him like he wasn't present, Sawyer wasn't sure which one of them Locke was speaking to, so he didn't respond or visibly react when Locke left.

"Here you go, Detective," Levi said, handing his salted caramel coffee to him.

"Thank you, Levi." The man truly had a lovely smile and the square, black glasses made his blue eyes stand out more.

"Come on, Romeo," Kelsey said, hooking her arm through his and steering him toward computer twenty-seven. She sat down in the chair then pulled out a large bottle of Advil from her purse. "Here you go."

Sawyer shook out three tablets then handed the bottle back to her. He popped the tablets in his mouth and washed them down with a sip of very hot, but delicious, coffee. "Do you think our person was silly enough to leave us a clue?" he asked.

"Doubt it, but we have to try." Kelsey's slender fingers danced over the keyboard, and the clacking of her hot pink fingernails reminded Sawyer of his niece's tap dance recitals. "Mmm-hmm. It's what we thought. Let me check one other place." She typed a few more seconds then scrolled through some fields. More typing and an administrator login box popped up. "Why don't you ask your new friend to come over here and assist us for a second?"

Sawyer turned around and caught Levi watching them. The man smiled nervously when Sawyer busted him ogling his ass, but Levi didn't hesitate to join them when Sawyer waved him over.

"Our person cleared the history but wouldn't have been able to permanently delete the browsing data without administrator privileges. Do you mind logging in so we can see what they cleared?"

"Please tell me they checked their Facebook account," Sawyer said.

Levi entered the password then stood off to the side.

"Unfortunately, not," Kelsey said. "The only thing our person accessed during the timeframe was the website to upload the podcast."

"Damn," Levi said. "I'm sorry I couldn't be more helpful."

"You've been very helpful, Levi," Kelsey said. "You've given Detective Key the name of someone to talk to tomorrow."

"And this coffee is amazing. Thank you."

"My pleasure," Levi said. Sawyer really liked the earnest appraisal he saw in the man's blue gaze. It helped take his mind off his abrasive, dickhead for a partner. "I guess I'll see you in the morning."

"You will."

Levi started to say something else, but the bells above the door chimed. "Good morning, Mr. Pettigrew," he said to the elderly man who shuffled in.

"Almost afternoon," the man replied. "You got any of that chicken salad I like so much, or is it too early still?"

Levi smiled at Sawyer and Kelsey then followed Mr. Pettigrew to the counter. "I have some ready for you. Croissant, wrap, or bread?"

"Are you really going to ask me that?" the older man groused.

"It's always better to ask than assume," Levi replied, but he was looking once more in Sawyer's direction.

"Croissant. Always the croissant."

"Want to stick around for lunch?" Kelsey asked.

Chicken salad on a croissant sounded delicious, but he was eager to return to the station. "Nah. I need to look through the file of evidence Putz's widow gave me." Interviewing the yoga instructor was his next priority, with the private investigator ranking a close second.

Kelsey kept the conversation light on the way back to the precinct. Sawyer learned she was originally from Atlanta and hadn't moved to Savannah until after she'd graduated college. "It's far enough away to give myself much-needed freedom and independence from my family but close enough that I can visit them frequently."

"Wise," Sawyer said. "I should've tried that." Not that there was any place on the planet he could hide where his mother wouldn't find him.

"Your family lives close by?"

"Close enough," Sawyer quipped. "Have you listened to Putz's final podcast yet?" he asked, steering the conversation away from his personal life. He liked Kelsey and felt they had clicked, but he was slow to trust these days.

"Not yet," Kelsey said. "I'm not sure I can stomach hearing it."

"It sounds pretty gruesome."

"I was referring to whatever vitriol the man was spewing before someone killed him. Jerry is the one who's scrubbing the tape to see if he can find any clues. He's the very best." Sawyer detected a hint of something else besides professional admiration in her tone of voice.

A dozen or more news vans lined the streets surrounding the precinct, creating a traffic nightmare with gawkers straining their necks to see what was going on. Sawyer noticed a few reporters standing in front of cameras outside the station when Kelsey drove by. Even though the local news wouldn't be airing updates until noon, the national networks would be looking for live updates every thirty minutes or hour. No reporter would give up the opportunity to go live on the big networks. It could be the big break they knew was just around the corner.

"Vultures," Kelsey muttered. Sawyer didn't disagree.

His headache had started to recede by the time Kelsey pulled into the parking lot behind the building until he saw a familiar red convertible BMW parked next to his Audi.

"Are you okay?" Kelsey asked.

"Did I groan out loud?"

"Yeah. Is it the headache?"

"Not exactly. It would seem my mother has decided to visit me at work today."

"That's a bad thing?"

"More like bad timing."

"I could keep driving," Kelsey offered.

"Tempting. So very tempting."

Kelsey laughed and pulled into a parking spot. "Don't say I didn't try to help."

"I won't forget your kindness."

Kelsey's delightful laugh put a smile on his face. Her reaction to seeing his mother in the bullpen visiting with detectives he hadn't even met yet was even better. "Oh my God! Do you know who that is? What's she doing here?"

"Who?" Sawyer asked, playing dumb.

"How gay are you?" she asked. "That's Evangeline O'Neal. One of the most famous supermodels in the history of supermodels. Civil rights activist. Animal lover. She's so kickass. She must be getting close to sixty-five, but you wouldn't know it to look at her."

"You better not let her hear you say that, Kelsey. My mother isn't a day over fifty-nine."

She looked like a cartoon character when her mouth fell open. "Mother?"

Evangeline turned just then and spotted them. She excused herself and crossed the room. "There's my boy."

CHAPTER 7

"Hello, Mom," Sawyer said, hugging her. He loved the way she always smelled—like jasmine and vanilla. As frustrating as she could be at times, there were two things he knew about his mother: she would love him unconditionally beyond her last breath, and her signature perfume stirred a sense of peace and happiness within him.

"Do you have time for lunch today? The nice detectives in your unit told me you caught a real humdinger on your first day with SPD." Sawyer had planned to eat at his desk while looking through Melody Jameson's file, but he could tell by his mother's expression she wouldn't take no for an answer. "I know you're trying to solve a crime, but a detective still has to eat, especially on his birthday." *Yep. Not taking no for an answer and playing dirty to get her way.*

"Today's your birthday?" Kelsey asked, grabbing Evangeline's attention.

"Son, introduce me to this magnificent woman? Why am I running into you at a police station and not on the runway at fashion week in Milan?"

"Mother, please allow me to introduce you to Kelsey Hightower. She's one of our cyber techs who helps us solve crimes."

"Beautiful *and* brilliant. I love that in a woman."

Kelsey covered her chest with both hands. "Ms. O'Neal..." It seemed Kelsey was too emotional to continue.

"No formalities. Please call me Evangeline."

"Oh, I couldn't possibly," Kelsey said, shaking her head. "I just want to say how much I appreciate all the things you do to make the world a better place. You don't just throw your money and name behind a cause, you take to the streets and make a difference."

"Kelsey, thank you so much. Do you know who inspires me to do great things? I'll give you a hint. He's tall, brooding, and is really upset with his mother for letting it slip that today is his birthday. He's a remarkable man, my son."

"I agree wholeheartedly," Kelsey said, earning a disbelieving look from Sawyer. They'd just met; there's no way she could know that.

"It's almost twelve thirty, so can you grab a quick bite to eat now?"

Locke had disappeared for who knew how long to do who knew what. Surely, no one would begrudge Sawyer having a quick lunch with his mother on his birthday.

"Now is fine, ma'am," Chief Rigby said, stepping up beside him. She smiled at everyone then focused on Sawyer. "You'll get to spend many days hunkered over your desk while looking through evidence. Today doesn't have to be one of them. Locke called me a few minutes ago and informed me he needed to handle a personal matter. Go have a nice lunch with your mother."

Evangeline aimed her widest smile at Sawyer's superior officer. "Hello, Chief Rigby. I don't know if you remember, but we met at a charity event last year."

"How could I forget? It was a lovely evening. It's nice to see you again, ma'am."

"And you also. Please tell your lovely wife I said hello." Evangeline turned to Sawyer. "Both these smart women highly recommend you have lunch with me. What do you say?"

"There's no way I can refuse you," Sawyer said, kissing his

mother's cheek. "I won't be long, Chief. There are a few more interviews I'd like to conduct today. Would you prefer I wait for Detective Locke or proceed on my own?"

"Run the investigation however you see fit. If Locke doesn't like it, he can come see me."

"Yes, ma'am."

"Enjoy lunch," Chief Rigby said before walking away.

"I'm going to head back to my cubicle," Kelsey said, taking a few steps backward. "Thank you for allowing me to work in the field with you today."

"My pleasure. I'll keep you posted on what we find."

"You'll have to join us for lunch next time," Evangeline told Kelsey.

"That would be lovely. You guys have a wonderful lunch."

"See you later, Kels."

He knew every eye was on them when they left the precinct, but he was used to it after thirty-four years.

"I made a reservation at Giancarlo's since it's your favorite," Evangeline said when they walked outside into the sweltering heat. His mother looked resplendent in a white, flowy dress and strappy sandals. She looked cool and immaculate while Sawyer's clothes stuck to him.

"Reservations, huh? You didn't just happen to be in the neighborhood?"

"Have you ever known me to play coy? I had every intention of treating you to lunch for your birthday, even if I had to drag you out of there kicking and screaming."

"As if I'd ever embarrass Evangeline O'Neal in public," Sawyer scoffed.

"You've always been such a delightful person, Sawyer. I meant every word I said to Kelsey. You make me want to be a better human too."

Sawyer's heart squeezed in his chest. "You humble me, Mom."

"Enough of this over-the-top emotional stuff. The heat is threatening to ruin my makeup. The last thing I need to do is add tears to the mix." Once they were in the car and driving toward Giancarlo's, she asked, "What do you think about your new partner?"

"He's an insufferable dickhead."

"Whoa," Evangeline said. "Why don't you tell me how you really feel?"

"There's no way to sugarcoat it." Sawyer told her about his first meeting with Locke then followed it up by repeating the "I don't want to be friends" speech.

"Uh oh."

"Uh oh?" Sawyer repeated.

Evangeline stopped at the red light and turned to look at her son. "You can't resist rescuing wounded things, and Detective Locke sounds like the most wounded of them all."

"I don't disagree with your assessment, but even I know a lost cause when I see one."

"Many people would've discounted your precious Bones, but you saved him, and look how he turned out. He is over twenty pounds of fur, rumbling purrs, and cuddles."

"Locke is nothing like my cat," Sawyer said, but inwardly grinned because he'd used the same analogy earlier in the day. Locke would never lie against Sawyer's chest, purring in pleasure like Bones did. His traitorous brain painted a picture of just how beautiful the moment could be, and Sawyer's visceral reaction went straight to his balls. He was grateful for the distraction when his mother pulled beneath the portico at Giancarlo's.

"Good afternoon, Ms. O'Neal," the valet attendant said when he opened her door.

"Good afternoon, Roberto. Take good care of my baby." The valet's attention shifted to Sawyer. "Not *that* one," Evangeline told the kid who couldn't be older than twenty. "It must be the scruff you're sporting these days," she told Sawyer when they were walking to the entrance. "Makes you look a little edgy and dangerous. The boys can't seem to resist it."

"I'm not interested in dating boys, Mom."

"Who said anything about *dating*? As long as they're consenting adults, whose business is it? Or do you have someone else in mind?"

Sawyer's brain started to form a picture of Locke, but he forcibly changed the image to a sweet man with nerdy glasses, blue eyes, and the prettiest blush Sawyer had ever seen. "Maybe. We'll see."

Evangeline let out a sigh that sounded hopeful. She'd never pressured Sawyer to move on after Victor died of colon cancer two years ago. She'd said he would know when his heart had healed enough to love again. Sawyer wasn't sure Levi was the one he'd fall for, but it was the first time he was interested in going on a real date since losing his husband. It was a step in the right direction.

When Sawyer returned to the precinct after lunch, his stomach felt full and heavy, but his spirits were much lighter. Earlier that morning, most of the detectives were already out in the field by the time he left Rigby's office. After lunch, the heat and humidity chased them all back inside to work at their desks, if their investigations permitted.

Sawyer introduced himself around, receiving many "welcome to the team" and "happy birthday" messages. He wondered how they all knew it was his birthday since his mother hadn't announced the occasion through a bullhorn. Then he saw the birthday balloons and the bakery box on his desk. Kelsey had to be the culprit behind it.

Sawyer opened the large pink box and found two dozen, brightly colored cupcakes. He was stuffed from lunch but knew he'd find room for one. He could resist cookies, cakes, pies, and doughnuts but cupcakes were his kryptonite.

"Anyone in the mood for a cupcake?" Sawyer asked.

He went from being the new guy to the favorite guy in seconds. Across the bullpen, Locke leaned against his desk with his arms crossed over his chest. His eyes shifted to the cheerful mylar balloons announcing his celebration. Locke looked like he wanted to stomp across the room and stab the balloons with a pair of scissors.

Sawyer took a big bite from a chocolate cupcake with fluffy lilac-colored frosting. Resigned to being the bigger man, Sawyer held the box out toward Locke as a peace offering. Locke slowly straightened to his full height and crossed the room.

"I'm not surprised you'd pick the cupcake that matches your shirt. I bet your underwear is the same color," Locke said, picking up a vanilla cupcake with mint green icing.

Several responses came to mind: Sawyer could tell him it was none of his business, he could inform Locke his comment was inappropriate for the workplace, or he could tell him to go choke on his cupcake. He chose none of those. Instead, he leaned forward, lowered his voice to barely a whisper, and said, "You're assuming I wear them."

Locke had just taken a bite of the cupcake and choked. Sawyer had killed two birds with one stone; he gained the upper hand and made Locke choke without voicing his petty thought out loud.

His partner coughed a bit but recovered easily enough. "I had that coming," he reluctantly admitted.

"And more," Sawyer tossed back.

"Grab the folder Melody Jameson dropped off and meet me in the conference room at the end of the hall. I put the boxes we brought from Putz's storage locker in there already. Mrs. Hanover's flash drive arrived while you were out, so I set up my laptop in there. There are thousands upon thousands of letters. I guess we'll make it our command center until the chief boots us out.

"Sure, but I need to make a quick detour upstairs. I know Kelsey is responsible for the cupcakes and balloons, so I'd like to thank her in person and offer her a cupcake."

"No problem." Locke seemed much more relaxed than he was

that morning. If Sawyer didn't know better, he'd say Locke's "personal business" included him letting off some steam. Sawyer refused to think of the ways his partner achieved it.

Sawyer's visit with Kelsey was brief. He hugged and thanked her for the treats and passed the pastry box around, making fast friends with the cyber tech team. He stopped by his desk long enough to unlock the bottom drawer and grab the file before heading to the conference room.

"Where do you want to start?" Sawyer asked, dropping down in the chair opposite from Locke's.

"The only update I have so far is from Jerry, who's our most seasoned analyst on the tech team. He was unable to detect any background noises that gave our guy away. I asked him to email the scrubbed version to me, and I couldn't detect anything. I'll cue it up for you to listen to if you want, but I want to warn you it's really disturbing."

"The brutal murder or the message Putz was spewing before he died?" Sawyer asked, thinking of what Kelsey said earlier.

"Both. Would you like me to recap it for you, or do you want to hear it?"

"Recap," Sawyer said without hesitation. "If the trained professional couldn't pick out background clues using high-tech equipment, I certainly won't."

"The hate message of the week was that gays are the cause of the hurricane barreling toward the southeast Atlantic Coast states. Savannah has become overrun with them, and this is God's way of cleaning house," Locke said somberly.

"That's not a new message," Sawyer said, rolling his eyes.

"That's as far as he got before someone started cracking his skull. You don't even hear a door open or footsteps. You just hear Putz getting cut off by a loud thump and what sounds like his body crashing to the floor. The loud thumping continues for about ninety seconds. The assailant doesn't let out a peep the entire time—not a grunt, a curse, or a groan. They just keep clobbering him. Ninety seconds doesn't sound like a long time, but a person can strike something with a bat dozens of times in that span."

"Jesus," Sawyer said. "Did Jerry think the recording was too clean?"

"He didn't rule out the possibility it was scrubbed before it was uploaded, but he said it would have to be high-end equipment to erase the signs of editing from him. He found no evidence someone had tampered with it."

"So, no clues from the recording. I think the next two likely interviews need to be Jacque, the yoga instructor, and Rocky Jacobs, the private investigator. Who first?"

"I'd say Jacque," Locke replied. "The PI could be in the field. I'm not a fan of investigators, but some of them are good guys. It's best not to piss them off needlessly, so I'll call his office and request a meeting if you call and see if the yoga instructor is at his studio. I imagine he does in-home sessions for clients, and it makes no sense to drive to his studio if he's not going to be there. I'm sure Melody has informed him of our conversation today, so he might have gone to ground."

"Deal." Sawyer dialed the number to the studio and listened to it ring while Locke did the same with the PI. A receptionist picked up on the third ring. Rather than tip her off he was a cop, Sawyer softened his voice and said, "Hello, sugar. Can I please speak to Jacque? My best friend told me he is the master at what he does, and honey, I'm in desperate need of his *help*." The receptionist politely told Sawyer that Jacque wasn't in and wouldn't be available for a few days. "Oh, surely he has a private number for his best clients. I know my girl wasn't playing with me about that. Come on; help a queen out." It was no good. The receptionist was trained well to guard her employer's information. "I'll just call him back later this week. Thank you, sugar."

When Sawyer disconnected the call, he looked up and caught Locke staring at him with his mouth hanging open.

"No luck. Jacque isn't scheduled to be in the studio for a few days. I guess we'll need to go knock on his door. Did you reach the PI?"

"I had to leave a voicemail message," Locke replied without blinking.

Sawyer snapped his fingers, breaking his partner's trance. "What's your problem?"

"Am I dreaming right now?"

"How about I slug you and we find out?" Sawyer suggested. "So what? I can get campy if the situation calls for it."

"Funny," Locke said dryly. "I'm serious, Key. Who are you really?" He held up a finger. "Asshole." *Two fingers.* "Speaks legal shit and computer geek." *Three fingers.* "Attracted to nerds." *Four fingers.* "Son of a legendary supermodel." *Five fingers.* "Campy on cue."

"You forgot the sexy-voiced Adonis part."

"That's your list, not mine. How the hell didn't I know that Evangeline Freaking O'Neal is your mother after the paper ran all those articles about you for nearly a year?"

"It's Evangeline Frances O'Neal. They didn't print the familial connection because my mother is the sweetheart of the South and above reproach."

"Huh."

"Attracted to nerds?" Sawyer questioned.

"I'm a detective. I didn't miss the cute little exchange between you and the café owner. He has something for your headache all right."

"Listen, Locke. You can keep a running tally on my attributes, or lack thereof, all you want, but I'm drawing the line at you removing your shoes and socks to count them out with your toes."

"How about this finger?" Locke asked, flipping him off.

A well-lubed middle finger was one of Sawyer's favorite things in the world, but it wasn't something he'd tell Locke. Just thinking about it made him want to squirm in his chair. He tapped a few things into the laptop and pulled up Jacque's home address. "Come on," Sawyer said, scooting his chair back and getting to his feet. "Let's drop by the yoga master's house. Maybe we'll get lucky."

Locke snorted, forcing Sawyer's eyes up to meet his. "Something tells me you'd have better luck if you stopped by the cybercafé on your way home."

"I'm dropping by in the morning to interview Becca, who is a potential witness," Sawyer said, not taking the bait.

Locke opened the conference room door and gestured for Sawyer to precede him. "According to the grapevine, you're now older than I am. Age before beauty."

It was Sawyer's turn to brandish his middle finger.

CHAPTER 8

"**A**RE YOU SURE YOU LOOKED UP THE RIGHT GUY," LOCKE ASKED when he pulled the Charger up to the guardhouse in front of the ornate gates keeping unwanted visitors away from the ritzy gated community in Isle of Hope. "This guard shack looks more like a miniature castle. I think it's constructed of real stone and not that fake stuff."

"We're in the right place. Jacque, the yoga master, lives here. His business and home are registered under the name Clark Seaver," Sawyer said.

"Yeah, Jacque sounds more pretentious than Clark, which allows him to charge more per hour for his *sessions*."

"Are you implying his yoga studio is a front for an escort service or something?" Sawyer asked his partner.

Locke didn't answer him because a guard ambled over to the window and opened it. Frigid air Sawyer associated with a meat locker rolled out of the guardhouse, but he understood the need for excessive chilled air when he saw the guard was dressed in fine livery that would rival the best-dressed doorman in New York City. Only the guards at Buckingham Palace dressed better than this guy. At least he wasn't forced to wear one of those big hats.

"Gentlemen," the guard said. "What can I do for you?"

Locke showed him his badge. "We're here to interview a resident. Will you kindly open the gate?"

"Which resident?" the man asked.

"I'm not required to answer that, so I won't." They didn't want Clark Seaver, aka Jacque, going to ground.

The guard held up his hands in mock surrender. "I was only asking. There's no need to get testy." The man punched a button and the gates opened. "Have a good day, Officers."

Locke closed the window and drove through them. "Can you believe the way he's dressed. Does the queen live back here?"

"I know a few queens who live back here, but I don't think that's what you meant," Sawyer quipped. Many of the prominent members of the LGBTQ+ community lived in this neighborhood. Even though he'd attended several parties here over the years, he wasn't familiar with all the street names or the layout, so Sawyer had entered the address in the car's GPS back at the station.

Locke followed the directions, navigating the pristine paved roads winding past immaculate homes for a few minutes before answering the question Sawyer had asked when at the guardhouse.

"I didn't mean to imply the guy is up to anything illegal or sleazy, but it's hard for me to believe he has enough clients like Melody to make this possible," Locke said.

"He could be a trust fund baby," Sawyer suggested. "Maybe he's financially free to follow his passion."

"Which is teaching people to stretch and breathe?"

"There's more to yoga than stretching and breathing." Sawyer looked out the passenger window, catching a glimpse of the palatial estates between breaks in the dense trees surrounding them, and remembering the last time he'd been back here.

It was before Victor was diagnosed with cancer, and they'd only been married for a little over a year. They were still in the honeymoon phase where they couldn't get enough of each other. Victor had kept his hand possessively on Sawyer's thigh during the entire trip unless

74

he needed it to drive. They'd pulled up in front of their friend's home and kissed like they might never get another chance before going inside.

Sawyer swallowed down a lump of sorrow. He knew this day was going to be difficult for so many reasons, and he dreaded going home to a quiet house. He used to love his birthday because Vic made them so special, but now he wished he could forget he had them. *Breathe in. Hold. Release.*

"You'll get to use your yoga skills a lot around me."

"I already have," Sawyer said when Locke made the final turn on to a winding, paved driveway. Sawyer let out a sharp whistle when the house came into view. The large two-story stone and glass structure sat at the top of a hill overlooking an immaculately groomed yard.

"How do you get grass this green?"

"It looks like the same kind they use for professional baseball fields. He's even hired a landscaper to cut it in the same kinds of lines you see at ballparks."

"It makes me want to stomp across it," Locke shamelessly admitted.

"Piss on it too?"

Locke chuckled. "Busted." Locke parked the Charger in the middle of the circle drive in front of the house. "I hope this guy is home and is willing to talk."

"I guess we'll find out," Sawyer said, pushing open his door. "Damn. Could it get any hotter out here?" He slid his finger beneath the neck of his shirt, trying to peel it away from his damp skin.

"I told you to lose the tie earlier. It's only going to get more humid because another storm is rolling in," Locke said, gesturing to the dark clouds in the distance. "I figure we have about forty-five minutes to an hour before it hits. Hopefully, we'll be back at the station poring over threatening emails, hate letters, and the neighborhood canvas notes from the uniforms. I wouldn't refuse coffee and a second round of cupcakes."

Sawyer followed his partner up the broad set of steps leading to the front door. "I shouldn't eat another one, especially after eating one of those bear claws Chief Rigby's wife made."

Locke stopped suddenly and turned to face Sawyer with a stern scowl on his face, making him lurch to a halt too. "Are you fucking with me right now because I was a jerk to you earlier?"

"You were a dickhead to me earlier, but no, I'm not jerking around with you."

"Chief Rigby gave you one of her coveted bear claws?"

Sawyer studied Locke's expression to see if he was the one fucking around. His astonishment looked sincere. "Yes. They are delicious, so I guess I can see why she doesn't share...often."

Locke narrowed his eyes. "You asked for one, didn't you?"

"No. She offered, and I accepted."

"I've worked for Rigby for five years, and I've looked longingly at those bear claws dozens of times. She's never once offered one to me or anyone else in the precinct."

"That you know of," Sawyer countered. "Maybe they've all had a crack at her bear claws, and they're just not telling you."

"That's cruel."

"You should try playing hard to get and stop drooling in her office."

"You—"

"Detectives Locke and Key, I presume." Locke spun around, and both detectives stared at the shirtless, sweaty man standing in the doorway. Sawyer would recognize that voice and body anywhere but hoped like hell he was playing it cool. On the job or not, he couldn't resist letting his gaze roam over the chiseled pecs, tight abs, and bulging biceps on display. At least Sawyer kept his eyes above the waistband of the man's mesh shorts, although he knew what he'd find if he allowed his eyes to keep traveling south. "Melody told me you'd probably stop by. Come on in." The glistening hunk turned around and headed inside his house, leaving the door open for them to follow.

"You don't get a body like his working on a yoga mat," Locke said. When Sawyer didn't respond, he turned and looked at him curiously. "What's wrong with you? Do you know him or something?"

Sawyer cleared his throat. "Something like that."

"This isn't the time to be coy," Locke said tersely. "Did you pick this guy up at a club or something? If so, you can't be involved in questioning him."

"No," Sawyer assured him. "I've never met the guy before today."

"But you do recognize him from someplace. Where?" Locke's eyes widened suddenly. "Porn?" he guessed. Sawyer nodded. "Gay porn?" Sawyer nodded again. "Is his junk as big as the rest of him?"

That wasn't a question Sawyer expected a straight man to ask, but it snapped him out of his daze. *And made him question those rumors again.* "Jesus. I'm not answering that. Come on, dickhead."

Sawyer left Locke standing there gaping and wondering while he went in search of Clark, aka Jacque, aka Randy Dagger. As soon as he walked inside Clark's home, Sawyer noticed a gorgeous black-and-white photo of a naked Clark Seaver wrapped in the embrace of an equally stunning nude man.

"That's a gorgeous photo, Mr. Seaver," Sawyer said, not bothering to hide his admiration. He didn't have to confess he recognized the photo from Vic's all-time-favorite porn scene.

"Thank you. It feels like a lifetime has passed since we took the photo."

Sawyer heard Locke enter the house then stutter to a stop. He knew if he turned and looked, Locke would be staring at the sexy picture. It was hard to miss since it was at least five feet tall and three feet wide.

Clark Seaver chuckled and said, "Can I interest either of you in something to drink? I have lemonade, water, soda, and iced coffee."

"I would love a glass of lemonade," Sawyer said.

"I'll take one too," Locke added.

"Follow me to the kitchen, and you can interview me there."

Locke didn't say anything until they reached the kitchen. "I must say, this is a beautiful home, Mr. Seaver. Forgive me for my boldness, but I didn't realize yoga instructors earned this kind of money."

Seaver blew out a breath. "You're wondering how many other scams I've run besides the one I helped Melody with, right?"

"The thought had crossed my mind," Locke admitted.

"The answer is zero. Are you Locke or Key?" Seaver asked him.

Sawyer reached over the kitchen island and offered his hand. "I'm Detective Key, and this is my partner, Detective Locke." Locke might not like him throwing the word partner around, but it was true, and he could get over it. "Sorry for the lack of introductions."

"No problem," he told Sawyer then turned to Locke. "I only helped Melody out because she's my friend."

"Not just your client?" Sawyer asked.

"No," Seaver said. "To paint a clear picture, I need to set the stage a bit. I met Melody Jameson during our freshman year in college, and we became immediate friends. She was bright, smart, and full of life and she didn't care I was gay and fucking other guys on camera to pay my way through college. She is the most loyal person I've ever met." Seaver paused, searching the detectives for any signs of derision or surprise. "You either knew it already, or you have the best poker faces I've ever seen."

"Or both," Locke said ambiguously. "What does this have to do with Melody Jameson's marriage and your willingness to help her out with Roland Putzinski?"

"Mel and I lost touch after graduation. It was just sheer luck when we ran into each other at a coffee shop here in Savannah. She'd changed so much I almost didn't recognize her."

"We've seen her before-and-after plastic surgery pictures," Sawyer said. "I can see why you might not have known it was her right away."

"It was more than her looks, Detectives. Her confidence and spar-kle were gone. Instead of looking into vibrant blue eyes, I was looking into the lifeless, dull eyes of a doll. I had to know what happened to my friend, but she wasn't willing to talk about it. I offered to help her work through her stress with yoga, and she started opening up to me after a few months. Discovering she was married to that monster was a complete shock."

Sawyer accepted the glass of lemonade from him without managing to stare at his broad chest. "Did you train her at your studio or her home?"

"We started out at my studio but then moved the sessions to her house while Roland was at work. This was before he was fired from his job. I had no desire to run into the son of a bitch. He left for the radio station each morning around seven thirty, and I would arrive at their home around nine."

"Five days a week?" Locke asked, writing down notes.

Seaver set the glass of lemonade in front of Locke then poured himself a glass too. "Three."

"How did you go from teaching Melody yoga techniques to accepting money from her to let Putz blow you so a PI could catch it on camera?" Locke wasn't pulling any punches.

"One day, Putz returned home for his briefcase while I was working out with Melody. I got the impression he thought he'd catch us fucking or something, but instead of proving she was unfaithful, Putz outed himself."

Locke stopped writing and looked up at Seaver. "Outed himself how?"

A lightbulb went off in Sawyer's head. "He recognized you as Randy Dagger."

Seaver nodded then smiled wolfishly. "He did, and so did you." Sawyer shrugged like it was no big deal, but he felt heat creeping up his neck. "At first, I thought his stunned expression was because of my size, but he slipped and called me Randy even after Melody introduced me as Jacque."

"Oh fuck," Locke said. "Since Melody knew about your earlier porn days, she knew there was only one way Putz would recognize you."

"Then it all started making sense to her," Sawyer said. "The years of supposed impotence because of her physical appearance had nothing to do with her looks and everything to do with her gender."

"Can you believe the son of a bitch? Emotionally abusing a sweet, young woman because he hated himself for being gay. To make matters worse, he got off on gay porn then turned around and talked about homosexuals being the downfall of society. Melody didn't ask me to set that fucker up; I volunteered."

"How?" Locke asked.

"How'd I what? Get it up for him? There were plenty of times I wasn't in the mood during my porn career, and I still managed to film scenes. I took a Viagra, closed my eyes, and pretended I was with someone else."

"What about the money?" Sawyer asked. "Melody told us she paid you a few thousand dollars."

"Look around, Detectives," Seaver said, gesturing to a luxurious kitchen as grand as any you'd see in a *Better Homes and Gardens* magazine spread. "Does it look like I needed the money?"

"Then why'd you take it?" Locke asked.

"Melody insisted on compensating me. She didn't believe me when I said helping her get away from him meant more to me than any sum she could pay me. She paid me two thousand dollars each time, and I turned around and donated the money to a local LGBTQ shelter. I can show the money going in my account then going right back out."

"How did you feel when she changed her mind about exposing Putz's sexuality?" Sawyer asked.

"Her exposing him would only make her a target. His zealot fans wouldn't believe Putz liked to suck cock even if they watched it live on Pay Per View."

"True," Locke admitted.

"Let's talk alibis," Sawyer said.

"I was in Vegas this weekend for a bachelor party. I took a red-eye flight home Sunday night, with a three-hour layover in Charlottesville from six to nine this morning. I'll happily provide any documentation you need. I hated the fucker, but I'm not your killer, Detectives."

"Thank you for your time," Locke said, sliding a business card to him. "Scan and email your airline tickets and credit card statements showing your hotel reservations to me. Call me if you think of anything else."

Seaver turned an expectant gaze to Sawyer. "Aren't you going to give me a card too?"

"Sure," Sawyer said, retrieving one and handing it to him. "Thanks for the lemonade."

"My pleasure." Sawyer didn't mistake the little purr in Seaver's voice.

"We'll show ourselves out," Locke said. "Looks like we interrupted you mid-workout."

"Just finished. A few minutes later, and I would've been in the shower."

Don't think about water sluicing over his hard body.

"How did you know we were here?" Locke asked. It was a fair question since they hadn't told the guard who they were there to visit.

"I have trail cameras set up along the driveway, and I also have a motion-sensor alarm that gets tripped when a car reaches a certain point."

"Nice setup," Locke admitted. "Too bad Putz didn't believe in home security."

"Maybe," Seaver said, shrugging his massive shoulders. "I might not have killed the guy, but I won't pretend to mourn him. The world is a better place without his brand of hate."

While Sawyer didn't disagree, he would never condone vigilante justice. "Have a good afternoon," he said politely then headed toward the front of the house.

As soon as they cleared the front door, Locke said, "There's no way a gay porn star made enough money during his college years to afford this house twelve years later. No fucking way."

Sawyer laughed. "Maybe he invested the money well. You never asked what his major was."

"You think he invested his money in the stock market and is now a millionaire?"

"I think he invested his money by starting his own porn production company, used his fame to grow memberships, then sold it for a huge profit once it became the most popular site."

Locke quietly contemplated what Sawyer said while driving around the circle and heading down the long driveway. "Is that what he really did?"

"Yep. Randy Dagger's name is still attached to the porn business, so he's probably making a profit there too."

More silence from Locke. "Randy Dagger?"

"Yep."

"So, his porn name meant horny, short knife."

"Not short," Sawyer said, managing to keep a straight face. "Maybe he thought Randy Claymore didn't have the same ring to it. Sounds like an accountant or something."

"Claymore? That's like the longest sword."

"Uh-huh."

"I have so many questions, but none of them would be appropriate," Locke said.

"Then don't ask," Sawyer said firmly. "Google them like the rest of us do. Kelsey can teach you how to erase your search history."

"Fuck you, smart-ass. You know he wants to ask you out," Locke said suddenly. "I don't need to remind you how inappropriate it would be for you to accept."

"Yes, Dad," Sawyer replied, rolling his eyes. "Besides, he's not my type."

"You're not into big, muscular dudes?"

"I prefer wiry blonds," Sawyer said, turning the table on him from that morning. *Stew on that, partner.*

Locke didn't say another word during the drive back to the station, and Sawyer did a mental victory lap.

CHAPTER 9

"I CAN'T BELIEVE NONE OF PUTZ'S NEIGHBORS WITNESSED HIS ASSAILANT lurking around his house," Sawyer said after reading the reports from the officers who canvased the neighborhood. "Not even a strange vehicle."

"It was dark and rainy," Locke replied. "They were probably watching trashy reality television or catching the last innings of the Braves game. They're up in Philly right now, and you can count on great games when those two rivals meet."

"I don't buy it. There's always a nosy neighbor in every community. They seem to know everything happening in their neighborhood regardless of the time of day."

Locke tossed a file onto the conference table and ran his hands through his hair. "Maybe they saw our perp and are too scared to talk to the police, or maybe they invited them in to dry off and drink a cup of coffee to celebrate a job well done."

Sawyer shook his head. "I'm serious."

Locke sat up straight and stretched his arms over his head, working kinks out in his shoulders and upper back. "I am too. It's hard to get witnesses to come forward when someone they like is a victim of a homicide. They're often scared of payback if the killer finds out, and sometimes people are afraid of pointing the finger at a person who could be innocent." He gestured to the stacks of boxes in the corner of the conference room. "Putz was a well-hated man."

"You make a good point," Sawyer agreed.

"I normally do, which is why you should listen when you hear the magnanimous gesture I'm about to make."

"*Magnanimous* gesture?"

"Hey, you're not the only one who knows big words, Golden Boy. I just wait to use mine when it really matters."

"And it matters right this moment?" Sawyer asked.

"Yes, so are you ready to hear what I have to say?"

Sawyer dramatically gripped the conference table like he was bracing himself. "Ready."

"He's got jokes, folks," Locke yelled through the open conference room door.

"Give him hell, Key," Detective Blue from arson said as he passed by. He was built like a tank and spoke in a deep voice, reminding Sawyer of the late actor Michael Clarke Duncan.

Locke gave Blue the middle finger then looked at Sawyer once more. "Go home."

"Or I'll regret it?" Sawyer asked, uncertain where the hell Locke was going.

"Go home because it's your birthday, and there has to be a thousand things you'd rather do than sit here and sift through Putz's hate mail."

Going home to his quiet house was the last thing Sawyer wanted to do. "Nah, my family celebrated my birthday over the weekend. I'm good to look through letters and emails."

Locke studied him, instinctively recognizing there was more than dedication to his job keeping Sawyer at the precinct. "Well, you get the first crack at the delivery method then. Would you prefer to read the snail mail or email?"

Sawyer grinned. "I'll kick it old school and go with snail mail." He slid on a pair of latex gloves then carried the box with the most recent dates on top. "What kind of system are we going with?"

"What do you mean?"

"We'll need to sort the correspondence into categories," Sawyer replied.

Locke thought about it. "'Keep' or 'discard' categories?"

"I was thinking more like 'harmless rants,' 'hits close to home,' and 'read again' categories."

Locke pondered the suggestion for a minute. "Harmless rants because there's no violence included, hits close to home could be a match, but what do you mean with the read again category? Save to take a second look after our initial pass?"

Sawyer smirked at Locke. "Save for bad days when you need a good laugh."

"Got it, but I doubt Rigby or IA would appreciate that one."

"Too true," Sawyer said. "We'll call it maybe instead."

Locke typed away on his laptop. "The digital files are set and ready to go."

Sawyer ripped out three sheets of paper from the legal pad and wrote the categories on them. He spaced them evenly in the center of the table. "I'm ready too."

Locke clicked the mouse to view an email, and Sawyer pulled an envelope out of the box. He scanned the content but didn't find anything worth noting, so he put it in the harmless pile then reached for the next envelope.

"This woman put a curse on his dick," Locke said. "What do you think?"

"Ouch," Sawyer said, grimacing. "I don't see how it relates to the case unless the ME tells us the real cause of death was due to his shrunken penis and not the blunt force trauma she first suspected."

Locke shrugged. "I'll consider it a maybe because it's pretty damn entertaining."

They continued going through the correspondence for hours, only stopping to read the interesting ones out loud, go to the bathroom, or get something to drink. By seven o'clock, they'd looked through the last six months of hateful emails and letters, and the only two categories collecting letters were harmless and save. Not a single person threatened to cause physical harm to Putz.

"I don't think I actually expected to find a smoking gun here," Locke said, "but I had hoped for a clue. Most of these people are trying to reason with the man or possibly enlighten him. That wasn't at all what I expected to find."

"Me either," Sawyer said, pushing back from the chair and standing up to stretch again. "Are you hungry?" he asked Locke without thinking.

Locke looked at him as if he were giving it thought then shook his head. "I was invited to a friend's house for dinner. It's not too late to grab a burger there, so I think I'm going to head over."

"Yeah, okay. I'll see you tomorrow."

Locke shifted his attention powering down his laptop. "See you tomorrow."

Sawyer left the conference room and retrieved his personal cell phone from his locked desk. He had voicemail messages from his brother, sister, father, and several friends who wanted to wish him a happy birthday, but the one person he needed to talk to the most hadn't called him. Maybe it was for the best because hearing Imelda Ruiz's voice was bittersweet. He loved the woman as much as his own mother, but they were tied together by grief and sorrow. Maybe clinging to Vic's mom had made it harder for him to heal.

The thunderstorms Locke had predicted hadn't shown up until his drive home. "Just fucking great," Sawyer groused. The torrential downpour made visibility nearly impossible, but he made it home without incident, and he had never been more grateful to have an attached garage. "Where's my boy?" Sawyer asked, entering the kitchen through the garage door.

His humongous, gray cat lazily strolled into the room, stopped to stretch his long body, then continued toward Sawyer. Bones stood up on his hind legs and placed his paws on Sawyer's thighs, giving his human permission to pick him up.

"How's my big boy?" Sawyer said, cradling the heavy feline against his chest. Bones purred and rubbed his head against Sawyer's chin. "That good, huh? There must've been a lot of birds and squirrels visiting the feeder outside your favorite window." The placement of the feeder wasn't an accident, and Sawyer didn't feel guilty about it since Bones was inside and couldn't hurt the birds or squirrels. He figured it was like television for cats. Bones dug his claws in Sawyer's shirt and purred louder. "You're just charming me so I'll shut up and feed you, huh, big boy?" Sawyer set the cat down by his bowl and retrieved the fancy food from the cabinet beside the refrigerator. Bones performed a figure eight between Sawyer's legs while waiting to hear the pull tab breaking the sealed can. "Looks like it's lamb and rice tonight." *Meow.*

Once Bones was settled, Sawyer headed upstairs to shower off the day. The heat and humidity always made him feel dirty, but the Putzinski case made him want to bathe in bleach. How were such vile people created? Nature or nurture? Both?

As it always did, the hot water cascading over Sawyer's body released his tension and cleared his mind. He suddenly realized he and his partner might be looking for the wrong motive. They were looking for a suspect who'd retaliated against Putz's hateful rhetoric, but maybe that wasn't right. What if Melody Jameson wasn't the only one who'd found out her husband liked cock? What were the odds Clark was his first male lover? If proof had landed in the wrong hands, someone could've felt betrayed that Putz's message was fake. Maybe his hateful vitriol did come from his heartless soul, but why would they believe him? He fervently blamed homosexuals for everything wrong with the country but eagerly dropped to his knees to blow his favorite gay porn star. It would've been the ultimate slap in the face to someone who ardently believed in Putz and his message.

Someone like Shirley Hanover.

No one believed in Putz more than Shirley, and probably no one had more to lose if the truth about him went public. What better way to deflect attention away from herself than to point her finger at Melody while bending over backward to assist the detectives investigating the crime? It was the oldest ploy in the book. How can I be guilty when I'm so helpful? Melody and Clark both had airtight alibis, and it was time to take a closer look at Shirley Hanover. Sawyer's first instinct was to call Locke and discuss it, but they hadn't reached that level of comfort yet, and he knew it was possible they never would. If Sawyer had something stronger to go on than a hunch, then he wouldn't have hesitated to call his partner. Well, he would've called dispatch to put him through to Locke's cell since they hadn't exchanged numbers.

Sawyer went to work making a mental list of things he wanted to find out about Shirley Hanover first thing the next morning. Satisfied he'd gotten as far as he could for now, he turned off the shower, dried off and dressed. Once back downstairs, he debated his choices for dinner: frozen meals, takeout, or a quick breakfast. No matter how bare his cupboards or refrigerator were, Sawyer always had eggs, milk, breakfast meat, and a block of cheese he could shred to make a fancy egg scramble. Checking the bread cabinet, he discovered he had one English muffin left. Sawyer would have to keep an eye on Bones because his cat was addicted to bread. If he allowed himself to become distracted, Bones would snatch the English muffin off his plate.

"Breakfast for dinner," Sawyer said out loud. The one thing he hated most about living alone was the silence.

Even after a rough day, he missed the noise he'd come to expect from his married life. Before he'd met Vic, he had preferred a serene home and only turned on the television when he'd wanted to watch a program. He had never played the radio to fill the silence. Sawyer had grown up with two rowdy siblings and had loved that his adult space was the exact opposite of his childhood home. Vic had always needed background noise, even when he'd been reading. His husband's television choices had usually been low-intensity things like cooking or DIY shows because he'd found them soothing. Sawyer had rarely watched television, but when he had, he'd preferred the world news or a documentary about things that interested him. Vic had teased him mercilessly about his passion for true crime shows.

"You spend all day long wading in people's depravity then choose to watch it for pleasure too?" Vic had asked.

Vic hadn't been a shallow man. He'd cared about politics, social injustice, and wanted the world to be a better place, but he'd known when to step away to preserve his sanity. In his eyes, you fought the things you feared and hated with everything you had, but you didn't let it consume your every thought.

Seeing the merit in Vic's convictions, Sawyer had given it a shot. He'd done his best to check the negativity and depravity at the door each night when he had come home. He'd watched some of Vic's favorite DIY shows, and Vic had watched documentaries on the History channel with him. They'd found a compromise as they had on most things. On Sunday mornings, they'd shared the local paper and the *USA Today* over coffee before whipping up a decadent brunch and discussing important political or social issues impacting their community and lives. They'd cared, they had been activists, but they'd found peace and balance in a world of constant strife.

After Vic died, it had hurt too much even to hear the hosts' voices on the shows his husband loved, so he had stopped watching them. He'd also stopped turning on the radio because they had always played a song that had reminded him of the man he'd loved and lost. He'd canceled his daily and weekly newspaper subscriptions because there was no fun in doing the crosswords and sudoku puzzles by himself. The silence he'd once found comforting and calming felt like the heavy, oppressive lull that had hovered at the funeral home when people gathered to mourn and pay respects. Two years later, Sawyer felt like he was still in the private viewing room spending his last moments with his husband, wondering how in the hell he would ever come to grips with the fact Vic was gone at thirty-six years old.

Sawyer wiped away his tears and released a shaky breath. "Vic would be so disappointed," he said, pulling out the ingredients he needed to make dinner.

Vic was the most selfless man Sawyer had ever known. He hadn't worried about dying; he'd worried Sawyer would stop living. "These past eight years with you have been the best of my life, babe. I want you to promise me you'll find love and happiness again. You have too much love inside you to keep it to yourself," Vic had whispered hours before his heart stopped beating. "I mean, I want you to mourn me properly, but then I want you to find an epic love. Promise me right now, Sawyer."

Sawyer had shaken his head, unable to speak words he knew would be a lie. He couldn't imagine a day when he'd want to love someone other than Vic. "I can't."

Vic's breath had become labored as he'd struggled to stay with Sawyer because Vic knew his husband wasn't ready to let go. "You'd rob me of my dying wish?" Vic had tried for a teasing smile, but it came out as a grimace.

Sawyer had hated his selfishness. Instead of resting comfortably, Vic was fighting tooth and nail to comfort him—the one who wasn't dying. Wiping the tears from his face, Sawyer had leaned forward and pressed his lips to Vic's for a soft kiss. "I promise to do my best, Vic. You've set a really high standard, love, so it's not all my fault if it doesn't happen easily."

"Fair enough," Vic had said, serenely smiling when he drifted to sleep.

Sawyer had remained in the chair beside Vic's bed, holding his husband's hand and watching his chest move. He'd fallen asleep at some point, and a nurse had gently nudged him awake to let him know Vic would be passing soon. She'd been a hospice nurse long enough to recognize the signs. Vic's inconsolable parents had been in and out during the day, only taking breaks in the bedside vigil to compose themselves so they wouldn't upset Vic. Too afraid to leave Vic for a second, Sawyer had asked the nurse to please find his in-laws.

They'd spent the next hour, Sawyer on one side of the bed and his parents on the other, holding Vic's hands and telling him how much they loved him. Sawyer had turned on the DIY network to give Vic the precious background noise he had loved one more time.

"I made him a promise, Bones," Sawyer said to his cat. "I told him I would try, but I haven't." He'd embraced the loneliness instead of trying to move past it. Sawyer's body and soul had started to cry out for more, but he'd refused to act on it.

Vic had always made a big deal out of birthdays; he'd viewed them as fresh starts. Did Sawyer want to spend his thirty-fourth year as lonely as he spent his thirty-second and thirty-third? "No, I don't," he admitted softly. Saying it out loud brought on a new rush of tears, but they felt more like cleansing and healing tears than ones wrought from sorrow and sadness.

Sawyer pulled out his phone and opened his Audible app. Listening to a DIY show didn't feel right, and he wasn't in the mood for a documentary or a baseball game, but a well-narrated book was the perfect choice to entertain him and break the silence in his kitchen while he cooked dinner. He started *A Ferry of Bones and Gold* by Hailey Turner and kept listening while he ate dinner, cleaned the kitchen, and started a load of laundry.

It was close to ten when his phone rang, cutting off the book in the middle of an excellent battle. He would've been annoyed if he wasn't so relieved at seeing the name on the caller ID.

"Hola, Mama Ruiz," Sawyer said when he answered.

"How's my beautiful birthday boy?" Imelda Ruiz asked.

"I'm doing good," he told her and actually meant it for the first time.

He told her about the parts of the day he could discuss then got caught up on what was going on with her and Vic senior. He remarked that she sounded happier than he'd heard in a long time.

"We're healing, sweetheart," Imelda said gently. "That's how Vic would've wanted it."

"I know," Sawyer said. "I still miss him every day, but I'm going to fulfill the promise I made to him."

"That warms my heart so much, Sawyer," Imelda said tearfully. "Vic lives through us now, so we need to experience all the things he no longer can."

Sawyer knew she was right, but he just hadn't been ready to embrace it until recently. "Will I see you at the ball diamond dedication on Saturday?"

Sawyer's parents, Baron Key and Evangeline O'Neal, had established a large charity in Vic's name that did many wonderful things. They supported community outreach programs benefiting at-risk LGBTQ+ youth, children's literacy programs at the local libraries, and also established a scholarship at the high school where Vic had passionately taught and coached baseball. Their current project was revitalizing youth sporting complexes, and Sawyer couldn't wait to throw out the first pitch at the Victor Ruiz Junior ball diamond. Sawyer had worried Imelda and Vic senior would think his parents were overstepping, but Evangeline had involved them in every project to ensure they approved of how they delegated the funds.

"Of course," Imelda said. "We wouldn't miss it."

They talked for a little while longer until Imelda let out a soft yawn. They parted with the same words of love they had always shared, but they felt different. Affection between them since Vic died had never been forced or strained, but the words had always held a hint of sadness. That night, they felt more like hope.

Sawyer continued listening to *A Ferry of Bones and Gold* until it was time to get ready for bed. It wasn't until he was tucked between the sheets with Bones curled up on the pillow beside him that he realized he'd forgotten to take the trash down to the curb.

"Damn it," he groused, pulling a pair of pajama pants on over his briefs and tugging an old T-shirt over his head so he wouldn't shock any neighbors who might have also forgotten to take out the trash.

He startled some nocturnal critters hoping to find a feast when he rolled his trash bin to the curb. Down the street, a woman wearing overnight curlers and a robe approached her bins with two small plastic bags in her hands. He didn't think many women still wore those types of curlers to bed, but he could think of a few who probably did. Shirley Hanover was one of them.

Shirley.

A thought suddenly occurred to him. Whoever had killed Putz hadn't thrown their bloody clothes in his trash can along with the bat. They would be looking to discard the evidence as discreetly and as quickly as they could.

"Fuck."

Sawyer sprinted back inside his house and took the stairs two at a time to reach his bedroom quickly. Bones looked up at him with annoyance when he slid through the door and began rifling through his drawers for a pair of jeans. Sawyer had forgotten to throw his clothes in the dryer, which left him with a faded, holey pair that weren't appropriate to wear on the job, but they were still more professional than his pajama bottoms.

Sawyer put on his belt then secured his gun, badge, and cuffs in place before turning off his bedroom light and heading to the garage to get in his car. Shirley had provided her home address, which happened to be in a neighborhood close to Sawyer's. He realized he might be too late to catch her in the act, but he was betting she would wait until she thought everyone was sleeping before stashing the evidence of her crime in the trash bins. Sawyer drove past her house and saw a few lights were still on inside. He parked farther down the street— close enough to see her house but not so close it drew attention. The houses closest to him were all dark, and he felt certain the neighbors were sleeping or not home.

He had no idea how long his stakeout would take, so he started his audiobook again to entertain him. Sawyer saw a shadow emerge around the rear corner of the Hanovers' house around one in the morning just as Patrick and Jono were about to get their freak on.

"Are you fucking serious?" Sawyer groused, pausing the audiobook and quietly exiting his car.

Sawyer pulled his gun free from the holster and slid the safety off. He doubted Shirley was carrying a weapon or that she'd put up much of a fight, but it never paid to take any suspect for granted. The Hanovers hadn't turned on their lamppost that was strategically set at the corner where their driveway met the sidewalk. Since the city had placed their streetlights every two or three houses on the block, the area was pretty dark without the lamppost turned on. The front porch lights were also left off, and the shadowy figure hadn't tripped any motion-sensor lights.

Sawyer suspected the added darkness was intentional to help cover Shirley's attempt to hide her crime. Putz lived in a similar neighborhood with the same city lighting setup. She would've been familiar with how she could access his house without tipping anyone off. Under the cover of darkness, Sawyer couldn't tell simply by looking if what she held in her hand was something other than a last-minute addition to the trash like his neighbor lady down the street. His gut told him he was right though.

Sawyer hid in the shadows, watching as his suspect stopped halfway down the dark driveway as if she could feel his regard. After a minute, she hurried toward the trash cans at the curb. Sawyer knew he had to make his move. Keeping his gun pointed down, Sawyer silently ran on the balls of his feet while keeping as close to the shadows as he could for maximum surprise.

He stepped out of the shadows just as his prime suspect reached for the lid of the trash can with their free hand. "Police! Step away from the trash cans, drop the items on the ground, put your hands in the air, and don't move," he said firmly.

A masculine gasp sounded from the shadows, momentarily catching Sawyer by surprise. "Oh God!" Carl Hanover said. "I should've known better than to think I could get away with it."

Sawyer recognized a confession was about to occur. "Mr.

Hanover, I'm placing you under arrest for the murder of Roland Putzinski. You have the right to remain silent." Sawyer finished reading him his Miranda rights while keeping his gun aimed at the shaking man. "Do you understand these rights as I've read them to you?"

"Yes, Detective. I waive my rights. I killed that son of a bitch for what he did to my wife. I'm not even sorry."

"Okay. I need you to stay still for me, sir." Sawyer holstered his gun and secured Mr. Hanover's hands behind his back then called dispatch for a cruiser when he detected the strong odor of urine. He had literally scared the piss out of Carl Hanover. Sawyer was all about justice, but he wasn't ruining his leather seats.

CHAPTER 10

WHAT SHOULD'VE BEEN AN EASY APPREHENSION TURNED OUT TO BE anything but. Before the squad car arrived, Shirley Hanover woke up to find her husband missing from bed. After searching the house with no success, she had flipped on all the exterior lights, flooding the lawn, driveway, and sidewalk with bright LED lights.

"Fuck!" Sawyer said, raising his arm up to shield his eyes.

"Step away from my husband, or I'll blow your head off," Shirley screamed frantically. Sawyer heard the distinctive sound of someone pumping a shotgun.

"Mrs. Hanover, it's Detective Key." Sawyer had adjusted to the light by then and held his hands up shoulder high to show his weapon was holstered. "Put the gun down, Mrs. Hanover."

"You don't look like Detective Key in those clothes."

"I'd gone home for the day and changed into something casual, ma'am. The SPD is sending out a cruiser to assist me. I don't want to see you taken into custody also." Mrs. Hanover set the gun down just inside the house, which meant it was still in arm's reach. "I need you to step onto the front porch and shut the door. I want your hands where I can see them." She complied but genuine confusion registered on her face.

"I don't understand, Detective Key. What are you doing at my home? Why is my husband kneeling on the ground with his hands cuffed behind his back?"

"I did it, Shirl," Carl said.

"Did what, honey?" Shirley asked, sounding completely dumbstruck.

"I killed that no good, lying son of a bitch for what he did to you. After all these years, you stood behind him." *The plot thickens.*

Sawyer's attention was piqued, but he wanted to make sure he made this arrest by the book. "Mr. Hanover, as much as I appreciate your street-side confession, I'd prefer to have this conversation at the precinct."

"Carl, don't you say another cotton-picking word," Shirley said. "I'm going to call our attorney."

"I already waived my rights," Carl said.

"Rescind them," she said. "Lawyer up like they do on television."

"Can I do that?" Carl asked me, sounding a little hopeful.

"You can, but that's only going to delay the inevitable since I caught you getting ready to throw out the evidence that places you at Putz's house. I'm also hours away from interviewing a witness who can place you at the café where the podcast was uploaded." Sawyer's bluff worked because Carl Hanover's shoulders slumped in surrender. "Why don't you just think it over while we wait for the patrol car?"

"Oh my God! What will the neighbors think?" Shirley asked, covering her face with her hands. If she was really worried about them not finding out, she would have stopped yelling across the yard.

"I specifically asked for them not to come in with their lights blazing and their sirens blaring. Mr. Hanover peacefully surrendered, so it's not necessary."

"I pissed my pants, Shirley. Will you bring a change of clothes to the station for me?"

"Detective Key, surely you'll let my husband clean up before you take him to the police station."

"Ma'am, I'm afraid I can't. I already know there's a shotgun just inside the door, and there could be countless more weapons inside the home which pose a threat to my safety."

The distinct sound of a Harley Davidson motorcycle reverberated off the houses and grew louder as the bike drove nearer. Sawyer assumed it was someone who lived in the neighborhood until it pulled up to the curb in front of the Hanovers' house. Sawyer put his hand on the butt of his gun, prepared to pull it quickly if the stranger was hostile. The man swung his leg over the bike and ambled over with a loose-limbed walk that Sawyer easily recognized after only working with the man for a day. Long legs encased in dark denim and a black motorcycle jacket ratcheted up Royce Locke's sexy factor from one hundred to one hundred thousand. He removed his helmet, shook his head then ran his hand through his longish strands of blond hair. His partner kept his hair short on the sides and back but let it grow longer on top. During the day, he used a product to sweep the strands back and keep the hair out of his eyes. But Locke was off duty and his long bangs hung loose around his face.

Locke had the kind of hair a lover wanted to grip while he fucked his face or rode his ass hard. *Damn it. I can't be thinking about this kind of shit.*

"Lucy," Locke said, imitating a thick Cuban accent, "you have some serious 'splaining to do." His words and voice were light, but the expression on his face was thunderous. He was not happy Sawyer hadn't called him, and maybe he'd feel the same way if the situation were reversed. "But first you might want to catch your fleeing suspect."

"What?" Sawyer asked, thinking Locke was only razzing him.

"Run, Carl!" Shirley yelled from the porch.

"Goddamn it," Sawyer snarled. "Keep an eye on her, Locke. She has a shotgun just inside the door." Sawyer took off down the street after Carl, who was moving a lot faster than he expected him capable of. "Freeze, Mr. Hanover," he yelled. Sawyer didn't pull his gun because the older man was unarmed, cuffed, and running barefoot down the sidewalk. It was only a matter of time before he stepped on a limb or slipped on a walnut.

Carl pulled up short suddenly and began hopping on one foot. "Son of a bitch!" With his hands behind his back, it was hard for him to balance, and he toppled forward. Carl's face kissed the sidewalk hard.

"Damn it," Sawyer groused. The last thing he wanted was to drag a bleeding suspect from a high-profile case into the precinct. The papers would be filled with allegations that he beat up Mr. Hanover. Sawyer gripped Carl by the shoulders and helped him to his feet. Sure enough, Carl had busted his nose and blood gushed down his face. Sawyer pulled his phone out of his pocket and called for an EMT. "So much for no lights and sirens."

Instead of guiding Mr. Hanover back in front of his house, Sawyer led him over to his car where he kept a first aid kit in the trunk. Carl fought to get free from his grasp, so Sawyer gripped the older man's bicep tighter.

"Knock it off before you hurt yourself worse," Sawyer bit out. "I have a first aid kit in the trunk, and I'm going to clean you up before we take you in."

By this point, Carl had started to sob so mucus mixed with the blood still oozing from his nose. "I'm sorry."

"I said you had a right to remain silent, and I highly suggest you abide by that until we get to the station."

Carl nodded and didn't say a word while Sawyer slid on latex gloves, gently inserted cotton plugs up his nose to staunch the bleeding, and washed the blood off his face. Sawyer sealed the gloves and bloody wipes inside a hazmat bag and tossed it in his trunk until he could properly dispose of it later. Then he marched Carl back to where Locke stood on the sidewalk.

A cruiser pulled up seconds after he reached Locke and two uniforms got out of the car. "Evening, Detectives."

"This is Carl Hanover. He's confessed to murdering Roland

Putzinski." Ambulance sirens sounded in the distance. "I called for an EMT because he fell and hit his nose while fleeing."

"I think you tackled him," Shirley Hanover yelled from the porch.

"No, he didn't," a woman yelled from across the street. "Don't even try to pull that shit, Shirley. Right, girls?" A chorus of agreement followed her question.

Sawyer and Locke turned and saw five ladies dressed in their bathrobes standing across the street. It was nice to have witnesses, but he hoped they wouldn't be needed.

"You cleaned me up and plugged up my nose, so why do I need an ambulance?" Carl asked nasally.

"You hit the ground hard, I just want to make sure you didn't give yourself a concussion, Mr. Hanover."

"Why do you need us then, Detectives?" one of the officers said.

"We only have our personal vehicles," Locke said. "I'm not putting Hanover on the back of my Harley."

"Why did you bring personal vehicles to a stakeout?" the other asked.

"It's not really your job to question us, is it?" Locke countered.

"It was a spur-of-the-moment hunch," Sawyer said, playing nice detective to Locke's dickhead detective. The ambulance sirens grew louder as it neared the neighborhood, but luckily, they shut them off once they turned onto the street. "After the paramedics clear Mr. Hanover, I need you to escort him back to the precinct while Locke and I collect evidence."

"Let me get Carl a change of clothes. It's inhumane to let him sit in his own urine," Shirley yelled from the porch.

"Are you freaking kidding me right now?" one of the officers said, realizing the real reason Sawyer called for a cruiser. Locke pinned the cop with a malicious glare, and he backed off.

While the EMTs checked Carl over, Locke unzipped his jacket to reveal his shoulder holster and badge hanging from the chain around his neck. "I'll escort Mrs. Hanover inside to get Carl's change of clothes while you collect the evidence on *your* collar."

Sawyer tipped his head to the side, gesturing for Locke to follow him. "That's not what this is. It's not *my* collar; it's *our* collar."

"It sure doesn't look like it from where I stand."

Ignoring Locke's blatant attempt to pick a fight, Sawyer asked, "How'd you even know I was here?"

"Dispatch called me after you requested the squad car because I'm your partner."

Sawyer snorted. "So now you want to be partners?"

Locke took his sweet time raking his eyes over Sawyer's threadbare, old university T-shirt, which was a size or two too small, and his worn, holey jeans. When Locke's gray eyes finally met Sawyer's again, his lips tilted up in a sneer. "I didn't say I wanted to be your partner, but neither of us can help the hand we were dealt. Let's get on with our tasks so we can wrap this up. Dispatch interrupted me at a particularly bad moment, and I'm hoping the lady will forgive me and welcome me back with open arms." Sawyer fought the urge to roll his eyes.

Locke didn't smell like sex but maybe he hadn't reached that pivotal moment yet. A devilish smile spread across his face as a plan formed in his mind. Locke was eager to get back to his lady friend, and Sawyer was suddenly determined to cross every T and dot every I before they questioned Carl at the precinct. A confession alone wasn't enough to convict in Georgia; Sawyer needed to collect corroborating evidence to ensure Hanover went to prison for his crime.

CHAPTER 11

BY THE TIME LOCKE AND KEY RETURNED TO THE PRECINCT, WORD HAD gotten out about their arrest. Media outlet vans and their crews were back in front of the station, which was expected with any sensational homicide and subsequent arrests. Chief Rigby and the district attorney, Gillian Babineaux, were also waiting for Sawyer and Locke in the chief's office.

"Motive?" Gillian asked.

The African American woman in her mid-thirties was dressed immaculately in a lavender tailored suit, which she'd paired with stilettos in a darker purple shade. Since it was close to midnight, Sawyer assumed someone interrupted her at home, and she dressed for the possibility of facing cameras after the interview was over. Then again, for all he knew, this was casual wear for Babineaux. She was newer to Savannah but had made a big name for herself as she worked her way up from rookie counselor in the district attorney's office to the one the people of Chatham County elected as their top lawyer. Brilliant. Relentless. Honest. Sawyer figured she had her eyes set on becoming a federal judge someday, but her ambitions never seemed to detract from her current position.

"He said he killed the son of a bitch for what he did to his wife," Sawyer told the DA.

"Could it be that simple?" Babineaux asked, her dark, shrewd gaze made Sawyer feel like she was trying to read his mind.

"It seems so on the surface," Sawyer replied.

A dark brow shot up. "'On the surface.' What do you mean?"

"It seems like an open-shut case, but we won't know more until we interview the suspect."

"What kind of corroborating evidence did you collect at the scene?"

"Bloody clothes and latex gloves he tried to throw away in the trash can. The lab will compare samples to match the blood to Putz's," Locke said. Rigby grimaced over Locke's nickname for Putzinski while Babineaux struggled to keep her twitching lips from becoming a full-blown smile. "We're having his car towed in so our crime scene techs can go over it. Putzinski's blood should be found in the car even if Hanover attempted to clean it this morning. Finding fingerprints or other proof Carl Hanover was in Putz's house won't do us any good since he likely visited the property with his wife. Explaining Putz's blood in Hanover's car will be much harder to do if he recants his confession."

"I'll do my best to expedite those tests. I have some contacts at the local GBI lab, and I won't hesitate to call in some favors." The Georgia Bureau of Investigation could be a detective's best friend or worst enemy. Sawyer hoped this interaction fell into the former category. "Let's get on with the interview, shall we?" Babineaux asked.

"I'll watch from the interview room," Chief Rigby said. "We don't need to overwhelm him by cramming unfamiliar faces in the room. Maybe Locke should come with me too since Sawyer was the one who initially made contact."

Sawyer could feel his partner's tension rising, and with their partnership already strained, he thought it would be in his best interest if Locke participated also. "Ma'am, with all due respect, I would prefer to include my partner in the interview."

"As you wish," Chief Rigby said, gesturing to the door.

Sawyer held back, allowing the ladies to walk out of the room first so he could speak to Locke. "Look, I—"

"I'm not sure whose ass you're trying to kiss, but you can knock it off. If you'd wanted my participation, you would've called me," Locke snarled. His body was coiled with tension and ready to spring into a fight at the slightest trigger. "You can try to show Rigby you're team Locke and Key, but I know better."

"There's just one big flaw in your little poor-pitiful-me tirade, Locke. You didn't give me your personal cell number nor is your police-issued number programmed into the phone IT gave me. Yeah, I could've called dispatch and asked them to put me through to you, but I couldn't justify doing it on a *hunch*." Sawyer loosened his shoulders and tried a less combative tone. "You made it clear how you felt about my arrival on the force. Was I going to risk every gain I'd made today by pulling you away from a night with your girl?"

Locke released a sharp breath then turned his back to Sawyer, scrubbing his hands over his face. After a few seconds, Locke turned around and met his partner's gaze. "It's pretty fucking arrogant of you to think you made any gains with me today, asshole." The corner of his mouth twitched, and Sawyer knew their sorta-truce was back on. "Let's go nail this guy's balls to the wall so I can get back to my babysitting duties."

"Babysitting?" Sawyer asked. "What about the lady who will forgive you with open arms?"

"She's six months old, so there's no accounting for her taste," Locke said. When Sawyer stood there staring at him as if they'd fallen into *The Twilight Zone,* Locke said, "I was watching Candi's kids for her so she could pick up an extra shift at the hospital. Her sister usually is the one she calls, but Crystal has stayed the past three nights while Candi worked over the weekend." Candi, as in Candace Wilkes, Marcus Wilkes's widow. "Marc is seven, Daniel is five, and baby Bailey is just six months old. I'm their godfather, so who else would she call when she needed an extra hand? The kids were also the personal business I had to take care of this afternoon. Marc had a dentist appointment, and Candi needed to get some sleep for her shift. I can't let Candi down. She's been through enough."

Sawyer didn't want to think about the relief spreading through his body after learning Locke wasn't out getting fucked during their shift or before he arrived at the Hanovers' house. "Who's with the kids now?"

"Candi's mom came over to relieve me until I can get back. Adele is a sweet woman, and she means well, but she drives Candi a little crazy with her unsolicited advice. Her solution to Candi's problem is to marry the first nice guy who comes along."

"A new man isn't always the solution," Sawyer quipped.

Locke smirked then headed toward the door. "I'll have to take your word on that one. Personally, I know I'm not the solution to anyone's problem unless they're looking for strings-free sex. Then maybe," Locke tossed over his shoulder as he walked out of the room.

Sold. Sawyer mentally shook his head, scattering the fragmented images taking shape in his brain before a complete picture of Locke stretched out on his bed could form.

When they reached the interrogation room, Babineaux was waiting for them in the hallway with her arms crossed over her chest. Rigby was nowhere in sight, so Sawyer assumed she was already in the observation room. "Thought maybe you got lost," Babineaux murmured wryly. "Ready to do this?"

"Our apologies for keeping you waiting, ma'am," Locke said. He held open the door and gestured for her to precede before falling into step behind her, leaving Sawyer to catch the door for himself. He was so distracted by the way Locke's ass looked in his tight jeans the door nearly hit him in the face.

Locke glanced over his shoulder and smirked at his partner. Was he grinning because he knew Sawyer was thinking about sinking his teeth into his taut globes or because he nearly went face-first into the door?

Sawyer took a seat across the table from Hanover, and Locke dropped into the chair beside him. Babineaux remained standing in the corner of the room looking in charge and imposing. Carl kept nervously glancing at her like she was his judge, jury, and executioner. "Do you need anything before we begin, Mr. Hanover?" Sawyer asked. "Something to drink?"

"A cigarette. I gave them up two decades ago, but I'd kill for one right about now." Realizing what he said, Carl seemed to shrink tighter inside himself.

"This is a non-smoking facility, Mr. Hanover," Babineaux said.

Carl shook his head. "I wasn't serious anyway. Go ahead and ask your questions. I haven't changed my mind about waiving my rights to an attorney, and I'm not recanting my confession."

"I appreciate your cooperation, sir. I want to inform you this interview is being recorded. My name is Gillian Babineaux, and I'm the district attorney for Chatham County."

"I know who you are," Carl said, averting his gaze from her.

"I'm going to reread your rights for the recording to document that you fully understand them before we continue." Carl nodded but kept his eyes glued on the table in front of him while Gillian read him his Miranda rights. "Do you understand these rights as I've read them to you?"

Carl lifted his head and met her gaze head-on. "I do, and I'm waiving my right to an attorney."

"Okay," Gillian said. They all knew he could recant his statement and revoke his waiver at any time. It happened a lot once people had time to think about it. "Walk us through the events of June fourteenth from the moment you arrived at Roland Putzinski's house."

"His back door was unlocked like it usually is, so I entered his house without him knowing it. I knew from speaking to Shirley that Roland would be recording his show between nine thirty and ten thirty, so I waited until I was sure he'd be in his booth so I could take him by surprise. I yanked open the sound booth door, startling Roland, then I hit him in the head with the bat I brought with me."

"Let me stop you there. The bat used to kill Mr. Putzinski was yours? You brought it from home?" Babineaux asked.

"I got the bat from the sporting goods store earlier that day. I stored it in my trunk until it was time to rid the world of someone like him," Hanover said. *Someone like him.* Those three words could mean a host of different things.

Sawyer had to bite the inside of his cheek to keep from gasping, and beside him, Locke tensed, bumping his leg against Sawyer's beneath the table. Carl Hanover didn't just admit to murdering Roland Putzinski; he confessed to premeditated murder, which was a capital offense, making the death penalty a possibility. Sawyer wasn't sure what stunned him most: Carl's boldness or Locke not removing his leg the moment they touched.

"You're admitting to planning and carrying out the murder of Roland Putzinski?" Babineaux confirmed.

"Isn't that what I just said?" Carl asked. "Why haven't you asked me why? Isn't motive important?"

"It's more important to confirm you committed the crime you confessed to by having you explain in great detail what happened when you arrived at Roland Putzinski's home with the intent to kill him."

Carl's face scrunched up in confusion. "Confirm my confession? I thought you'd be happy to wrap this case up quickly."

"While expediency is nice, I prefer we lock up the right person, sir."

"I am the right person," Carl said, raising his voice. "Why would I lie?"

"To protect someone else who might have committed the crime," Babineaux replied.

"False confessions happen a lot," Sawyer said to the older man, whose face was turning an alarming shade of red. Hanover was either working up toward rage, a heart attack, or a stroke. "What happened after you hit Roland?"

"He fell out of the chair."

"Did he fall forward, backward, to the left or right?" Locke asked.

Carl pursed his lips together and narrowed his eyes like he was replaying the sequence of events. "He fell back and to the left. His head landed near my feet." That was exactly how Putzinski fell out of the chair, so either Carl had been the one who struck Putz, or he helped cover up the crime for the one who did.

"How many times did you strike Mr. Putzinski?" Sawyer asked.

Carl met his gaze with an unflinching stare. "Until his head looked like a smashed watermelon and my rage was gone." His voice was remorseless, and his eyes were as cold as a shark's. Breaking eye contact with Sawyer, Carl turned his head to look at Babineaux. "Is that close enough to the murder scene to please you, ma'am? The clothes and shoes the detectives confiscated were mine and much too large to fit my wife, which is who you think I'm covering for. I did protect her but not until it was too late."

"Explain," Babineaux said, ready to hear the motive.

"I suspect you already know the truth about Roland Putzinski, don't you?" Carl asked then chuckled when none of us took the bait. "He was a closeted gay man whose betrayal was going to ruin my wife's reputation. People would assume Shirley wasn't a good judge of character if she couldn't see the truth about Roland, and what good is an agent without their reputation? How could her clients trust her to have their best interests at heart when she'd been blinded by Roland all these years? If word got out that he liked to suck cock and take it up the ass, Shirley's career would've been over." Carl took a deep breath and released it slowly. "It would've broken her heart."

Sawyer recalled the comments Melody had made about Shirley's personal feelings for Putz. Had Roland been aware of them too and used this as an opportunity to get Putz out of the picture? Sawyer knew he might be poking the bear but decided the truth needed to come out. "It would've broken her heart how? I can understand disappointment if a client turns out to be someone other than they led you to believe, but brokenhearted sounds more personal than I'd expect from a professional relationship. What makes you say that?"

Carl's face turned even redder. Beneath the table, Locke's leg bumped Sawyer's again. It felt like a what-the-hell-are-you-doing nudge, but Sawyer wasn't backing down. He liked his confessions tied up with a pretty bow. "Are you asking if my wife was having sexual relations with Roland?"

"I'm asking if your wife *wanted* to have sexual relations with him?"

All the fight left Carl, and he slumped back against his chair. "Probably, but that wasn't what I meant." He shook his head, and it looked like he'd had enough. Carl released a long sigh. "Roland was going to fire Shirley and replace her with a young gay dude from Atlanta. It would've broken her heart."

"How do you know this, Mr. Hanover?"

"Roland told me last week. He wanted to give me a heads-up because he knew I'd have a hysterical woman on my hands. Can you believe the gall of that man? I'd usually say balls, but now I know he doesn't have them. My wife was with Roland since the beginning. Without her, he wouldn't have had the syndicated radio show and the book deals. Without Shirley, he'd still be beating off to gay porn in his parents' basement. He owed everything to her but was ready to toss her aside because he had a hard-on for the young pup who was eager to please him."

Sawyer wanted to know the name of the gay man willing to work for Putz. The guy fell into two categories: self-hating gay or money-over-substance gay.

"You planned and carried out Roland Putzinski's murder because he was gay and was going to fire your wife?" Babineaux asked. "Did I understand you correctly?"

"I knew you wouldn't understand a word I said," Carl spat out. He turned to Locke and Sawyer. "You heard me correctly, didn't you, fellas? I couldn't let my wife's reputation get ruined, and I wouldn't stand by and watch Roland break her heart."

Locke folded his arms on the table and leaned forward. "Do not disrespect DA Babineaux again, Mr. Hanover. She's the one standing between you and the death penalty." All color leeched from Hanover's face.

Babineaux did a cutesy little finger wave then gestured to the notebook and pen in front of him. "Write it all down and sign it, please."

"But I just told you everything," Carl countered.

"And now I'd like a signed confession, Mr. Hanover."

Hanover engaged Babineaux in a staredown that only lasted for a few seconds before he looked away and reached for the notepad and pen. After he signed his confession with an exaggerated flourish, Babineaux walked to the door, opened it, and gestured for a uniformed officer to take Hanover to lockup until we were ready to transport him to the county jail. "I'm sure we'll speak again."

"What's going to happen next?" Carl asked, looking and sounding less confident once the officer pulled him to his feet.

"You'll be arraigned before a judge where you'll plead guilty or not guilty to the charges I file against you. The judge will decide if you're granted bail or will remain incarcerated before and during your trial."

"Are you going to seek the death penalty?" Carl asked, notching up his chin defiantly.

"I haven't decided yet. I strongly recommend you hire an attorney, Mr. Hanover."

"I'm sure my wife will make the arrangements."

"We're going to transfer you to the county jail until the arraignment. Your attorney can visit you there."

Carl shuffled out of the room with his armed escort, which meant Sawyer had no reason to continue sitting at the table hoping Locke would bump his leg again. No sooner had the thought popped into his head, Locke scooted his chair back and rose to his feet.

"Well, this has been an interesting night," Locke said.

"To say the least," Babineaux agreed. "Great job, guys." She spun on her stilettos and headed out the door without a backward glance.

"Thank you," Sawyer and Locke both said even though she was already gone.

"Not one to stick around and chitchat, is she?" Locke asked him.

Sawyer rose to his feet and stretched, feeling the hem of his shirt rise a few inches. Since he was looking at Locke, he didn't miss his partner looking at the exposed flesh.

"Were you out clubbing when you got the idea to stake out the Hanovers' home?" Locke asked, a blond brow quirked.

"Fuck no," Sawyer replied. "I'm too old for that shit. I like nice quiet evenings at home."

"What's with the tight, holey jeans, and too-thin shirt. Did you wear the outfit in eighth grade?"

"I've had the jeans since high school and the shirt since my freshman year of college," Sawyer said with a shrug. "I needed to do laundry." Sawyer nodded toward Locke's motorcycle jacket and tight-as-sin jeans. "What about you, Easy Rider?"

"You should reserve judgment until after you've ridden one."

Sawyer knew Locke meant a motorcycle, but it wasn't the image that came to the forefront of Sawyer's mind.

Locke lifted his hand in a farewell wave then headed to the door. "See you back here in a few hours."

Sawyer grumbled then followed Locke out the door. "I was hoping we'd get to report for duty a few hours later since we made the big arrest."

"Not even for you, Golden Boy."

The two men went their separate ways once they reached the parking lot. Sawyer sighed in relief when he started the car. His audiobook picked right back up where he'd left off. The fictional characters were engaging in sexy shenanigans up against the wall.

I really need to get laid. It's been too long. Sawyer questioned his sanity for listening to something that would rev him up without having anyone to help him unload. The narrator moaned loudly about the same time someone knocked sharply on his window. Sawyer turned his head so fast he felt his neck pop. Locke stood on the other side, grinning like a fool while the narrator vividly detailed the hot sex scene.

"Fuck me," Sawyer growled before he turned off the radio and rolled down the window.

"I'm not sure about you, but someone is getting action," Locke said.

"You're supposed to be grossed out by two guys getting it on," Sawyer informed him. The look in Locke's eyes was the opposite of repulsion.

"Am I now?" Locke countered. "Thanks for letting me know how I'm supposed to feel, Key. I just came over to apologize for being a dick earlier, but I'm not going to now. You and your assumptions can have a good night. I have a little girl waiting for me who has her days and nights confused." He nodded toward the radio. "You and…"

"Patrick and Jono."

"You, Patrick, and Jono have a good night."

Sawyer rolled his window up as Locke walked away, his long sensual strides doing more to rev up his libido than the sexy audiobook. Sawyer couldn't tear his eyes away when his partner smoothly straddled the metal beast and fired it to life. He felt like an idiot for watching him ride away, but Sawyer felt rattled by everything that had occurred that day.

Locke hated him, tolerated him, resented him, and then *wanted* him all in the same day? No. There had to be another explanation for the heat flashing in Locke's gray eyes when he looked at the strip of exposed flesh between Sawyer's waistband and T-shirt. He couldn't have seen lust followed quickly by disappointment when Sawyer commented on Locke's laid-back reaction to overhearing the grunts and groans of two men—fictional or not—engaging in hot sex.

Every argument about why Sawyer shouldn't want Locke dissipated. Every brick Sawyer had added to shore up his defenses against the enigmatic man crumbled. He felt exposed, raw, and ignorant in his assumptions. The problem was Sawyer wasn't sure what he was willing to do about it.

CHAPTER 12

LOCKE IN HIS TIGHT BLACK TEE AND SHOULDER HOLSTER. LOCKE SITTING astride his motorcycle. Locke staring at Sawyer's strip of exposed skin. Locke's sexy voice when he'd admonished him for making assumptions about his acceptance levels or possibly even his sexuality. The last one reached Sawyer at the deepest level. The dreams went on and on until Sawyer woke with a leaking, aching dick with only himself to relieve it.

There would be no going back to sleep until he took care of his body's demands. He hadn't been this aroused since... He couldn't finish the thought, wouldn't allow anything to disrupt his driving need for release. Bones made a grumbling noise and jumped off the bed when Sawyer yanked open the bedside drawer at an ungodly, predawn hour. *Smart cat.* He fumbled around, searching for the lube to rub one out but paused when his hand bumped into the flesh-like dildo. It had a suction cup on the base, and Sawyer took it into the shower when the need for penetration overwhelmed him. This was one of those times.

Throwing back the covers, Sawyer grabbed the dildo and lube before padding across his room to the bathroom, his swaying balls so heavy and full they ached. While waiting for the water temperature to heat up, he ran a hand over his chest, sucking in a sharp breath when his fingers brushed over hardened nipples. He closed his eyes and pictured Locke's face pressed against his pecs, licking and sucking his nipples while Sawyer fisted his blond hair.

Fantasies of Locke kissing a path down his body, stopping to dip his tongue inside his navel before running his nose through his happy trail, made him moan out loud. Sawyer fisted his throbbing cock, wanting to put himself out of his misery but not eager for the fantasy to end. Using his precum to ease the way, Sawyer started stroking with a steady rhythm that took him to the edge in seconds. He opened his eyes when the warmth built at the base of his spine and his taut balls drew tighter against his body. Shuttling his fist faster, Sawyer reached up with his free hand to pinch and roll his nipple between his thumb and forefinger.

He bit his lip to keep from crying out Locke's name when his semen jetted from his cock in thick ropes, painting the gray and cream marble countertops. He'd always had a visceral, animalistic reaction to seeing his own cum, and marking his lovers made sex that much more intense. Sawyer leaned forward, bracing his hands on the vanity while he caught his breath. Guilt rose swift and unwelcome inside him, but he shoved it aside. His one-time fantasy didn't hurt anyone. Regardless of Locke's behavior the previous night, Sawyer knew the score. Locke was off-limits to him and would always be, so he would work off his fantasies solo and none would be the wiser. *Including you,* his conscience said.

Sawyer shoved away from the vanity, ignoring the voice of reason, and headed into the shower where the dildo, still suctioned to the marble bench, mocked him. Knowing he was good and spent, Sawyer went about washing like usual, doing his best to ignore the pressing urge he felt for penetration. The need clawed at his guts, unwilling to fade away even after a hard climax. *It's right there. Use it.* His dick started hardening again at the thought. *Fucking traitor.*

The best way to counter his attraction to Locke would be to get this out of his system before seeing him again. Sawyer growled his surrender then slicked the toy with lube before working two fingers inside his tight hole. *God, it had been so long. Too long.* Once he was stretched as far as the awkward position allowed, Sawyer turned around. Stabilizing the dildo with one hand and gripping the bench to brace his weight with the other, Sawyer lowered himself down until the broad head of the toy pressed against his greedy pucker.

The penetration stretched and burned as Sawyer slowly lowered himself onto the slick toy. The sensations were familiar and good, but not the same as a real cock. He missed firm hands gripping his hips, holding him down to receive a fierce fucking or guiding him up and down a hard cock. Sawyer wanted to see possessive finger bruises on his skin and feel the burn of a lover's teeth sinking into his flesh as seeking pleasure overrode all other senses.

Sawyer's cries of pain and pleasure echoed in the tile and glass enclosure as he rode the dildo up and down, grinding the toy against his prostate until stars danced behind his closed eyelids. God, how he missed the euphoric pleasure of being filled and mastered by a man whose primary concern was seeing him shatter with pleasure. Locke's smirking face appeared in Sawyer's mind, and he instinctively knew the man would play dirty. Locke would use filthy words and skillful hands to get Sawyer off.

He tried to replace Locke's face with Levi's, but the images flickered like a holograph until his partner was once again solid and so real Sawyer could almost feel his hot breath on his neck and his fingers tugging his nipples until…

"Locke! Fuck, yes!" Sawyer roared as he came hard for the second time that morning.

He rutted and ground his ass against the toy until he had nothing left to give and every bit of strength fled him, following his spunk down the drain. It took him a few minutes to recover enough to ease off the toy and rinse his body. Sawyer turned the water off, dried his body, and flopped back down in bed buck-ass naked—too exhausted and satiated to even cover himself.

When his alarm went off a few hours later, Sawyer rolled over to slap it off and found Bones staring at him with disdain and judgment.

"I couldn't help myself," Sawyer groused, his voice thick with hard sleep. "He's so fucking hot, Bones. You'd understand if you saw him."

Meow.

"Oh, right. This isn't about me; it's about your belly."

Meow.

"Fine."

After feeding Bones, Sawyer decided to skip his morning workout. His glutes would testify that riding the dildo was equivalent to a few reps of squats. He was sore and satiated in a way he hadn't been in a long time. Rather than tuck the toy away, he decided to leave it out. No one would see it, and Sawyer was tired of denying himself something that made him feel complete.

After Vic died, Sawyer had lived in a state of depression for several months and hadn't experienced a desire to even masturbate. His mind had started mending before his broken heart, and his sexual urges soon followed. Ignoring the need to climax became physically painful, but seeking release made him sick with guilt. He had cried the first time he'd jerked off but couldn't deny how much better he felt physically. After a year, relieving himself wasn't enough, so he had allowed friends to talk him into going to a club. He wasn't ready to date or fall in love, but he missed the feel of a man's hands on his body.

The first hookup after Vic died had been the hardest and Sawyer had vomited and cried from the guilt once he returned to the home he had once shared with Vic. The guilt lessened after a few tries, but the releases were empty and cold, so he'd just gone back to taking care of business himself.

Sawyer finally felt ready to date again and enjoy every aspect of a relationship. He just needed to stop fantasizing about his straight-ish partner and find a man he could build something with. Levi's sweet face, adorable blue eyes, and nerdy glasses came to mind.

The café owner had seemed interested in him, but Sawyer had been out of the game so long it was possible he misread the signs. "Guess I'll find out when I return to the café this morning," Sawyer said to Bones, who ignored him to watch birds and squirrels battle it out for bird seed from the feeder. Bones' tail twitched from left to right as his head shifted up, down, and side to side as he watched the birds dive-bomb the squirrels. Sawyer made machine gun noises and simulated nosediving-engine sounds to add to his cat's entertainment. "And don't come back," he said prissily when the squirrel ran down the feeder pole and darted into the bushes.

Bones looked up at his human. Sawyer didn't think it was possible for an animal to look more scornful than his feline did at that moment.

Meow.

"I'm going, Bones."

Traffic was light since rush hour hadn't begun, so Sawyer reached Bytes and Brew before he got to finish the next Chapter in his audiobook. Sawyer was surprised by how many people were sipping coffee and working on computers when he walked in. Levi looked at the door with an automatic smile when Sawyer walked in. The café owner's blue eyes widened, and his smile grew from pleasant to delighted in a heartbeat. *Okay, he hadn't imagined his interest.* In the next instant, Levi nodded his head toward a computer where a young lady sat staring at her monitor. Sawyer winked at Levi then walked toward his witness. He kept his stride casual and was careful not to loom over the woman.

"Is your name Becca?" Sawyer asked, showing her the badge clipped on his belt.

Becca's eyes widened slightly, but she nodded. "Rebecca Brenner is my legal name."

Sawyer gestured to the empty chair beside her—the same one he suspected Carl Hanover sat in to upload the recorded podcast to Putz's website. "My name is Sawyer Key, and I'm a detective with the Savannah PD. Mind if I sit down?"

"Um, sure," she hesitantly said. "Am I in trouble?"

"Not at all," Sawyer assured her with a smile. "Do you remember the man who sat in this chair yesterday morning?"

"I do," Becca said with a nod. "Normally, I wouldn't pay attention because making eye contact with strangers is just asking for it these days, but he needed some help figuring out how to access the internet. I guess he uses an older form of Windows." I pulled up Carl's arrest mugshot on my phone and turned it to show her. "That's him!" The color drained from her face. "Oh my God. Did I witness a crime? Did I almost die yesterday?" She covered her mouth with both hands to stifle her squeak. Becca dropped her hands and leaned forward. "Did I unknowingly help him commit a crime. Oddly, that upsets me more than almost dying."

"I don't believe you were in any danger, and you're not responsible for any of his actions. The crime he is accused of committing occurred before he showed up at the café," Sawyer assured her.

"I'm so relieved."

"I would like for you to come to the Midtown police station and formally identify him and make a statement."

"I can do that," Becca said, nodding her head. "When? Now? I have class in an hour."

Sawyer pulled a card from his wallet. "Sometime today would be great. Here's my number. Call me, and we can set up a time for you to meet me at the station."

Accepting the card, Becca stared at it a few seconds before lifting her head to meet Sawyer's gaze. "Will there be a formal lineup like on television?"

"We'll use photographs. You'll make a statement about your interaction with the accused and sign it," Sawyer replied.

Becca furrowed her brow and nibbled on her bottom lip. "Will I need to testify in court?"

Sawyer tilted his head slightly. "I'd love to assure you it won't be necessary, but I won't lie to you. There's always a possibility you'll be called to testify if you witness any part of a crime or the subsequent cover-up."

Becca gave a curt nod. "I'll call you after my next class. I have a window of time early this afternoon."

"Sounds perfect. Take care, Miss Brenner."

"You too, Detective Key."

Confident he'd hear from her soon, Sawyer stood up and strolled over toward the counter to order a coffee and say hello to Levi. Even though he'd only talked to Becca for a few minutes, the café had gained nearly a dozen more coffee drinkers. Levi and his staff worked efficiently, taking orders and filling them with Levi operating the espresso machine like he'd been doing it all his life. Sawyer was disappointed when he reached the counter and Levi remained at the other end making drinks.

Realizing it wasn't the time or place for flirting, Sawyer placed his drink order before moving down to the end of the counter to wait with the others. Levi handed each cup off with a smile, thanking each customer and wishing them a great day. When it came to Sawyer's turn, he couldn't help but notice Levi's eyes were warmer, and his smile was more inviting than thankful.

"It's good to see you again. Here's your salted caramel coffee," Levi said. "I hope you have a fabulous day, Sawyer."

"It's starting pretty good," Sawyer replied, lifting his cup to toast the man who made it. "See you later."

"I hope so."

Sawyer didn't understand the full meaning behind the twinkle in Levi's eyes until he saw where Levi had written his phone number beneath his name on the cup. In case Sawyer wasn't clear about his intention, Levi had written: Call Me!

Sawyer was in a spectacular mood when he walked into the precinct. Seeing Locke slumped back in his chair looking haggard made his sometimes-petty heart even happier. The charcoal gray T-shirt stretched tightly across Locke's impressive shoulders and chest made his gray eyes appear lighter. Sawyer wanted to kick himself for noticing.

"Jesus," Locke grimaced when Sawyer stopped by his desk to say hello. "Dial it down a little, will you?" Locke held up his hand like he was shielding his eyes from a bright light.

"Dial what down?" Sawyer replied with a raised brow.

"You're strutting around here like an alley cat, and your smile is blinding me. Did you stop by your dentist to get your teeth whitened before coming to work?"

"Takes an alley cat to know one, Locke," Blue said as he passed by them with a drink carrier in one hand and a pastry bag in the other. "Congratulations on the collar, Key."

"It's my collar too, asshole, and mind your own business," Locke told him good-naturedly. Then he turned his gaze back to his partner, eyes zeroing in on Sawyer's cup, and he knew what his partner saw. Locke flicked his gaze back up to his, and Sawyer was too happy about the annoyance he saw there. "You always going to be so chipper in the morning?"

"You always going to be such a dick?" Sawyer asked then nearly choked on his words when they triggered a memory from the shower.

A corner of Locke's mouth curved up into a wry smile, making it seem like he'd read Sawyer's mind. *God, I hope not.* "Probably," Locke said. "At least on the mornings after only catching a few hours of rest on a sofa more made for looks than sleeping."

The phone on Locke's desk rang, giving Sawyer an excuse to walk away without it feeling awkward. He needed to gather himself and get his head on straight so he could focus on his damn job. The first thing he did was enter Levi's contact information into his personal phone before locking it in his desk. He couldn't make out what Locke was saying, but Sawyer could tell by his serious tone it was probably related to one of his active cases.

Sawyer's desk phone beeped twice in rapid succession, signaling an internal call. He didn't recognize the extension on the caller ID since he didn't have them memorized yet. Picking up the phone, he said, "Detective Key."

"Can you come to my office?" Chief Rigby asked.

"Sure. Locke is on the phone right now. Do you want me to wait for him to wrap up his call first?"

"Come alone," Rigby firmly said before hanging up.

Sawyer took the last sip of his coffee then rose swiftly from his desk and made his way to the chief's office. He felt Locke's intense gaze on him when he walked past him and rapped on Rigby's door, announcing his presence. Sawyer didn't turn and meet his partner's stare; he opened the door and entered their chief's office once she granted him entrance.

The next fifteen minutes were a lecture on proper protocol and how she expected the detectives in her unit to follow it.

"There are no rogue detectives here. If I wanted Locke on the street without a partner, I wouldn't have hired you. That means if you feel the need to investigate someone, regardless of the hour, you call in for support. If Locke isn't available, one of the other MCU detectives will provide backup. Am I clear, Detective?"

"Yes, ma'am. I won't do it again."

Rigby gave a curt nod. "Good. Better get back out there before Locke starts wondering if you're in here eating my bear claws."

Sawyer laughed hard. "You know about his obsession."

"Of course. Why do you think I don't share them with him? His looks and charm get him too much in life. He'll have to dig deep to earn a bear claw from me."

"You've made my day, Chief."

When Sawyer left Rigby's office, he noticed Locke wasn't at his desk. His chair was pushed in, and his computer was dark.

When he reached his desk, Sawyer saw that the coffee cup with Levi's phone number on it was gone. He hadn't thrown it away before he went to Rigby's office, which meant someone else had. Then he noticed barely legible words scrolled on a Post-it note stuck to the middle of his desk. Sawyer picked it up and tried to decipher it.

"What's this?" Sawyer asked Blue, whose desk was closest to his.

Blue pivoted in his chair and grinned. "That's Locke's shitty handwriting. He should come with his very own translator. I have pretty good luck deciphering his bullshit though." Sawyer handed the neon green square of paper to Blue. "Damn, he's a childish dickhead. Are you sure you want to work with him?"

"He'll soon learn I'm relentless in pursuit of the things I want," Sawyer replied. "Are those Roman numerals mixed in with the chicken-scratch letters?"

"Yep. It's an address." Blue squinted and turned the square slightly to the right. "Thirty-five twenty-nine Sussex Place. He must've taken a call while you were in Rigby's office."

"Thanks, Blue," Sawyer said, slapping the guy on the back.

"No problem. Good luck."

When Sawyer tossed the crumpled note in the trash can, he noticed it landed next to the coffee cup he hadn't put there. What the hell was Locke's problem, and why did he care?

CHAPTER 13

THE CRIME SCENE AT SUSSEX PLACE WAS MOSTLY A REPEAT FROM THE previous day sans the media circus and with a much smaller crowd gathered across the street. Sawyer noticed crime scene tape wasn't used as a barricade along the perimeter of the property to keep people back nor was Officer Andrews there to keep the bold onlookers from getting too close.

"We meet again, Officer Jones," Sawyer said when he jogged up the few porch steps to the pale yellow, two-story house. The exterior was quaint and cheerful with white shutters and window-box planters filled with a variety of colorful flowers. It was the kind of place a person looked at and couldn't imagine anything horrific happening there. The police presence and ME's coroner van were a reminder that no neighborhood was exempt from crime.

"I wish it were over a beer and not because of another homicide," Jones replied. "You know the routine."

Sawyer signed in then put on gloves and booties. "What do we have?"

"DeShaun Benson, age thirty-two, and Caroline Wembley, age twenty-eight. It looks like a murder-suicide, but DeShaun's mother isn't buying it." What mother wanted to believe their child could be either the victim or perpetrator of a murder-suicide?

As if on cue, a heartbroken voice rang out from the crowd. "I'm not going to let you tarnish my boy's reputation just so you can close the case and dust off your hands. I know how this goes down every time. It's always the black man who did it. My boy didn't do drugs. My boy wasn't violent. He was a respected doctor, and he loved every hair on that girl's head."

Sawyer looked over his shoulder and saw Officer Andrews wrap her arms around the bereaved woman then guide her over to a cruiser. Rather than just put her inside the car and shut the door, Andrews squatted down beside the passenger seat and took both the sobbing woman's hands in her own. Sawyer couldn't hear what Andrews was saying, but it had an immediate effect on the mother, who nodded her head. Andrews stood up, shut the door, then walked around and got in behind the wheel. She'd assessed the situation when she arrived on the scene and decided where she was needed most. Sawyer respected that.

"Mrs. Benson found the bodies and called nine-one-one. Bless her heart, I wouldn't wish that on any mother," Jones said somberly.

"Nor would I," Sawyer agreed then stepped inside the home.

The first thing he noticed was how cold the house was. Sawyer noted the windows were fogged up due to the drastic difference in internal and external temperatures. Water rivulets dripping down the windowpanes from condensation made it look like the house was weeping. Sawyer heard voices coming from the hallway to the right of the living room and followed them. Lining the walls were dozens of photos of a young, interracial couple who looked happily in love. Big smiles and affectionate touches were captured in every shot. The final frame outside their bedroom was a collage of photos starting with DeShaun down on one knee presenting an open ring box to Caroline, then him sliding an engagement ring on her finger, and ended with DeShaun spinning Caroline in a circle while kissing her smiling lips. Sawyer's heart thudded heavily in his chest because he knew the scene in the bedroom would be anything but joyous. He preferred to remember the happy couple as they were captured in the photos, but his job didn't allow him to bury his head in the sand. He took a deep breath then stepped inside the bedroom.

Locke and Fawkes were squatting beside the body of a black male who'd died of a gunshot wound to the temple. Lying on the bed was a semi-nude white female who'd died from strangulation.

"At first glance, one would assume the young lady was killed by her boyfriend before he turned a gun on himself," Fawkes told Locke.

"That isn't what happened?" Sawyer asked, causing his partner and the ME to look at him.

"You walk quietly for a tall man," Fawkes said, narrowing her eyes at him. "The male victim doesn't have any gunpowder residue on his hands. Also, the slight bump on his middle left finger tells me he's lefthanded, but he was shot on the right side of his head. If a person were serious about killing themselves, they'd do it with their dominant hand. Even ambidextrous people often tend to favor one hand over the other."

Sawyer squatted down to examine the Desert Eagle 1911 used to kill DeShaun Benson and noticed the serial number had been filed off.

Fawkes pointed toward the bed. "The female victim doesn't show any signs of a struggle you'd expect to see with a strangled victim. She doesn't have blood or skin beneath her nails, and she didn't scratch her neck while trying to free herself from the scarf used to choke her. There are no ligature marks around her hands, so they don't appear to have been bound before strangulation. The petechial hemorrhaging associated with asphyxiation is present, so I think she was incapacitated first. Most likely taken by surprise. On the back of her skull, there's a large bump indicating she was struck, most likely rendering her unconscious. I think our killer placed her on the bed and strangled her, waited for Mr. Benson to arrive, then shot him point blank when he stepped through the door."

"Double homicide then," Sawyer said.

"Those are my initial findings, and I don't believe the autopsies will change my mind. Time of death will be trickier because of the tampered room temperature. I'm sure you noticed how cold the house is."

"I did."

"Someone turned the air-conditioning down to sixty degrees, which slows down the onset of both rigor and livor mortis. It also fucked up my body temperature readings and delayed decomposition. There are also no obvious signs of insects, which can be a medical examiner's best friend." Sawyer had to fight off a hard shiver. He could live the rest of his life without encountering maggots or any other insect associated with death. "I'll do additional testing in the morgue. The stomach contents can give us some big clues. We'll have to rely on eyewitness accounts to go with my forensic findings to determine a more accurate window of death," Fawkes said.

Locke rose to his feet and walked over to Sawyer. "We'll start interviewing friends, family, and coworkers to build a timeline. Both the victims' cell phones are present, and neither are passcode protected, so we'll be able to find phone numbers."

"Let's start with Mrs. Benson since she's already on the scene, then we'll have to notify Caroline's family if someone hasn't called them already," Sawyer said. The two of them left the room, discarded the gloves and booties, and disposed of them in the biohazard bag at the front door before heading to Andrews' cruiser to speak to Mrs. Benson.

When the woman saw the detectives walking toward her, she jumped out of the car and started walking to them. "DeShaun didn't do this, Detectives," she said firmly. "They had everything going for them. They'd just gotten engaged last month and were planning their wedding. My baby would never do something like this."

After several years in law enforcement, this part of the job never got easier. Sawyer at least found comfort that he could assure Mrs. Benson she wasn't wrong about her son. He couldn't say that to every grieving parent though.

"We're investigating DeShaun's and Caroline's deaths as a double homicide until evidence points to the contrary, Mrs. Benson. I'm so very sorry for your loss, and I wish like hell you weren't the one who found them."

"I'll never be able to unsee it," Mrs. Benson choked out then started sobbing again.

Locke surprised Sawyer when he wrapped his arm around the grieving woman and pulled her into his shoulder. "We won't stop until we find out who did this, ma'am. You have my word."

"Do you know if Caroline's parents were notified yet?" Sawyer asked.

Mrs. Benson lifted her head from Locke's shoulder and nodded. "Mary called me this morning and asked if I'd heard from either DeShaun or Caroline since I last saw them at lunch on Sunday. I hadn't, but it wasn't unusual with their busy schedules. Mary was adamant something was wrong because she and Caroline had been exchanging pictures of wedding dresses they liked. She got a sick feeling when Caroline didn't reply to the last text Mary sent. Like me, she figured Caroline was busy with a project at work. She's an architectural engineer." Mrs. Benson's face crumpled, and she started crying again. "*Was*. She was an architectural engineer." Locke patted her back, and Andrews joined them with a box of tissues. Mrs. Benson thanked her then wiped her eyes and tried to pull herself together. "Mary knew something was wrong when an entire day went without a response from Caroline. I promised Mary I would come over and check on them and…" Her words trailed off, and her body shook with silent tears. "Jim and Mary were vacationing in Palm Springs and are getting on the first flight home."

"Do you know of anyone who would want to hurt DeShaun and Caroline? Did they tell you about any threats they received from anyone? Were they having issues with coworkers or someone they used to date?" Locke asked.

"Not that either of them said to me, but DeShaun wouldn't have wanted to worry me about something he hadn't perceived as a real threat. Had he felt threatened, he would've filed a police report."

"Is there anyone we can call for you, Mrs. Benson?" Sawyer asked. She shook her head. "Why don't we go back to the station so you can help us establish a timeline. We'll need to know where they worked and get contact information for anyone they come into contact with regularly."

Mrs. Benson nodded. "I can help you with that."

"I'll drive her," Andrews said softly.

"Thank you," Locke said.

They waited for Andrews to guide Mrs. Benson back to her cruiser and drive away before speaking.

"We live in such a fucked-up world," Locke said, sounding despondent. "You better call me if you get a *hunch* in this case because it's my turn to body-tackle a fleeing suspect. You don't get to have all the fun." Or did he mean credit?

"I didn't tackle Carl Hanover; he fell," Sawyer said dryly. "See you back at the station." He didn't bring up the coffee cup incident because it wasn't the right time, and what would he say if it were? He was better off chalking it up to an innocent prank and focusing his energy on getting justice for DeShaun, Caroline, and their families than dwelling on imaginary hidden motives.

CHAPTER 14

MRS. BENSON'S HEARTBREAK WAS SOUL-CRUSHING, BUT SHE HELD herself together as best she could to give Sawyer and Locke as much information as possible in between body-racking sobs. Officer Keeley Andrews stayed with them the entire time, holding the grieving mother's hand. She'd impressed Sawyer and changed his less-than-stellar first impression of the woman.

When the interview was over, Locke and Sawyer assured Mrs. Benson they'd do everything within their power to get justice for DeShaun and Caroline. They left her with Andrews and a counselor from the victims' families outreach program then headed to the bullpen to put together a strategy. Locke stopped at his workstation since it was closer. Rather than sit in his late partner's chair, Sawyer leaned his hip against the edge of Locke's desk.

"We'll cover a lot more ground if we split the interviews between us," Locke said.

TV shows and movies always depicted detective partners as joined at the hip, and while it was mostly true, there were times it made sense to split up. Mrs. Benson had given them no less than a dozen names.

"Agreed," Sawyer said.

"Do you want their coworkers or friends?" Locke asked him.

"I'll take the coworkers."

Luckily, every name Mrs. Benson gave them was found in their phone contacts, and employment information for their friends outside the workplace was listed on their Facebook profiles.

"I'm going to head to St. Joseph's Hospital to talk to Dr. Benson's colleagues, then I'll hit up Grady, Keller, and Associates," Sawyer said.

"I'm going to notify their friends in person instead of calling them on the phone," Locke said. "I don't want to risk catching anyone while they're driving and causing an accident. Hopefully, they'll have a support system of work friends to help them cope with the shock."

"Meet back here later to compare notes?" Sawyer asked.

"Yeah, I'll pick up lunch for us. What do you feel like eating?"

"Surprise me," Sawyer said, amazed Locke would offer to pick up lunch for him.

"Ha. You already look surprised." Locke shook his head. "I'm aware we got off on the wrong foot yesterday, and I'm also certain I'm the reason. Buying your lunch is a peace offering."

"I'll take it," Sawyer said with a relaxed smile.

"Food allergies? Anything you have a deep affinity for or an aversion to?"

"Did you say perversion?" Detective Holly Stein asked as she passed through.

"You wish, Stein," Locke replied nonplussed. It was evident to Sawyer just how much the members of the MCU liked one another. Locke glanced over at the vice detective and did a double take. "How much for an hour?"

Holly glanced down at her denim cutoffs, fishnet stockings, thigh-high boots, and a barely there tank top. Sawyer had met her the day before and learned she was working undercover to arrest johns soliciting sex from prostitutes. "More than you could afford, champ." Holly winked suggestively at Locke, who laughed and shook his head before turning his attention back to Sawyer.

"Back to your likes and dislikes, Key." Sawyer quirked a brow. "For food," Locke clarified.

"Thanks for clearing it up. We both know what happens when I assume things," Sawyer quipped. *I go home and jerk off and ride a dildo until I can barely walk.* "I'm not aware of any food allergies, and I like everything."

"All right," Locke said, rising from his chair. "I've delayed the inevitable for as long as I can. Breaking these people's hearts fucking sucks."

"It does." Sawyer waited until Locke was nearly at the bullpen exit before speaking again. "Hey, Locke, maybe you should record your interviews or type your notes in your phone so I won't have to ask Blue to decipher them for me." Locke just held up a middle finger and kept walking.

Sawyer laughed, feeling like one of the team for the first time since he'd arrived. He made himself a cup of coffee before taking the same Charger he'd used the day before. What should've been a sixteen-minute drive to travel eleven miles turned out to be thirty-five minutes due to construction on Harry S. Truman Parkway and an accident on Abercorn Street. Police officers were directing traffic around the collision involving three cars and a motorcycle. The patrolman waved Sawyer through, and he flashed his headlights to thank him. He knew a lot of cops who would've flipped on their lights and sirens to get through the congestion quicker, but it only made an already hectic situation more chaotic. It would be one thing if he were responding to an emergency, but he wasn't.

Sawyer parked in the emergency room parking lot then headed toward the entrance. Just the brief walk between his car and the sliding doors had him sweating profusely in the oppressive heat. It triggered the memory of Locke's remark from the previous day about his choice to wear dress shirts and ties. He'd paid closer attention to what everyone else wore to work on his second day and noticed it was a mixed bag. Chief Rigby didn't strictly enforce the dress code for the detectives working in her department. Some wore suits like him while others wore polo shirts and dress pants. Locke was the only one besides vice who wore T-shirts and jeans. Stein's attire that day didn't count. Sawyer couldn't help but notice she was tall, brunette, and had an athletic build. She and Locke seemed to have natural chemistry, and he couldn't help but wonder if it stemmed from a closer relationship outside the precinct.

Stop it, dumbass, Sawyer chided.

"Can I help you?" asked a young woman with vibrant red hair and amber eyes working at the patient intake desk. Her nameplate identified her as S. Jenkins.

"I'm Detective Key, and I need to speak to doctors Rizzo, Justice, Grant, and Sherwood, please."

Ms. Jenkins smiled nervously. "It sounds like a law firm." When Sawyer didn't laugh, she apologized and picked up a phone. "Hailey, I have a detective here to see Rizzo, Justice, Grant, and Sherwood." She listened for a second then sucked in a harsh breath. "Oh no," she said, glancing up at Sawyer with widened, wet eyes. "Okay." Tears slid down her face when she hung up the phone. "Hailey is the physicians' assistant. She'll be here in just a minute." Ms. Jenkins swallowed hard. "Is it true? Is Dr. Benson dead?" Sawyer wasn't surprised word had reached them already. The only thing that traveled faster than the speed of light was terrible news.

"I'm afraid so, ma'am."

Her shoulders shook, and more tears spilled down her face. "But Dr. Benson was so nice and so young."

"I'm very sorry for your loss."

The double doors leading back to the ER opened with a whoosh. Sawyer assumed the tear-streaked woman in dark blue scrubs walking toward him was Hailey.

"Detective," she said with a soft voice. "I'm Hailey Perkins and I'm the physicians' assistant. I'll take you back to our breakroom, and then I'll find the doctors for you. They're all aware of the situation and probably have retreated to their offices for a few minutes of privacy." Hailey took a big shaky breath. "I cannot believe DeShaun is dead. This has to be a bad dream."

"I wish it was," Sawyer said gently. He also wished he'd chosen to speak to their friends and avoided the antiseptic smell and sterile lights of the hospital which never failed to remind him of Vic's last days at the hospice facility. He hadn't wanted to die at home. They'd just bought their house, and Vic had wanted Sawyer to only have good memories of him there.

"In here," Hailey said, gesturing to the open door of a small, unoccupied breakroom. "Do you have a preference which doctor you speak to first? Would you like to speak with all of them at once?"

"One at a time is great, and the order doesn't matter to me. I'll record these interviews on my phone unless they request otherwise," Sawyer replied. He didn't want the doctors' answers to influence each other. He wanted genuine reactions and responses. It wasn't the time to hold back because they didn't want to do or say anything that would tarnish DeShaun's image.

"I'll be right back."

The first doctor was Jessica Sherwood. As Hailey said, Dr. Sherwood's shock was evident in her wide eyes. It took her a few seconds to pull herself together and answer Sawyer's questions. She wasn't aware of anyone who would want to harm DeShaun or his lovely fiancée, as she referred to Caroline. Darren Justice met with him next, and his answers were all the same. DeShaun was happy, in love, and passionate about his work. If he had an enemy, Dr. Justice wasn't aware. Bonnie Rizzo followed him shortly and was so distraught her answers came out as hiccup-like chirps, and Sawyer learned nothing new. Mark Grant came in last, and even though he was equally as devastated as the others, he had maintained more control over his emotions.

"I think I'm the last one to see him alive," he said in a stunned voice once Sawyer officially told him what the ME believed to have happened the previous evening. "We walked to our vehicles together. I'd noticed he seemed a little distracted and teased him about wedding plans already causing stress."

"What did he say?"

"He laughed it off, but it didn't sound genuine. It was dry and felt more like he was appeasing me rather than finding real humor in my joke," Dr. Grant said.

"Did he give you any indication of what was bothering him?"

"DeShaun said he'd been trying to get ahold of Caroline to let her know he was running late but hadn't been able to reach her, and she hadn't responded to messages."

His answer grabbed Sawyer's attention. He needed details to help build an accurate timeline. DeShaun's phone would reveal a lot, but eyewitness interaction and perception could be helpful too. "Did he give you an idea of how long he had tried to contact her?"

"He said he'd chatted with Caroline at lunch when they made dinner plans, but DeShaun couldn't reach her a few hours later when he called to ask her to adjust their reservations. He assumed she was annoyed and knew the reason for his call and decided not to answer."

"Is that how she would commonly react?" Sawyer asked.

"I can't say," Dr. Grant replied. "It was the first time DeShaun mentioned the behavior to me."

It was possible Caroline wanted to delay the inevitable conversation, or it was possible she was already dead.

"Is there anything else you can think of? Was anyone giving him or Caroline trouble? Had he received threats from angry patients? Were there jealous exes or coworkers?"

"I'm not aware of any threats, Detective. I think there were plenty of ladies, and a few men, who would have loved to capture DeShaun's heart, but they knew a lost cause when they saw one. There was no one for him but Caroline. You couldn't help but love the man and want the very best for him. I'm going to miss his big smile and booming laugh." Dr. Grant choked up then and wiped furiously at his eyes. He released a shaky sigh and pinned Sawyer with a stern look. "You catch this animal, Detective."

"I'll do my very best, sir."

Sawyer rose to his feet and shook hands with the man. "Are there any nurses or other personnel you think I should talk to?"

Dr. Grant shook his head. "Dr. Benson was very friendly to the staff but maintained a professional distance. Unless they overheard a conversation not intended for their ears, they wouldn't be privy to anything going on in his personal life. You're more than welcome to ask around if you like."

"I'll chat with Hailey to see if she can think of anyone. Thank you for your time, Dr. Grant." The man nodded and exited the breakroom.

Sawyer gathered his thoughts, typed notes in his phone, then rose to his feet. Hailey was waiting for him outside the breakroom.

"Dr. Grant said you wanted to see me?" Hailey asked.

"So far, all I know is that DeShaun was a brilliant doctor and a good man who was crazy in love with his fiancée," Sawyer said. "Did you notice anything unusual about him yesterday? Did he seem distracted or upset by anything?"

"Not that I saw, but I only worked for half a day yesterday. My kids had orthodontist appointments, so I left as soon as everyone cycled back from lunch," Hailey said.

"Is there anyone on the nursing staff you think I should talk to?" Sawyer asked.

"I can't think of anyone who knew him better than the doctors you already spoke to, but you're welcome to pull them aside and speak to them."

"Why don't I leave a few business cards with you and they can call me if they think of anything helpful? I've given cards to each of the doctors also."

Hailey accepted the cards and nodded. "Thank you."

Sawyer nodded goodbye to the redhead at the desk and kept

walking, wanting away from the hospital smell and trying to outrun the sadness seeping into his soul after listening to one heartfelt remark after the other about DeShaun Benson. He hit the remote start to cool off the car then sat with the fan blowing on high for a few seconds.

The only thing he'd gleaned from his visit was that DeShaun hadn't been able to reach Caroline after lunch, but Sawyer wouldn't know what time he started calling or texting her until he was back at the station looking at DeShaun's cell phone.

Sufficiently cooled off, Sawyer shifted the Charger into drive and headed toward Grady, Keller, and Associates where he hoped Caroline's coworkers knew more personal details about her life than DeShaun's did.

Traffic was less congested when he turned left on Abercorn Street. Pedestrian flow on the sidewalks was practically nil because the heat and humidity would suck the life right out of a person. It felt more like August than June.

"Record heatwave," the radio DJ said like he could read Sawyer's mind. "There's a tropical depression forming south of the Bahamas and experts fear it could pick up enough steam to become a hurricane."

"Just what we need," Sawyer muttered when he turned left onto White Bluff.

The offices of Grady, Keller, and Associates were located inside an old, two-story home that had been rehabbed and converted to a business. The dove gray exterior with navy blue shutters was a nice contrast to the white, wraparound porch. When Sawyer reached the front door, he noticed a sign taped to the windowpane.

We apologize for the inconvenience, but our office is temporarily closed. We will reopen tomorrow.

Word had already reached Caroline's coworkers too.

There were several cars in the parking lot, and although the reception area was dark, lights were on deeper inside the business. Sawyer knocked firmly. No one answered right away, and he was preparing to walk around to the back of the property to try his luck when a woman poked her head around the doorway separating the office space from the reception room. Sawyer unclipped his badge and held it up for her to see. The woman nodded and walked to the door.

"Good morning, ma'am," Sawyer said once she opened it. "I'm Detective Sawyer Key with the Savannah Police Department. I suppose you know why I'm here."

She swallowed hard and nodded. "I'm Alice Barnes. I'm the office manager. Please come in. We're all back in the conference room trying to make sense of this tragedy." Alice Barnes's shoulders shook as he followed her down a hallway.

Several heads jerked up when they walked into the room. "I'm Detective Sawyer Key with Savannah PD. I've been assigned to investigate the double homicide of DeShaun Benson and Caroline Wembley."

"Double homicide?" a young, blonde woman in the back of the room asked. "We'd heard it was a murder-suicide."

"That's false information, ma'am," Sawyer said.

"I told you," said a severe-looking man with white hair sitting at the head of the conference room. "I knew DeShaun didn't kill Caroline."

"No one wanted to believe it, Mr. Keller," a brunette said in the front of the room. "It was stated as a rumor, not a fact."

Other emotions besides grief and shock stirred in the air, putting Sawyer on alert. The issue could be internal such as people not liking each other in general, or perhaps Caroline's death was the source of the additional tension in the room.

"Is it possible to use this conference room to conduct individual interviews?" Sawyer asked, counting heads as he searched the room to gauge reactions to his request. Twelve people. Mrs. Benson had only mentioned three by name. "Starting with Aubrey Frye, Jarrod Applegate, and Misha Ferrero."

"Absolutely," Mr. Keller stated. "My partner, Terrance Grady, is out of town on vacation but I can have him phone you."

"I appreciate it. I'm primarily concerned with what happened yesterday, but I'd love to chat with Mr. Grady if he's aware of anything that might help us solve the case like arguments she's had or threats she's received."

"Caroline?" Mr. Keller asked. "I can't even believe we're having this conversation. Who in the world would want to hurt either of them, let alone both of them?"

"That's what I'm trying to find out," Sawyer assured him.

"Let's get started then," Mr. Keller said, clapping his hands. Everyone, including him, rose to their feet. "Aubrey, you talk to the detective first since you knew her best. Misha and Jarrod will follow after."

"Okay," a young blonde woman said. She sat back down and waited for the rest of the employees to exit the room before speaking to Sawyer. "I did know her best. We were friends outside of work too, where the rest of the staff was more like work acquaintances."

Sawyer took a seat across the table from her. "I'd like to record this interview so I can type my case notes later. Is that okay with you?"

"Sure."

Sawyer tapped the voice-recording feature on his phone and stated his name, the date and time, the case, and the person he was interviewing as well as the location of where it was being conducted.

"Are you aware of anyone who harbored a grudge or ill will toward Caroline or DeShaun?"

"Wayne Miller," Aubrey said through gritted teeth. "I'd bet a month's salary he killed them."

Sawyer sat straighter in his seat. "Why do you think so?"

"He dated Caroline for three years. He thought her relationship with DeShaun was a phase, and that she'd come to her senses. He got nasty when she moved in with DeShaun six months ago, and I hear he flipped out when they got engaged last month. It's him, Detective Key. He killed Caroline and DeShaun."

CHAPTER 15

S AWYER IGNORED THE EXCITEMENT PULSING THROUGH HIS SYSTEM AND
focused on breathing. Most homicides were personal and
committed by lovers, ex-lovers, family members, or other
people close to the victim, but he couldn't allow statistics to sway his
judgment. What mattered were the facts, not conjecture.

"You said Caroline and Wayne dated for three years. How long
ago was that?" Sawyer asked.

"They dated for three years and had been broken up for about a
year," Aubrey said.

"And how much time passed after their breakup before Caroline
started dating DeShaun?"

Aubrey broke eye contact and looked down at her clasped hands
resting on the table. "Not long," she said softly.

"Ms. Frye, I'm not here to judge your friend. Nothing you say to
me will impact my determination to bring her killer to justice. The
only way I can do that is by putting together all the pieces of the puzzle. If we leave something out, we risk not solving the case or looking in the wrong direction. I won't think less of your friend for being
human."

Aubrey sniffed and looked up at him. "Caroline never admitted it
to me, but I think she and DeShaun started seeing each other before

she officially broke up with Wayne. If not before, then immediately after."

"What makes you think that?"

"It was obvious her relationship with Wayne was on its death bed." Realizing what she said, Aubrey covered her mouth and trembled as a fresh wave of tears flowed down her cheeks. Sawyer slid the box of Kleenex across the table toward her and waited patiently. After a minute or two, Aubrey sniffled and wiped her eyes with a tissue. "Caroline and Wayne had started fighting all the time. He was jealous and possessive; it stifled her personally and professionally."

"Can you give me specifics?"

"The personal impact was more obvious," Aubrey said. "Caroline rarely got to go anywhere with her friends, and when she did, she was always tense and watching the clock like she was out on a prison furlough or something. One of her other friends remarked on it once and referenced *Cinderella* by asking Caroline if her car would turn into a pumpkin if she stayed out too late. Caroline joked by saying her prince would turn into a frog."

"Did you see any signs of physical abuse?" Sawyer asked.

Aubrey swallowed then nodded. "I saw finger-shaped bruises around her wrist once. She'd worn a long-sleeved blouse to work to cover it up but spilled coffee on her sleeve. She'd tried to wash the stain out with cold water but couldn't, so she was forced to roll the sleeves up or wear stained clothes in front of our wealthy clients."

"Did you ask her about it?"

Aubrey's mouth pursed into an angry grimace. "I did. She tried to tell me her purse strap got wrapped around her wrist while she was carrying too many things to avoid an extra trip to the car. She claimed the strap got caught in the closed car door, but she didn't know it until she started to walk away and got jerked back. She was very fair like me, so I know how easily she bruised, but this looked more like someone gripping her wrist too hard. She made jokes about her middle name being Grace and how her mother should've chosen a different name."

"Any other times?" Sawyer asked.

"She had an odd bruise on the back of her neck once. She'd worn her hair up in a messy bun and wasn't even aware the bruise was there until Jarrod pointed it out to her when we were getting coffee."

"What did she say?"

Aubrey shook her head. "She waved it off and remarked on her clumsiness again."

It sounded like physical abuse to Sawyer too, but it was speculation at this point. "You said Wayne's behavior impacted her professional career also? How so?" Sawyer asked, although he had a good idea.

"A large part of this business is schmoozing," Aubrey quipped, showing the first sign of humor since they began talking. "I don't mean we're a bunch of blowhards and ass-kissers. We're the best architects in the state of Georgia and work with the wealthiest clients. That means we have to showcase how awesome we are with open houses and various other events. Clients will often throw parties once their projects are completed to thank us for a job well done. The partners expect our attendance at these events. Blowing them off and missing opportunities to secure new clients is cause for getting fired. Caroline nearly lost her job after missing a few in a row. It was only the quality of her character and work that saved her ass."

"And you feel her absences from those events were because of Wayne?"

"Caroline told me as much. Rather than attend the events with Caroline as her date, Wayne refused to go and wouldn't let her go either."

Sawyer's brow rose. "He wouldn't *let* her?"

Aubrey cringed while nodding. "One time, Wayne removed something on her car that prevented it from starting. Another time he hid both sets of keys. She told me the incidents were followed up with shouting matches and threats."

Sawyer went on full alert. *This* was the information he needed. "What kind of threats?"

"He would scream and rant about Caroline's supposed plans to leave him. He threatened to kill himself if she did," Aubrey said softly. "Caroline called his family multiple times for help, but they dismissed the remarks as Wayne being dramatic. His mother even blamed Caroline for them. If she were a better girlfriend, Wayne would feel more secure."

"Complete bullshit," Sawyer said, momentarily losing his objectivity. "Tell me about the end of their relationship."

"What Wayne feared would happen actually did," Aubrey said.

"Meaning?"

"Caroline met DeShaun at a party thrown by his colleague who'd used our services. Dr. Mark Grant is his name. Caroline said Dr. Grant specifically introduced them and made a big fuss about how much they had in common. He and DeShaun seemed close from what I could tell, so you'll want to interview him if you haven't already." Aubrey's face turned pink. "Sorry. I don't mean to tell you how to do your job."

"It's okay," Sawyer said good-naturedly. "You'll be happy to know I talked to Dr. Grant before coming here." Sawyer wondered why Dr. Grant left off the part about introducing Caroline and DeShaun, although it probably didn't seem relevant to him. "It was love at first sight?"

"Yes," Aubrey said wistfully, sounding like a woman who'd like to make that same kind of connection. "Caroline's demeanor changed after that party. Rather than join us for lunch as usual, she went elsewhere. She said she took clients to business lunches, but she never turned in expense reports for them. Caroline started glowing with happiness for the first time since I'd known her, so I honestly didn't care who put the smile on her face. She left Wayne and moved in with her parents within two weeks, then the flower and chocolate deliveries started showing up at the office."

"From?" Sawyer asked. It could go either way since both men would want to show her they deserved her—one to win her back, and the other to win her heart.

Aubrey snorted. "Wayne wouldn't buy her chocolates or flowers. He thought she should be grateful he loved her."

"Wow."

"Yeah," Aubrey said sadly. "I won't ever understand what she saw in him, but then again, Caroline only wanted to see the best in everyone. It was probably her fatal flaw."

"So, DeShaun poured on the charm right out of the gate."

"It was genuine, Detective. He sent her flowers every single week to show her how special she was to him." Aubrey broke down again. "I knew he wouldn't have hurt her, but Wayne... He's the kind of person who could and would."

While it sounded like the case, Sawyer didn't know of too many violent people who waited a year to get even. It could've happened precisely how Aubrey described. Wayne could've lived in a state of denial until Caroline got engaged to DeShaun. Even so, there would've been signs of instability along the way.

"I know you said Wayne acted out when she moved in with DeShaun and then seemed to go over the edge after their engagement, but were there any other indicators leading up to that point? It all goes back to the puzzle I'm trying to piece together."

Aubrey looked down at her hands once more. "Wayne left hateful voicemail messages and sent disgusting texts to Caroline at first, but they seemed to die down pretty quickly because she ignored him."

"Hateful and disgusting how?" Again, Sawyer thought he knew, but he wasn't willing to lead her.

Aubrey looked up and met Sawyer's gaze. "Racist remarks about her choosing a black man over him."

Sawyer nodded. "Did he ever do anything other than leave messages or send texts? Did he ever approach her at home or work?"

"Not that she ever said, but she never told me about the physical abuse when they were together."

"Do you know if DeShaun was aware of the hateful messages when they first started happening?" Sawyer asked.

Aubrey tilted her head to the right while she thought it over. "I can't recall a specific conversation, but I'm sure I would've asked her what DeShaun thought about it. Wouldn't I? It seems like such a logical thing to ask, but I was just so damn happy for her. It was also obvious to me she didn't take Wayne's antics seriously until later."

"What specifically happened with Wayne when Caroline moved in with DeShaun then later got engaged? You mentioned he got nasty then flipped out. Can you tell me about that?"

"The exterior of their home was vandalized after Caroline moved in with DeShaun. Someone threw a large rock through the big picture window, and they painted hateful messages on the exterior of the house. She couldn't prove Wayne did it, but I know that's who she suspected because she told me so. When they got engaged, Wayne went on a social media tirade about biracial children never finding acceptance. He never mentioned Caroline or DeShaun specifically, of course, but a mutual friend of Wayne and Caroline's saw it and pointed it out to her."

Sawyer had so many questions. He was dying to know how Caroline met Wayne and how long ago? Were they childhood friends who grew up together but didn't start dating until after college? Had she met him at college and realized too late what a monster he was? Then he thought back to his conversation with Mrs. Benson. She'd mentioned DeShaun wouldn't have said anything to her unless he felt threatened. Did she not know about the vandalism, or did she discount it because it happened six months prior? Had DeShaun and Caroline even gone to the police with their suspicions, or did they worry it would just cause more trouble? Unfortunately, Aubrey couldn't answer any of those questions when Sawyer asked her.

"Can we talk about Caroline's day yesterday so I can put a

timeline together?" Aubrey nodded. "Was there anything unusual about Caroline's day? Was her routine unexpectedly disrupted or plans changed suddenly?"

"Not that I can think of," Aubrey stated. "Yesterday morning started like any other Monday. We had our weekly staff meeting for project updates then parted so each of us could do our thing. Depending on the phase of our projects, our tasks can take us to meet with contractors or clients on jobsites, in their homes, offices, or even over lunch. We sometimes need to meet with public officials when questions arise about our blueprints during the building permit process. When we're not on the phone or meeting with various people for each project, we are at our desks drinking coffee and working on new designs. We're seldom all here at the same time, but there's a group of us that try to meet for lunch each day."

"Caroline, Jarrod, Misha, and yourself?"

Aubrey smiled sadly and nodded. "We chat about where we'll be around midday so we can decide on a place to meet. We all looked forward to the hour together each day. We got to vent about our jobs and clients before gossiping over the things going on around us."

"Did you all meet for lunch yesterday?"

"We met at Clancy's. Are you familiar with it?"

"Very," Sawyer replied. "They have the best sandwiches and kettle chips. What time would you say you ate lunch?" The information could be vital for the ME's autopsy since the temperature at the crime scene had been altered to throw off their findings. Fawkes would rely heavier on internal factors such as stomach contents and rate of digestion to help nail down the timeline.

"I think she arrived a little after noon, and she ordered her food right away. I'd say we were eating by twelve thirty. Caroline was a little late because she was chatting with DeShaun on the phone in her car. He was between patients, and she wanted to talk to him while she could. Caroline said they'd made plans for dinner that night at Grimaldi's. It's a new restaurant they'd been eyeing for a few weeks but were waiting for the mania to die down. She was excited that she'd easily snagged a reservation for dinner at seven. She ordered a chef salad for lunch since she was trying to watch her figure and had planned to blow her caloric intake at the restaurant."

That fell in line with Dr. Grant's timeline of leaving at six thirty. DeShaun would need more than thirty minutes to get home, shower, change for dinner, and drive to the restaurant. Depending on traffic and how quickly he could get ready, they would've been at least fifteen minutes late. If DeShaun saw the writing on the wall early on, it made sense that he wanted to tip off Caroline so she could adjust their reservation, if possible. Most restaurants had a policy that allowed for slightly late arrivals, but beyond the window, their table would be given away. If this dinner were important to Caroline, DeShaun would've been worried about displeasing her. Not reaching her would cause him to worry.

"Caroline joked and said DeShaun would probably be late, so she had a backup plan in place so she wouldn't lose her table," Aubrey said, breaking into his thoughts.

"And that was?"

"They'd drive separately. Caroline said she'd grab their table and drink some wine until DeShaun could join her."

"Sounds reasonable," Sawyer replied. "Did anything unusual occur at lunch? Any conversation that stands out?" Sawyer was trying to find out why Caroline would've neglected DeShaun's attempts to reach her if she wasn't upset he could potentially be late to dinner. "Did she seem distracted or was she worried about meeting with a client?"

"Her afternoon appointments were with her favorite clients, and she was looking forward to them. As for the lunchtime conversation, the only thing that stands out is how irritated Caroline was with her mom. They didn't see eye-to-eye on the type of wedding Caroline should have, and especially didn't agree with the style of dress she should wear. Caroline joked that her mother's ideal dress looked like a ball gown from the eighteen hundreds. She laughed and said she'd elope with DeShaun to Vegas before wearing a wedding dress that required her to wear a corset or a hoop skirt beneath the fabric, and she was turning off her phone so she could concentrate on her appointments."

Aha. Caroline had turned off her phone and probably forgot to turn it back on. She had no idea DeShaun was trying to reach her. That piece of information was extremely helpful. After lunch, Aubrey stated she had returned to the office and remained there until seven. At no point did Caroline show up, call, or email her.

"I'm going to need the names and contact information for the clients she was scheduled to see yesterday afternoon."

"Our receptionist, Roberta, can help you with that."

"Excellent," Sawyer said. "You've been very helpful, Ms. Frye." He removed several cards from his wallet and laid them on the conference table. "Please call me if you can think of anything else."

The rest of the interviews with the staff at Grady, Keller, and Associates didn't reveal any additional information. Aubrey had been the one with the best insight, and he thanked her again before leaving the office. Once outside, Sawyer's cell phone vibrated with an incoming text. He didn't check his message until he was back in his car with the air-conditioning blasting on high.

It wasn't a number programmed into his contacts, but it was from a local cell phone. Sawyer opened it up then laughed out loud when he read the message.

Hey, asshole. Lunch in thirty minutes.

Sawyer smiled while he tapped out a response. *Who's this?*

Locke's response was immediate. *The nerdy guy from the coffee shop.* So, he had seen the phone number on the coffee cup before throwing it away. Sawyer refused to analyze Locke's actions right then.

Nah. I already have his number programmed in my phone. Of course, Sawyer had the contact saved on his personal phone, but why ruin good banter with facts? *This must be Detective Dickhead.*

Busted. You're so smart. You should be a detective. This is me officially giving you my number, asshole. Don't abuse it.

Sawyer snorted. *Roger that, Detective Dickhead.*

Guess it's better than Detective Dick Breath.

Sawyer's mind spun with how to respond. He typed out a response then hovered his thumb over the send arrow. *Don't knock it until you've tried it.* Sawyer knew he shouldn't send it but couldn't seem to stop himself. He sent the message, tossed the phone onto his passenger seat, and backed out of the parking spot. He'd find out in twenty minutes if he'd just made the biggest mistake of his professional career.

CHAPTER 16

WHILE WAITING FOR LOCKE TO ARRIVE WITH LUNCH, SAWYER CALLED Caroline's clients on the list Roberta provided him and confirmed she'd arrived at all her appointments on time and was in good spirits when she left. None of them detected anything out of the ordinary about her demeanor. She was her typical self—punctual, upbeat, and professional.

She had left her last appointment at five thirty, which would have given her plenty of time to go home and unwind a little bit before she had to get ready for dinner. Sawyer confirmed with the manager at Grimaldi's that neither Caroline nor DeShaun made it to their dinner reservation. They'd get warrants for her credit card and bank statements to see if she made any purchases that would place her anywhere else after her last appointment.

He heard the carryout bags rustling to announce Locke's arrival before he stepped inside the conference room they'd used the previous night to go through Putz's hate mail. The boxes were still stacked neatly along one wall, and they'd need to either enter them in as evidence or ask the chief what she wanted to do with them.

"Feels like we just left this room," Locke said, not meeting Sawyer's gaze.

"Sure does," Sawyer replied then noticed the familiar red logo on gray plastic bags. "You went to Clancy's?"

"Yep." Still no eye contact.

Sawyer wanted to think Locke was busy sorting their food orders, but he kept his gaze averted even after the bags were empty. He worried he'd gone too far with his last text and wasn't sure how to bring it up, or if he should. Deciding to set it aside for the time being, Sawyer said, "That might also be the last place Caroline Wembley ate."

Locke snapped his head up then. "Might?"

"Last confirmed place. Caroline met her work friends there for lunch yesterday. I also got a promising lead on a suspect."

"Me too. We can compare notes as soon as I fix my low blood sugar," Locke said, dropping down into a chair and reaching for his carryout container. "I hope you like lobster salad on a French roll. It seemed fancy enough for you."

"Fancy?" Sawyer asked, sitting down and reaching for his lunch. "Because I'm gay?"

"Don't be an idiot," Locke countered, failing to meet Sawyer's gaze once more. "Not everything is about your sexual preferences, asshole. Your mom is a supermodel. It's doubtful you grew up eating macaroni and cheese from the blue box like the rest of us."

"Don't bet on it. Evangeline liked to keep it real with us," Sawyer quipped. "Not to sound preachy, but I believe you meant my sexual *orientation*. Preference implies I have a choice on who I'm attracted to, and I don't." He unwrapped his sandwich and took a big bite, moaning when his taste buds came alive.

Locke stopped chewing and pinned Sawyer with the oddest look before he resumed eating.

"What?" Sawyer asked once he washed the bite down with a sip from the bottle of water Locke had brought him. His partner shook his head. "Why were you looking at me funny?"

Locke took a long swig of his water, and Sawyer couldn't tear his eyes away from his Adam's apple working up and down as he did. Locke put the cap back on his bottle and set it down on the table. "I'd heard the term food porn before but never realized what it meant until you started moaning like those characters in your audiobook."

"Sorry," Sawyer said sheepishly. "I'll try to tone it down a notch or two." He nodded toward the catfish sandwich Locke had purchased for himself. "That was my husband's favorite sandwich. It was the last thing Vic requested before we admitted him into the hospice center. He loved the aioli mayo. I tried to duplicate it for him but never could."

Locke briefly looked at his sandwich before returning his turbulent gray gaze to meet Sawyer's. "I'm sorry for your loss too. I should've realized how much you can relate to the way I'm grappling with Marcus's death."

"Thanks," Sawyer said, regretting he'd made the awkward moment more so by mentioning his late husband and reminding Locke of the pain that still consumes him—the only reason they were partners.

"Your husband had excellent taste," Locke said, looking back at his sandwich. It seemed like he was debating if he should eat it or not.

"He was quite the foodie," Sawyer said with a smile. "I didn't mean to ruin your lunch with my rambling. Eat. Enjoy. Vic would want you to."

Locke picked up his sandwich but didn't take a bite right away. "Vic had good taste in other things too." Locke's gray eyes widened as if he couldn't believe he'd said that, or he worried Sawyer would take it the wrong way.

He was grateful he hadn't been eating or drinking when the words came out of Locke's mouth. Sawyer knew, or was reasonably sure, Locke wasn't hitting on him, but he couldn't stop the flood of naughty images attacking his brain. Sawyer figured Locke was referring to his character, but he suddenly wanted to lie across the conference table and offer himself up as a buffet. A bright flush spread up Locke's neck and face. Sawyer decided to take pity on the man. "He was a snazzy dresser also."

"I bet he dressed appropriately for the weather though," Locke said, gripping the life raft Sawyer tossed to him.

"I've reconsidered my work attire," Sawyer told him before popping a hush puppy into his mouth.

"You're going to stop wearing an undershirt beneath the dress shirt?" Locke teased.

"Nah, I was thinking more along the line of Stein's getup. Those fishnet stockings would allow a lot of air flow. I can turn those jeans I wore last night into denim cutoffs."

Locke choked on a bite of catfish sandwich. Once he got control of his coughing, he wadded up his napkin and threw it at his partner, hitting Sawyer square in the chest. "I really want to hate your guts, Key."

"I know," Sawyer said. "I can't help it if I'm irresistible. Good genetics, remember?"

"Let's not get carried away here. I'm just sorry for the way I acted yesterday. That speech... I'm horrified." Locke chuckled and shook his head. "Candi smacked me in the back of the head when I told her about it."

Like someone stabbed a balloon with a needle, Sawyer's sudden high spirits popped. While it was nice Marcus's widow didn't hate Sawyer's guts for filling his vacated position on the force, it rankled that Locke hadn't concluded his behavior was bullshit on his own. Beggars couldn't be choosers, and Sawyer didn't want to harbor resentment toward his partner. It would only fester and become cancerous to his soul.

Sawyer smirked. "It was probably long past due."

"I'm also sorry for the Detective Dick Breath comment. I didn't mean it in a homophobic way. It's okay if you have dick breath as opposed to...um..."

"Locke," Sawyer said, cutting him off before the conversation got worse. "I didn't take it as a homophobic remark. Relax. In all fairness, my remark was just as unprofessional."

"Maybe, but I provoked it."

"Agreed," Sawyer said.

Locke smile, nearly robbing Sawyer of his breath. "You didn't take much convincing."

Sawyer shrugged. "I'm easy." When Locke chuckled, Sawyer met his gaze. "To get along with."

"Now that we've cleared that up, let's compare notes."

Sawyer spent the next fifteen minutes telling Locke what he learned and the unanswered questions he had while devouring the food.

"I can answer some of those," Locke said, wiping his mouth with a napkin then tossing his empty container and trash inside the plastic takeout bag. "Wayne and Caroline dated in high school but broke up when Caroline went to college. According to Christina, Caroline's best friend since the fifth grade, the breakup had been Wayne's idea. He thought they should see other people but really meant *he* should see other people. Christina said he showed up at Caroline's college and threatened the guy she started dating. The new boyfriend preferred keeping his face intact to dating Caroline and broke up with her. It was a small, private college, and once word got around about Wayne's jealous rage, no one wanted to date Caroline. Somehow, the asshole convinced her they should date again four or five years ago."

"According to her work friend, it was four years ago," Sawyer said. "It's hard to imagine a seemingly lovely person like Caroline dating a guy like Wayne once let alone twice. Were her friends aware of what was going on?"

"DeShaun's best friend is also his cousin. His name is Lance Chauncy, and he provided the most concise information. The guy is crushed like everyone else, but getting justice for DeShaun and Caroline is the most important thing to him right now. It seems like Caroline has a history of keeping negative things from her friends. They had suspected she was physically and verbally abused by Wayne, but anytime they brought it up to Caroline, she got defensive and pulled away from them. She didn't try to keep the vandalism a secret but said there was no evidence pointing to a particular person."

"Was she in denial?" Sawyer asked. "Aubrey said she wanted to see the best in everyone, but why would she keep giving Wayne the benefit of the doubt?"

"I don't know if she was giving him the benefit of the doubt," Locke said. "According to Lance, she was only repeating what the cop had told DeShaun and Caroline when they filed a vandalism report."

"The vandal didn't sign his name to the hate messages left on the house?" Sawyer teased.

"Nope. We'll have to get a copy of the report, but according to Lance, an officer did take photographs of the crime scene and canvassed the neighborhood, but no one saw anything. Lance also said the officer had informed the couple there were similar incidents with biracial couples in the surrounding neighborhoods, so it didn't seem like an isolated event."

Sawyer shook his head. "I doubt very much that DeShaun and Caroline found any comfort in the knowledge."

Locke smirked. "They didn't, and DeShaun didn't take it lying down. Despite the officer's opinion, DeShaun visited Wayne at his work. Lance went with him to make sure DeShaun didn't lose his cool."

"Really?" Sawyer sat up straighter. "Where does Miller work?"

"Beauregard Buick."

"The dealership with the cheesy commercials?" Sawyer asked.

"That's the one. Wayne works as a mechanic there. According to Lance, DeShaun outright asked him if he was the one harassing them. Wayne denied it, of course, and claimed he wouldn't take Caroline back if DeShaun offered him cash because she was damaged goods."

"Whoa," Sawyer said. "Such an incendiary thing to say. Did DeShaun take the bait?"

"Lance said DeShaun just laughed at Wayne, which really pissed the racist off. He'd hoped DeShaun would jump in his face or hit him so he could have him arrested. Lance said he and DeShaun left without incident."

"Explain to me how Mrs. Benson either didn't know about this or didn't make the connection."

Locke grimaced. "DeShaun's grandmother was dying of cancer at the time the house was vandalized, so Mrs. Benson was spending every spare minute with her. Both DeShaun's and Caroline's friends said the couple had deliberately kept the incident quiet to avoid upsetting her. As time went on without further incident, they chalked it up to a one-time thing. They also noted that the racist rant after the couple got engaged was part of the daily posts Wayne made during his 'white pride month.' They couldn't say for sure it was directed at Caroline and Wayne specifically."

"Why were any of her friends still associating with him—social media or otherwise?"

"Keep your friends close and your enemies closer."

"That makes sense," Sawyer said, nodding his head. "How do you feel about a trip to Beauregard's?"

"I'm too young for a Buick," Locke quipped.

"I was thinking about solving a double homicide, but if you're too cool to step onto a Buick dealership's lot…" Sawyer let his words drift off as he rose to his feet.

"Like hell you're solving this without me, asshole."

"Detective Adonis Asshole," Sawyer reminded him. "If you're a good detective, I'll let you body tackle Wayne if he makes a run for it."

"Yeah?" Locke asked excitedly. He looked heavenward and held his hands up in prayer. "I believe in miracles. I believe in miracles."

Sawyer laughed. After the night-and-day difference between his first and second day on the job, he had to admit he was a believer too.

CHAPTER 17

"**W**ELL, HELLO, SUGARS," SAID THE DOLLY PARTON LOOKALIKE sitting behind the reception counter in Beauregard's dealer service area. The nameplate nestled between the antibacterial gel and a collection of Disney Funko Pops identified her as Marla. "What can I do for you today?"

You can start by not calling me sugar, Sawyer thought. Rather than voicing his thought, he said, "We're here to speak to Wayne Miller, ma'am."

Marla's eyes widened. "What's this about?"

Sawyer unclipped his badge and showed it to her in case she missed the shield on the chain around Locke's neck. "We're here on official police business, and we need to speak to Mr. Miller privately, please."

"Oh, sure," Marla said. "Let me show you to the breakroom. It's empty at the moment since the guys have all just finished their lunch breaks."

"Thank you, Marla," Locke said.

She walked out from behind the tall counter and gestured for them to follow her. Marla wore a hot pink, ruffled tank top, a tight pair of white capri pants, and hot pink wedges. It wasn't the outfit so much that caught Sawyer's attention as it was the black, greasy handprint on her right ass cheek. Sawyer glanced over at Locke and caught his smirk. Feeling his partner's attention, Locke met Sawyer's gaze with a sneer before turning his eyes back to Marla's well-toned ass. Sawyer had to admit it was hard to look away, which was why they both got caught when she stopped at an open door and turned to face them.

"I want to be flattered by your attention, but I can tell by your expressions that you weren't really admiring my ass. Wayne put a big, greasy handprint on me again, didn't he?" Locke and Sawyer both nodded. Marla released a loud huff. "I'm going to kill him. Marking his territory like I'm a fire hydrant and he's a dog. You'd think after eight months of dating he'd feel less insecure. Make yourselves comfortable. Would you like something to drink? We have soda, water, coffee, and tea."

Sawyer shook his head. "No, thank you."

"I'm good also," Locke replied.

"I'll just be a minute." Marla turned and walked in the other direction.

Sawyer elbowed Locke in the ribs to get his attention off Marla's ass and back on their case. He tipped his head toward the breakroom, and Locke led the way inside, a low chuckle rumbling from his chest.

"You couldn't stop staring either," Locke said.

"True, but I probably wasn't having the same thoughts as you."

Locke released a long sigh. "There you go with your assumptions again. I was thinking it was a shitty thing to do to a woman. Someone's dick is so tiny he needed to ruin her pants to make sure the world knows she's his. Pathetic." Of course, Locke would never have to resort to such drastic measures with the women he pursued. "You owe me an apology for your shallow opinion of my character."

Sawyer chuckled because he couldn't take his partner seriously when he wore that mock outraged expression on his handsome face. "I'm sorry."

"See that it doesn't happen again," Locke said condescendingly. "You did notice she said Wayne was the one who placed the handprint there, right?"

"Of course. I also heard Marla say she's been dating Wayne for eight months."

"I thought maybe you were too outraged about my supposed ogling to pick up on it." When Sawyer rolled his eyes, Locke added, "Okay, I went too far."

"She said Wayne, but we don't know if it's the same guy. Maybe there's more than one guy with that name working here."

"We'll find out."

And they did, five minutes later, when their prime suspect appeared in the doorway with a pissed-off Marla standing behind him. "I found the asshole for you, Detectives." Yep. Same Wayne. She spun on her heels and marched down the hallway. Miller stepped inside the breakroom and closed the door.

He wasn't anything like Sawyer had imagined—a lot less ogre and more like a charming prince. Instead of medium height, thinning hair, and a beer belly testing the mettle of the buttons on his navy blue work shirt, Wayne was tall, had thick wavy hair that probably made the ladies sigh, and a physical build that rivaled Sawyer's. He greeted them with a toothy grin like the ones in toothpaste commercials. Sawyer had worked in law enforcement long enough to know that ugliness was often well hidden behind a handsome veneer. It still managed to catch him off guard sometimes. His name tag read: TheWayne. Was he mocking DeShaun's name or was it another way of saying *the man*? Either way, the guy repulsed Sawyer.

"I'd offer to shake your hands, but mine are filthy," Miller said after the two detectives introduced themselves. Too bad he hadn't shown Marla the same consideration, but then again, he wasn't trying to teach Sawyer and Locke a lesson.

"Have a seat, Mr. Miller," Sawyer said.

"What's this about?" Miller asked, pulling a chair out from the table and dropping down into it. Sawyer and Locke took the seats across from him. "Am I in some kind of trouble?"

"Should you be?" Locke quipped.

"Nah." Miller's lips spread into a calm smile. "What can I do for you?"

"Are you the Wayne Miller who dated Caroline Wembley?" Sawyer asked.

Miller's shoulders stiffened, and his eyes narrowed. "What did that crazy bitch say I did now?" *Now his true ugliness begins to shine through.*

"She didn't say anything," Locke said tersely. "She's dead." Locke was deliberately cold so he could gauge the man's reaction. Of course, if Miller killed them, he'd had plenty of time to fake his response. Maybe he was too stupid to think they wouldn't look in his direction, but Sawyer doubted it.

Miller's eyes bulged but in alarm instead of shock. "Hey now," he said defensively. "You think *I* did it? I haven't seen or spoken to Caroline in months. We broke up a year ago, and I've got a new girl now. You need to be looking at her *fiancé*. The man has a temper on him. Showed up here one day threatening me because he said I vandalized their house. I couldn't be bothered with such petty shit. She was dead to me the minute she started dating *him*." Realizing what he said, Miller choked on his saliva. "I didn't mean it like that, Detectives."

"We'd look really hard at Dr. Benson if he weren't also dead," Sawyer stated.

"Huh. No shit?" Miller asked flatly. "Well, I can't say I'm surprised. If you lie with riffraff, you're bound to get bitten by fleas."

Rage flowed through Sawyer's veins, and he clenched his jaw so he didn't say something stupid.

Locke had no trouble expressing his disgust, but Sawyer had been warned plenty that he was a bit of a wild card. "*Riffraff?* He was a well-respected doctor."

Miller sneered. "It's not his *profession* I take issue with, Detective."

"Listen here," Locke began but stopped when Sawyer nudged him with his knee beneath the table.

Miller lifted his hands in a bring-it-on gesture. "I've got nothing to hide so ask me anything you want."

Locke laid his phone in the center of the table then hit the record button. After identifying himself and the other people in the room, he nodded for Sawyer to kick things off.

"My partner and I appreciate your cooperation, Mr. Miller," Sawyer calmly said, even if he wanted to flip the table and punch the son of a bitch in his smug face. "Let's start with your whereabouts yesterday."

"From when to when?" Miller asked. Now, that might've seemed like a legitimate question, because any lawyer would advise you not to volunteer information to the police. By forcing them to give him a timeline, he avoided the risk of shooting himself in the foot. On the other hand, it could've also been a fishing expedition to see if they'd accurately determined the time of death.

"From the time you woke up until the time you went to bed," Locke said.

"Well, my alarm clock went off at six o'clock. I started my day off with a blow job from my girlfriend, Marla, whom you've just met. Caffeine has nothing on my girl's mouth when it comes to firing up the blood. And those tits!" *Gross.* "Afterward, I did my normal shit-shower-and-shave routine." *Nasty son of a bitch.* "Are those the kind of details you want?"

"Don't do that," Locke growled.

"Do what? Tell the truth?"

"Demoralize your girlfriend just to make your dick look bigger," Locke said.

"I'm just giving you what you asked for," Miller said, eyes wide with false innocence. Then he briefly glanced in Sawyer's direction before meeting Locke's stare again. "Or does hearing about my girlfriend going down on me insult your faggot partner's tender sensibilities. I know all about Detective Key. I read in the papers how the sheriff ran his sissy ass off." *Wow. Miller could read.* Sawyer wasn't going to waste his time or breath on correcting him. It was much better if Miller underestimated Sawyer.

Locke tensed, and Sawyer could tell his partner was seconds away from lunging across the table at Miller, which was precisely what people like him wanted. Then he'd play the victim and attempt to discredit a lawful arrest and trial. Sawyer nudged Locke again, and he seemed to relax.

"Are you a sissy boy too?" Miller asked. "I didn't take you for one."

"Where did you go after you left home?" Sawyer asked, steering them back on track.

Miller sneered at him, and Sawyer thought for a moment he was going to ignore his question. "I came directly to work. Marla rode with me. She can vouch that I stayed at work all day long. When it was quitting time, I went home and stayed there for the rest of the night."

"You said 'I' and not we. Marla didn't ride home with you?" Locke asked.

"She had a church thing. Her mama picked her up at work then dropped her off at our house around eight o'clock."

"What time did you leave work?" Sawyer asked.

Miller tilted his head like he had to think hard. "I stayed a little later than usual because Marla accidentally double-booked our final service slot for the day. Rather than piss off a customer and risk Marla getting fired I stayed and completed the job. I can print off paperwork to prove I was here until five." *Such a gentleman. Did he punish her later for it? Wasn't that how abusers acted?*

"We'll take it," Locke said. "Did you make any stops on the way home?"

"No, I—" Miller paused. He either remembered something or

162

realized they would see any charges on his bank statements if they obtained a warrant. "I stopped for gas, beer, and chew." *Of course, he did.*

Sawyer kept his expression neutral. "What time did you arrive home?"

"Five thirty. Give or take a few minutes," Miller said.

"Do you have anyone who can corroborate your story and place you in your home from five thirty to eight when Marla returned home?" Locke asked. "Neighbors?"

"I don't have any immediate neighbors. I live off the road, and my property is surrounded by trees. We like the privacy." He waggled his brows suggestively, and it made Sawyer want to puke. "I'd love to give you guys proof I was home, but I can't. Quite honestly, I'm not doing your work for you. I didn't kill them, Detectives, so there's no way you can pin this on me."

"We don't *pin* things on innocent people," Locke said defensively.

"Whatever." Miller scooted his chair back and rose to his feet. "I'm done cooperating now. Bring a warrant if you want to talk to me again."

"Aren't you remotely curious how they died?" Sawyer asked just as Miller reached the door.

Without turning to meet Sawyer's gaze, Miller shrugged his shoulders and said, "It makes no difference to me."

Locke and Sawyer locked gazes once they were alone again. The silent communication exchanged said "he's our guy" but both of them knew they had a lot of work to do before they could prove it.

On the way out, they stopped by Marla's desk. She confirmed what Miller said then handed them a printout showing the last job Miller had entered into the system, and it showed the client paying for service just before five. They knew from client statements Caroline was still working then, so the printout didn't help or hurt Miller. He still had time to kill Caroline and DeShaun and get home before Marla arrived home at eight.

"How did Mr. Miller seem when you returned home from your church activities?" Sawyer asked.

Her face turned red, and she broke eye contact. "He was the same ole Wayne. Hungry and horny." She looked back up and softly said, "Wayne just told me about his ex-girlfriend and her fiancé. That's really sad. I wish I could help you solve their murders, but I don't have any information to give you."

Sawyer slid a business card across the desk. "Will you call me if you think of something—anything—that might help us?"

"Of course."

Sawyer nodded, and they returned to their car, which felt as hot as the surface on the sun. "Blow harder," Sawyer said, loosening his tie. Realizing his error, Sawyer dropped his head forward in embarrassed shame.

Locke snorted. "There are so many things I could say, but I'll just inform you the fan is already set for maximum blow."

Steering them back to a safer topic, Sawyer said, "We're going to need evidence pointing to Miller if we hope to get a warrant to search his home. Caroline and DeShaun live in a neighborhood of young professionals, so it's not likely a neighborhood canvas during this time of day will benefit us."

"We need to do the interviews around the time we think Caroline arrived home. See if any of the neighbors noticed a suspicious vehicle or activity."

Sawyer nodded. "Agreed. If you have plans tonight, I can go by myself."

Locke shifted the Charger in drive. "I don't have plans, but you could."

Sawyer pictured the note Levi wrote on his cup and recalled his commitment to Chief Rigby. He could have plans that night, but they would wait. "Nah. I'm game."

On the way back to the station, the desk sergeant, Officer Peters, called to let Sawyer know Becca had arrived at the station for the formal lineup. Sawyer checked his phone and didn't have any missed calls or texts, which meant she just came to the station without calling first.

"We're on our way back," Sawyer said. "Tell her I'll be there in fifteen minutes or less."

"Will do, Detective. Caroline Wembley's parents just arrived too."

"Thanks, Peters," Sawyer said before hanging up.

Talk about the highs and lows of the job. With Becca, Sawyer was adding another piece of incriminating evidence to put Carl Hanover in prison. For the Wembleys, Sawyer and Locke were witnessing the worst day in their lives, just as they had done for Mrs. Benson. He just hoped they'd have real answers for them soon.

CHAPTER 18

THE PHOTO LINEUP WITH BECCA WENT QUICK AND SMOOTH ONCE SHE got past Locke's charm and good looks long enough to look at the photos. Sawyer couldn't blame the young woman. The interview with Caroline's parents was as horrible as he expected. The middle-aged couple never envisioned a world without their daughter in it. Like Caroline's coworkers and friends, they felt like Wayne was the only person who would want to harm their daughter and her fiancé.

"Tell us about Caroline," Sawyer gently urged.

"She was a late bloomer," Mrs. Wembley said with a sad smile and a distant look in her eyes. "All her friends were getting boyfriends as early as their freshman year of high school, and some a little earlier, but not Caroline. Her heart broke each time one of her friends chose to spend time with a boy instead of her. I tried explaining to Caroline that it was typical behavior, and her friends didn't love her less. I was right too because she was still very close to those young ladies. She loved them, and they loved her." Fresh tears began to fall, and Mr. Wembley held his wife close to his chest. It looked like he was trying so hard to hold his grief inside him as men are taught to do. "Wayne was the absolute opposite of Caroline in every way. He peaked early and was a popular boy in school as well as handsome. When he

Locke snorted. "You were too busy solving crimes and listening to two dudes go at it to have time to watch television."

"Maybe watching cop shows is how I wind down after a bust."

Locke leveled Sawyer with a quirked brow and wry grin. If Vic had a hard time understanding Sawyer's habit, then Locke would really find it odd. Luckily, Locke let it go, and they got back down to business. "We need to kick it old school and trace Caroline's route home, and since her cell phone was most likely turned off, phone towers won't help us. Let's get a warrant for her bank and credit card activity. See if she made any stops along the way home. They might have camera footage that could offer clues. She could've had an unfortunate encounter with a stranger who followed her home. DeShaun could've walked in on the act."

"Right," Sawyer said, exchanging a look with Locke that said the scenario was possible but unlikely.

"After we talk to Dottie, I'd like to get fresh eyes on some outstanding cases."

"Sure. Um, who is Dottie?" Sawyer asked.

"She's one of the ladies on our staff who requests our warrants. Dottie is my favorite, but don't tell the others."

"Why? Is she a tall brunette with an athletic build?"

Locke rolled his eyes. "Hardy har har." He gestured for Sawyer to follow him. "I can't believe no one gave you a tour of the building and introduced you around yesterday."

"I think you were supposed to do that," Sawyer shot back.

"Keep twisting the knife, Key."

Sawyer snickered. "I guess there's no time like the present for introductions to people I haven't met yet."

Their first stop was a small office space shared by four women who had very different reactions to seeing Locke enter their space. There was a tall brunette named Shelly who didn't look at all happy to see Locke, but she aimed a kind smile at Sawyer and shook his hand. Donna and Dottie were next, sisters who appeared to be close in age

"I'll let you know as soon as Judge Ballard signs off on it."

"Thanks, sweetheart," Locke said, giving her a hug. "I'll probably be at my desk for a few more hours, but you can always reach me on my cell. Have a good afternoon, ladies," Locke said, earning a wink from Dottie, a smile from Donna, an eyeroll from Kirsten, and the middle finger from Shelly.

Sawyer thought he and Shelly were going to get along great and hoped his smile conveyed as much. "Where to now?"

Locke showed him the evidence locker next. "Officer Tobias guards our evidence like Fort Knox during the day. I'll have to introduce you to Melvin who works the night shift." He slapped the older man on the shoulder, and said, "Follow Tobias's rules and you'll get along just fine."

"Which is why I don't like you," Tobias countered with a wry grin. He offered his hand to Sawyer. "It's good to meet you."

"Likewise."

The tour continued with the small jail, a nicely equipped gym, and a locker room. "Ready to take a look at some of my files?"

"Sure."

When they reached Locke's desk, he unlocked the bottom drawer and pulled out three files. "I wouldn't call these cold cases, but they're definitely lukewarm by now." To Sawyer's surprise, he tossed them on the desk facing his—Marcus's desk. When Sawyer only stared at the files, Locke said, "Look, I appreciate what you did yesterday, but it's not necessary for you to sit at the opposite end of the bullpen just to spare my feelings. It's not practical either."

"You don't want to shout your insults at me across the bullpen?" Sawyer asked, trying to lighten the tense moment.

Locke chuckled. "Nah, that's not it. If we're going to do this, we're going to do it right."

"So, are you going to invite me to your house for a cookout now?"

"Let's not get carried away, smart-ass," Locke replied. "I'm talking about our partnership. Just move your shit already and quit busting my balls."

"On one condition, Locke," Sawyer said.

"Name it, Key."

"You don't ever throw away a coffee cup with a cute guy's phone number on it until you've made sure I saved it to my phone."

Locke grinned. "Yeah, okay. Deal."

It didn't take Sawyer long to move his belongings to his new desk. Then they spent the next few hours going over the cases looking for any avenues left unchecked. Even though Sawyer felt Locke had been extremely thorough, he had a few confidential informants from his days at the sheriff's office he wanted to reach out to. It took Sawyer a while to understand that some people didn't trust cops, so they withheld evidence, fearing retribution from both the criminals and dirty cops protecting them. Only an idiot would believe citizens didn't want to live in safer neighborhoods. It took Sawyer a while to build trust within the minority communities, and he was careful to never betray that trust.

"It's worth a shot," Sawyer said after he left the final message.

"I appreciate it," Locke said. "Let's head out and start knocking on doors in Caroline and DeShaun's neighborhood. I want to make sure to hit the neighbors on the street behind them too. The bastard might've entered the back door."

"In broad daylight, no less," Sawyer added. "That's either ballsy or stupid."

"I think the vandalism was a trial run," Locke said after a few seconds. "If he could launch something through their picture window and spray-paint racial slurs on their house during the day, then he could walk inside their house and murder them."

Sawyer thought about it then began typing on his computer. He easily found the vandalism report and saw where the responding officer noted a similar crime in the same area weeks before Caroline and DeShaun's house was struck. "One house in their neighborhood was targeted, not multiple," he told Locke. "That means the cop exaggerated the coincidence, or Caroline chose to latch on to that rather than believe Wayne was harassing them."

"She might've also just downplayed it for her friends," Locke countered. "Either way, DeShaun wasn't buying the cop's theory."

"I'm going to run a search for vandalism reports around that time and see if any match theirs or were documented as racially motivated."

"Add a month before the first known vandalism and choose yesterday for the end date," Locke said.

"Nearly two dozen vandalism reports have been filed over the past seven months." It didn't take Sawyer long to look through them and determine that only one of them matched Caroline and DeShaun's and it was the incident the responding officer cited. "Just those two."

"Test run," Locke repeated.

"I think so too. I'm curious how close the other house is to Caroline and DeShaun's."

Locke swiftly rose to his feet. "It's time to find out. Knowing your good fortune, we're likely to stumble onto Wayne trying to cover up his tracks."

Sawyer snorted. "I don't always get that lucky."

"But when you do, you hit it big-time. You should play the lottery." Locke thought for a minute. "Then again, maybe that café cutie is your prize."

"Could be." Sawyer hoped he sounded casual and Locke would drop it. Deciding to take the bull by the horns, he said, "If history repeats itself, you get to tackle Miller."

"Nah," Locke said, shaking his head. "I changed my mind. Besides, I'd hate to deprive you of doing something you're really good at."

"So considerate," Sawyer said, not bothering to suppress the shudder that came with picturing himself tackling the disgusting piece of shit also known as Wayne Miller.

"That's my middle name," Locke said when they stepped outside the precinct.

"What? Asshole?" Detective Blue asked as he approached them from the parking lot. "I can picture your mom seeing you for the first time and knowing Asshole is a name you would hear often. Why not work it into your legal name. Royce Asshole Locke." Then he started laughing. "Sounds like a chastity belt for anuses."

It took Locke a few seconds to stop laughing before he could speak again. "Blue, I'm starting to think your harassment is a sign of deeper feelings for me."

"You should be so lucky," Blue retorted as he stopped by the door. "Congratulations, Key."

"Um, thanks. Can I ask why you're congratulating me?"

"You lasted longer than a day with this guy," Blue said, hooking his thumb in Locke's direction. "It was more than most people picked for the office pool."

"There's an office pool?" Locke and Sawyer asked at the same time.

"A bet to see how long I'd last?" Sawyer clarified.

"Yep," Blue said. "There's a hundred dollars for the person who wins, and nearly fifty percent have already been eliminated. I got my eye set on a new fishing pole and that money will come in handy."

"Which means you haven't been eliminated yet," Locke said, narrowing his eyes in thought. "Thanks for the vote of confidence, Blue."

"It has nothing to do with you, hotshot." Blue tilted his head in Sawyer's direction. "I recognize a stubborn man when I see one."

"I prefer relentless," Sawyer quipped.

"That works too," Blue said with an easy laugh.

"Come on, Relentless," Locke said, walking toward the parking lot. "We have a neighborhood to canvas."

"Catch you later, Blue," Sawyer tossed over his shoulder as he followed Locke.

Do not stare at his ass. Do not stare at his ass. Do not... Too late. Sawyer couldn't tear his eyes off that denim-covered masterpiece or prevent himself from imagining his hands sliding the jeans down to reveal the flesh beneath them.

Get a grip. Sawyer forced himself to recall the grisly case and focus his energy on solving the crime instead of lusting after a man he'd never have.

CHAPTER 19

"**S**o, about Shelly," Sawyer said once they pulled out of the parking lot.

"What about her?" Locke obviously wasn't going to make this easy for him.

"I couldn't help but notice her hostility."

"Nah. Shelly's crazy about me." Locke was either in denial, just liked yanking Sawyer's chain, or was purposely evading the question. Possibly all three. "Her sister, though… She hates my fucking guts."

"Wow. That's intense."

"It's childish is what it is," Locke replied. "Who carries a grudge for bullshit from high school?"

Sawyer thought about it. "It depends on the situation. Some kids are bullied pretty hard and carry those scars with them for a long time, sometimes forever."

Locke glanced over at him. "Sounds like you're speaking from experience."

Sawyer shrugged. "I was the quiet kid who observed everything. We all carry baggage around. Some of us just aren't as aware of it as others."

"I'm trying not to be an assumptive asshole like you, but I figured you went to a pricey private school."

"I did," Sawyer admitted. "That doesn't mean there wasn't pressure to fit in. This isn't where I break out a violin and give you a woe-is-me story, but I can promise you that having wealth comes with a whole new level of problems. Everything is a fucking pissing contest. You'd think because everyone wore school uniforms it would level the playing field, right? That couldn't be further from the truth. You aren't comparing labels on jeans and shoes; you're comparing car brands and the number of vacation homes your family has. It's so shallow, and everything is built on lies and fragile egos. The thing is, I never cared about any of that shit. I still don't. Let's just say the kids I went to school with cared about them a great deal and made me the social pariah."

"The grass is always greener on the other side, isn't it?" Locke asked quietly.

"I didn't mean to sound so poor, poor pitiful me. Things worked out well for me. I don't talk to anyone I went to school with unless forced to at a social function I'm not able to worm my way out of. I carved out my own path just as my parents encouraged." After a few minutes of silence, Sawyer tried again to get the scoop on Shelly. "So, Shelly's sister..."

Locke chuckled. The warm vibrations in his chest made Sawyer think of the other sounds he could provoke from his partner's throat. "Not going to let it go, are you?"

"I could be persuaded, I guess, but it would require you to share a different secret."

Locke braked at a red light then turned his head to study Sawyer. "Secret? Are you going to freeze my bra if I fall asleep?"

"Huh?"

"It was a teenage slumber party reference. Lord knows my older sister had enough of them. I hated the parties when I was little, but admittedly came to look forward to them when I was old enough to appreciate the scantily clad girls lingering around my house, especially the ones who *mistook* my bedroom door for the bathroom the summer I turned sixteen." Locke laughed, so Sawyer did too, even if he faked it. "Lisa Sue is Shelly's older sister. She was my first real girlfriend in every sense of the word. Dates, kissing, and eventually sex..." Locke's voice drifted off, and Sawyer knew he was remembering.

"Green light," Sawyer said when the light changed and he hadn't moved his foot from the brake to the gas pedal.

"Yeah, she sure gave me that." *Honk. Honk.* The lady behind them in a Prius expressed her displeasure, but it snapped Locke out of his trip down memory lane. "We went to junior prom and everything. I picked up extra shifts at my old man's company to afford the tuxedo rental and flowers. The way Lisa Sue looked at me when I showed up at her house was totally worth the sacrifice. She looked like an angel in her ice blue dress too. It was supposed to be an extraordinary night for us." Locke got quiet again. "Then I ruined it when I drank too much of the spiked punch. Instead of a romantic night in our special place, I vomited all over her dress. I hadn't known it, but her parents hadn't been able to afford to buy it, so she'd kept the tag on the dress so she could return it to the store. I guess it was tucked discreetly inside, and I wouldn't have seen it until I took it off her."

"That didn't happen, huh?"

"Hell no. Lisa Sue broke up with me, and her parents were so mad they wouldn't let Shelly go to the prom when she reached high school."

"It was just an accident," Sawyer said in disbelief.

"There's more to the story. I'd at least gotten as far as removing Lisa Sue's panties from beneath the dress. She'd been so distraught when we arrived at her house she'd forgotten she was carrying them in her hand. I returned their daughter panty-less, wearing a dress with a huge stain on the front, and reeking of booze. Lisa Sue told them she hadn't been drinking. I told them she hadn't taken a drink. They didn't believe a guy from a family with the reputation mine had, even after I offered to reimburse them for the dress."

"Rough crowd. I guess I still don't understand why Lisa Sue hates your guts. Sure, you made a mistake, but you were young and stupid."

"I didn't handle the breakup well," Locke said sheepishly.

"How bad are we talking here? Did you sing sappy love songs outside her window at night or write dramatic poems?"

"I just made it hard for her to find a new boyfriend. I wasn't quite as fucked up as Wayne. I didn't beat anyone up or threaten them, but there were other ways of intimidating a guy," Locke replied.

"Do I want to know?"

Locke shrugged. "As captain of the football, basketball, and baseball teams, I made practices harder for any guy I saw talking to her. Lisa Sue wasn't fooled, and she resented my interference."

"I could see how that would make her unhappy."

"The worst part was that I dated other girls like our breakup was no big deal while sabotaging any chance she had with other guys."

"Total dick move," Sawyer said. "I can understand the grudge now."

"She's crazy about the man she married, and they have four adorable kids. She's only angry out of spite. Anyway, I've come a long way since high school."

Sawyer turned and met his partner's smiling gaze. "The jury is still out on that one."

"Fair enough," Locke said, parking in front of the pretty little home where DeShaun and Caroline Wembley lived. "You can think about it while we split up. Do you want this street or the one behind their house?"

"You can have this street," Sawyer said, opening the passenger door. "Let me know if you find out anything."

"Likewise," Locke replied.

The way the neighborhood was set up, you couldn't access Sussex Place without driving along Tremont Street. Built in different eras, the two streets in the area were a blend of two-story and ranch-style homes. Some houses sat on two lots while others were crammed closer together on single lots. Caroline and DeShaun's house was on a large lot on Sussex Place while most of the homes on Tremont Street sat on smaller lots. Sawyer crossed through their back yard and the side yards between the two houses directly behind them. Sawyer kept walking until he stood in the middle of Tremont Street, assessing the homes and judging which of the houses on both sides of the street had a clear view of DeShaun and Caroline's back yard. Sawyer determined that six of them were his best hope, but he wouldn't limit his canvas to those houses. Even though the others couldn't see the victims' home from their property, it didn't exclude them from seeing something critical to their case.

A boy with hair as bright red as the flames on his bike stopped on the sidewalk near Sawyer. "Hey, mister. What are you doing?"

"My name is Sawyer, and I'm a police detective," Sawyer said to the boy who looked to be around ten years old. "I'm investigating a crime. What's your name?"

"I don't talk to strangers," the kid answered.

"You're talking to one now," Sawyer pointed out.

The kid's eyes widened as if he hadn't thought about that until Sawyer asked for his name. The kid lifted his feet from the sidewalk then began pedaling furiously in the opposite direction. He pulled his bike to a stop in front of a porch five houses down then darted inside like his pants were on fire. Sawyer prepared for a worried mother or father to come outside and check things out, but they didn't.

Sawyer started his canvas with the first two houses whose back yards butted up against DeShaun and Caroline's. Neither of them were home during the window of time Locke and Key thought the victims were killed. Sawyer then visited the houses on both sides of theirs. One lady reported a Jeep Wrangler in the neighborhood she'd never seen before. When asked what made it stand out to her, she replied it was the camo paint scheme. Sawyer's heart began to speed up because he'd seen a Wrangler matching the description parked outside the service garage at Beauregard Buick. What were the odds? *Could he be this lucky two homicides in a row?*

Sawyer thanked her for her time then kept moving along the street. He saved the two homes on the opposite side of Tremont with the best views of the victims' back door for last. He struck out at the first one. Neither of the women living there saw anything out of the ordinary. He tried his luck at the last house, but no one answered the door. He noticed they had one of those Ring Doorbells equipped with a camera aimed at their porch. When someone rang the bell, the camera activated and alerted the homeowner. It also had a motion sensor that triggered an alert if it detected motion within thirty feet of the door. They could use their phone or tablet to communicate with the visitor through the built-in microphone. Sawyer scribbled a note on his business card and left it in their mailbox. Just as he stepped off the porch, a dark red minivan pulled up and parked in front of the garage. A harried mom and her five kids got out of the vehicle and approached slowly.

"I'm Detective Key with Savannah PD," he said, showing her his ID. "It looks like your hands are full right now, but I'd like to ask you a few questions if you have a minute."

"Of course," the brunette said, wiping sweat off her forehead with the hand that wasn't clutching her toddler against her chest. The older kids took advantage of their mom's distraction and started heading down the driveway. "Not so fast," she said firmly. The four of them halted immediately. "Help carry in groceries, get your chores done, then I'll think about letting you play with your friends."

They weren't pleased about it, but they listened.

"I'm Alicia O'Malley, by the way," she said to Sawyer. "Why don't you come on in and cool off while you ask your questions. I'll even pour you a glass of lemonade."

The inside of the O'Malleys' house was as hectic as you'd expect with five kids, but it was tidy and cold enough to trigger goose bumps.

Alicia put her sleepy little girl in a pack-n-play inside the kitchen and started putting groceries away, but not before she poured Sawyer a tall glass of lemonade. He chugged half of it before explaining why he was canvassing the neighborhood and asked if she'd seen anything out of the norm the previous evening. Alicia was horrified to hear about what happened to DeShaun and Caroline and wished she'd seen something to help Sawyer.

"We were at our church getting ready for bible school next week." The doorbell rang, and her cell phone lit up with an alert. "It's Simon. He conveniently shows up here every night at this time, knowing I'm going to invite him for dinner. I might as well give him a house key. Drink your lemonade. I'll be right back."

Simon turned out to be the redheaded boy with the bike. "Oh, it's you."

"Hello, again," Sawyer said.

"Simon, did you happen to see anything unusual yesterday when you stopped by when we weren't home? Any strange vehicles or people?" Alicia asked him.

Simon thought about it for a few seconds then shook his head. "I don't think so." He turned big eyes back to Alicia. "Can Stevie play or is it too close to dinnertime?"

Alicia smiled and ruffled his hair. "Stevie is in his room cleaning. Help him tidy up the mess you contributed to, and you can stay for dinner."

Simon tilted his head and considered Alicia's offer. "What are you eating?"

"Does it matter, kid?" Alicia asked dryly.

Simon smiled up at her adoringly. "Not really. Thanks, Mrs. O'Malley." He darted down a hallway.

"Might as well call me Mom," Alicia yelled after him. "I'll expect you to draw me a card for Mother's Day next year like the rest of the knuckleheads."

"Okay, Mom," Simon's voice came from deeper inside the house.

Alicia shook her head and smiled back at Sawyer. "We have this conversation every night. He'll call me Mom for the rest of the evening then he'll revert to Mrs. O'Malley tomorrow."

"Rough home life?" Sawyer asked.

"Single mom who does the best she can working two jobs. When she's not working, she's sleeping. She looks like skin and bones, but I truly believe it's from exhaustion and not drug use or an eating disorder. She tries hard, but I worry so much about Simon. We'd keep him in a heartbeat."

"He's lucky to have your family looking out for him," Sawyer said.

"It's the right thing to do. Besides, we're the lucky ones; he's a great kid."

"How'd you know he stopped by when you weren't home?" Sawyer asked. "Your Ring Doorbell app?"

"Yes," Alicia said, nodding.

"Do you have the video recording plan or basic?"

A smile ghosted across Alicia's face. "We have the video recording plan. Maybe I can help after all." She pulled up her app, and they went through each recording on her phone from the previous day. As if fate were smiling down on him that week, Sawyer and Alicia could see the image of a man walking around the side of DeShaun and Caroline's house as soon as Simon stepped out of the frame.

Got him! The distance was too far to make out the features, but the height and build were identical to Wayne Miller's. The recording cut out just as the man approached the back door, so Sawyer never saw him enter, but with another neighbor seeing a Jeep Wrangler like the one Sawyer suspected Miller owned, it was a coincidence he couldn't ignore. "Can you go back and screenshot those images and either text or email them to me?"

"Of course. I can also send you the videos." Sawyer pulled a business card from his wallet while she captured the images on her camera roll. "What's your preference?" she asked when she accepted Sawyer's card.

"Doesn't matter."

"Email is probably more professional," she said as she tapped away on her phone. "I hope someone can help you get a clearer image of this guy."

"We'll see what we can do."

Alicia snapped her head up. "You already know who this is, or you at least have a pretty good idea, don't you?"

Sawyer wondered if she'd heard something in his tone. "I can't comment. I'm sorry."

Alicia stopped tapping and set her phone on the counter. A second later, Sawyer's phone chimed to let him know he had a new email. She waved off Sawyer's apology. "Don't worry about it. Just catch the bastard. Would you like more lemonade before you go?"

He would love to drink another glass or two, but Sawyer settled for finishing what was already in the glass after he verified the photos and videos came through okay. "I'm good," Sawyer said. "Thank you for the lemonade, photos, and video clips."

Alicia walked him to the door and wished him luck. As soon as Sawyer was on the sidewalk, he dialed Locke. "Miller is our guy," Sawyer said when Locke answered. "I think I have enough to get a warrant to search his residence."

"Meet me at the Charger," Locke said excitedly.

Sawyer jogged across the street and through the yards and discovered Locke was already sitting in the driver seat of their car. The engine was running, which meant he probably had the air-conditioning running full blast.

"How long have you been sitting here?" Sawyer asked once he lowered himself onto the passenger seat and closed the door.

"Just a few minutes. My canvas was a bust. What do you have?"

Sawyer smiled, drawing out his big moment. "A witness placed a camo Wrangler in the vicinity. We saw one of those at the dealership. What do you bet we find one registered to Miller?"

"Well, it's the South and there are a lot of camo-painted vehicles, but I'm not taking that bet," Locke said. "What else. You're too smug for just a Jeep sighting." Sawyer pulled up his email and showed Locke the images captured by the Ring Doorbell. "Son of a bitch. I bet we can get one of our super nerdy tech people to clean up the images a bit. Zoom in for a closer look maybe."

"Zooming in too far will only make the images blurrier. Let's find out what vehicles are registered to Miller and see what we can do to clear up the images and videos. Maybe we can find a nice judge to issue a warrant tonight."

"Your family knows people. Do you have a connection who can help us out?" Locke asked.

"Possibly, but I'm wary of throwing my weight around. Then again, solving a double homicide is worth it."

"Attaboy," Locke said, patting his shoulder. "Let's do this."

CHAPTER 20

T HE SEARCH WARRANT WAS SIGNED BY JUDGE GRIMSHAW WITHIN AN hour of Sawyer requesting it. He wouldn't allow himself to think about what the special favor might cost him. Probably a dinner with the judge's grandson who'd recently come out as gay.

Joining Locke and Key were four of the detectives from the MCU—Blue and Tara South from arson and Shawn Ashcroft and Kyomo Chen from vice.

"Always ready to bring down a neo-Nazi," Blue had said when he swapped out his suit jacket for a bulletproof vest with Savannah Police Department emblazoned on the front. His big smile looked exceptionally bright at the prospect.

"You know we're going to ask you boys to return the favor," Kyomo Chen said, sliding his .40 in his leg holster.

"We'd be happy to," Sawyer replied.

"Ky means an early morning bust where we end up seeing a lot of the scum buck-ass naked when we drag them out of bed and cuff them," Locke informed his partner.

"Sounds like a party to me," Holly Stein said, sauntering into the bullpen. She had replaced her fishnets, cutoffs, and thigh-high boots with a black tactical uniform and combat boots. "Room for one more?"

"Always got room for you, pretty girl," Locke replied with a purr that made Sawyer wince inwardly, at least he hoped his disdain didn't show.

Fifteen minutes after they received the signed warrant, they filed out of the precinct and into their cars. Carpooling wasn't something cops did when heading to execute a warrant or bust unless it was the SWAT team in their armored vehicles, so Sawyer was surprised when Holly decided to ride along with them. Maybe it was because she was without her partner or perhaps she just wanted to verbally fuck Locke during the ride. Either way, Sawyer was annoyed and decided to tune out their incessant flirting by looking out the window and thinking about anything besides the way Locke made him feel.

Locke pulled Sawyer into the conversation a few times when they veered away from the sexy banter that made him feel uncomfortable. Neither Locke nor Stein ever crossed the line into an inappropriate territory, but it was too close for Sawyer's liking. He would've felt the same way even if he weren't jealous. Damn. Sawyer hated the green monster growing inside him and couldn't remember the last time he'd felt that way.

Liar. You wanted to punch the flirty art teacher who couldn't seem to keep his hands off Vic. Sawyer didn't like remembering the fights that had always escalated whenever Sawyer felt threatened by their close relationship. That was different. Vic had been Sawyer's husband, and he'd only known Locke for less than two days.

"Not much of a talker?" Stein asked Sawyer, which made him feel bad because the woman had done nothing wrong. It wasn't her fault he was insanely attracted to his partner who couldn't seem to stop glancing at Stein in the rearview mirror when they chatted.

Pulling his head out of his ass, Sawyer said, "I'm usually a lot more talkative, but my brain tends to go into overdrive in situations like these. Guys like Miller are fucking dangerous, so I tend to plan things out in my head. We looked up the property layout on the auditor's website, so I'm thinking about the best ways to protect our asses while approaching his home."

"At least the bastard doesn't have a basement where he can hide and pick us off one by one as we try to come down the stairs," Locke added.

"We got this, fellas," Stein said positively. "I have a good feeling about this. You do good work, Key," she said, leaning forward and patting him on the shoulder.

"What about me? I helped," Locke whined, sounding like a toddler.

"Yeah, you too," Stein said, ruffling Locke's hair. "Maybe we can celebrate later."

"Sounds great. Oh, Key has probably never been inside Joe's Pub since the sheriff's department has their own haunt. Joe's is much better than Reno's," Locke said. "Wait. You probably have better plans for tonight with the café owner."

Sawyer shrugged. "I've been to Joe's plenty of times, and any plans I might make with Levi would depend on how long this search takes. With any luck—"

"Which you seem to have a lot of," Locke interjected.

"—we'll end up arresting the son of a bitch. It'll take another few hours to process and interview him. I think I'll stop by and see Levi in the morning on my way to the station instead of calling him late tonight."

"In person is a nice approach," Stein added. "It's more meaningful. Take notes, Locke. This guy is smooth."

"Thanks," Sawyer replied.

"I don't need to take notes, Stein. I don't hear many complaints."

Stein snorted. "Not to your face."

"Kids," Sawyer said firmly. "Let's not lose our focus."

"Yes, Dad," Locke and Stein mumbled, making Sawyer smile for the first time since they got in the car.

A Chatham County deputy cruiser was parked at the end of Miller's road waiting for them. Even though the homicide had been committed in city limits, Wayne lived outside their jurisdiction. As a courtesy, Sawyer phoned the Chatham County Sheriff's Department to make them aware of the arrest warrant. It looked like they decided to provide backup.

Locke pulled up beside them in the lead car and rolled down his window. "It's a great evening to execute a search warrant, right, fellas?" he asked.

"We're just here to provide backup if you need it," the deputy said, gesturing between his partner and himself. "Is that you, Key?"

Sawyer looked around Locke and waved at deputies Knight and Dayton. "How's it going, guys?"

"Better than you, I think," Dayton said from the passenger seat. "Who'd you piss off to get stuck with Locke?"

"They decided our last names would make us good partners," Locke quipped dryly. "You guys with Knight and *Dayton* are pretty close, but not as cutesy as us. We ready to do this, or do you need to crack a few more jokes and chat with Key like long-lost pals?"

"We're ready," Knight said with a cocky grin.

They didn't pull up to Miller's house with lights flashing and sirens blaring because it would give him extra time to mount his defenses. When Locke put the Charger in park, Sawyer exited with his right hand resting on the butt of his .40 Smith and Wesson and clutching the search warrant in his left. Sawyer noticed the Jeep Wrangler registered to Miller was nowhere in sight, but there were plenty of outbuildings he could've parked it in. The only vehicle there was a silver Chevrolet sedan which matched the description of the car registered to Marla. Sawyer felt eyes watching him from inside the house as he approached the steps up to the front deck.

His footfalls on the warped wooden steps and deck boards sounded loud, and there was no way whoever was inside the tiny house hadn't heard him approach. The rest of the team got into position. Locke had his back while Blue and South went around back to guard any rear entrances. Chen, Stein, and Ashcroft placed themselves where they could watch the front door while keeping the sides of the house in their periphery—Stein went left and Ashcroft and Chen took the right.

Knight and Dayton acted as sentinels in the driveway, making sure unwanted visitors don't ambush them from behind.

Before Sawyer could knock, the ruffled curtains over the door window parted to reveal Marla, but she looked nothing like the woman they'd seen that morning. Fury raged through Sawyer when he cataloged the bruises, cuts, and dried blood marring her swollen face. *Fucking bastard.*

Sawyer tamped down the urge to rage and roar and held up the piece of paper in his hand instead. "We have a warrant to search the house and outbuildings, Marla," he spoke through the door.

She slowly nodded as if the motion had cost her a significant amount of energy or pain to execute. Sawyer heard the metal slide of a chain lock and click of a deadbolt before Marla opened the door.

"Come on in," Marla mumbled, barely moving her jaw. "He's not here. He took a stash of cash and drove off in his Jeep a few hours ago."

Heavy footsteps vibrated the sketchy deck, indicating Locke was coming up behind him. "Call for an EMT," Sawyer said over his shoulder. "Marla needs medical care."

"No, I don't. I'm fine, Detective," Marla said weakly.

Locke came up to stand directly behind Sawyer and sucked in a sharp breath. "I'm calling them." He stepped off to the side and radioed in for an ambulance.

"Can you step outside?" Sawyer asked. In response, Marla hobbled out of the door then started to topple forward, but Sawyer's quick reflexes prevented her from falling. "I got you, Marla."

She buried her head against Sawyer's chest and cried heartbroken pitiful sounds. After a few minutes, Marla pulled back and looked up at Sawyer. "I think he did it, Detective. I think he killed that woman and her fiancé."

Sawyer guided her over to an old metal glider and helped her sit down. He crouched down in front of her and noticed her right ankle was swollen to twice the size of the left one. "Why do you think so?" He gestured for Chen, Ashcroft, and Stein to go on inside the house and begin the search.

She pointed to her face. "This is the result of me asking Wayne if he did it." Marla's words were measured and slow, and her voice trembled.

"What made you decide to ask him?" Locke asked her.

"Wayne has a bad habit of talking in his sleep. I've known every time he's cheated on me because he rats himself out. Sometimes I'm barely aware of his early-morning ramblings, but he woke me up this time because his body was jerking and twitching hard enough to shake the bed. I flipped on the small lamp next to my side of the bed and looked over at him. He was still sound asleep and wore the evilest grin I'd ever seen. His words shocked me. He said, 'I'm glad the bitch is dead.' Now, I know you're wondering why I didn't tell you this morning, but I didn't know someone he'd dated had been killed until after you showed up at the dealership. I thought maybe he was dreaming about a movie or television show he'd watched. I wrestled with what to do all day long. Wayne noticed my unusual quietness and asked about it when we got home tonight. That's when I confronted him. It was the stupidest thing I've ever done, and I am thanking the good Lord I'm still alive. Afterward, he left me lying on the floor while he grabbed his emergency go bag he keeps filled with cash, a few guns, and clothes."

"Do you have any idea where he might've gone? Does he, or anyone he knows, own a secluded property he might use as a hideout?" Locke asked.

"Most of his family members and friends own fishing cabins on various lakes around the state. I don't think he's stupid enough to go to any of them."

"Why?" Sawyer asked. Wayne didn't strike him as a particularly smart man.

"Those would be logical places you or the state police would look," Marla said.

"You think Miller is smart enough to think it through or is he just running on instinct right now?" Locke countered.

"He's much smarter and more manipulative than either of you are giving him credit for, Detectives. If Wayne killed Caroline Wembley and her fiancé, then he would've been planning this for a while. He had a bag packed and an escape route planned out. He's dangerous, Detectives. Very dangerous."

Chen stepped out onto the deck and said, "There's something you need to see, guys."

"Be right there," Locke told him, looking hesitant to walk away from the interview with Marla. "Is there anything else you can think of, any hint he might've given you?"

Marla shook her head then winced. "Wayne only said for me to keep my fucking mouth shut. He said he'd come back and kill me if he found out I'd talked to anyone about my suspicions."

Stein stepped out on the porch. "I can wait with her for the ambulance if you guys want to go inside."

Sawyer rose to his feet but didn't look away from Marla's face. "We're going to catch him, Marla. He's going to pay for what he did. Do you have someplace you can stay? Family or a friend?"

Marla sniffled. "I'll call my mom to pick me up after you leave."

"Call her now, honey," Stein said, extending her phone. "We're not leaving here until we know you're going someplace safe. There's no guarantee Miller won't come back here to silence you for good."

A shudder racked Marla's body, and she began to cry again. Stein met Sawyer's narrowed gaze with a firm and unapologetic expression. It wasn't that he thought she was wrong. Misleading Marla could have fatal consequences. Sawyer just wouldn't have said it so bluntly.

"Detective Stein is right, Marla," Sawyer said gently. "You can't stay here. After you get checked out, Detective Stein will pack a bag for you. Tell her what you want and where she can find it, and she'll make it happen for you." Marla sniffled but nodded slowly. "Don't come back here alone. Don't come back here with only your mother. If you need to get some of your possessions, you need to call the county sheriff's office and request an escort. If they don't cooperate, I want you to call Locke or me."

"All right," Marla said, unable to meet Sawyer's gaze.

Sawyer and Locke left Marla with Stein and entered the house. The interior of the house reminded Sawyer of The Putz's—tidy but with outdated furniture. Instead of lewd posters on the wall, Miller chose mounted deer heads, turkeys, and largemouth bass as decorations.

"In here," Chen yelled from the back of the house.

Locke and Sawyer found him in a spare bedroom that Miller had converted to a gun room. Every type of gun imaginable hung on all four walls. In the center of the room was a table with cleaning materials and tools to maintain and restore the firearms. Tucked in the corner was an open filing cabinet where Ashcroft stood looking at several sheets of paper.

"He has meticulous records of his purchases, sales, and trades," Ashcroft said. "Guess which gun is on the list but nowhere in the room?"

"Desert Eagle 1911?"

"Bingo," Ashcroft said. "Granted, they're a popular handgun, but the metal file and shavings on the worktable makes the missing gun look more suspicious."

"I saw a technique on an episode of *Forensic Files* where they used a chemical to restore the serial number. The stamp goes deeper in the metal than people realize. Maybe our guys can pull that off too," Chen said. "What I really wanted you to see was this." He raised a golf club with his latex-gloved hand.

"You want us to buy you a putter for Christmas?" Locke asked.

"It's a wedge," Sawyer corrected, approaching Chen for a closer look. "A very expensive custom-made club. Let me guess, Chen, it's the only one you found."

"Right again, Key. Guess whose name is engraved on the shaft?" Chen asked.

"DeShaun Benson," Locke said. "So much for Wayne being smart and planning well. The ME said Caroline was hit in the back of the head and most likely rendered unconscious before she was strangled because there were no defensive wounds on her body."

"But there's more," Chen said, pointing to the long strands of blonde hair caught where the metal of the wedge connected to the shaft."

"Let's bag it and tag it," Sawyer said. "Collect the file and shavings as well as the master list of guns."

They searched the house and outbuildings for another hour. Sawyer nearly had a heart attack when he opened a freezer inside the largest of the buildings and saw a bunch of animal heads. Based on the tools and chemicals, it looked like Miller operated a small taxidermy business. Other than the creepy heads and instruments that looked like torture devices, they didn't find anything interesting.

By the time they finished, Marla had already been treated by the EMTs and left with her mother, but not before she provided Stein with the names of Miller's closest friends and family. As bad as her injuries looked, they weren't severe enough for hospitalization. Her bruises, cuts, and sprained ankle would heal, but the emotional trauma would last much longer. Sawyer truly hoped she found someone to help her navigate the roller-coaster ride of recovering from an abusive relationship.

They locked up everything as best they could and headed out.

"Miller is your guy," Stein said. "There's not much you guys can do besides issuing an APB and BOLO. Do you want to start interviews tonight? We can help you?"

"As much as I want to take this fucker down, I'd rather wait until daylight to improve our chances of not getting shot by a squirrely family member," Locke said. "I hate the idea of him getting farther away, but he's probably hunkered down someplace. We'll flush him out, but not at the expense of our safety."

Sawyer drummed his fingers against his thighs. He knew Locke was right, but it wasn't in his nature to go home and wait it out.

"Isn't that right, Key?" Locke said tersely. "No Rambo, superhero bullshit that could cost someone their life."

"Okay," Sawyer said through gritted teeth.

"Come have a drink with us to unwind or call Levi to make dinner plans. Don't go home and skulk and don't take it upon yourself to solve this case."

"I already agreed."

"So, what's it going to be," Stein asked. "Drinks with us or a call to the cute guy?"

Sawyer wanted to bond with his new team, but he needed space from Locke to regroup. "I think I'll take a rain check on the drink and give Levi a call."

Sawyer expected Locke to say something smart or snarky, but he remained silent. Sawyer glanced over at him but couldn't read his expression. Maybe it was a trick of the dashboard lights, but Locke looked irritated. Why? He agreed not to go off on his own. Was it because he wasn't having a drink with them? Was it because of Levi? *Nah.* The last thought nearly made him laugh out loud. It'd had been a long day, without much to show for it, and Locke hadn't slept well the previous night. Locke was probably just cranky. Sawyer shoved all thoughts of Locke aside to preserve his sanity.

Back at the station, Sawyer quickly retrieved his personal cell phone from his desk then wished everyone a good night. Alone in his car, he leaned his head back against the rest and closed his eyes while waiting for the air conditioner to cool his car. Noticing the time on the dashboard, he decided it was too late to call Levi. Stein, Locke, Chen, and Blue walked out of the station together a few minutes later, but none of them looked in his direction. He could head over to Joe's on

Broughton Street and get to know his team better or go home to his cat and his audiobooks. Sawyer recalled how deafening the silence had become in his house and knew he had to make changes in his life like make new friends that weren't tied to his old life. Could he find that with his new team on the Savannah PD? Exhausted from a long day, he didn't trust himself to make the best choices and alcohol surely wouldn't help. The temptation to see what Locke was like away from the job was almost too much for him to resist, but he shifted his car in drive and headed home.

CHAPTER 21

L EVI'S SPARKLING BLUE EYES AND DELIGHTED SMILE GREETED SAWYER when he walked through the café door the next morning. Feeling wanted and desired created a liveliness and vigor inside his body stronger than any cup of coffee could provide. It was almost like he'd grabbed on to a live wire. A part of his brain, a very loud part, reminded him that Levi wasn't the one he'd been thinking of when he'd taken himself in hand during his morning shower. Using Levi was the last thing Sawyer wanted to do, but he felt like he needed to give the man a fighting chance. Whatever he felt for Royce Locke was temporary, and it wouldn't be wise to blow a chance with a guy who honestly wanted to get to know him better. Fantasy versus future. Sawyer had always made smart decisions, why should this one be any different?

"I'll take care of this guy, Terrance," Levi said to the employee who was poised to take his drink order. Nothing about his tone was suggestive, but Sawyer's brow quirked up anyway. The pink blush blooming across Levi's cheeks was adorable and possibly addictive. "You've earned a break," Levi added.

Terrance glanced between his boss and Sawyer, reading the situation correctly as evidenced by his broad grin. "Sure thing, boss. Would now be a good time to ask if I can leave early?"

"Don't push your luck, kid," Levi replied without taking his eyes off Sawyer. Terrance chuckled and mumbled something about not blaming a guy for trying. Once it was just the two of them at the counter, Levi ran his gaze over Sawyer's torso. "This is a different look for you."

Sawyer glanced down at the black T-shirt stretched across his chest and neatly tucked inside his black tactical pants. His badge hung around his neck on a chain, and his black shoulder holster hugged his torso. "Do you prefer suits?"

Levi swallowed hard and ran a finger under his collar. "Both have merits. I can't say I prefer one over the other. Damn. You must work out a lot." Levi sounded more nervous than complimentary. Did he think Sawyer would judge him or find him less attractive if his body wasn't as rock hard? If so, Levi couldn't be further from the truth. That was something left to discuss during the getting-to-know-you phase of dinner.

Downplaying his physique, Sawyer shrugged and said, "It's a necessity for my job. Not only does it help with the physical parts like chasing perps, but it also relieves stress."

"Relieves stress," Levi repeated, eyes lit with mirth or maybe lust. Sawyer didn't know the man well enough to read him. Yet. "What's your poison this morning? Another salted caramel?"

"Yes, please. Can I also get a black coffee with two sugars for my partner?" Sawyer glanced down at the pastry display and noticed a few bear claw pastries left. "And two of your bear claws."

"Absolutely," Levi said, turning to fill the orders.

"Hey, Levi," Sawyer said, stopping him. "The only reason I didn't call you last night was because I didn't finish working a case until nine thirty. I knew you had to get up early to open the café and didn't want to risk waking you. I'm dressed like this today because I expect to have a very long day in the field. I have every intention of calling and inviting you to dinner."

Levi's grin grew impossibly bigger. "When?"

"When am I going to call you? I'm hoping I get home at a decent time tonight so we can make plans."

"No. When would you like to have dinner? Talking to you sounds great, and I promise to answer no matter what time you call me. Sleep be damned. While I have your undivided attention, let's make dinner plans."

"Yeah, that works too." Sawyer hadn't dated in so long, and he felt rusty as fuck. "I have a feeling today could be just as long as yesterday, so I don't want to make plans then have to cancel. That's no way to start things off. Why don't we shoot for Friday night? Will that work?"

"Friday sounds amazing. I promise not to hold a grudge if your work interferes. I fully understand you don't work a nine-to-five job," Levi replied softly. He understood it now, but it didn't mean he wouldn't grow increasingly frustrated every time the phone rang and interrupted a dinner or nixed plans they made. Vic had been astonishingly patient, but even he lost his cool on more than one occasion.

Whoa. It's one dinner. Don't put the cart before the horse. "I'll call you tonight so we can work out the details."

"Perfect."

Sawyer watched Levi make the drinks. His movements were smooth, sure, and practiced, and it was apparent how much he loved his job. When he turned around to carry the coffees over, Sawyer noticed his flush had grown deeper, and he had teeth marks in his bottom lip. Sawyer's attention had made the man nervous, even if he'd never let on.

Picking up the coffee tray and pastry bag, Sawyer smiled again at Levi. "Talk to you later."

Levi winked. "Later."

Sawyer was still whistling when he walked into the precinct fifteen minutes later. Locke glanced up quickly then did a double take, raking his gaze over Sawyer's attire before meeting his eyes. Locke looked like someone had ridden him hard and put him away wet.

Sawyer immediately regretted thinking the familiar phrase. Even though it referenced horses, people could be ridden hard and exhausted too.

"Wow. I know I accused you of going Rambo, but I didn't think you'd show up dressed like him," Locke said.

"Rambo wore fewer clothes than this. Besides, aren't you the one who said I had overdressed for the heat. Now you're complaining because I chose clothes for the field."

"Is one of those cups of coffee for me?" Locke asked, letting the subject drop.

Sawyer set the carrier and pastry bag on his desk then handed Locke's coffee to him. "Black. Two sugars."

"How'd you know?" Locke asked before taking a sip.

"Really? I'm a detective. I notice things." Sawyer moved the pastry bag to Locke's desk. "One of those bear claws is mine."

Locke tore into the bag, pulled out a pasty the size of his head, and took a massive bite. "So you think," he said around a mouthful of food. Even though he didn't make further remarks about Sawyer's attire, he seemed to have a hard time looking away from his chest. It made it really difficult for Sawyer to remember to make smart choices when he had that laser-like focus aimed on him.

Sawyer sat down at his desk, booted up his computer, and reached for the pastry bag. Locke jerked it out of his reach. "I'm not playing with you, Locke." His partner quirked a brow but relented. Sawyer scrutinized Locke's appearance. His blond hair was messier than usual. A few of the longer strands in the front broke free from the style and fell over his forehead. Dark blond stubble dusted his jawline, indicating Locke hadn't shaved. Was it because he didn't wake up at his own house? *Not your business.* "Rough night? Too many drinks? You look out of sorts?" *So much for minding my own business.*

Locke snapped his eyes up to meet Sawyer's gaze. "You could say that." He punctuated the admission with a crooked smirk.

Sawyer chose to bite into his pastry rather than comment further. He didn't want to know what, or who, Locke had gotten up to.

"Does your boyfriend make bears claws better than the chief's wife?"

"Levi isn't my boyfriend. I barely know the guy." Sawyer took another bite then washed it down with a drink of delicious coffee. "One bear claw is far superior to the other."

Locke narrowed his eyes. "You're not going to tell me which is better, are you?"

"Hell no. You'll have to earn the privilege to sample the baked goods in the chief's office."

"Asshole," Locke muttered under his breath.

"*Adonis* Asshole."

Locke lifted the hand not holding the pastry, probably to flip him off, but stopped when he saw someone or something behind Sawyer. A huge smile spread across his face, making Sawyer's chest tight. "There are my best girls," Locke said, setting his pastry down and rising to his feet. "Candi, come over here so I can introduce you to Sawyer."

Fuck me. Suddenly, Sawyer regretted moving to Marcus's desk. Yes, he wanted to be closer to Locke—for *professional* reasons—but he didn't want to upset Marcus's widow. Unsure what to expect, Sawyer slowly turned his chair and rose to his feet.

Candace Wilkes was beautiful, even in her grief and exhaustion. Tall. Brunette. Athletic build. She had the kind of face that made angels weep. The smile she gave Sawyer was tired, but her dark brown eyes were warm when she extended her hand toward him. "I've heard great things about you," she said.

"I've heard wonderful things about you too." Sawyer looked at the infant resting her head on her mother's shoulder. "Especially this little beauty."

"This is Bailey, and she's the light of my life. Aren't you, darling?" Locke asked, reaching out his hands toward her. Bailey giggled and launched herself in his direction so fast Locke had to hustle to catch her. "Easy does it, pumpkin," Locke said, cradling her against his chest and kissing the top of her head. He looked ridiculously good holding a baby, and it did wicked things to Sawyer's heart. He resented the fact he had to remind himself ten times a day that Locke wasn't his and would never be his. "To what do I owe this honor, Candi Corn?" *Candi Corn?*

"I'd love to say that we're here to see you, but I'm here to talk to someone in human resources," Candi said.

"Is everything okay?" Locke had gone into protector mode, and there went reminder number eleven. Sawyer was curious what the hell was going on there. "Want me to hang on to the little nugget for you? We'll be heading into a briefing in a few minutes, but I can take her with me." Bailey reached a chubby hand toward Locke's mouth, and he made a growly noise and acted like he was going to chomp her fingers. The baby squealed and kicked her feet, reaching for his face with both hands.

Candi and Sawyer laughed at the pair's antics, but Candi quickly grew somber. "It's better I take her with me. The assholes should see who they're screwing over. I should've brought the boys with me too, but they had plans to swim with my sister and their cousins. I couldn't ruin a good day for them."

Ah. The department must've been dragging their heels on paying out Marcus's benefits to her. Why? Because he committed suicide? Sawyer knew there were suicide clauses with most life insurance policies, but Marcus had other benefits that should've been paid to his widow. She had a right to be upset.

"You let me know if you need me to talk to someone," Locke said, passing Bailey back to her mom. The infant wanted no part of it. She began crying and reaching for Locke—a testament to how much time they spent together.

Candi was too busy quieting her daughter for a few seconds to respond. Once Bailey settled down, Candi smiled at Locke. "You do too much already."

"It's not enough. It will never be enough," Locke replied. He leaned forward and kissed Candi on the forehead before kissing Bailey's chubby cheek. "Just call, okay?"

"I will."

After the two special ladies in Locke's life left them alone, Sawyer broke the silence. "What's this about a debriefing?"

"We're going to coordinate with CSSO and GBI to spread out and knock on as many doors as we can until we find out where the hell Miller is hiding. Reps from those departments are due to arrive..." Locke checked his watch. "Any minute now." As if he'd conjured them out of the air, four deputies and six GBI agents strode into the bullpen. "Now if only I could get SPD to pay Candi what they owe her as quickly as I summoned our help."

Sawyer shook his head and followed Locke. He recognized the deputies but had never met the GBI agents who had shown up to assist them. After everyone introduced themselves, the MCU detectives assigned to Miller's apprehension showed the deputies and agents to the conference room so they could get their meeting started and get on the road quicker.

"It's official," Locke said ten hours later, looking and sounding as haggard as Sawyer felt. "Miller is in the wind. He's had plenty of time to get out of Georgia. The question is: did he go north or south?"

The team had knocked on the doors of every known associate, friend, or family member. They were spat at, cussed out, and cursed. The group spread out to stake out every remote cabin registered to any of them which encompassed a two-hundred-and-fifty-mile radius. Cities and asphalt gave way to rural areas and dirt roads. Miller was nowhere to be found, and Sawyer felt like he wore every mile of grit they had traveled. Coming up with nothing after a long day was a horrible feeling.

Sawyer wanted a hot shower, a cold beer, and something delicious to eat.

"We learned a valuable lesson today," Locke said, patting Sawyer's shoulder as they headed to their vehicles.

"That you couldn't carry a tune in a bucket?" Sawyer asked.

"I sing along with Johnny Cash damn well, and you know it." He did, but Sawyer didn't want to add to Locke's already inflated ego. "The next time we're in the field like this, we'll do the Johnny and June duets. You can be June."

"Thanks," Sawyer said drolly. "What did we learn today, Locke?"

"We can work ten hours straight and not kill each other. How awesome is that?"

Sawyer smirked and shook his head. "It'll do."

"Do you have plans tonight?" Locke's question took him by surprise, but he worked hard not to show it.

"I need to call Levi at some point to finalize plans for Friday. What did you have in mind?"

"I think you should invite me over for dinner. I'll bring beer," Locke said.

"Did I hear you correctly? You asked me if I had plans then invited yourself over to my house for dinner?"

"Yeah. You game?"

Sawyer knew what his answer should be. Ten straight hours, most of it spent in a confined space with Locke, had worked on his nerves. He learned a lot about Locke's teenage exploits, his favorite music, and discovered he was as much of a foodie as Sawyer. Locke talked about Candi and the kids, Daniel, Marc, and Bailey, until he felt like he knew them. Locke talked about everything that was important to him except the person who had meant the most—the ghost elephant in the car. *Marcus.* Locke's silence on the subject spoke volumes. *There was no one I loved more than him.* Sawyer was grateful Locke hadn't picked up on his internal struggle but knew he needed to break away and regroup. It was so much easier to ignore his attraction to his partner when Locke was being an asshole, but funny stories, personal anecdotes, and smelling his cologne had worked on his nerves. Before Sawyer could respond, Locke's cell phone rang.

"It's Candi. I better take this in case she needs an emergency sitter," Locke said, hitting the accept button. "Hey there, Candi Crush. What's up?" Sawyer chuckled at the nickname. Locke's expression morphed from happy to thunderous in seconds. The scowl on his face reminded Sawyer of his first day on the job. "Just breathe, honey. I'll be right there," Locke said, storming off toward his vehicle.

"Rain check then?" Sawyer asked after his partner tucked his phone back in his pants pocket.

Locke stopped and spun around. "Fuck! I'm sorry. Is that okay?"

"Sure," Sawyer said casually. "Another time."

He drove home, fed his cat, took a cold beer into the shower with him, then made himself a double-decker bacon sandwich. Some days he worried a lot about what he put into his body, and others he couldn't give a fuck less. Sawyer's call to Levi was brief. He was tired and talking over the phone didn't hold the same allure as speaking to him in person. Sawyer wanted to see those pretty pink blushes and look into his expressive eyes. He wanted to magically stop investing emotional energy in people and situations that weren't healthy for him. They confirmed their dinner plans, and Sawyer genuinely looked forward to their date. After hanging up, Sawyer fell asleep in his recliner while watching a Braves game. Someone ringing his doorbell jolted him awake sometime later, dislodging a pissed-off Bones. A glance at the clock on his cable box said it was twelve thirty.

"Who the hell?" he sleepily asked on his way to the front door. Glancing through the peephole left him just as baffled as when he hadn't known the identity of his visitor. Sawyer opened his door, and a drunk and very uncoordinated Royce Locke fell into his arms. "Whoa there."

"Sorry for stopping by so late. Were you sleeping?" Locke's words were slightly slurred as hot beer breath blasted against Sawyer's face and neck.

"Yeah, but it's okay. What's wrong?" Sawyer asked. "Please tell me you didn't drive here in this condition."

"Hell no. I took a Lyft. Might've taken me a few tries to type in your address," Locke slurred.

"How'd you know where I live?" It seemed like a dumb thing for him to ask, considering his maybe-straight, very drunk partner was in his arms and pressed against him. Shouldn't he be asking why he was here?

"I'm a detective. I know things." Locke nestled deeper into Sawyer's hold. "You feel so fucking good. Warm. Strong." Locke buried his nose in Sawyer's throat and inhaled deeply. "Smell good too."

Sawyer somehow managed to chuckle even though it felt like he'd stopped breathing. "And you're very wasted."

"A little, but it doesn't make it less true. Booze is truth serum or some shit. There's a lot I could say."

"There's a lot I won't let you say."

Locke lifted his head and peered up at Sawyer. "Fine. I'll just use my mouth to do other things." Then he pressed his lips to Sawyer's.

CHAPTER 22

LUST—HOT AND ADDICTIVE—SPIKED SAWYER'S BLOOD AND SENT IT racing through his veins, threatening to obliterate reason and logic. His brain screamed "pull back," but Sawyer threaded his hands through Locke's silky blond strands instead, holding him still so he could deepen the kiss. Sawyer's knees weakened when their tongues met, causing him to stumble back against the foyer table. Locke's arms tightened around Sawyer's waist, and he shoved a denim leg between Sawyer's, nestling his firm, toned thigh just beneath his balls. Locke's body heat seeped through the thin fabric of Sawyer's mesh basketball shorts. Stars exploded behind his closed eyelids, and his grip on sanity diminished a little more.

Sawyer had only known Locke for three fucking days, and much of the time was spent wondering what the man tasted like. The answer: so fucking good. Even the taste of beer couldn't detract from Sawyer's pleasure. *Beer. Fuck!* This wasn't right. His conscience surged forward, scrabbling for purchase.

Sawyer tried to break the kiss and pull away, but Locke, sensing his intention, firmly gripped the back of his neck, holding him in place. Even drunk, Locke's kissing skills were impressive. His tongue was aggressive and playful at the same time—sweeping in boldly one second then darting back out just to flick the tip against Sawyer's.

Someone growled lustily—maybe it was both of them—then they angled their heads to deepen their kiss as the touching began. Locke slid both hands beneath Sawyer's tank top, ghosting his fingers over the ridges of his abdomen to reach his pecs. Sawyer kept one fist tangled in Locke's messy hair but slid the other hand down to grip his taut ass, holding him in place. *Friction. Just need a bit more friction.* Sawyer canted his hip ever so slightly and… *Right fucking there.* He felt the whimper in the back of his throat. There was no earthly being or heavenly power that could've prevented him from rutting against Locke's rock-hard thigh.

Sawyer ripped his mouth away from Locke's, letting his head fall back and exposing his throat. Sawyer cried out when Locke circled an erect nipple with his thumb before pinching and tugging it. Sawyer gripped Locke's ass hard enough to leave finger marks while riding his thigh harder. Locke dropped his head to Sawyer's neck. Dark blond scruff scraped over sensitive flesh in his wake, then he sank his teeth into a tendon.

"Oh God," Sawyer moaned, getting embarrassingly close to coming in his shorts. Locke responded by chuckling against his hammering pulse. Something about his partner's rumble penetrated Sawyer's lust-saturated brain. "I… You… We…"

Locke chuckled harder, but before Sawyer could comment further, he recaptured Sawyer's mouth in a bruising kiss. The hand on his chest slowly slid down his torso until it reached his waistband. Teasing fingers toyed with the drawstring of his shorts. One smooth tug and there would be nothing keeping Locke from touching his bare, leaking cock.

Stop. This isn't right. Sawyer could barely hear his soul's pleas over the blood rushing through his veins. *So close. Just a little more.* Curious fingertips dipped beneath Sawyer's waistband and grazed the wet head of his dick. Locke simultaneously broke the kiss and jerked his hand out of Sawyer's pants at the same time. He stared at his wet fingers with both a dazed and curious expression. Then Locke stuck his fingers inside his mouth, sucking Sawyer's precum off them.

The gesture stunned Sawyer so much that his hips stilled. He waited in breathless anticipation for Locke's next move. *This was it.* They had reached the point of no return—the zero hour. If they crossed the line, there would be no going back. Was Sawyer willing to risk his career to appease Locke's curiosity? Isn't that what this was? Sawyer had nothing to base his opinion on other than his instinct, which rarely steered him wrong. He suspected Locke's attraction to men wasn't new, but his willingness to explore it was.

"You're drunk," Sawyer said, trying to inject sanity and reason into the situation. "I think we need to slow this down."

Locke grinned wryly but didn't budge an inch. "I'm not that drunk; I'm tipsy. Tell me you don't want me, and I'll walk away. No harm done and no hurt feelings."

Sawyer opened his mouth to form the lie that would preserve his sanity and save their partnership but could only manage a sigh. Locke aimed his pirate's smile at him, and they were kissing again, harder than the first time—teeth gnashing and tongues dueling. Locke tugged the drawstrings loose then shoved his hand inside Sawyer's shorts, fisting his cock and jacking him with sure strokes.

Determined not to come alone, Sawyer unfastened Locke's jeans and slid his hand beneath the waistband of his underwear. The heat of Locke's thick erection seared his palm and ratcheted up his desire. He matched him stroke for stroke, both of them driving each other to the edge.

A song suddenly started playing in the foyer, and they jolted apart. Sawyer glanced around the room looking for the source of the old song he hadn't heard in years. He thought it was called "Sugar, Sugar."

"Fuck," Locke groused, figuring out the source of their interruption before Sawyer could. Locke pulled his ringing phone out of his pocket and stared at it. He flicked his apologetic gaze to Sawyer briefly before accepting the call. "Hey, Candi Land," Locke said softly, stepping away from Sawyer and taking his body heat with him.

It was for the best, Sawyer said to himself while retying his drawstring. No irreparable damage had been committed, and he had more accurate spank bank material. Silver linings and all that shit. Sawyer looked down at his hand, expecting to see scorch marks on his palm.

"I'm okay, honey. I'm sorry I scared you," Locke said, sounding slightly less drunk—tipsy—than when he'd arrived. Whatever Candi had said to him put a sappy smile on his face that made Sawyer want to vomit. "Sorry I snuck out of there, but I didn't want to wake you or the kids. I didn't drive. I left my Harley at your place and called a Lyft to take me home."

Sawyer pushed off the wall and walked deeper into his home. Watching hearts and moonbeams shine from Locke's eyes when he talked to Candi Wilkes was terrible enough, but listening to his lies about where he went after he left her house was more than Sawyer could handle. He sent up a silent prayer of thanks that the universe had been looking out for him. He had no idea how he'd handle it if Locke wanted to pick up right where they left off once he completed the call. It turned out he had nothing to worry about when Locke found him a few minutes later peering into his refrigerator like it held the answers to all of life's mysteries.

"What's that?" Locke asked, hooking his thumb over his shoulder in the direction of Sawyer's living room.

Sawyer shut the refrigerator door and turned to face him. "That was you inviting yourself into my home and helping yourself to my body."

Locke's face grew scarlet red, but he didn't look angry or remorseful. "I didn't ask what *that was*; I asked 'what's that' as in what the hell is that huge gray beast glaring at me from the back of the sofa."

Grateful for a safer topic, Sawyer said, "The gray beast is Bones. He's my cat."

"That isn't a cat," Locke said, shaking his head. "At least not a breed I've ever seen."

"I don't know Bones' full story, but the veterinarian said he's part Maine Coon, and the breed is exceptionally larger than your typical domestic house cat."

"I think he wants to chew my dick off."

Sawyer chuckled. "You're safe unless you have bread tucked in your underwear. And since I know you don't…" He let his words trail off. Cracking jokes about their near mishap felt wiser than demanding to know what the fuck Locke had been thinking. "Want me to make you some coffee, or do you just want some cold water?"

"Water," Locke said. "Otherwise, I'll be up all night." He snorted. "Who am I kidding. There's no chance in hell I'll get any sleep tonight." Glancing at the clock on the microwave, he amended, "This morning."

Sawyer looked at him, really looked at him for the first time since Locke got off the phone. His mouth looked pinched, and a deep V furrowed his brow. Whatever prompted Candi to call Locke earlier that evening had rocked his world. Sawyer longed to smooth the grooves away with his fingers, but wisely kept the expanse of the kitchen between them.

"On second thought, do you have any beer?" Locke asked. "I'm feeling way too sober right now."

"I think you've had enough beer for tonight."

Locke stiffened, and his countenance darkened. "Don't tell me what my limits are, Key. We're not to that stage in our partnership." *Ouch.*

"I see. We're just at the drunk-kiss-and-fondle stage." Locke flinched like Sawyer slapped him, and he immediately regretted his spiteful words.

"I'm just going to head out. I'll order another Lyft." Locke turned around and headed back toward the living room.

"Stay," Sawyer said. "Please. Just a little longer."

Locke slowly turned around and blew out a frustrated breath with enough force to ruffle the messy strands of blond hair hanging over his forehead. "I messed up here tonight, Key. I'm sorry. I didn't want to be alone and coming here felt right. I shouldn't have kissed you or touched you."

Sawyer's mouth tipped up into a half smirk. "It wasn't that bad."

Locke glared at him. "It was damn good. Don't bother trying to deny it with the giant wet spot on the front of your shorts."

Sawyer shook his head. "God, you're a dickhead."

"I'm not going to bother disputing that."

Reopening the fridge, Sawyer pulled out two bottles of beer then crossed the kitchen to hand one to Locke, who twisted the cap off and took a long drink. "I can tell you're upset by whatever happened tonight. I know we're virtual strangers at this point, maybe a little closer since you nearly stroked me off—" Locke choked then spat a mouthful of beer all over Sawyer's tank top, cutting off the rest of what he was going to say. "Damn. Now I need another shower."

"Make it a cold one, asshole. You're not getting any more of this," Locke said, making a big circle over his chest and groin.

"Anyway," Sawyer continued, "I'm a good listener when you're ready." *If he's ever ready.* "I promise to keep what you tell me confidential."

Locke's eyes were a smoky gray, and Sawyer couldn't read the expression. Relief? Pleasure. "I'm not ready yet, but soon, okay?"

"Sure," Sawyer said with a firm nod. "I have a spare bedroom if you want to crash here tonight."

"I don't want to impose." At Sawyer's quirked brow, Locke added, "More than I already have."

Sawyer took a long pull from his beer. Common sense said he should order Locke a ride then firmly shut the door on this night, but he couldn't. There had been so much vulnerability in Locke's confession about him not wanting to be alone, especially in the words that followed. "You're not an imposition. You said coming here felt right, and I want you here. Finish your beer, and I'll show you to the spare bedroom." A thought hit him. "Have you eaten?"

"Yeah." Locke didn't sound convincing, so Sawyer quirked a brow. "At lunch," Locke admitted grudgingly.

Sawyer returned to his refrigerator and pulled out the rest of the uncooked bacon. "How do you like it?" he asked Locke who grinned sheepishly. "Your bacon, dickhead. Chewy or crispy?"

"You don't have to cook anything for me."

Sawyer pulled Vic's favorite old cast iron skillet from the cabinet. A random thought came out of nowhere. *Vic would like him.* Sawyer didn't know enough about Locke to confirm or dispute the thought. It could just be fanciful thinking. "If you don't tell me, then you'll leave me to guess. Might as well get a bacon sandwich you're going to like."

Locke moaned a little. "Crispy."

"Would you like a fried egg too?" When Locke didn't answer right away, Sawyer looked over his shoulder and caught his partner staring at his ass. "Eyes up here, sweetheart." Sawyer snapped his fingers, and Locke jerked his head up to meet his gaze. "Fried egg on your sandwich?"

Locke swallowed hard, and his expression became unreadable again. "That sounds great. Um, do you have any tomatoes?"

"Was I born and raised in the South?"

"I don't know," Locke quipped. "We have a lot to learn about each other. I have more to learn than you do because you let me ramble on for ten hours today."

While it was true, Sawyer had a feeling he'd only learned surface things. He wanted to learn so much more but recognized he had to be patient. "One day at a time, yeah?"

"Yeah."

Locke wolfed down the bacon sandwich and drank another beer before Sawyer showed him to the spare room.

"You have your own bathroom. There should be soap and shampoo in there. I'll grab you a pair of basketball shorts for you to sleep in."

"Maybe I like sleeping naked." Locke hadn't slurred his words, but he was definitely feeling the additional alcohol. Then he laughed and reached for the hem of his T-shirt. "Just toss them on the bed, and I'll grab them when I get out of the shower." Locke reached for the button at the top of his jeans, making it obvious he was getting undressed even if Sawyer was in the room.

"Be right back," Sawyer said. Locke's chuckle followed him down the hallway.

Stopping in the peace and serenity of his bedroom, Sawyer pressed a hand over his racing heart. He had to be dreaming. There was no other explanation for the things that happened. Instead of pinching himself to test his theory, Sawyer grabbed a pair of shorts from his drawer and returned to the bedroom down the hall from his. He'd planned to drop the shorts on the bed and leave, but Locke had left the bathroom door open a foot, giving Sawyer an eyeful of toned, tan skin beneath the hot water. Steam had already started to fill the room, but it didn't prevent Sawyer from seeing Locke reach down and start stroking his cock. Sawyer stood transfixed, staring at Locke plea-suring himself and feeling like a sexual deviant. He might've stayed for the entire show if Locke's deep, lusty moan hadn't startled him.

Sawyer hauled ass back to his bathroom where he needed to shower the smell of beer off his skin. The downside was washing away Locke's touch, which made him sadder than it should. *Levi. Think about Levi and all the potential there.* But it wasn't images of Levi he took into the shower with him or that followed him into his dreams when they finally came a few hours later.

Royce Locke, what am I going to do about you? Better yet, what am I going to do to you?

CHAPTER 23

SAWYER WAS AWAKE LONG BEFORE HIS ALARM WENT OFF. THE FEW hours he'd slept were fitful at best, and he knew there was no way in hell he could relax back into sleep knowing Locke was just down the hall. Naked? Was he wearing his shorts? Both images tormented his mind and chased him out of bed much earlier than even he preferred.

Bones, his constant shadow, was nowhere to be found in his room. There was no way in hell he'd given up his spot on the bed to sleep anywhere else in the house unless his innate feline curiosity was too much for him to resist. A persistent voice told Sawyer to stay clear of Locke's borrowed bedroom, but that's exactly where he headed after dressing for a workout and brushing his teeth.

The carpet runner in the center of the hallway muffled his footsteps, but they still sounded loud to him. When he and Vic renovated the home, an electrician had tucked tape lighting with motion sensors along the baseboard in the hallway. Even though the area was softly lit, it seemed glaringly bright to Sawyer's overstimulated senses. He noticed the door to the spare bedroom was opened wide enough for his big bruiser to fit through. He knew damn well he'd pulled the door shut when he left the room the night before. Sure, Locke might've opened the door before going to bed, but he doubted it.

Sawyer suspected the appeal of a stranger in his home lured Bones, who was tall enough when he stood on his hind legs to reach the handle, and smart enough to know he could easily open it with the swipe of his paw. Sawyer had witnessed his bold intelligence enough to know nothing would stop his cat when he made up his mind that he wanted something.

Aided by the light in the hallway, Sawyer eased the door open slightly wider and peered inside the room. Locke lay facedown on the bed with his head turned in the opposite direction of the door. The shorts Sawyer had loaned him were on the floor next to the clothes, underwear, and shoes he'd worn the previous night. Locke had shoved the sheet and duvet down, exposing the upper curve of his ass. God, the man was beautiful. *Fucking pervert.* Sawyer felt a little less creepy and slightly more vindicated when he spotted his best furry friend curled into a ball at the base of Locke's spine. Bones lifted his head, giving Sawyer his don't-even-think-about-it look.

Curiosity had lured Bones to the room, but he stayed out of necessity. Bones thought Locke needed him, and who the hell was he to argue? Animals had heightened senses that detected things humans didn't notice. Sawyer had known Locke was a fucked-up mess when he showed up drunk, but Bones' insistence he was needed drove home just how deep the hurt went.

Sawyer backed out of the room and headed down to the kitchen to start the coffee brewing before he hit his home gym. Pushing his earbuds in place, Sawyer turned on his playlist, which consisted of high-octane rock to stimulate his brain, and started warming up his muscles on the treadmill.

After two miles of cardio, he hit the weights. It was shoulder day, so he concentrated all his energy on those groups of muscles. He cycled through the presses, raises, and rows then repeated until every inch of his body was covered in sweat. He was on his last set of rear delt raises when he glanced up in the mirror and found Locke standing in the doorway behind him. His partner was so busy staring at his ass he hadn't realized Sawyer stopped the reps until he lowered the heavy barbells to the ground and stood to his full height.

Their eyes met and held in the mirror for several seconds. Locke's expression was unreadable once more, or maybe it was more like Sawyer was afraid to read too much into the heat he saw in the other man's turbulent eyes.

"You come here often?" Locke asked, sauntering into the room wearing the borrowed shorts. Sawyer had a bigger build, so they hung lower on Locke's hips, showing off the definition of his pelvis and broadcasting that he wore nothing beneath them. "This is a nice set-up." Locke ran his finger over the bench press bar, and Sawyer would swear he felt the touch in his groin.

His heart rate spiked even harder when he could no longer deny the lust in his partner's eyes. In the light of the morning, he was more determined to resist his attraction to Locke. To do so, he'd need distance and clarity. He needed Locke out of his house before his touch and smell permeated everything—every room. Planting a friendly smile on his face, Sawyer turned around and faced Locke. "I just need to grab a shower, then I can drop you off at your place."

"So eager to get rid of me?" Locke teased, but the light in his eyes dimmed a little. Sawyer had hurt him with his dismissal.

"I just need time to prepare myself for which Royce Locke I'm going to meet today."

Locke stiffened and lowered his hand to his side. "What the hell does that mean?" Those gray eyes darkened like storm clouds. Anger. Now that emotion was easier for Sawyer to swallow.

"It means exactly what you think it does."

Locke placed his hands on his narrow hips, and the shorts slid precariously lower, the thin fabric outlining his straining erection. Sawyer jerked his gaze up to meet Locke's sneer. "You think I'm mentally unstable or have a personality disorder?"

Sawyer rolled his eyes. "No."

"Then what the hell do you mean?" Locke demanded.

Sawyer held up his index finger. "On Monday, you made it clear you didn't want me for a partner, and you resented my very existence." A slight exaggeration. Sawyer held up a second finger. "On Tuesday, we struck a truce, but things were still tense." A third finger went up. "Wednesday, you get a call from Candi that upsets you which later prompts you to show up at my place drunk and ready to fuck."

Locke flinched but never looked away. "Okay, maybe some of those things are true."

"Some of them?" Sawyer's eyebrow rose with his voice. "Which of those things aren't true."

"I didn't come here to fuck you," Locke groused. "I came here because I needed a…"

"Friend?" Sawyer supplied. "I was happy the tension between us had eased. I even started to feel like we would be friends someday, but we aren't there yet. So why me? Why not Stein?"

"I didn't want to give Holly the wrong idea about our relationship."

Sawyer laughed, but it was full of disdain instead of humor. "The wrong idea? The two of you verbally fuck one another every time you're in the same space. It's borderline disgusting and completely inappropriate for the workplace. How dare you act like she's this delicate flower who has jumped to wrong conclusions. You can lie to yourself all you want, but don't sling that bullshit in my direction, and don't you dare insult her—deliberately or by accident." The fury raging through his system blindsided him.

"I never said—"

Sawyer didn't let him finish. "Don't! You need to own up to your fucking behavior. What about me? Was your tongue down my throat and your thigh between my legs giving me the wrong or right idea? Which is it, Locke?"

"You weren't complaining?" Locke countered angrily. "You could've said no. You're a strong guy who could've pushed me off you at any time. Did you? Fuck no. You gripped my ass and nearly rubbed one out on my offensive thigh. No one has ever kissed me the way you did, so don't act like you're some pitiful victim. Yeah, I might've made the first move, but you were right there with me the whole time. Right. There. With. Me." Locke raked his eyes over Sawyer's sweaty, bare chest then stopped at his groin. "Your outrage might be more believable if your dick wasn't trying to tear its way out of your shorts."

Sawyer looked down at his crotch and discovered he was hard as a spike. He'd never found arguing particularly arousing before, but he was in unchartered territory in many ways. "Huh. What do you know?"

"I know I need to come right now, and I'd prefer to not do it alone." Locke didn't move; he waited for Sawyer to decide and take the lead.

In response, Sawyer crossed the room and captured Locke's lips in a hard kiss. Logic. Reason. Self-preservation. All those things bailed on him, leaving him with a need so intense it drove him to the brink of insanity. All that warm, sexy male flesh on display was irresistible, and Sawyer had to touch Locke everywhere, and his partner met his boldness with his own seeking fingers. His mind spun with all the ways he could make Locke shatter apart and cry out his name. Blow job. Jack them off together with his big fist? Frotting against him until they both blew? Full penetration was off the table. No lube or condoms on hand, and he thought Locke might be a virgin to anal sex.

Locke broke the kiss and moaned, "Please. Put me out of my misery, Sawyer."

Locke had finally spoken his first name, and it drove him over the edge. Sawyer maneuvered Locke over to the leg curl bench with the reclining back that would keep their faces in proximity. Sawyer wanted to rock his world but do it in a position which would allow him to taste Locke's moans and groans.

Sawyer pushed Locke's shorts down his legs. "On your back," he said, pointing to the padded bench.

Locke smiled wickedly then did as commanded. He gasped when his bare flesh touched the vinyl. "Fuck, that's cold."

"You won't be cold for long," Sawyer said arrogantly, shoving his shorts off and stepping out of his shoes. He straddled Locke's hips, aligning their cocks together perfectly, and began thrusting. Sawyer's slick skin aided the glide, and Locke's mouth went slack and his eyes rolled back in his head. "Warm enough yet?"

Digging his fingers into Sawyer's hips, Locke said, "Getting warmer."

Sawyer gripped the back of the bench above Locke's head for leverage and rode him harder and faster, trapping their cocks between their bodies for optimal friction.

"Going to come," Locke said. "Come hard."

Sawyer lowered his mouth to Locke's, reclaiming those lips and catching the moans and whimpers as he moved closer and closer to the precipice. Sawyer's body shook, and his balls drew tight, signaling he was about to erupt too. He wanted—needed—them to come together. Thankfully, Locke was right there with him. Sawyer felt Locke's body tense beneath him, and he relaxed and quit fighting his body.

Locke dropped his hands from Sawyer's hips to circle his arms around his waist, clutching Sawyer tightly. Together they grunted, groaned, and came in a slide of hot, sticky cum. Sawyer continued to kiss Locke long after their sated bodies stilled. Locke kissed him just as eagerly until their breathing and racing hearts returned to normal speeds. Sawyer wasn't sure what he expected to see in Locke's eyes when he broke the kiss and raised his head, but his expression made his breath hitch in his throat. Awe, surprise, and the eagerness to do it all again stared back at Sawyer. *Pull back,* his brain urged. Locke seemed to hold him tighter as if he sensed Sawyer's internal struggle.

Sawyer wanted to tease him and say something that would ease the tension building inside him. He could've gone with something like *we have to separate at some point,* but instead, he said, "I didn't take you for a guy who likes to cuddle."

Some of the joy dimmed in Locke's eyes, but he recovered quick-ly. "Do you think about me often?"

"More than what's healthy," Sawyer admitted.

"You're very direct."

Sawyer shrugged then straightened fully, breaking the hold Locke had on his waist. Staring down at the mess of combined cum on both their stomachs made him forget what he had been about to say. Locke couldn't seem to tear his eyes off Sawyer's messy abs, which stroked his ego far more than he should've allowed. They'd gotten off togeth-er, but what had it changed? The answer was nothing. Remembering himself, Sawyer said, "I've learned it's the only way. Running and hid-ing from things never made them go away." Locke narrowed his eyes like perhaps Sawyer was accusing him of doing that, but he didn't challenge him or push further.

Looking to avoid a confrontation, Sawyer rose on shaking legs then dismounted the bench. He'd never be able to work out there again without remembering the way Locke felt in his arms or how he sounded when he climaxed. He picked up their shorts from the ground and tossed Locke's to him while he used his pair to wipe the cum off his stomach. Not tearing his eyes off Sawyer's hands, Locke did the same thing with his shorts.

"What now?" Locke asked, sounding unsure for the first time since he showed up on Sawyer's front porch.

"We shower, dress, grab a bite to eat, and I drop you off at your place so you can get ready for work. Then we go about our day like we normally would." *This changes nothing* were his unspoken words, but it was a bald-face lie. What they shared changed every-fucking-thing.

Locke swung his legs over the bench and stood up. "Your shower or mine?" His cockiness returned and fuck if Sawyer wasn't turned on by it. "I'll wash your cock, and you can wash mine."

"That isn't how the phrase goes, and I think we should probably shower separately. Put some distance between us so this doesn't bleed into our workday."

"Stuff the genie back inside the bottle without getting your three wishes?" Locke asked, quirking a brow. "Or maybe you received a few wishes without voicing them out loud…"

"Arrogant ass."

Locke flicked his shorts, snapping the end against Sawyer's thigh and landing much too close to his cock for his comfort. Sawyer strode toward him, but Locke held up his hand. "You said we needed to go to separate showers. It's too late to change your mind now."

"You're going to pay for this, Royce." A telling tremor worked through his partner. Locke liked hearing his first name roll off Sawyer's tongue.

"I'm walking out of here now before we're both late for work. We have a double homicide to solve," Locke said. "Don't think about following me, big guy."

Sawyer imagined himself following Locke into the shower, dropping to his knees, and showing him that no one knew how to blow a dick better than him. Sawyer knew all the places to press his tongue as well as the perfect suction to maximize Locke's pleasure. Gag reflex? Nonexistent. He wanted to demonstrate his skills but knew it wasn't the right time. There was too much between them that needed to be aired out. So he waited until Locke had time to reach the spare bedroom before retreating to the sanctity of the master bathroom.

He made quick work of washing his hair and body then shaving. It took him longer to pick out what he was going to wear. They weren't supposed to be knocking on doors and kicking rocks all day, so a suit would look more professional, but he couldn't get past the heat in Locke's eyes when he raked his gaze over his tight-fitting T-shirt the previous day. Sawyer chose a light gray tee and paired it with a pair of black designer jeans he knew hugged his ass perfectly.

When he returned to the kitchen, Locke sat at one of the barstools sipping his coffee while Bones twined around his feet.

"Your cat likes me," Locke said, not bothering to hide his lusty gaze as he checked Sawyer out from head to toe. "We have the same pair of boots."

"Yeah. I noticed that on my first day." Sawyer made a cup of coffee then faced Locke again. "Hungry?"

Locke licked his lips like Bones did after eating his gourmet food. "Uh-huh."

"For food," Sawyer amended.

"Not really. I make a big deal out of wanting the chief's bear claws, but I'm not much of a breakfast eater."

"That's because you're not doing it right."

"Yeah?" Locke asked. "I suppose you're going to show me how to do it right."

Were they still talking about breakfast? "I am. Do you like spinach, feta cheese, and tomatoes?" Locke nodded. Sawyer went to the refrigerator and pulled those items out along with the carton of eggs. "Egg white omelet and an English muffin. It's quick, delicious, and good for you."

"Let's see what you got, hotshot," Locke teased.

Sawyer got the last laugh when Locke's first bite elicited a moan almost as loud as the one he'd let out when he came.

"Shut up and eat your breakfast," Locke groused. "Smug, know-it-all bastard."

His grumpiness only made Sawyer laugh harder. Knowing they were running out of time, he tucked into his food. Locke pinched off a piece of his English muffin and held it up for silent approval. Sawyer nodded his head, and he leaned down, offering the bread to Bones, who snatched it and ran into the living room to enjoy his bounty. After they finished, Locke insisted on helping him tidy up the kitchen before they headed out, but not before Bones made a real slut of himself by throwing his big body down and exposing his belly for Locke to rub.

Sawyer debated on warning him about the belly trap but decided against it. He smugly waited for Bones to go from *rub my belly* to *how fucking dare you*, which he'd finish with biting or scratching Locke. It didn't happen. Instead, Bones purred loud enough to rattle the windows while Locke told him what a pretty, pretty kitty he was.

When Locke straightened up, Bones looked at Sawyer expectantly. Sawyer knelt beside him and started rubbing his furry belly. He got one and a half passes, maybe two, before Bones hissed and bit the fleshy part of his hand between his thumb and forefinger before scampering off toward his perch in front of the window.

"Damn brat," Sawyer said, shaking out his hand. At least he hadn't bitten him hard enough to break the skin.

"Your cat likes me better than you."

"Shut up and get in the car," Sawyer said, mimicking Locke's grouchiness from earlier.

They said very little during the drive to Locke's house. Locke spoke only to give directions, and Sawyer asked if the temperature in the car was okay. Sawyer offered to take him back to Candi's to pick up his Harley, but Locke said he'd drive his car to work and get it later. The farther they drove from Sawyer's house, the more awkward things felt between them. Locke lived in a quaint bungalow-style home with gingerbread trim surrounded by flowerbeds with riotous explosions of color everywhere. Sawyer realized he knew very little about Locke, but this surprised the hell out of him.

"You live here?"

"Don't be an asshole about it, okay?"

"I'm not trying to be an asshole. I'm just surprised. Did you plant all the flowers yourself?"

Locke shook his head, and a wistful expression briefly crossed his face before he slipped his neutral mask back into place. "No, my aunt did. This was her home, and she left it to me when she died. I work hard to keep up with her flowers to honor her memory, but they're running amok. I should hire a landscaper, but I feel like it's something I need to do. I think she'd be disappointed."

"I don't," Sawyer said softly. "It's obvious you care about honoring her memory and taking care of her flowers."

"I need to do better." Locke sighed. "About a lot of things." He smiled at Sawyer, but it didn't reach his eyes. "See you in a bit."

"Yep."

Sawyer drove to the station and greeted the MCU detectives in the bullpen, hoping he wasn't broadcasting how much his world had been tilted on its axis overnight. He made coffee, sat at his desk, and booted up his computer. While waiting for his partner to arrive, he dug out one of the cold cases Locke was trying to solve. It didn't take long for the case to absorb Sawyer's interest, and he lost track of time. His cell phone vibrated with an incoming text, interrupting his thoughts. Sawyer's heart sank when he read the message from Levi.

Sorry I missed you this morning. I hope you have a great day. Looking forward to tomorrow night.

Fuck! He'd told Levi during their conversation he would stop by to say hello and get coffee on his way to work. He hadn't thought once about Levi and their date the following night because he'd been thoroughly distracted. Sawyer continued staring at the message wondering how to respond. Did he apologize for not showing up at the café? Cancel their plans? He couldn't take Levi out when he had so many conflicting emotions about his partner.

Sawyer became aware of someone looming over him, casting a shadow over his desk. He didn't need to turn to see who stood behind him. The way his body came alive told him everything he needed to know. Locke set a cup of coffee on his desk. Sawyer recognized the logo on the cup and nearly groaned.

"Levi sends his best," Locke said. "You better respond to his message and let him know you're looking forward to the date too. You don't want him to get the idea you changed your mind."

Locke walked around and sat at his desk facing Sawyer's. "Would you?"

CHAPTER 24

"**W**HAT DID YOU DO?" SAWYER DEMANDED IN A LOW TONE.

A smug smile split Locke's face. "I don't understand the question or the harsh tone. You're making me feel naughty when all I wanted to do was return your thoughtful gesture from yesterday morning. What better place to buy your coffee than from your favorite café? You were supposed to stop by there this morning, by the way."

"In the conference room right now," Sawyer said tersely. He swiftly rose from his chair and exited the bullpen without waiting to make sure Locke followed him. Keeping his back to the open door, Sawyer took deep, cleansing breaths to try and calm down. *Breathe in. Hold. Release.*

Sawyer spun around to face Locke as soon as the door closed. The urge to fist his shirt and slam him against the wall was overwhelming, but he didn't dare lay his hands anywhere on his partner's body.

"I don't know why you're so upset, I only—" Locke's words died in his throat when Sawyer leveled him with a don't-fuck-with-me glare. "That's kind of sexy."

"Don't."

"Don't what? Speak the truth?" Locke asked. "I think it's sexy."

"Don't hurt Levi. Don't toy with him like he's a fucking mouse and you're the badass alley cat."

"Are you mad at yourself or at me?" Locke asked. "I don't think Levi was on your mind last night or this morning, or things would've turned out very differently. You wouldn't have forgotten to stop by his café either."

"I fucking hate you right now," Sawyer growled.

"I don't think that's hate, Key." Locke took the few steps toward him, closing the distance.

Sawyer bristled with anger. "Don't toy with me either. What happened between us meant nothing to you."

"God, you really are an asshole, Key. I'd been joking all along, but now I mean it. Grade A asshole."

"Are you going to deny it?"

Locke opened his mouth to reply, but a loud knock rattled the door. They jerked apart, both seemingly shocked at how close they'd moved together. Sawyer turned and looked away while Locke stomped over and wrenched the door open. "What?" he asked angrily.

"Whoa," Blue said in his deep voice. "Trouble in paradise?"

"What do you want, Blue?"

"I came to tell you they found Miller's Jeep abandoned at a gas station in Byrdstown, Tennessee, near the Kentucky border. The chief is on the phone now trying to sort out if law enforcement in Tennessee will process the Jeep and send us any evidence they find, or if we are going to have it towed back here for processing. There's also a PI here to see you. Says his name is Rocky Jacobs."

"Thanks, Blue," Locke said. "Mr. Jacobs can wait. I left a message for him on Monday regarding Putz's case, and the asshole never called me back. He can go stew in his sweat for a while. Miller's abandoned car takes precedence."

With their argument temporarily forgotten, Sawyer turned around and was prepared to follow Locke out the door, but Blue still stood in the doorway.

"Rocky isn't here about The Putz. Caroline Wembley's family hired him to help track down Miller. He's either already heard about the latest development or will have discovered it by the time I return to the bullpen."

"Great," Locke groused. "A private dick interfering with our case is exactly what we need right now." Blue still hadn't budged. "What?"

"The two of you might want to conduct your private business away from the precinct. You weren't exactly yelling, but you weren't being discreet either. Luckily, I was the one who overheard bits and pieces of the argument instead of the chief or someone who likes to spread rumors and innuendo."

"Thanks, Blue. We'll pay closer attention next time."

Blue nodded and shut the door, sensing that they had more to say to each other before returning to the bullpen.

"You once told me the only thing you're good for is no-strings sex," Sawyer said. "Is that what this morning was to you?"

Locke placed his hands on his hips and looked at the ceiling for a few seconds before meeting Sawyer's gaze again. "You want honesty?" Sawyer nodded. "I don't know what this morning was about except it felt really fucking good. I come from a long line of bastards, Key. Lockes aren't good at love, because we're notorious for making shitty choices. We tend to ruin anything good that comes into our lives, but I'm having a hard time digging up remorse for what we did. You, on the other hand, have regret written all over your face."

"It's confusion," Sawyer countered. "This hot and cold bullshit isn't good for either one of us. You're giving me vibes that tell me to touch and take, but you're telling me I shouldn't want those things. It fucks with my head. We're bickering one minute and borderline flirting the next."

"What do you want to do about it?"

"We put it behind us and work together, or I apply for a position with GBI."

Locke flinched but didn't look away from him. "We'll work through it."

Sawyer nodded and stepped around Locke, needing the fuck away from his partner before he said more things he couldn't take back. He'd just gripped the doorknob when Locke's growl of frustration stopped him in his tracks.

"Wait." Locke's voice had been so soft Sawyer almost hadn't heard him. "I didn't go to the café this morning to toy with Levi or spill the dirty details on what we did. I'm not really a dickhead, and you're not really an asshole. We just have our moments."

Sawyer released the knob but didn't face Locke. "Why did you go then?"

"Curiosity. I wanted to see the kind of man you liked."

"Interesting move from a guy who doesn't like strings. Is that the only reason?"

"No," Locke said hoarsely. "I also wanted to make sure he was good enough for you. I hope things work out between you."

Sawyer nodded once then left the room. When he reached the bullpen, a tall man with sandy hair and a bullshitter's smile was kicked back in Sawyer's chair with his feet propped up on his desk. Sawyer wanted to punch him. He knew the visceral reaction was a result of the conversation with Locke, but this jackass would make an excellent alternate target for his rage.

"Jacobs, I presume?" Sawyer asked.

"The one and only."

"Get the fuck out of my chair and show some damn respect by getting your feet off my desk." Sawyer felt every pair of eyes in the bullpen aimed at him.

"Rough crowd," Rocky Jacobs said, making a big production of lowering his legs and rising to his feet with his hands up in the air like he was surrendering. "I'm unarmed, Detective. Don't shoot."

"Pretending I'd shoot an unarmed man isn't giving me the warm and fuzzies, Jacobs."

"Wow, we got off on the wrong foot," the private investigator said, looking and sounding baffled. "Wait. You're partners with Locke." He nodded as if he'd just solved a big case. "That explains everything. Where is your illustrious partner?"

"Right here, asshat," Locke said, joining them. "What do you want? We have real investigating to do."

"Well, if you don't want to hear how I can get pings from Wayne Miller's cell phone faster than you can, then I'll just be going."

Jacobs took two steps before Locke said, "Not so fast. I'm going to show you to the conference room while Key retrieves some information."

"You mean how Miller's Jeep was abandoned near the Tennessee-Kentucky border?"

Locke narrowed his eyes. "I can neither—"

Jacobs cut him off. "Confirm nor deny. I know the routine. If you want to catch Miller, then you'll want to cooperate with me." Jacobs headed for the bullpen door. "I know the way to the conference room. This isn't my first rodeo. Talk amongst yourselves, and I'll be waiting patiently for you."

Once Rocky Jacobs left, Locke said, "How do you want to play this?"

"You think he was telling the truth about accessing the pings, or is he blowing smoke up our asses? We don't have that information from the phone company yet, so how does he?"

"I've heard there are companies that have developed the software to track cell phone pings more efficiently than any of the mobile service providers can. The only thing Jacobs needs is Miller's phone number, which is easy enough for a PI to obtain. What are we willing to share in return?"

"I guess we can tell him what we have so far and see where it gets us. Let's see what he knows, then we'll find out more about the abandoned Jeep."

Sawyer nodded and followed Locke to the conference room. Jacobs was sipping coffee at the head of the table. He waved his hand dramatically in front of his nose. "Smell that?"

"I don't smell anything," Sawyer said.

"Did you shit your pants?" Locke asked. "The bathroom is down the hallway."

"It's the pheromones bouncing off the walls in here. They're so hot it's burning my nostrils. Somebody should fuck already."

Sawyer didn't dare risk a glance at Locke's face. "Stop being an asshole and tell us what you have."

"That's no way to build a beautiful relationship," Jacobs countered.

"You would've returned the message I left you on Monday if you had wanted to establish a good working relationship with us," Locke pointed out.

"I heard you caught the killer the next day. What was the point?"

"If I have to tell you, then I think this 'relationship' is going to be a little too one-sided for my liking," Locke told him.

"I agree," Sawyer said.

"Let's start over, shall we?" Jacobs said, straightening in his chair and dropping his wiseass expression and tone of voice. "The first thing I need you to know is that the Wembleys didn't hire me because they felt you're incompetent, which usually isn't the case. They know you have to follow the rules, and I don't. We all know that Wayne Miller killed Caroline Wembley and her fiancé, DeShaun Benson. We're not even going to pretend another person on this earth would want to harm them. I have sources in the department, and I know you have a pretty solid case right now, but what good is it if you can't capture Miller? I have the tools to find him, and you have the resources to bring him in when I do."

Locke snorted and shook his head. "If you illegally obtain information that leads to Miller's arrest, it will be inadmissible in court, Jacobs."

The PI shrugged. "If this information happens to come from an anonymous tipster…"

"What do you know so far?" Sawyer asked.

"Nothing yet. I was just put on retainer this morning. When I leave here, I'm going to ask my buddy to run Miller's cell phone number to see if he gets any pings. If not, we already know he's made it as far as Tennessee, but probably traveled into Kentucky. From what

I've been able to glean, there were no vehicles reported stolen where Miller ditched his Jeep."

"Someone probably picked him up," Locke said.

"You can contact the gas station and inquire on obtaining video footage to see if Miller is spotted getting in another vehicle. You can do an extensive search for any friends Miller might have in the Tennessee or Kentucky area. I'd start with friends on social media. If I can get a ping and you can find a likely accomplice in that area, then we can contact local police and have them take a look around. If all that fails, maybe his girlfriend can—"

"No," Sawyer and Locke said at the same time.

"No fucking way," Locke groused.

"She's been through too much already. She's lucky to be alive, so there's no way we're using Marla as bait to get Miller back here," Sawyer said.

"Whoa, guys," Jacobs said, holding up his hand. "I wouldn't ask you to put her in danger. I was thinking a Facebook message or a text feeding him false information so he'd relax and slip up a little."

"Still too dangerous," Sawyer said.

"What if I could help tuck Marla away someplace safe and clone her phone to send the messages?"

"Maybe," Locke said.

"Last resort," Sawyer added.

Jacobs offered a genuine smile instead of the smarmy ones from earlier. "Fair enough."

"What do you get out of this?" Sawyer asked.

Jacobs scrubbed a hand over his mouth. "Pride that I helped get a killer off the street. Prove that not all PIs are go-it-alone rogues. We all want the same thing here—justice for Caroline and DeShaun. What do you say?"

Sawyer looked at Locke for the first time since entering the room. His partner didn't like it either, but they couldn't turn away invaluable resources if they wanted to find Miller.

"Fine," Locke said. "Don't interfere in our investigation or give out information to your clients without getting permission from us."

"Fair enough."

The men shook on the deal, then Jacobs left the conference room, leaving Sawyer and Locke alone. They had a lot of work to do, but Sawyer realized he had something important he needed to get off his chest so he could fully focus on finding Miller.

"I'm sorry for what I said."

"You were wrong, Sawyer." How did he make his name sound so sexy?

"About what, Royce?"

"What happened between us meant something to me. How could it not? You're the gold standard when it comes to men."

Sawyer's heart sank because the compliment was said with so much regret in Locke's voice. He knew damn well what it meant. "But you're a no-strings kind of guy?"

"I am."

"Why'd you do it then? You saw how much I was attracted to you and decided to experiment."

Locke flinched. "Like I said last night, I was acting on instinct, even when I knew I shouldn't. I also meant what I said about Levi. He's a sweet guy, and he's so into you it's almost ridiculous. He probably doesn't have a shit ton of baggage or hang-ups preventing him from having something outstanding in his life."

Seeing Locke expose his vulnerabilities only made Sawyer want him more, even though he knew it was a lost cause. Fighting the urge to pull his partner into his arms, Sawyer said, "Everyone has baggage and hang-ups, Royce. We all battle things that go bump in the night and scare us shitless."

"Even you?"

"Especially me. Maybe someday I'll share them with you."

Locke grinned. "Fair enough. Ready to catch a killer?"

"I'm always ready for that."

Locke called the gas station in Byrdstown, Tennessee, where Miller's Jeep was found and requested copies of the camera footage. He explained the situation to the employee who answered the phone, then to the manager the first person passed the call to, only to be told he'd have to wait to speak to the owner when he came in at noon.

"Wayne is friends with thousands of people, so you can help me look," Sawyer said when Locke finished his call. "It's shocking his profile and his friends list are set to public. From the few profiles I've clicked through, they don't mind filling in the bio information including where they live, work, went to school, their favorite teams, the clubs they're involved with, and their hobbies. I would've expected them to be a bit more…secretive."

"Maybe they're hiding in plain sight or deflecting the ugliness with something shiny. How does an asshole like Miller have that many friends?"

"Laws of attraction or something scientific, I'm sure. Like-minded people attract similar kinds. I'm sure there's a perfectly good explanation."

Locke snorted. "Yeah, science."

"I meant what I said about Marla. She's been through enough."

Locke met his gaze. "I agree."

They spent the next few hours going through Miller's list of friends and jotting down the name of anyone who lived in Tennessee, Kentucky, or Ohio. He might have intended to keep traveling north to put as much distance between himself and Georgia. The list was whittled down to two hundred and twenty people.

"That's more than I expected," Locke said, flopping back in his chair.

"Let's hope the gas station footage comes through and gives us the license plate number of the person who picked him up."

Locke glanced at his watch then straightened in his chair. "It's past noon. They must not have given the owner my phone number." Locke phoned the gas station again and went through the same process as the first time except the manager put the owner on the phone instead of taking a message they never intended to pass along. Locke repeated the reason for his call then listened patiently. A smile spread across his face, and he winked at Sawyer. "That would be perfect. Let me give you my email address." Locke rattled it off then listened again. "An hour is fine. Thank you very much." Locke hung up the phone. "He'll send the footage within the hour. He said the car wasn't there when he left work yesterday evening at around seven o'clock. The night manager noticed it when she arrived a few hours later at eleven o'clock. She called the police when it was still there when her shift ended at eight o'clock."

"Why didn't she assume someone had pulled over to get some sleep before getting back on the road?" Sawyer asked.

"They have a designated spot for that, but Miller hadn't parked there. She told Mr. Patel she had a bad feeling. He's just grateful she called the police instead of approaching the car on her own. He's going to pull the footage from seven o'clock on to see when Wayne showed up and when he might've gotten a ride."

"He's sending it in an hour?"

Locke nodded but didn't look away from his screen. "Gives us time to grab some lunch. You could make it up to Levi and pop in for a sandwich."

He needed to put more time between the orgasm he'd shared with Locke and seeing Levi again. "I was thinking about seeing what plans Kelsey had. I haven't had a chance to talk to her since Monday," Sawyer said casually. Locke met his gaze then. Maybe it was a trick of the blue light from his computer, but Locke looked relieved he wasn't meeting Levi, and Sawyer couldn't allow himself to go there. Locke had indirectly told Sawyer he was a lousy risk by pointing out that Levi was a safer bet for him.

"Kels is good people."

Rising to his feet, Sawyer asked, "Do you want to join us?"

"Nah. I have some personal stuff to deal with anyway. Meet you back here?"

"Sure." Sawyer felt Locke's eyes on him when he walked away. He was so fucking confused about what to do and hoped lunch with Kelsey would cheer him up.

Kels took one look at his face and knew something was wrong. "Guy problems, huh?"

"Something like that."

She pulled her purse out of her bottom drawer and stood up. "You've come to the right person because I know the perfect place for emotional eating."

She drove them to a Mexican restaurant he'd never heard of, and Sawyer ate the best salsa he'd had in his life. He and Kels mowed through two baskets of chips and ate huge entrees that came with rice and beans.

"All we're missing is a pitcher of margaritas," Kelsey said, lounging back in her chair, rubbing her belly. "We have to do this again when we're off the clock."

"Deal. What are you doing tonight?" Sawyer teased.

She laughed. "So, you and Locke or you and Levi? Which one is the source of your guy problems? Both? One at the job and one at home?"

"Levi and I haven't gone on a date yet," Sawyer replied.

"Locke is the issue then. Is he playing hardball still?"

Sawyer choked on his drink of sweet tea when he remembered the sound Locke made when he emptied his balls. "You could say that," he managed to croak out after a coughing fit.

Kelsey stared at him with a look of utter disbelief on her face. She blinked twice then a sly smile slowly spread across her face. "Are you serious?"

"I didn't say anything."

"You didn't have to, sweetheart. You should see your face right now."

"What's wrong with my face?" Sawyer asked, reaching up to touch his cheeks.

"Flushed face. Enlarged pupils. Nearly choked on your drink. I was referring to professional conflict, but it's obvious I was off there."

"Kels, it's not like that. It's…" Sawyer shook his head. "Hell, I don't know what it is except that it's bad for me. Levi seems so sweet, and he's the kind of man I should want."

Kelsey's laughter was deep and rich, attracting the attention of everyone around them. "Honey, you know that's not how life goes. You can't force something that isn't there."

"But I can resist someone who isn't good for me."

"Who says he's not good for you?" Kelsey pressed.

"He did." Sawyer felt a brief flash of guilt for talking about this to Kelsey, but he trusted her and needed advice.

"Did he say that because he believes it or because it's the easier way out?"

"I don't know," Sawyer replied, shaking his head. "What do I do about Levi? I asked him out on a date."

"Go on your date. How the hell are you going to know if there's something special unless you try? Right now, you're wowed by Locke's good looks and charisma, but it takes more than that to make a relationship work."

"The words 'Locke' and 'relationship' don't even belong in the same sentence together," Sawyer quipped.

"Every dog has his day. Maybe Locke's number is up."

Sawyer's phone rang, and he glanced at the caller ID. "Speak of the devil," he said to Kels then answered the phone. "What's up?"

"I have the video footage," Locke said.

"We're ready to head back now," Sawyer said, signaling for the check. "See you soon." He hung up then smiled at Kels. "Cross your fingers we found a break in this case."

"Crossing everything."

Locke looked antsy when Sawyer returned from lunch with Kelsey. "It's about fucking time."

"Seems like someone has already said that to me this week."

"Pull your chair around here so we can look through it together."

Sawyer wheeled his chair over and sat beside Locke, careful not to sit too close. It took everything in his power to focus on the task at hand and not let his mind drift to that morning when there had been nothing between them but sweat and cum. Beside him, Locke cleared his throat and Sawyer knew his mind had drifted too.

They slowly went through the footage and saw Wayne pull in around eight thirty. He parked and nothing happened for two hours until a red Ford Explorer pulled up behind his Jeep and parked. From the angle of the camera, they could only see the side of the Explorer. Wayne got out of the Jeep with his duffle bag and got into the passenger seat of the red SUV, which pulled forward almost before Wayne shut the door. A semi-truck drove by from the opposite direction, blocking the SUV from the camera. By the time the semi was out of the frame, the Explorer was too.

"Damn it. We might've been able to catch a partial on the license plate when it drove by," Locke growled. He checked the footage from the other security cameras but the SUV either didn't appear or the angle prohibited them from seeing the license plates.

"Go back to the first footage where it had a closer shot of the SUV. Something about it seems familiar."

Locke rewound the video then paused when the SUV appeared on the frame. "There are tens of thousands of red Explorers just like that everywhere."

"Can you zoom in on the rear quarter panel. Right there," Sawyer said, pointing to the screen once Locke got a closer look. "How many of them have bullet hole decals on the rear windows and also happen to be friends with Wayne Miller on Facebook?"

"Which one is it?"

"I'll have to look back through my names, but I know damn well I saw that SUV in the background on a profile pic. I think there's a deer head decal on the other side." Sawyer returned to his desk and started going through Wayne's friend lists again while Locke looked at the other camera feed and confirmed the deer decal was present.

"Nice catch, Key. Damn good catch," Locke said a minute later.

Sawyer clapped his hands. "Found him. Bart Travers who lives in Paducah, Kentucky. Even has his phone number in the bio. Who the hell includes that on their profile?"

"I'll run the guy through legitimate sources while you reach out to Jacobs."

"Me?" Sawyer asked. "You're his buddy."

"Use your personal phone and text the guy. With any luck, we'll be going on a road trip to collect our fugitive."

"Isn't that the US Marshals' job?"

"We're not going to miss our chance to catch this bastard."

Great. Another ten-hour day in the car with Locke. "Fine, but fair warning. I'm bringing my audiobooks with me, and I don't plan to use my earbuds."

Locke laughed and shook his head. "Text Jacobs so I can get Cinderfella back in time for his ball."

Sawyer flipped him off then texted Jacobs.

CHAPTER 25

JACOBS TOOK ANOTHER DAY TO COME THROUGH, BUT WHEN HE DID, IT paid off big-time. Sawyer had expected Miller to ditch his phone, but he either didn't think he could be traced, or he wanted them to follow him. The pings documented his journey from the rendezvous spot at the gas station in Byrdstown, Tennessee, to a destination nearly two hours north. Instead of heading to Paducah where Bart lived, they'd gone to an isolated area nestled near the base of the Daniel Boone National Forest outside Berea, Kentucky.

The anonymous tipster Jacobs scrounged up provided just enough detail that they could cross-reference the lead with the information they'd gathered from the video and Facebook search to show Chief Rigby. Sawyer and Locke were initially excited they'd found their guy until they gathered in Rigby's office Friday afternoon to call the local post of the Kentucky State Police. Chief requested they put eyes on the location until they could get an extraction team in place. Post Commander Davies' response in the form of laughter caught them off guard.

"Oh, wait. You're serious?" he asked.

"As a heart attack," Rigby replied with no humor in her voice. As a woman, she'd worked her ass off to achieve her position, and someone laughing at her, especially a man, probably made her blood boil.

"The Georgia Bureau of Investigation fast-tracked the DNA from the hair found on the murder weapon and matched it to the female victim, Caroline Wembley. It was enough for me to obtain an arrest warrant and an extradition order. I'm in the process of coordinating transportation with the US Marshal services, and in the meantime, I'm only asking for your guys to keep an eye on the place."

"I think I gave you the wrong impression when I laughed at your request, and for that, I do apologize. It's obvious you don't know the significance of where your suspect has chosen to hunker down. I'm also surprised your tipster didn't give you a heads-up. It makes me highly suspicious of the information they provided." Sawyer groaned inwardly.

"Enlighten me then, Commander," Rigby said, not sounding the least bit mollified by his apology.

Sawyer and Locke listened in horror as Davies described the cult slash militia compound where Miller had taken up residence. They referred to themselves as the Brethren of the Chosen Sons. He agreed to increase police presence in the towns closest to the compound in case Miller left to get food or go to a bar, but Davies warned it might be weeks before they saw any movement in or out of the place. "A full-scale battle with the Brethren would be on a larger scale than Waco and Ruby Ridge combined, and it could trigger a civil war in this country beyond our worst nightmares. I want to help you apprehend this bastard, but I won't put my people in the line of fire, nor will I be the one responsible for the shot that destroys our country." There was nothing any of them could say that would counter his objection, so Rigby thanked him for his assistance, and they agreed to keep in touch while people much higher on the law enforcement totem pole worked this out.

The commander's chilling words still echoed in Sawyer's ears hours later when he pulled up outside Levi's house to pick him up for dinner. Levi met him at the door when he approached the craftsman-style house located within walking distance of his café. Levi's happy smile eased some of the chill that had permeated Sawyer's soul that morning in Rigby's office.

Sawyer returned his smile. "Hi. You look handsome." Levi wore a gray dress shirt that made his eyes look bluer, white jeans, and gray leather loafers.

Levi's slow appraisal of Sawyer's pressed white shirt, black jeans, and black boots resulted in another one of those adorable blushes. "You look ridiculously sexy."

What came next? Should he hug Levi? Lean in for a quick kiss? *What the fuck was the proper dating etiquette these days?* As if realizing one of them needed to make the first move, they both leaned toward each other at the same time, and their chaste kiss landed clumsily and left of center. They pulled back and laughed, breaking the awkwardness.

"I'm complete shit at this," Sawyer admitted.

"No, you're not."

"Do you trust me to get us to the restaurant in one piece?"

Levi's soft laugh was delightful and contagious. After a few seconds, he reached up and cupped Sawyer's cheek. "Of course, I do."

Just like that, Sawyer was transported back in time. Vic had walked him to his front porch, and Sawyer had asked if he wanted to see him again. Vic leaned in and pressed the sweetest kiss on his lips before saying, "Of course, I do." Fast-forward a bit and the two men faced each other at an altar, promising to love, honor, and cherish one another in sickness and in health. When it was time for Vic to respond to the pastor's question about taking Sawyer as his husband, he had cupped Sawyer's face with both hands, ghosted his thumb over his lips, and said, "Of course, I do."

Instead of bringing Sawyer to his knees, the memory felt like a warm embrace—a reminder of a time he would always cherish. It also triggered the promise he'd made to Vic at the end.

This is me trying, Vic.

"Are you going to tell me where you're taking me?" Levi asked, snapping Sawyer back to the present.

"It's a surprise." Sawyer placed his hand at the small of Levi's back when they walked to his car then opened the passenger door for him.

Levi smiled up at him from his seat. "You're very good at this." Sawyer returned his smile before shutting the door and walking around to the driver's side. "Um, are those for me?" Levi asked, pointing to the bouquet in the back seat. "Or do you always keep fresh flowers in your car?"

Sawyer groaned and briefly rested his head on the steering wheel before turning apologetic eyes toward his date. "See. Horrible at dating. I should've read an article or something. I'm sure so much has changed since the last time I went on a first date. They have apps and stuff now." Sawyer looked over at Levi, whose body shook with laughter he tried to conceal behind his hand. "Jesus. Now I sound like I'm seventy-five years old. You should've seen me in the floral section at the market trying to figure out what kind of flowers you might like or even if you liked them. Some guys would probably get downright pissy if you bought them flowers. I can throw them out the window if you don't like them."

"Sawyer," Levi said, cutting into his rambling diatribe. "I love flowers, I'm not at all insulted, and I appreciate how much effort you put into the date. It means a lot to me. I want you to have a good time too, so maybe you take a deep breath and go with the flow."

"Go with the flow?" he repeated.

Levi nodded. "If we're right for each other, spending time together should feel as natural as breathing."

"Breathing. Yeah, I like that."

Levi giggled. "Good. Keep breathing." Then he sneezed. "Uh Oh." Before Sawyer could ask what he meant, Levi went on to sneeze five more times.

"Are you allergic to flowers?"

Levi sneezed again. "Cats. Allergic to cats."

"Oh."

Levi rolled down the car window to let fresh air into the car. "Bad allergy to cats. I tried taking shots and pills when I fell hard for a guy who owned three cats, but it was no good. There must be dander in here."

"There probably is. I have a cat. His name is Bones."

"Oh," Levi said, sounding dejected. "I bet you're really attached to him."

"As pathetic as it sounds, the cat is my best friend."

Levi released a soft sigh. "It sounds adorably sweet, but it also means I've been friend-zoned once more."

"I'm sorry," Sawyer said, and meant it.

"You're still buying dinner, right?" Levi teased.

"Absolutely."

Once first-date jitters were no longer present, conversation flowed smoothly during the short drive to Grimaldi's with the typical getting-to-know-you chitchat. They discovered they had similar tastes in movies, music, and audiobooks.

"Grimaldi's, huh? I've heard it's great."

"We're about to find out."

They walked into the restaurant and were quickly shown to their table. Sawyer had explicitly requested a quiet corner. Some people liked being seen and wanted to sit in the center of it all. He wasn't one of them. Give him a quiet corner where he could enjoy his food in private.

He couldn't help but think about Caroline and DeShaun when they walked to their table. They had been so happy, planning the rest of their lives together. It hurt to think of their smiling faces in the photographs hanging on the walls. Wayne Miller had ended their dreams when he killed them in cold blood. There would be no more dinner reservations, or a wedding, or babies. The idea that Wayne could get away with it made Sawyer sick to his stomach.

"Are you okay?" Levi asked, penetrating his thoughts.

Sawyer smiled. "Sorry. Work temporarily intruded. It won't happen again."

"It's okay."

They ordered a bottle of pinot noir to share with their meals. Levi went with the traditional spaghetti and meatballs while Sawyer chose chicken tetrazzini. Once the waiter left, awkward silence took over until Levi said, "Tell me something silly about yourself."

Sawyer raised a suspicious brow. "Why do I have to go first? What if I tell you something embarrassing while you tell me something funny?"

Levi laughed and rolled his eyes. "You're such a cop. No leaping before looking. Fine. I'll go first. I wrote a love letter to my teacher in second grade."

Sawyer smiled. "That's pretty common."

"My teacher was a man, so I outed myself at an early age," Levi said, waggling his brows. They laughed together, then Levi gestured for Sawyer to have a turn.

"I don't have anything remotely that cute to share."

"Then share something salacious," Levi teased.

"I don't have anything salacious to share either. I'm a boring person." His brain called him a liar then replayed his morning with Locke in his home gym. That was salacious as hell, but it was also a treasured memory he wouldn't share with anyone. It was even more special since there was no way in hell it would happen again.

"Sawyer," Levi said gently. He snapped his head up and met the man's blue gaze. "Where'd you go just now?"

Sawyer took a drink of ice water to quench his suddenly dry mouth. "I'm right here."

"Tell me something you feel comfortable sharing. Show me pictures of your dream wrecker, I mean Bones."

Sawyer laughed and pulled his phone out of his pocket. "Here he is," he said, opening up the photo album titled: Bones Kitty.

"Wow. He's so beautiful and so big."

"He weighed twenty-four pounds at his last checkup," Sawyer said as proudly as any father would.

"Look at all his fur? I feel the urge to sneeze again just looking at his pictures. I bet you have to brush him a lot."

"Daily, and he's a fucking diva who demands it." Sawyer flipped to the next picture where Bones struck his otter pose showing off his belly. "That's the belly trap."

Levi laughed. "Belly trap?"

"He presents his belly and dares you to resist him. Once someone gives in, and they always do, he either scratches or bites them." Sawyer tilted his head to the side as another memory from the previous day inserted itself on their conversation. "Except for Locke yesterday morning. Bones didn't—"

Levi chuckled and shook his head. "I knew there was a reason Locke showed up at my café yesterday out of the blue. I'd never laid eyes on the man until the day you guys arrived to check out the computers. I sensed the tension between you then but didn't realize it was sexual. Locke even smelled like you. I noticed it right away, but my heart didn't want to believe what my gut was saying. Lots of guys use the same soap and shampoo. I'd mentioned that I hoped to see you and he said you were running late because of him. Or he'd thrown you off your morning routine or something. Look, we're not a couple, so you don't owe me any explanations. I'm just sharing my observations."

Sawyer wasn't a liar or a manipulator. As awkward as the truth was, he felt he owed Levi that much. "Things with Locke are complicated, and I'm not sure what to do about it. Life with my late husband was easy for the most part. Sure, we had problems and fights, but we both knew what we wanted and worked together to achieve it. I never questioned where I stood in his life. Vic never doubted my love for him. It's taken me two years to arrive at the point where I want to date again. I miss being half of a happy couple. I want date nights and cuddling under blankets during a storm. I crave a person who's going to love me no matter what life throws at us. I need a man who is proud to call me his."

"You can't have those things with Locke?" Levi asked softly, sounding more curious than upset.

"No."

Levi shook his head slowly. "I wouldn't write him off just yet. He came to the café to size up his competition."

"Probably, but you'll be happy to know he judged you the winner."

"Get out of here," Levi said. His timing was terrible because the waiter approached with their food. "Not you, sir," Levi quickly corrected. "It was a figure of speech." Once they were alone again, Levi said, "Regardless of Locke's opinion, we both know who has snagged your attention. I can't be mad about it. I'm getting a delicious meal and hopefully a new friend."

"I like you, Levi. I've struggled hard to move past my grief, and I think part of the reason was that all my friends were so closely tied to the life I shared with Vic. I cherish those friendships, but I need more in my life. I would really like to be your friend."

After dinner, Sawyer drove Levi home and walked him to the door. "Let's have lunch soon."

"Sounds great. Drive safe," Levi said then kissed him on the cheek.

Sawyer had every intention of going straight home until he replayed the dinner conversation with Levi again in his head. Locke had gone there to stir up trouble despite what he said. Sawyer had the urge to call him out on it and decided there was no time like the present to confront him. Sawyer drove to Locke's house but didn't stop because there wasn't a single light on inside the house and his black Camaro wasn't in the driveway. He wasn't home. He was free to do anything to anyone who wasn't Sawyer, which only made Locke's behavior with Levi more confusing. Why sabotage things between Sawyer and Levi then later pretend he hoped it would work out between them? Or maybe Levi was exaggerating what had happened or had allowed his insecurities to misinterpret Locke's words and demeanor. Sawyer's head spun with the possibilities.

Fuck it. Sawyer didn't need Locke's kind of crazy in his life. He drove home then drank until he passed out.

CHAPTER 26

MEOW.

Sawyer glanced up from where he sat on the cold tile floor hugging the toilet. "I don't need your judgment right now, Bones."

Meow.

Sawyer would've commented, but dry heaves wracked his body, prohibiting talking for a few more minutes. By the time he slumped to the floor, he couldn't remember what he'd been about to say. Bones gracefully jumped to the tile floor and planted his furry ass far enough away from Sawyer's head that he could read his feline's disdain without having to lift his pounding head. He hadn't woken with a hangover this severe since the morning after Vic's funeral.

"I'm never doing it again, okay?"

Meow.

"At least it's Saturday," Sawyer mumbled. "I can lie around and recover as long as there are no new murders and no breaks in the DeShaun-Wembley case. Is it so wrong for me to want Miller to lie low one more fucking day?" From his bedroom, Sawyer's phone rang. "I hate my life."

Meow.

Sawyer slowly pushed off from the floor to stand on shaky legs.

Gripping his head in both hands like it might somehow stop the jack-hammering, he staggered into his room to retrieve his phone. "No new murders. No new murders. No new murders," he chanted.

The missed call was from his mother. He started to call her back, but she beat him to the punch. It wasn't like her to call back-to-back instead of leaving a message. The pain in Sawyer's brain increased as he turned over every possible bad thing. His brother was in a car accident. His father had a heart attack. One of his nieces or nephews broke a bone. His sister discovered a suspicious lump. It was frightening how many tragedies he could imagine in seconds. And that was on a bad day. *Imagine what you could accomplish if your brain weren't threatening to split in two.*

"Mom," Sawyer croaked. "What's wrong?"

His mother released a frustrated growl. "Here I was worried to death something bad had happened to you, and you're just hungover."

Sawyer didn't risk permanent brain damage or waste energy trying to figure out how she knew. Evangeline O'Neal knew everything. "That *is* the something bad that happened to me."

"I've been calling you for a few hours. I've left several messages. Why didn't you call me back and put me out of my misery, you ungrateful ass? I gave you life, and this is how you repay me?"

"I didn't hear the phone ring until now. I'm sorry."

"I'm coming over there to help you get ready," Evangeline said all businesslike.

"Ready for what?" Better to admit his forgetfulness and ask instead of trying to figure it out himself. Silence accompanied his question. It was loud and very judgmental somehow. "Mom, are you still there?"

"I'm here, and I'm also more concerned now than before you answered. I can't believe you forgot."

"Forgot what?" he repeated. Panic raced through him, making his heart pound as hard as his head. What did he forget? Then the memory slammed into him like the Titanic hitting the iceberg. "Vic's field dedication." It was also their wedding anniversary. His nostrils and eyes stung with impending tears. How could he have forgotten such meaningful events? "Oh God," he groaned into the phone, pain making his words barely audible.

"I'm coming over." Evangeline, the powerful celebrity who had ruled their home like an empire, exited the conversation; Mom, the woman who'd nurtured him through all his illnesses, disappointments, and heartbreaks, entered it. "Be there in twenty."

Sawyer didn't argue because it wouldn't do any good. He needed her and wasn't afraid to admit it. They disconnected without a proper goodbye, but that's what happened when Hurricane Evangeline, as his father referred to her, was on the scene. Some kids had mama bears who wanted to protect their cubs, but he had a mother with enough energy and purpose to match the mighty winds of at least a category two hurricane.

He stumbled back to the bathroom to shower and make himself as presentable as possible, thinking that seeing him would alleviate some of her concern. Then he looked in the mirror and groaned. He hardly recognized the man with bloodshot eyes, snarled dark hair, and sallow skin. "Oh fuck. I need a miracle instead of a shower."

True to her word, his mother arrived in twenty minutes on the dot looking fabulous in a pale pink sundress and high-heeled, braided sandals made with various shades of pink leather. She slid her oversized sunglasses on top of her head, pushing her long, black curls away from her face. Sawyer hated the worry he saw in the dark eyes that looked so much like his. "It's worse than I thought. Step aside."

Sawyer would've laughed at her sharp tone, but he didn't want to jostle anything. He settled for a grin.

"How could you let this happen, Bones?" Evangeline tossed over her shoulder on the way to the kitchen. Bones glared at Sawyer from his princely perch in front of the window. It was a silent fuck you if ever he saw one. Sawyer shrugged but immediately regretted it. "Sit."

Evangeline pointed to the barstool at the island—the same one Locke used two days before—and he dropped down on it.

His mother pulled out several items from her large tote bag, also pink. Sawyer recognized the bottle of Excedrin and knew the rest were oils and supplements but didn't know which ones. "It's not a miracle cure, but it will help." She went to his freezer and pulled out a can of concentrated orange juice and freezer bags with frozen strawberries and bananas stored in them. Next, she grabbed the vanilla Greek yogurt and skim milk from the refrigerator. He was about to receive one of Mom's Medicinal Smoothies. She had one for nearly every occasion, but this was the first time she made him one for a hangover.

She dumped a spoonful of orange concentrate into the Bullet blender, then added the frozen fruit, a healthy scoop of yogurt, a splash of milk, and liquid essential oils and supplements. She aimed a somewhat-apologetic glance at him before turning the blender on. Sawyer covered his ears like a toddler, but the pain was still excruciating. Once it was thoroughly mixed, she checked the consistency. "Needs ice."

The ice dispenser in the refrigerator sounded like boulders were tumbling out of it instead of ice cubes. His mother grinned gleefully when she fired up the blender again. She was finding too much pleasure in his suffering. While pouring the concoction into a tall glass, she said, "Let this be a reminder not to act like a dumb college kid whenever something upsets you."

Sawyer's lips twitched at the corner. "Yes, ma'am."

Evangeline handed him two Excedrin tablets with his smoothie. "Take the pills and chase it down with the smoothie while I make coffee and fix you an omelet." Sawyer started to object to the food, but she quelled him with a fierce look. "Trust me."

Sawyer answered by swallowing the tablets and chasing them with the smoothie. He smacked his lips while trying to determine if he liked the taste or not. The predominant flavor was the fruit, but the texture was a little iffy because of the yogurt. A vitamin-y taste lingered, and slick oil coated his mouth. He continued to sip the drink while Evangeline moved gracefully through his kitchen preparing a southwest omelet and toast.

By the time she plated his food, Sawyer felt a little better. The Excedrin was working on his headache, and whatever was in the smoothie helped ease his nausea. He pinched off a corner of his toast and fed it to Bones. "You could probably bottle that and make a killing," Sawyer said.

"And encourage moronic behavior? How long have you known me, Sawyer?"

"Thirty-four years."

"Which is long enough to know better." Evangeline slid a cup of black coffee to him, and he graciously accepted it without protesting the lack of sugar and sweet creamer. "Tell me everything."

So he did. Like always, she listened without comment or question, allowing him to get everything off his chest.

"This Levi was the guy you were feeling hopeful about when we had lunch on Monday?" *Had it only been five days ago?*

"Yes, but we'll have to settle for friendship. Levi is allergic to cats, and Bones is here to stay."

"Naturally," Evangeline drawled. "Then there's the fact you're falling for your partner."

A protest rose quickly but died just as fast. For one thing, she'd sniff out a lie a million miles away, and what good would it do? "I'm not sure my *feelings* are the kind you build something on. It might just be lust. I don't even fucking know Locke. He's an impenetrable fortress. Every time I think I've worked a brick loose, a new one slides in its place."

"Better than a booby trap, I guess."

"Mom, really?"

"I hate to be corny here, but you're the key to his lock. Get it?" She paused for effect. "Tough crowd tonight," she said when Sawyer didn't respond. "You only have two choices: you be patient and allow time to build trust so he can open up to you, or you kick down the fucking door." Sawyer stared at her in shock. "What? I cuss."

"Rarely."

"This situation calls for emphatic language."

Sawyer took a deep breath then said, "I'm surprised one of your options wasn't for me to move on."

"Sawyer, if that were possible you would've done it already instead of getting drunk. Something bigger than your brain is preventing that from happening, and it extends beyond your weakness for wounded things. His soul is speaking to yours. If it were just physical, you could screw it out of your system. Be honest, was what you shared Thursday morning enough, or did it only make you hungrier?"

Sawyer felt himself blush. He hadn't told his mother they'd been physical, but she had read between the lines when he had recounted the conversation with Levi. "He's closeted at best and in denial at worst." Thinking about Locke's remarks the day before, Sawyer dropped his head forward and groaned. "It has taken me two years to work up the courage to date again, and the guy who captures my attention is the one who might not ever be able to give me what I want."

"Do you want to live the rest of your life without finding out?"

Sawyer thought about it and remembered the way he felt when Locke kissed and touched him. If the connection he felt to Locke were only physical, he wouldn't care so much about the man's secrets. He wouldn't worry about lessening his pain. He wouldn't have drunk himself into a stupor.

"Patience it is then."

"That's my boy."

Relentless.

When Sawyer stepped onto the pitcher's mound on Victor Ruiz Jr Field four hours later, he felt much better. The headache and fatigue had disappeared, and his nausea hadn't returned. His slightly red eyes were the only telltale sign of his wild night. Luckily, he could hide them behind sunglasses on a bright, sunny afternoon.

The announcer had extolled his late husband's virtues as an educator, coach, citizen, husband, and a son over the PA system before Sawyer strode out onto the field wearing a jersey with Vic's baseball number and last name embroidered on the back. Sawyer adjusted the brim of his hat and nodded dramatically as the seven-year-old catcher squatting behind home plate. The boy ran through a few signs Sawyer shook off for show before nodding on the sign for the fastpitch. Sawyer went through the familiar motions of a wind-up then released the ball at half the usual velocity so he didn't accidentally hurt the kid.

The pitch crossed home plate as a perfect strike, landing in the catcher's mitt with a solid snap. The crowd for both teams cheered as Sawyer jogged over to shake the catcher's hand and wish him luck, When the boy turned around to join his teammates, Sawyer saw the name Wilkes stitched on the back of his jersey. It was probably a common enough name, but then he got that tingling sensation. *Fuck.* He tried to ignore his spidey sense that told him Royce Locke was near, but he couldn't help himself.

After hugging Vic's parents and his family, Sawyer gave in and glanced around the ballpark. Locke was easy to spot with his messy hair and bad boy aura softened by the little boy sitting on one leg and Bailey sleeping against his chest. Beside him, Candi clapped and cheered on her son and his teammates as they took the field. Sawyer didn't need Locke to take off his sunglasses to know he was looking at him. Sawyer felt it to his core.

"Is that him?" Evangeline whispered.

"Yep."

"Oh my."

"Yep."

The two families had lunch together to celebrate the new field and catch up. They raised their champagne glasses in a toast to Vic and had an enjoyable meal. No one brought up the fact that it was Vic and Sawyer's anniversary, but Imelda's brown eyes shimmered with bittersweet memories. She hugged him tightly when they said their goodbyes outside the restaurant.

"I love you," Imelda whispered in his ear. Then she thanked his parents for honoring Vic in such a beautiful way. "I know he's smiling down on us right now."

Maybe not all of us, Sawyer thought wryly. His mother smirked, letting him know she'd read his mind. *Get out of my head, woman.*

His sister and brother-in-law invited him over for dinner, and as much as he wanted to spend time with his nieces and nephews, he needed some quiet time. He assured them all he wouldn't be moping and promised his mother he'd spend his Saturday night sober. When his doorbell rang a few hours later, he expected one of his well-meaning family members was checking up on him.

He flung open his door and said, "Not moping. Not dr—" His words skidded to a halt as did his ability to think when he saw Locke standing on his porch.

"Hi." Locke sounded nervous and looked uncertain. "I'm not drunk either. I assume that's what you were going to say."

Sawyer swallowed hard. "What are you doing here?" he asked.

"I just came by to see how you are doing. I figured the field dedication might've been tough. The kids loved you, by the way." That made Sawyer smile because he had enjoyed giving them a pep talk before throwing the first pitch.

"Do you want to come in, or are you satisfied I'm okay now?" He sounded pricklier than he meant and groaned. "Scratch that. Come in and have a beer with me."

Locke eyed him suspiciously. "Are you trying to get me drunk so I'll take advantage of you?"

Sawyer laughed then walked back toward the kitchen, leaving the door open for Locke to leave or follow him. "Idiot," he tossed over his shoulder.

The front door clicked closed, and he heard Locke following him. "That's an improvement over dickhead. I'm glad your date last night put you in a better mood."

Sawyer pulled two bottles of beer from the fridge and handed one to Locke. "My date was a fucking disaster, but you made sure of that, didn't you?"

Locke blinked in surprise. Sawyer wasn't sure if it was due to his bluntness or lack of animosity in his voice. If he wanted something with Locke, he couldn't be pissed that the idiot ruined his chances with Levi. Could he?

"At the risk of causing an argument, how did I ensure your date was a disaster?"

"According to Levi, you showed up at his café smelling like me and insinuating you were the reason I didn't make it in to see him."

Locke shrugged. "What part of that was a lie? It wasn't like I told him you pinned me to the leg curl bench and rode me until we both came. I might've smelled like you, but he smelled your soap on my skin instead of your dry cum."

Sawyer had loved feeling their combined releases on his skin, had loved the way they smelled. His nostrils flared as did the desire to do it all again.

"Oh God," Locke groaned, turning his back on Sawyer while running his fingers through his hair. "I honestly didn't come here to pick up where we left off in your gym."

"Then why did you come here?"

Locke faced him and lowered his hands. "I meant what I said. Today had to be tough, and I wanted to make sure you were feeling okay."

"You don't know the half of it," Sawyer said. "Today is also our wedding anniversary."

"Tell me about him," Locke said. "From the things the announcer said, Vic Ruiz was a great man. I already knew that though because you loved him. Not just anyone is going to win your heart." Sawyer thought he detected a longing tone in Locke's voice, but he chalked it up to wishful thinking. "Tell me about the Vic you knew, and when I'm stronger, I'll tell you about the Marcus I knew."

It was a deal Sawyer couldn't resist. They moved into the living room where Bones waited for them on the back of the sofa. His cat made a real slut of himself purring and preening while Locke repeatedly petted his sleek fur from ears to tail, stopping only to scratch his ears or chin. Watching them interact was soothing, and he opened his mouth and let it all spill out.

"I met Vic not long after I graduated from law school. It was love at first sight. I felt like someone had run me over with a Mack truck. Everything just clicked between us. We moved in together not long after we started dating and built a life together. Marriage was something we never dreamed we could have until the Supreme Court ruling in 2015. We got married at the courthouse the very next week much to our mothers' ire. Suddenly, dreams of a family were also coming true. We had just taken the first legal steps to become parents. We'd researched and discussed using a surrogate or adopting overseas but decided to become foster parents and adopt the kids as our children. A few weeks later, Vic was diagnosed with stage four colon cancer. He had already started planning rooms for our future kids we hadn't met and couldn't wait to coach Little League baseball. When he died three months later, I didn't just lose Vic, I lost the family we were supposed to have. I couldn't function for months. That's when my problems started at the sheriff's department. The old bastard could deal with me being gay as long as I was doing things that garnered good press.

"He thought I was a weak pussy for needing time off to grieve for Vic. When I returned to work, Wheeler made my life hell. He gave me shit tasks and wrote me up for anything and everything he could, trying to get me to quit. I wouldn't let him win. I couldn't. One day, he went too far. He'd made a remark that colon cancer was the least punishment fags deserved." Beside him, Locke sucked in a sharp breath. "It took four deputies to pull me off him. It was the final straw. My father is one of the most respected litigators in the state, and we sued the county. They settled out of court on two provisions: I was to keep quiet about what happened, and Wheeler was to undergo *sensitivity* training. I donated the hush money to the charity my parents established in Vic's name. I kept my end of the bargain, and he did too as far as I know." Sawyer looked at Locke. "I don't know who went to Felix Franklin with the story, but it wasn't me. I kept my word."

Locke gently set Bones on the arm of the couch then slid over until they were pressed together. Looping his arm around his shoulders, Locke pulled Sawyer into an embrace. "I know you kept your word, Golden Boy. I also know you're going to meet another guy someday, and although he probably won't be as awesome as Vic, he's going to love you like crazy. You'll have a houseful of kids together. I'll be their favorite uncle, regardless of how many they have. There will be birthday parties, sleepovers, Little League games, and more chaos than you can imagine. You'll doubt your sanity and tell me all about it while we're chasing down leads. Then I'll remind you how much you wanted a family, and I'll try really hard not to resent the air your husband breathes. No promises though."

The mental images created by Locke's words were beautiful and heart-wrenching. He would be a bystander, a favorite uncle, a partner on the force, and a friend, but he wouldn't be the one building a life with Sawyer. He hardly knew anything about Royce Locke, so it was totally stupid for him to grieve a relationship that would never be, but mourn it he did.

He recalled what his mom said about their souls recognizing each other and his commitment to be patient while Locke figured things out. So, instead of admitting defeat or acting on the attraction they both felt, Sawyer gave him a squeeze then eased out of his arms.

"Do you want me to talk to Levi and assure him I'm not a threat to him? Maybe you guys can give it another go?"

"First, there's no way you could convince him of that. Second, he's allergic to my cat."

"He's gotta go then. Bones comes first." Getting over Royce Locke just became that much harder.

"Are you hungry?" he asked, signaling that deep conversation time was over.

"There are two things I'm always in the mood for, and eating is one of them."

Sawyer chuckled. "Come on, I'll wow you with my burger-grilling skills."

"I love a good burger almost as much as I love—"

"Locke," Sawyer warned.

"Okay."

Grilling burgers and watching baseball with Locke turned out to be a fantastic remedy for the tough day, even if it didn't include touching or kissing or mutually pleasing orgasms.

Patience, Sawyer.

CHAPTER 27

HE'S LATE AGAIN.

Sawyer had lost track of how many times Locke hadn't shown up for work on time during the next two weeks. That alone would be enough to raise a red flag, but he went on high alert once Locke started disappearing after receiving mysterious phone calls, and witnessing Locke and Stein huddled together having private chats in her car behind the precinct. She'd even tracked them down in the field. There was nothing sexual about their demeanor, so either Locke was assisting her with undercover work, or they were both on the take.

Don't be ridiculous.

Locke always had a valid excuse for why he'd been late or had to step away from the job for a few minutes. Candi had needed him, or he had an appointment, or a family matter to handle. Locke had always been referred to as a wild card, but the words "dirty cop" had never been used to describe him. Sawyer needed to believe his behavior was legitimate, but that brought up a different set of concerns.

Sawyer had hoped they would grow closer if he were just patient enough. Locke had sought him out to offer friendship and a broad shoulder to lean on the day of the diamond dedication. He'd seen it as a step toward something special, but he'd had the rug yanked out from under him the following Monday when he'd shown up at work. Locke wasn't as cold and dismissive as he had been the prior week, but he was more distant and aloof than Sawyer expected after the time they'd shared at his house.

He chalked it up to Locke not being a Monday person, but Tuesday hadn't brought an improvement, and neither had Wednesday. Locke had grown more distant with each passing day until they barely spoke unless it had something to do with a case. The other detectives in their unit noticed and looked at Sawyer with pity in their eyes, which had only pissed him off. He desperately needed something to happen to get his mind off his partner.

Sawyer got just that when Rocky Jacobs had texted his personal cell phone Friday morning before he left the house and requested a meeting away from the precinct. Sawyer had a feeling the private investigator had found something significant and hoped it was the break in the case they needed to bring Miller to justice for his crimes. Jacobs wanted to meet at eight at a bookstore slash café called Great Grinds and Book Finds located a few blocks from the precinct. Sawyer agreed to the time and place then forwarded the details to Locke.

"He's late," Rocky said, glancing at his watch for the dozenth time since they sat down. "Should I just tell you what I've found out or—"

"We wait," Sawyer said firmly then took a sip of the salted caramel coffee. It wasn't in the same ballpark as Levi's. Just thinking the man's name caused a twinge in Sawyer's chest. Levi had expressed a desire to be friends with him but hadn't responded to any of his texts or returned his calls since their failed date. Sawyer had figured it was a lost cause and had given up. He just wished he could do the same with Locke. "He'll be here."

Locke arrived a minute later and sat in the chair next to him, reeking of sweat, booze, and something else Sawyer was afraid to name.

"Rough night?" Jacobs asked him.

"Something like that," Locke said with a leer that made Sawyer's

261

stomach clench. "Get to the point of this clandestine meeting so I can get a shower before my shift starts."

"An all-nighter, huh?" Jacobs asked, ignoring Locke's terse command. "She wouldn't even let you use her shower? Tough lady. Your prowess in bed must be highly exaggerated."

"Fuck you." Locke scooted his chair back and started to rise until Sawyer placed his hand over his forearm, stilling him.

It was impossible to deny the energy crackling between them, but Sawyer pushed it aside to focus on the meeting. "What do you have for us?"

"You're not going to like it," Rocky said.

"We seldom do in these situations, Jacobs," Locke said tersely. "Quit dicking around and get to the point."

"Marla Edwards isn't the damsel in distress you believe her to be," Jacob said, pulling no punches. "She's been in contact with Miller."

"How do you know this?" Locke asked in disbelief.

"You're better off not knowing."

Sawyer snorted. "And you just expect us to take your word for it."

"Nah," Jacobs said, pulling a small MP3 player out of his pocket and a set of wireless earbuds. "You need to listen to this." Sawyer took one earbud, and Locke took the other. Once they were in place, Jacobs hit the play button.

"Baby, I know you're mad at me, but please hear me out." The sound of Miller's voice made Sawyer's skin crawl. Beside him, Locke tensed, but Sawyer didn't look at him.

"There's nothing left for us to say, Wayne," Marla said. Her tone wasn't the least bit set or firm, and Wayne sensed his opening.

"I shouldn't have hit you, baby. It was wrong of me, and I promise it will never happen again if you give me another chance."

"You said that the last time and look what happened. I still have bruises on my face, and my ankle is swollen from where I twisted it when you knocked me down." Marla's voice cracked, and she started to cry. "I thought you loved me, but if you did, you wouldn't have hurt me."

"Baby, my emotions were running extremely high. The cops are trying to pin something on me I didn't do. I thought they'd turned you against me too, and I reacted badly. I'm very sorry. I miss you so much, Marla. I can't stop thinking about you. I can't sleep at night, and I can hardly eat. I'm so lonely. My body aches for you, baby, and jerking off while fantasizing about fucking your big titties isn't working for me." Fucking gross, but they were getting to the real reason Wayne was calling Marla. He must not have found a replacement for her on the compound.

Marla released a long sigh. "I miss you too, but what can we do about it? You left me alone here."

"Just hearing your voice is helping me." Wayne lowered his voice a few octaves. "And making my dick hard. Are you wearing that sexy nightie I got you for your birthday?"

"Yes," she replied breathlessly.

Sawyer thought he might be fucked up for life if he was forced to listen to them having phone sex. Beside him, Locke must've known what he felt because he started to chuckle. It was the first sign of humor he'd seen out of his partner in two weeks, so maybe he could sit through the shit show if it meant seeing happiness in Locke's eyes. He risked a glance at Locke then regretted it because he was dying to kiss his smirking lips—consequences be damned. Marla's next words broke the spell.

"Is that why you called me? You just want me to talk dirty in your ear while you beat your meat?"

"Not the only reason," Wayne said shakily then groaned.

"If you want me back, you're going to have to come and get me," Marla said firmly. "Prove you love me and want to be with me. Prove you're sorry."

"Baby, I can't," Wayne whined. It was apparent Marla's demand was killing his mood. "The cops are watching me. Or is that what you want? You want me to go to prison for something I didn't do? They'll paint me a Nazi and a racist then throw me into general population where some guy named Tiny, who happens to be the size of Montana, will decide to make me his bitch. He'll pass me around to all his friends. Is that what you want for me, Marla? You want me to die a broken and battered man on a cold prison floor?"

Marla sobbed. "Stop saying that, baby. Of course I don't want you to get caught and go to prison. I only want to be with you. Surely someone as smart as you can find a way for us to be together."

"I will, baby. I promise. I need a little something from you now. Touch yourself and let me hear it." Marla responded with a long moan that made both men pull the earbuds out of their ears.

"Jacobs, is there anything important after the phone sex?" Sawyer asked.

The PI grinned wryly. "Just Wayne promising to call back with a plan for them to be together."

"I don't want to know how you illegally recorded these conversations, but I do want to know when it occurred," Locke told him.

"Last Wednesday," Jacobs replied. "Marla attended church then came home and committed several sins with Wayne over the phone."

"Have there been more calls since then?"

"No more phone calls, but my three partners and I have been taking turns tailing Marla to see if we can detect any changes in her activities."

"And," Sawyer prodded.

"She's received a floral bouquet every day this week, which is highly unusual according to gossip one of my partners heard when he got his car serviced yesterday. We knew what time Marla took her lunch, so he scheduled his appointment during that time. The lady who covers Marla's lunch breaks isn't her biggest fan."

Locke leaned forward. "I don't suppose your partner happened to get a peek at the card that arrived with the bouquet."

"He didn't need to because the gal he spoke to was so helpful. Marla claimed the flowers were from a new guy. Deidre, being curious and concerned after the last disaster—her words, not ours—checked one of the cards to see who had sent them. She said there were just a few random words typed on the card."

Sawyer's heart sped up. "Did she remember what they were?"

"Not all of them, but she did remember seeing Kentucky."

"She's going to him," Locke said. "He can't come back here, but he can meet her."

Jacobs nodded. "Marla left her mama's house at her normal time this morning, but she didn't go to work. She headed north on the 404."

Locke growled low in his throat. "Son of a bitch. She merged on to US 17 and crossed into South Carolina."

"Did she take luggage?" Sawyer asked.

"She parks in the garage so she could've filled her trunk with personal belongings, and we wouldn't have known. I put in a request for my buddy to ping her phone. We'll be able to track her."

"Unless she tosses the phone for a burner," Locke pointed out.

"We also have eyes on Miller. If he moves, we'll know it," Jacobs said. "We'll nab them when they meet up away from the compound. Miller won't have her drive up to the gate and ring a buzzer. Even if he wanted to, the Brethren wouldn't allow it."

"What the fuck are we supposed to take to our chief, Jacobs? We have a sex tape, flowers with fragmented words we think spell out a rendezvous point, and Marla heading north. Did the flowers come from a local florist where you might be able to sweet-talk them into revealing what the other cards said?"

"Ordered online with a prepaid card. Hear me out," Jacobs said when Sawyer and Locke grumbled. "I'm working on the florist angle. My partner does know which service he used, and I know people who are really good with computers." Meaning a hacker. "I should have the information for you this afternoon as well as the pings to confirm her location."

"You want us to take the information you gained illegally to our chief and hope she'll send us north to intervene?" Sawyer looked at Locke. "Can you imagine that call to the Marshals service?"

Locke didn't look at Sawyer or acknowledge his question; he kept staring at Jacobs. "It better be one hell of a convincing anonymous tip to the hotline this time."

"Keep your personal cell handy," Jacobs told Sawyer before he stood up and left them alone.

Locke rose from his chair and started walking away. Sawyer rose and swiftly followed. "You're willing to put our careers on the line based on what Jacobs has given us?"

Locke stopped suddenly and pivoted to face Sawyer. Unprepared for it, Sawyer nearly stumbled into him. He caught a whiff of cheap perfume and realized it was the annoying scent he'd detected in the café.

"I trust my gut, and it tells me Marla has had a change of heart and wants to be with her man. This might be our best chance of catching him. So, yeah, I want more concrete evidence to show the chief before we go get him."

"We?" Sawyer asked. "You think she's going to send us to Kentucky?"

"She might not let us join the task force that apprehends him, but if the Marshals can't bring him back to Georgia for any reason, she'll send us to go get him. I wouldn't make any big plans this weekend." Locke turned around and strode off without another word.

The hurt, confusion, and disappointment that had been simmering for two weeks started to boil over and become full-blown rage. By the time he reached the precinct, he was spoiling for a fight. Locke wasn't at his desk, but he knew where to find him.

The locker room was empty because the shift change was about to occur, and Locke was the only one dragging his ass. Locke's motorcycle helmet and a backpack sat on the bench in front of his locker. Sawyer didn't find his partner in the open showering area but heard water running in one of the private stalls. Locke had chosen the one farthest away from anyone who entered the area. Sawyer stood on the other side of the curtain, feeling like the worst kind of pervert, but he fucking needed answers. He was done waiting.

"Glad you found me, Key. You can wash my back. Give me a minute though to finish up. Unless you want to watch like you did the night I stayed at your house. I left the door open on purpose to rile you up," Locke said snidely, making Sawyer see red. He yanked the curtain hard to make the metal shower curtain rings screech across the bar. He took one look at Locke, and his anger died.

He stood beneath the spray with his head hung forward in a pose resembling shame. Locke's posture was so shockingly different from his gloating tone that it took Sawyer a moment to notice the bruises marring his partner's perfect body. Some contusions were older and yellowish green in color while others were new and mottled red or violet blue against his skin. Locke slowly lifted his head and met Sawyer's gaze, and utter devastation stared back at him. *Wounded.*

He temporarily forgot the revelation Locke had dropped at his feet, hoping to push him away, and focused on the tears streaming down his partner's face. Sawyer ached to step beneath the spray— consequences be damned—and take Locke in his arms to console him over... What? Locke had shut him out so completely he had no clue what was going on, but for something to cut him this deep, it had to involve Marcus.

"Enough is enough," Sawyer said firmly. "You've been distant, cold, and downright hateful to me for nearly two weeks. You show up late and disappear whenever it pleases you. Today you reek of sweat and cheap perfume and are covered in bruises. You're going to tell me what's going on, Locke."

Locke scrubbed the tears from his face. "I just need some time to process things."

"Time's up, Royce."

Locke closed his eyes and shivered like he was freezing, even though hot water sent steam billowing between them. "Not here, okay?"

"You have twenty-five minutes to wash the stench off and pull yourself together. Then we're going to run down leads which is code for getting this bullshit out in the open."

Locke's lips quirked on one end. "You're kind of hot when you're bossy."

You should see me in bed, Sawyer thought. "I'm fucking hot all the time, and you know it. Tick tock. Twenty-four minutes now. I will drag you out by your—"

"Okay," Locke said, raising his hands palms up. "Save the kinky shit for when we're alone."

Twenty-one minutes later, they pulled out of the station with Sawyer behind the wheel. "Tell me everything."

"Where are we going?"

"We really are chasing down a lead."

"Where? Who?" Locke asked. Sawyer could tell he was desperate to avoid the conversation, but Sawyer wasn't budging.

"You'll find out when we get there. Talk, Royce."

Locke heaved a heavy sigh. "Do you remember the call I got from Candi that prompted me to show up drunk at your door?"

"How could I forget?"

"Do you also remember Candi stopping by the bullpen to say hello that same morning?"

Sawyer nodded. "She said she was on her way to see someone in human resources because they hadn't paid out any of Marcus's benefits."

"Yeah," Locke said tersely. "The human resources rep was very vague with her and wouldn't give any information. When Candi called me that evening, it was because IA had just shown up at her door with a search warrant."

"Internal affairs? Why? They thought Marcus was dirty?"

"I drove straight over there, of course, but they wouldn't tell me anything. The assholes had uniformed officers bar me from entering the house or even speaking to Candi while they interviewed her."

"Because they think you're dirty too?"

"That's what I thought, but Officer Dykstra told me they'd already cleared me," Locke said. "I asked what they thought Marcus had done, but they refused to share the smallest detail with me."

"Did they take anything from his home?"

"Their computers and a few boxes of paperwork that Candi said were their personal finances and tax returns. If they find out he was dirty, they'll find a way not to pay out his benefits to her."

"She'll get an attorney and fight it."

"With what money?" Locke asked. "She can barely afford to cover the bills on her own. Marcus handled the finances, and she had no idea they'd racked up so much credit card debt."

"If they're broke, then he probably wasn't on the take. It's usually the other way around and cops have unexplained wealth." Sawyer glanced over at Locke. "I understand why you were so upset that night, but what's happened since then to justify your behavior lately?" Sawyer stiffened when he realized the answer. "You've been doing some digging on your own. That's why you and Stein were acting so secretive."

"You really don't like her, do you?"

Sawyer shrugged. "I like her just fine, but that doesn't change the facts. I saw you guys sitting in her car in the parking lot a few times, plus she showed up at some of our crime scenes unexpectedly. I'm guessing those mysterious calls were from her too."

"Jealous?"

"It didn't feel sexual. I've been around Stein enough to know she doesn't reek of cheap perfume."

"I'll be sure to pass along your high praise," Locke said drolly.

"Tell me the truth, Royce. Is Stein using her undercover connections to help you find out if Marcus was dirty?"

"Yes."

"And?"

Locke blew out a shaky breath, and Sawyer's heart fell. Locke had found something out—recently if the bruises and tears in the shower were any indications. "I don't know if Marcus was dirty yet, but I did discover something that blew my world apart."

What could be worse than finding out he was a dirty cop? Then the truth slammed into Sawyer with the force of a sledgehammer. "Marcus was having an affair."

"I knew he and Candi were having marital problems. They'd been fighting a lot, especially after Candi got pregnant with Bailey. She wanted more kids, but Marcus didn't, and he'd accused her of getting pregnant on purpose. Candi swore she hadn't, but I don't think he believed her. She had been convinced Marcus would come around once Bailey was born, but it wasn't the miracle she thought it would be. It drove a bigger wedge between them, but Candi was determined to make their marriage work." Locke growled and punched the dashboard nearly hard enough to crack it. "He swore up and down he still loved Candi and was committed to his marriage. He lied to me, Sawyer. Fucking lied right to my face."

"How do you know for sure?"

"I worked the leads Holly found for me and tracked her down. She's a stripper at The Alley Cat, which is a suspected front for seedier activities. Let's just say the owner didn't like me showing up there last night asking questions. He emphasized with every blow he'd landed just how angry he was that I'd made Crystal cry so hard she couldn't perform for the rest of the night. I tried to point out I'd paid good money for a few lap dances while asking my questions, but he said it was a drop in the bucket compared to what she usually brought in nightly."

"You'd think a popular girl like that would wear nicer perfume," Sawyer managed to say like it was no big deal, even though he wanted his turn at punching the dashboard.

"Now all I have to show for my trouble is five hundred fewer dollars in my wallet, a busted-up body, and a bruised heart after finding out Marcus isn't the man I thought he was."

"How'd the owner get the drop on you? Catch you by surprise?"

Sawyer asked, recalling there were no defensive bruises or cuts on Locke's hands.

"You could say that," his partner said sheepishly. "I should've known better when Crystal brought out the handcuffs during part of her lap dance. I thought she was just emphasizing the 'no hands' rules. I was distracted."

Sawyer snorted. "I bet."

"Not for the reason you're thinking." Locke paused and added, "Well, partially for that reason, but I was thrown more by hearing Marcus lived a double life. They'd dated for three fucking years, Sawyer. Three years. I never knew it. No one who knew Marcus would ever suspect he was unfaithful to Candi. He was the epitome of a perfect husband and father."

"And you're wondering what other secrets Marcus kept or what else you or Candi didn't see," Sawyer said.

"Exactly. I want to rage and make accusations about IA harassing Candi, but I can't. While I'm not their biggest fan, I've never known them to be wrong when they've suspected a cop is shady. Dykstra is an arrogant asshole, but he's a straight shooter. He didn't have to tell me I'd been investigated and cleared."

"True, or he might've told you that because he wants you to relax so he can catch you in the act."

"There's no act to catch me in."

"What about me? Why'd you push me away?" He thought he knew but needed to hear Locke say it. Sawyer wished he could be looking in his eyes when he answered.

"I knew Marcus since we were little kids, Sawyer. The part I neglected to include in my big spiel on the day we met was that Marcus was my first crush and case of unrequited love. I eventually got over it, and he became my best friend and the person I trusted most in the world. He loved me as much as he was capable of, and it was enough for me because he wasn't supposed to be mine. Not like that, anyway."

"You didn't have to tell me that, Royce. I heard the truth in your voice."

Locke released a deep breath, and it sounded a lot like relief. "I haven't been able to stop thinking about the weekend he died. I've asked myself a thousand times how I couldn't see he was despondent or calling out for help in some way. How could I know him but not see any of these things? I didn't know about the affair, or potential shady shit on the force, and I didn't know he thought Candi, the kids, his family, and I would be better off without him. If I was so blind to him, how could I trust my judgment when it came to someone I'd only known for a few days? As much as I wanted to hate your existence, I couldn't." *His soul is speaking to yours.* "Trust is something I'm struggling to come by right now."

Sawyer longed to reach over and squeeze his hand or pat his leg to reassure him. "You seemed okay at my house on Saturday."

"I still felt like it was just a big misunderstanding then. It was only a few days after the raid, and I was convinced Stein would do some digging and clear Marcus's name."

"That wasn't what happened?" Sawyer asked gently.

"Stein called me after I left your place. She couldn't definitively say Marcus was or wasn't dirty, but there were rumors. I started pulling strings and following leads that weekend which eventually led me to Crystal and The Alley Cat last night."

This was a truth Sawyer could work with. He could be patient while Locke realized he was trustworthy. *Or he could prove it.* "I'll help you uncover the truth."

"I can't ask—"

Sawyer banged his fist on the steering wheel. "You didn't. I'm telling you."

"So bossy."

"You should see me in bed."

Locke moaned and shifted in his seat, which triggered Sawyer to do the same. Suddenly, the air-conditioning in the car seemed to be insufficient to battle the rising temperatures inside the Charger.

"What about the older bruises?" Sawyer asked, steering their conversation back on course. "Some of them are a week old or longer."

Locke shrugged. "Family dinner that got out of hand last weekend. My punk-ass, kid brother said some shit I didn't like, so we took it out in the yard."

Sawyer laughed for the first time that morning. "Is that how your family always handles disagreements?"

"Pretty much."

"Did you teach his punk ass a lesson?"

Locke chuckled. "Fuck, yes." Then he looked at the house they'd stopped in front of. "Who lives here?"

"Marla's mother. We're going to ring the doorbell and tell her that her daughter didn't show up for work."

"We're going to tattle on Marla to her mommy?" Locke asked incredulously.

"Yes. Then we're going to ask her to show us to Marla's room so she can help us determine if it looks like Marla left on a long trip."

"We know that she has," Locke said.

"We *think* she has based on bits and pieces that Jacobs has collected illegally. We need Marla's mom to report that her daughter is going to meet Wayne so we can start using the legal channels to track them down too. Her connection to Wayne will waive the standard waiting period for a missing person. This way, the 'anonymous tip' looks more credible."

Locke grinned at him, and for a moment, awe replaced the tension and hurt in his expression. "You're an evil genius."

Sawyer killed the engine and winked. "You haven't seen anything yet."

CHAPTER 28

SAWYER'S PLAN WORKED. UPON LEARNING MARLA HADN'T SHOWN UP to work, Rachel Edwards did all the things a worried mother would do. She invited them in to search her room for clues. Marla's bedroom looked unchanged from high school. There were so many posters of '90s heartthrobs hanging on the wall you couldn't even tell what the wall color was beneath them, although Sawyer suspected a shade of pink to go with the bedding and the carpet. Everywhere they looked, Mark-Paul Gosselaar, Mario Lopez, Jason Priestley, Luke Perry, and several boy bands stared at them. It was the creepiest fucking feeling. Then it occurred to Sawyer that Marla was older than he realized, or she'd gone boy crazy when she was a preteen.

"There are a lot of trophies in here," Locke commented, looking at the overstuffed shelves lining three of the walls.

"Beauty pageants, dance competitions, and baton-twirling championships. My Marla was really something." *Was.* Rachel spoke about her daughter in the past tense, but Marla wasn't dead. Maybe the dreams she had for her daughter were though.

It didn't take them long to locate proof Marla hadn't just skipped work to go shopping at the mall. Her closet and drawers were mostly empty, and the bathroom was devoid of makeup, hair care products, and grooming tools. Rachel noted that her luggage was also missing. The woman's panic increased when she found proof Marla's departure wasn't short term. Written on pink paper, folded and left on a fuzzy pillow for Rachel to find was a letter from Marla. She dropped to the bed and unfolded the paper then sobbed as she read the words her daughter wrote.

"She left to meet him," Rachel said brokenly. "This is all my fault," Rachel said. "I stayed too long in an abusive marriage to her father, and now my daughter thinks it's perfectly acceptable for a man to hit a woman."

Locke walked over and squatted down, putting himself on eye level with Rachel. "Hey, but you did leave the abusive relationship, and that's an important lesson too," he said kindly. "That's a lot better than some parents do for their kids. You're strong and so is Marla. Maybe she just doesn't realize it yet."

It wasn't the first time Locke had said things that made Sawyer realize he was familiar with domestic abuse, and suddenly the yellow-green bruises started taking on a deeper meaning than just a brotherly quarrel that got out of hand. The more Sawyer learned about Locke, the harder it became to ignore all the ways the man tugged his heartstrings.

Locke stepped over to Sawyer so they could read it together. It was short and to the point.

Mama,

I know you don't understand, but I had to go. I love Wayne, and I know he loves me. He promised he'd change. I believe him this time. He didn't hurt those people, Mama. I can't tell you where I'm going, and I don't know when I can call you. I just want you to know you've been the best mama a girl could ever want. I love you so much. I hope to talk to you soon.

Love Always,
Your Baby Girl

Rachel looked up at Sawyer and Locke with tears streaming down her face. "I want my daughter back," she said fiercely. "Can you help me?"

"We'll do everything we can," Locke assured her.

Back at the station, they took Rachel Edwards and the pink note straight to Chief Rigby's office. She was the one holding all the cards, and they knew it would be more powerful for the chief to hear a scared mother's plea than Sawyer and Locke reciting what little they knew thus far.

Just as Sawyer predicted, Chief Rigby was motivated to move due to Marla's relationship to their prime suspect. She listened to what her detectives and Mrs. Edwards had to say then assured her she would get on the phone immediately and start making calls. "I will do my absolute best to get Marla back here, but she's a grown woman who's free to make her own decisions, even if we don't agree with them. I won't make promises I can't keep. I will present this as a grave situation since Marla's life could be in danger, but this will require decisions made at the federal level since she's crossed the state line."

"I understand, and that's all I can ask of you, Chief," Rachel said tearfully.

When the meeting was over, Sawyer and Locke rose to leave Rigby's office with Mrs. Edwards. "A word please, Detective Key," Chief said before they reached the door. Locke smirked at him then kept walking while Sawyer returned to the chair he'd just vacated.

"Yes, ma'am?"

"Remind me again the sequence of events leading up to this meeting in my office. Granted, I don't know what time Marla was due to arrive at work, but this feels fast to me. I'm willing to concede that her coworkers' concern would be elevated because of her relationship with Wayne, but I'm suspicious."

"How so?" Sawyer asked instead of repeating the bullshit timeline.

"I saw Rocky Jacobs in my precinct a few weeks ago, and rumor has it the Wembley family hired him to locate Wayne Miller. Is there anything you'd like to add to the stories Detective Locke and you have spoon-fed to me thus far?" she asked with a quirked brow, calling him out on their bullshit.

Like to add? "Not at this time, ma'am."

"When can I expect the next *anonymous tip* to come through the hotline?"

Busted. "I would assume when someone has valuable information that will help us capture Wayne Miller."

A slight and very brief twitch on the left side of her mouth was the only sign of emotion. "I will go to bat for the officers who serve under me, but don't make the mistake of thinking I'm stupid, and do not leave me hanging with my ass in the wind. Am I clear?"

"Crystal clear, ma'am."

"Now get out there and find the information our *tipster* needs to expedite the federal government's help." Sawyer rose from his chair. "But first," she said, reaching into her desk and pulling out a container. "Locke has been exceptionally asshole-ish the past few weeks. Have a bear claw on behalf of myself and the missus."

"Don't mind if I do," Sawyer said, accepting the pastry with a huge smile.

He had time to make a fresh cup of coffee and eat half the pastry before Locke returned to the bullpen. He jerked to a stop when he saw what Sawyer held in his hand. For his part, Sawyer made a show of licking his lips and enjoyed the heated look in his partner's eyes when Locke couldn't stop staring at his mouth.

"A reward for a job well done?" Locke asked.

"Seems that way," Sawyer said casually. "Oh, hey, do you want me to break off a piece for you?" He knew damned well Locke wouldn't accept his offer. He wanted one freely given to him by the chief.

"You can shove your bear claw—"

Sawyer gasped dramatically. "Is that any way to speak to your partner?"

"What did Rigby want?" Locke asked. Sawyer repeated the conversation for him. "She knows you're full of bullshit and she still gave you a bear claw. She's doing it on purpose, isn't she?"

"I can neither confirm nor deny."

The anonymous tip came a few hours later, prompting Rigby to make the necessary calls with Locke and Key present. The information was passed along the various chains of command until they reached SAC Kyler Matthews in the Louisville FBI office. By this time, Marla was likely halfway or more to her rendezvous point. They figured Wayne was a creature of habit and would probably want to meet Marla at the same location where he'd met Bart Travers.

"I have an agent who's infiltrated the Brethren. They got word to me last week that there's a hit out on a woman who might have information on one of their members," SAC Matthews said. "They must've been talking about Marla Edwards. My guy told me he's noticed a heightened sense of energy around the place, but he hasn't checked back in to report that he's overheard specific plans. We need to put a task force in place to intercept her before she meets Miller. Ideally, we take her into protective custody and put an undercover agent in her place to meet Wayne."

Chills ran up Sawyer's spine. Finding Marla's exact location became paramount. "We can locate her," Sawyer blurted without thinking it through. Beside him, Locke remained calm and showed no outward signs of annoyance or disbelief.

"How?" Rigby and Matthews demanded to know.

"The PI placed a tracking device on her car," Locke said, saving Sawyer from either lying or giving away the full truth. The FBI and Chief Rigby would swallow it slightly easier than the truth that a private company was assisting them in violating numerous privacy laws.

Rigby looked pissed but didn't comment while Matthews blew out a harsh breath. Chief cleared her throat and said, "Not to mention that we've had anonymous tips coming into our hotline that have been eerily accurate thus far."

Matthews chuckled. "God bless those tipsters. I'm going to get in touch with the local US Marshals office and come up with a game plan."

Locke rubbed his hands together and said, "We can hop a plane and be there—"

"No," Rigby and Matthews both said.

"This is a federal matter, Detectives," Matthews said firmly. "We will capture Miller and deliver him to you." Sawyer didn't like the man's smug tone, but there was nothing they could do about it.

Rigby disconnected the call then stared at them. "I stuck my neck out there for you."

"You did your job, Chief," Locke countered. "You were given actionable intelligence, and you moved on it. Now, let us do our jobs."

"Watch your tone of voice, Detective Locke. I don't think you want to hear my opinions about your *actionable intelligence* right now. You've always been a bit of a loose cannon, and I've allowed it as much as I could. I'm drawing the line this time. You are going to do your job by hitting the streets and investigating open homicide cases while the FBI and Marshals apprehend Wayne Miller. You can be pissed at me all you want, but I've made my decision, and it's final."

Locke stood up quickly. "Yes, ma'am." His tone was sharper than was respectful, but Rigby let it go.

"Now what?" Locke asked when they returned to their desks.

"We do our job like Rigby said."

"God damn Golden Boy," Locke grumbled. "No wonder she gives you the bear claws."

"She's not wrong, Locke. We've done everything within our power to see that Miller is brought to justice. Stop pouting. I'll call my pal Felix at the paper and make sure they write up a nice article about you." He'd do no such thing, because Felix was no friend of his.

"I'm not pouting," Locke denied, but he'd crossed his arms over his chest and looked like he was seconds away from stomping his feet.

"Come on," Sawyer said, crooking two fingers at him. "Let's go run down leads."

Locke quirked a brow, remembering their conversation from the morning. "Is that code for something else this time?" There was no mistaking the innuendo in his thickened voice.

"Not when you're only looking for a distraction to keep you from pouting," Sawyer said, walking away from their desks.

"I don't pout, Key."

But he was still pouting several hours later when they were hanging out at Sawyer's house. They'd learned from the ping tracker that Marla got held up in a large, nasty storm front that was moving through Kentucky and Tennessee and heading their way. She'd been forced to pull over at a truck stop ninety minutes south of Byrdstown. The task force had worked with local law enforcement to take her into custody. Once the weather passed, the undercover agent would drive the rest of the distance to the rendezvous point.

Since they were at a standstill waiting for updates, they'd decided to grill steaks and take a look at the notes Locke had made about Marcus's supposed dirty activities. The same storm that had created havoc for Marla showed up just as they were about to put the steaks on. Luckily, Sawyer had a vented indoor grill that made an excellent backup plan.

Sawyer grilled the steaks while Locke baked potatoes in the microwave and found the container with a leafy green salad Sawyer had tossed together earlier in the week. Sawyer had offered him a beer when they first arrived, but Locke declined one then and refilled his glass of sweet tea when dinner was finished. Was he worried that Sawyer thought he was an alcoholic?

Locke speared a piece of steak with his fork and chewed it slowly while looking a million miles away.

"You're still pouting," Sawyer whispered, earning a glare.

"This is my thinking face. You've already seen my orgasm face, so it's time you start seeing the others."

God, Sawyer wanted to see the orgasm face again so fucking badly. "What has you looking so pensive? Outraged that we have to wait for Miller updates while sitting around here with our thumbs up our asses, or are you thinking about Marcus?"

"Both," Locke admitted. "One angers me a lot more than the other."

Sawyer knew without being told that Marcus weighed heaviest on his mind. Sure, not being there to hear the handcuffs click around Miller's wrists sucked, but it was par for the course. They were outranked and outgunned. Marcus, though, was a totally different story.

"Well, we might as well make good use of our time while we wait for an update."

"Now you're talking."

Sawyer had detected heightened tension radiating off Locke. Some of it had to do with job stress, but a lot of it felt sexual to him. "I'm not sure we're there yet, Royce," Sawyer said, meeting Locke's gaze. He wanted Locke to see how much he wanted him, but he didn't want to be just another fuck-n-go to him. He also didn't want to be his distraction.

When Locke didn't comment, Sawyer returned his attention to his notes about Marcus. The storm had rolled in so fast Locke's pages were nearly ruined, so Sawyer retrieved his laptop from his office and started entering the details into a document he'd titled Thunder and Lightning. It was a fitting description because streaks of lightning arced through the dark clouds while thunder rumbled loud and long, vibrating the windows. Howling winds and heavy rain beat against the house, matching the tempo of Sawyer's racing pulse when Locke moved to stand behind him and leaned over the back of his chair. He was close enough that Locke's breath ghosted over his neck.

"You don't have a lot to go on," Sawyer said, studying the timeline

Locke made. "But not from lack of effort. All these details came from Stein's CIs?"

"The ones who were willing to talk to me. I still have a few more to talk to."

"*We* still have a few more to talk to. Some of my old CIs helped us close some of your cases these past few weeks. Maybe they know something about Marcus too."

Locke placed his big, warm hand on the back of Sawyer's neck and gently squeezed. "*We.*" The admission was a huge victory. "I think talking to your CIs is a good idea." Locke leaned closer and inhaled deeply. "Damn, you smell so good. And did you know you have an adorable freckle on the back of your neck? It's right here." Locke applied more pressure with his thumb, and Sawyer had to bite his lip to keep from moaning. "It gives a guy ideas."

"Yeah?" Sawyer asked hoarsely.

"Uh-huh." Locke removed his hand and pressed a brief kiss at the spot where his thumb used to be. Giving up the pretense of working, Sawyer dropped his arms to his lap and leaned into Locke's warm mouth. Locke's chuckle vibrated his flesh, sending electrical currents straight to his balls. Locke doubled down by sliding his hands around to Sawyer's chest, cupping his pecs and pinning him against the chair. Locke swirled his tongue over the freckle, making it nearly impossible to think or resist his pull. He had to try though.

"What's going on here?" Sawyer managed to ask without moaning.

Shifting his arms until he was hugging Sawyer, Locke propped his chin on his shoulder. "This is me no longer fighting the things I want to do with you."

Sawyer closed his eyes and leaned into his embrace. Locke nuzzled his lips against his neck. "After you've done all the things you want to do to me—"

"*With you,*" Locke said, interrupting him. "To you sounds pretty awesome also."

"Then what happens?"

"I don't smoke anymore so a cigarette is out. I was kind of hoping you wouldn't kick me out of your bed right away. I like the way you feel in my arms."

"And tomorrow?"

"We sleep in, and I make us breakfast."

Sawyer released a shaky breath. "I want you, Royce. I can't stop thinking about what it would be like to feel you inside me, but I can't handle 'no strings' with you. I don't want you looking at me like I'm a stranger on Monday. I don't want a sappy declaration from you; I just need to know you're not going to shut me out again."

"You make strings look damn good, Sawyer. Teach me to be the kind of guy who deserves you. Are you patient enough to stand beside me when my fight-or-flight instincts kick in? It's all I know, and miracles won't happen overnight. I never again want to see disappointment in your eyes and know that I put it there. I've been an insensitive dick to you many times since we met, but I'm not toying with you. I want this."

Sawyer leaned forward, breaking the embrace, then stood up. Locke straightened to his full height and pulled Sawyer into his arms when he turned to face him. Pressing his forehead to Locke's, Sawyer whispered, "You should know by now I'm relentless when it comes to pursuing the things I want. Right now, there's nothing in the world I want more than you."

Their mouths met and fused in a hungry kiss of teeth and tongues. Hands roamed over and under clothes and tangled in one another's hair as Sawyer led them to his bedroom. They shed any hesitation or fears as they bared each other's skin with confident, sure movements propelled by lust and the driving need to be with each other.

The raging storm matched the need thundering in his blood when Locke pinned him to the mattress and devoured his mouth. Sawyer spread his thighs, bringing him closer, aligning their bodies so their cocks were pressed together like they had been the first time.

Sawyer ripped his mouth away from Locke's, panting heavily. "As much as I loved our first orgasm, I need to come with your dick inside me this time."

"Really?" Locke rocked his hips forward, making Sawyer's eyes roll up in his head.

"It's all I've been able to think about since we met. You pinning me to the bed and filling me with your cock or bending me over and fucking me hard."

Locke's pupils expanded, and his nostrils flared. "But I've never… What if I let you down?" His vulnerability touched a place deep inside Sawyer's soul, where he tucked it away to cherish later—maybe always.

"Not possible. I'll guide you. Remember when I told you I was bossy in bed? I wasn't joking." Sawyer pointed to the drawer. "Condoms and lube."

"Don't you gay guys like foreplay?"

Sawyer snorted. "Of course, we do. I feel like the past three weeks have been endless foreplay between us. I'm good and edged. Now put me out of my fucking misery."

Locke chuckled and licked a path up Sawyer's neck then bit his ear. "I think our idea of foreplay is vastly different. No cock sucking or ass fingering, huh? I only need to throw insults or glare to rev you up."

"I've imagined sucking your dick more times than I can count, but I want to do it when I'm not on the verge of coming already. Drawer. Condoms. Lube. Now."

"Then you'll show me your oral skills?"

"Yes," Sawyer replied, but this time he sounded more desperate than demanding.

Locke lifted off Sawyer then leaned over to open the drawer. "What do we have here?"

"Oh fuck," Sawyer groaned, realizing what Locke had discovered.

Locke lifted the flesh-like dildo for closer inspection. "Fuck, indeed. I'm afraid I might not live up to your expectations." The smug smirk on his face said differently.

"I've seen your dick, Royce. It's perfect. Get back over here and fuck me with it."

"I'm sensing high intensity from you. If only I could figure out what you want from me."

Sawyer growled and fisted his cock. "Fuck me, or I fuck myself on that dildo while you watch. What's it going to be?" The dildo hit the drawer with a solid thunk, and Locke retrieved the condom and lube before shutting it. Sawyer rolled Locke to his back and straddled his hips.

Locke gripped Sawyer's hips then rocked up into him. Sawyer pulled Locke's right hand off his hip then drizzled lube over his first two fingers. "Slide your hand between my legs and smear the lube around my hole. Tease me really good."

Locke's hand brushed his aching balls and Sawyer moaned. "Like this?" He circled Sawyer's crinkled pucker, making him tremble.

"Hell yes," Sawyer said, staring into Locke's eyes. "Slide your middle finger inside me. Crook it up and peg my prostate."

"How will I know when I've found it?"

Sawyer could've given him a human biology lesson and describe the shape and feel of it, or he could've pushed Locke past any lingering trepidation to feel his way. "You'll know by the way I moan and fuck myself on your finger."

"You lubed two fingers."

"Once I start begging like a needy whore, you slip me a second finger and go to town on my prostate. You keep working in and out of me until my hole is relaxed and ready for your dick."

Locke shucked his wildcard persona and followed Sawyer's rules, stretching and preparing him until he was a shaking, begging mess on the verge of coming all over Locke's abdomen.

"Ready." Sawyer grabbed the condom, ripped it open, then slid it down Locke's dick. Instead of aligning his dick to his hole and sinking on him, Sawyer rolled to his back, catching Locke temporarily off guard. "This is the part where you pin me to the mattress and fuck me."

Locke moved between his legs, but instead of immediately pushing his dick inside Sawyer, he stared down at him. Knowing what a big moment this was for him, Sawyer slid his hands inside Locke's hair and pulled him down for a hot, wet kiss that told him more than mere words could convey. Yes, Sawyer was sure he wanted Locke. No, he wouldn't regret it.

Letting his instincts take over, Locke eased into Sawyer. He paused once his cock head breached the first ring of muscles, allowing him to adjust. Sawyer whimpered into his mouth, urging him deeper, but Locke took his time. Sawyer held him tightly against his body, feeling every tremor that racked Locke's body, tasting every groan of pleasure escaping his mouth as he learned how right it felt for them to be together.

Once Locke was fully buried inside him, he broke their kiss to stare into Sawyer's eyes. Brushing damp strands of hair off his forehead, Locke whispered, "It's about fucking time." Then he started to move—slowly at first then faster when delaying their pleasure was no longer possible. Grunts, jagged breaths, and the sounds of slick bodies slapping together filled Sawyer's room.

Sawyer reached between their bodies and began pumping his cock in rhythm with Locke's thrusts. It only took a few strokes before he climaxed so hard his vision dimmed. Locke followed right behind him—roaring, rutting in and out of him, and filling the condom.

Collapsing on top of Sawyer, Locke buried his head in the curve where Sawyer's neck and shoulder met. "Was I okay?" Locke asked, sounding rough and gravelly.

Sawyer tucked this precious moment away for safekeeping too. "You were perfect."

They lay kissing and touching until separation could no longer be delayed. Showering together was so much better than using different bathrooms. Sawyer fulfilled his fantasies by touching Locke in all the ways he'd imagined, and Locke seemed fascinated to discover all the erogenous parts on Sawyer's body. When the water started to get cold, they turned off the faucet, dried, then returned to the bed where Sawyer demonstrated his oral skills on Locke then allowed him to return the favor. Locke was a quick study who left Sawyer boneless, sated, and wondering how much longer it would be before his skills surpasses his teacher's.

The skies had calmed by the time they slid between the sheets. Sawyer lay on his back looking at the ceiling and listening to the whir of the ceiling fan and Locke's even breathing. Locke's head felt perfect on his shoulder, and he liked the heat of his palm resting possessively on his lower abdomen.

"Bet your dildosaurus in the drawer can't do this," Locke said sleepily, nestling closer still.

Laughing, Sawyer said, "Not even close." He lazily ran his hand up and down Locke's back, fingers trailing along the ridges of his spine. "Are you fighting the urge to run?"

"Not even close," Locke mimicked. "I was thinking it feels more like..." His words halted like maybe he was trying to pick the right words or phrases.

"Like it's about fucking time."

"Yeah, that."

Locke fell asleep soon after their cute exchange, but Sawyer continued to listen to the whirring fan and Locke's breathing. Knowing it was too early to fall for someone didn't prevent it from happening. It was scary as hell too.

Breathe in. Hold. Release.

"Sawyer. Wake up." Locke's sleep-roughened voice was sexier than he'd ever imagined. Sawyer burrowed deeper into the warm nest they'd made, loving the smell of the man on his sheets. "Got him."

Sawyer reached for Locke's hand and placed it over his cock. "Now you do."

Locke chuckled. "Miller. The Marshals and FBI nabbed him an hour ago." Sawyer jackknifed into a sitting position, nearly cracking his forehead on Locke's chin. Locke had left the bathroom door ajar to softly illuminate the bedroom. "Easy there, killer. I've stayed pretty for so long because I have one rule when it comes to fighting: leave my face alone."

"They got him? Really?"

"Yeah, I got up to use the restroom and decided to check my phone for updates. Rigby left a message."

"Just on your phone?" Sawyer asked.

Locke tossed Sawyer's cell phone on the bed. "You have missed calls and a voicemail message too. I'm curious if yours is the same."

Sawyer retrieved the message and played it on speakerphone. "I cannot believe neither of you are answering your phones," Rigby groused. "I'm going to tell you the same thing I told your partner. Your asses better not be on US 17 traveling north, or you'll be enforcing parking meters for the next year. Do you hear me? Marshals nabbed Miller and the Brethren's first lieutenant an hour ago without incident. Be at the station at one o'clock. I'm sure you don't mind giving up your Saturday afternoon to formally arrest Wayne Miller and process him. Don't be late. Parking meters. I mean it."

He looked up at Locke who nodded. "Verbatim." He took Sawyer's phone from his hand and set it on the nightstand beside his. "I'm wide awake now, and I'm in the mood to celebrate." Locke returned his hand to Sawyer's dick.

Adrenaline pumped through Sawyer's body, and his blood pooled south, making his dick hard as a spike. "What should we do?" Sawyer thought of all the sordid fantasies he'd played in his mind during the past three weeks. A wry smile played across his lips when his brain locked on the one thing he wanted most. "Ever heard of a rim job?"

"I've heard of a rim shot," Locke countered.

Sawyer smirked. "Similar concept. Get on your hands and knees and put your ass in the air."

Locke's eyebrow shot up. "What goes around and around my asshole before it sinks inside it?"

"My tongue. For now."

Unraveling Royce Locke by introducing him to all the pleasures his body held became Sawyer's new favorite passion. Holding the man in his arms afterward while they drifted to sleep became his new favorite way to celebrate life—something he stopped doing two years ago. In the calm space between wakefulness and sleep, Sawyer could almost feel Vic's blessing.

CHAPTER 29

THE WAYNE MILLER WHO STARED INTO SAWYER'S EYES IN THE INTERVIEW room wasn't the same man he met nearly three weeks ago. He'd dropped all pretenses since then. He'd shaved his head and added a new tattoo to his forearm which probably announced his commitment to the Brethren. The skin looked dry and irritated because Miller kept absently picking at the scabs while facing off with Sawyer across the table. There was no humanity in his cold, shark eyes, and the arrogant grin on his face said he was proud of what he'd done, and if given the opportunity, he'd do it all again. Unfortunately, juries would require more than just Sawyer's opinion about Miller's body language and demeanor. They liked physical evidence tying the accused to the crime, but they especially loved it when cops obtained a confession that corroborated the evidence.

"I want a lawyer," Miller said, pushing the yellow legal pad and pen back across the table. "How many times do I have to tell you? I don't have a fucking thing to say to you pigs." He pointed to Gillian Babineaux who sat on Sawyer's left side. "I especially don't have any-thing to say to her, except isn't there a field of cotton somewhere that needs picking?"

Locke, who had been standing in the corner observing, lunged forward. Gillian raised her hand, stopping him in his tracks without breaking eye contact with Miller. "Don't darken your record on my account, Detective. I've had this bullshit tossed at me for as long as I can remember, and yet, 'still I rise.' It's also clear the double homicide for which he's accused is a hate crime."

"Georgia doesn't have a current hate crime law, dumb bitch," Miller snarled.

"I don't need to have a state law to report you to the FBI," Babineaux repeated. "You're the one who fled across state lines after committing a hate crime which involved the federal government in your apprehension. Who's the dumb bitch now? Do you think I won't hand you back over to the men with the shiny, federal badges? I won't hesitate. I'm sure the FBI have many questions about your time with the Brethren. Regardless, you'll never taste freedom again." Babineaux rose to her feet and gestured for Sawyer to do the same. "We're done here. Miller doesn't want to play nice, and neither do we."

"I'll beat this rap and be back on the streets in no time. You have nothing on me."

Babineaux stopped halfway to the door then turned back around to face him. "Bet me. I have everything I need to prosecute you right here in Chatham County. It won't take long for the feds to file charges against you. Either way, you will be lucky if you see a trial courtroom in a year. That's a very long time to sit behind bars. A lot can happen in that time."

"Are you fucking threatening me?" Miller trembled all over, but Sawyer recalled the remarks he'd made to Marla and knew it was caused by fear, not rage.

"I'm stating facts. Ask your attorney how quickly the court systems move," Babineaux reported. She looked at us. "Call for transport. Take him to the county jail until the feds are ready to take him into custody."

"Wait! I'll talk."

"You've invoked your Miranda rights. You can't talk without your attorney present."

"I changed my mind."

"And be able to claim you were coerced later? I don't think so," Babineaux said firmly. She jerked her head, signaling she wanted Sawyer and Locke to follow her outside.

"Feds, really?" Locke asked once he shut the door. "You might've been able to get a confession out of him."

"Stop pouting, Detective Locke."

"I don't pout, ma'am."

Sawyer bit his bottom lip to keep from responding or touching Locke. It was hard enough to resist before he knew what Locke looked like sleeping on a pillow beside him or smiling proudly at him over the breakfast he'd made for them. It would be a struggle he'd happily combat daily to have this man in his life.

"Be real. Miller was a guest of the Brethren for the past few weeks and was arrested with their first lieutenant. This is the feds' first real chance to crack the organization wide open. You think they'll let us keep Wayne if he can help them?"

"Damn it," Locke said. "I know you're right."

"I usually am. Tell you what, I'll let you transport Miller to lockup so you can dance with the devil one more time."

Sawyer held up his forefinger when an idea occurred to him. "I think I know just the audiobook I can play on my phone."

Locke's smile was big and beautiful, making Sawyer want to pull him close and kiss him. "I'll take the long route, so he gets maximum enjoyment."

Babineaux's laughter and clicking of her high heels echoed off the sterile gray corridor. "I'll keep you in the loop, gentlemen," she tossed over her shoulder.

"I think I have a crush on her," Sawyer said.

"Hey now," Locke said. "I'm standing right here."

"Don't pout. It's a harmless crush born out of mad respect."

"I don't pout."

Their gazes met and held. Locke's gray eyes were darker than usual, reminding Sawyer of the clouds that had forced them inside to find alternative plans the previous evening. They hadn't known each other long, but he recognized the want and need staring back at him. Awareness stirred inside him, making his fingers twitch to slide inside Locke's blond hair and mess it up. He loved the way the strands fell forward around Locke's face when he leaned over Sawyer while moving deep inside him.

"You know what we need?" Locke asked.

"Pretty sure I do."

"Lunch. We haven't eaten since I made breakfast this morning. Breakfast wasn't much to hold us over for a long day like today."

Sawyer wasn't sure if Locke would be offended if he called his breakfast adorable, but it was. No one had ever made him slices of toast with poached eggs in the center. He'd called them birds in a nest and said his aunt Tipsy used to make them for him. Sawyer had lifted a brow at his aunt's nickname and Locke assured him she had earned it just how he'd guessed. Sawyer had eaten three nests and had slipped Bones one of the circles of toast Locke had cut to make room for an egg. It was the least he could do for locking the cat out of the bedroom overnight.

"I'm not that hungry." *For food.*

"Yeah, I guess it can wait until after we take Miller to county. Do you want to take him right now or let him stew a bit?"

They decided to let him sweat it out for an hour while they chatted, shook hands, and exchanged high fives with the detectives who were working. Miller was caught and Marla was safe and on her way home with her mother. It was a damn good day. It was after three when Sawyer and Locke marched a cuffed and shackled Miller out of the precinct. As they neared the Charger, Sawyer heard a guttural shriek, a war cry of sorts, erupt from the crowd that had gathered outside.

"You killed my son! I hope you rot in hell."

Sawyer jerked his head to the right and saw that Mrs. Benson had pushed through the crowd and was running in their direction.

"Keep your fucking mouth shut, Miller. Don't you dare say a word that will break that woman's heart more than you already have." Locke looked at Sawyer. "Go take care of her. I got him," he said, propelling Miller faster toward the car.

Sawyer broke away and intercepted Mrs. Benson, catching her in his arms. She sobbed brokenly against his chest. "He's going to pay, Mrs. Benson. I promise."

He glanced toward the Charger and saw Locke open the back door. Miller grinned evilly when he turned so Locke could place him in the back seat. Just as Miller started to bend, his head exploded, and Locke was thrown back onto the pavement. The world went completely still for a heartbeat then mass pandemonium broke out.

The crowd screamed and scattered, trampling anyone in their path. The officers went into live-shooter mode by pulling out their weapons, taking cover, and looking for the threat. Sawyer shoved Mrs. Benson behind the nearest car, drew his gun, then took off running toward Locke, not giving a damn about being in someone's crosshairs. He couldn't leave his…partner lying there with no help.

"Locke! Locke!" he shouted as he sprinted across the pavement. His boots felt heavy, making it seem like he was running in place. "Locke!" he yelled again, dropping to the ground beside him. Locke blinked and moved his lips, but no words came out. Was he shot in the lungs? Locke's face was covered with blood, but none of it appeared to be his. Relief flooded through Sawyer when he saw that Royce was shot in the shoulder, not his heart or lungs. An inch or two lower, and Locke would've died before he hit the ground. It was most likely shock and horrific pain that made it impossible for him to speak.

Grateful he'd skipped the shoulder holster that morning, Sawyer whipped his shirt over his head and pressed it to Locke's shoulder to staunch the blood until it was safe enough for the EMTs to arrive. Blue ran over and dropped down beside him, gun up and at the ready while he surveyed the area

"Locke, you okay?"

Locke's teeth started chattering, and he tried to reply with stuttering words that wouldn't form.

"It's okay, Royce. Help is on the way."

"What the fuck happened?" Blue asked. "You think the Brethren took him out so he couldn't talk?"

Sawyer looked around and saw that the only personnel around them were all uniform officers and detectives. Sirens sounded around them, but he couldn't tell if they were coming or going. "We need an ambulance, Blue," he shouted.

Blue radioed for assistance again and learned that an ambulance was in route.

Chief Rigby dropped to the pavement and covered Locke with a space blanket. "How is he?" She handed a clean shirt to Sawyer to put on too. It was a size too small, but it was better than going to the hospital half naked.

"C-c-chief," Locke said, fighting through the shock. "B-b-bear c-c-claw."

Rigby laughed in spite of the situation. "You can have a dozen once we get you taken care of, okay? Help is on the way." The look she exchanged with Sawyer acknowledged how damn lucky they were.

Sawyer rode in the back of the ambulance with Locke, whose pallor and blue lips scared the fuck out of him.

"Your partner is going to be okay," the EMT said as they rushed into the hospital—the same place Vic had gone for cancer treatments that hadn't been enough to combat his aggressive tumor.

Not again. Please, God. Not again.

They wouldn't let Sawyer back in the room with Locke, nor would they give him any information. Alone, all he could do was remember how horrific losing someone important to him felt. His heart pounded and his chest squeezed painfully, but he wasn't having a heart attack. Sawyer's face felt numb as his lungs laboriously worked to pull oxygen into them. He recognized what was happening to him.

Breathe in. Hold. Release. He kept chanting it to himself to regulate his breathing and work through the panic attack.

When Rigby showed up, she learned that they'd rushed Locke into surgery. The shot went clean through and caused significant damage to the muscles and tendons in his left shoulder. He had been lucky. So fucking lucky. Locke's family arrived not long after Rigby, and she introduced them to Sawyer before updating them on everything she knew.

The Locke clan all looked alike with various shades of blond hair and gray eyes. They gathered across the waiting room and looked at him with a mixture of hostility and mistrust, reminding Sawyer of the first day he and Locke met. Had he only known Locke for less than a month? Less than thirty days to remind Sawyer of what it felt like to really live again and how terrifying loss—or the potential of it—was?

Sawyer recalled the bruises on Locke's torso and the realization that Locke knew a lot about domestic violence and abuse. Which one of them was responsible for the bruises? Sawyer returned their glares with one of his own and the tension rose in the room until it neared the breaking point. One false move and it would all go up in flames.

Stein showed up looking frazzled and sick with worry. She made a beeline for Sawyer.

"I don't have any updates on Locke," he said when she dropped in the seat next to him.

"I'm here for you," she said then surprised him by reaching for his hand. "I've known Royce Locke since we were six years old. It will take more than a bullet through the shoulder to end him."

"You've known him that long?" he asked, desperate to think of something other than Locke on the operating table.

"Grew up next to each other." She glanced at Locke's family across the room. "It's amazing he turned out so good coming from that lot."

Sawyer thought of the healing bruises and his anger soared again. "I don't think they like me."

"They don't like anyone who is different than them. They don't care for me either because I rejected their idea of what a woman should want. A woman's job is to keep house, make her husband happy, and have babies. I'm not saying I won't do those things, but I'm not giving up my identity to make it happen."

"Interesting." The Locke family dynamics intrigued him, but he wouldn't ask Stein questions. It wasn't her place to tell him.

"What's more interesting is that you see me as your adversary."

"I don't."

"Maybe you don't now, but you did. There has never been anything between Locke and me. No, I couldn't fall for the good brother," she said wistfully, glancing across the room again. "You're good for Locke, and I'm pulling for you. Hang in there, okay?"

Unsure what else to do, Sawyer nodded. Stein patted his knee then rose from her chair and crossed the room. Sawyer was too lost in thought to pay attention to which brother had garnered her attention.

Hang in there.

He thought he'd been ready to love again, but today proved too much for him to handle. The scene kept replaying on an endless loop in his mind. If the trajectory of the bullet hadn't been altered by passing through Miller's skull, then Locke would be dead. Sawyer tortured himself over and over. Tears burned the back of his lids, but he held tight to his fear to release in private later.

A surgeon wearing dark scrubs came and spoke to the family and Rigby, who'd stayed even though the hunt for the shooter was underway. Her phone frequently rang with updates, which she stepped out of the room to take. Sawyer didn't ask her about them because he could only think about Locke, and how close he'd come to losing him. Locke's family showed very little change in emotion, but Rigby's smile told him everything he'd needed to know.

Sawyer rose to his feet and headed for the exit.

"Detective Key," Rigby called after him. "A word, please."

Sawyer felt the telltale signs that the tethers holding back his rage and fear were breaking. It started with a tiny tremor then built into full-body quakes. He had no intention of talking to Rigby in his current mood. He needed to be on the street looking for the person who'd nearly killed Locke.

"Detective Key, stop!" she said authoritatively. Sawyer jerked to a halt, allowing her to catch up. "I am too old and out of shape to be running after your ass." Rigby put her hands on her hips and pinned him with a stern gaze. "Don't you want to hear the news about Locke?"

"I could tell by your expression that his surgery went well. I'm going to go where I'm needed now."

"I think you're needed back inside the hospital," Rigby countered. "Locke will want to see you."

"He'd rather hear we caught the man who shot him."

"Then you can tell him we have the shooter in custody," Rigby said. "He turned himself in without incident."

"What? Who?"

"David Wembley."

Sawyer's mouth fell open in shock. "Caroline's father?" Then he recalled the vehemence in Mr. Wembley's voice when he told Sawyer and Locke he would've killed Wayne had he known Wayne was abusing his daughter. People toss that kind of phrase out all the time, but David Wembley had meant it.

"Former Army Ranger sniper. He still had his service .308 Winchester and decided to get justice for his daughter and DeShaun."

"And nearly killed Locke in the process," Sawyer bit out. "I can't be here, Chief. Locke's family doesn't want me there, and I sure as fuck don't want to be around them."

"Fuck them," she vehemently said, shocking Sawyer once more. "Locke will not want to wake up with only his family around. They're not close."

Sawyer hated the idea of disappointing Locke, but he had to put some distance between them to preserve his sanity. "They'll restrict his visitors to family only immediately after surgery. I'll come back tomorrow afternoon and see him."

Disappointment in Rigby's eyes made his stomach acid churn. "At least let me drive you back to the station since you rode here in the ambulance." He'd forgotten about that but would've realized it once he reached the parking lot and ordered a Lyft.

"Look," Rigby said once they were in her car headed toward the precinct. "This world has gone crazy, and ugliness is spilling out into the streets from every direction. The only term that comes close to describing the atmosphere is ground zero. There is violence and evil lurking everywhere around us, and here we are in the epicenter of it all. I know you're rattled; we all are. I need you in this fight, Key. Locke needs you too. It's why I planted the idea of you working for me when we met at the fundraiser. I could've promoted someone from inside the PD to be Locke's partner, but I knew you were the one he needed."

"How?" Sawyer asked.

"Intuition. I wasn't wrong about you, was I?"

Sawyer wanted to say yes and pretend he regretted the day he'd met Locke, but he couldn't lie. "No, Chief."

"That's what I thought," she said, pulling into the precinct parking lot. "Get some rest, then go see Locke. I need to go home and ask Leticia to make a dozen bear claws." That made him smile at least.

"Take care, Chief."

After retrieving his car, Sawyer swung by the liquor store for a bottle of Jameson. He had only intended to drink enough to help him sleep, but he kept drinking shots with every horrific memory that popped up. It was the worst drinking game ever. Recalling the way Vic looked the day he died. *Take a drink.* Miller's head exploding and Locke falling backward. *Take a drink.* Locke with blood and bone and brains splattered all over his face. *Take a drink.* The desolation and black hole his life had become after Vic's funeral? *Take a drink.* Remembering the promise he had made to Vic to love again. *Take two drinks.*

And since he hadn't eaten since breakfast, it didn't take him long to become shit-faced and pass out face-first in his sofa cushions.

A loud hammering woke Sawyer some hours later. At first, he thought it was his brain, then he realized it was coming from his front door. He figured they would go away if he lay on the couch long enough, but the pounding only got louder.

Sawyer pried his eyes open and noticed bright sunshine flooding his living room, which meant it had to be noon or later. He rolled off the couch and onto the floor with a jarring thud that nearly made him puke. He got to his hands and knees then used the coffee table as support to stand up on his feet. The pounding on the front door stopped, but his cell phone started ringing somewhere in the house, which meant his visitor had resorted to a different tactic.

"Coming," he rasped out, but his voice sounded so low no one besides him could hear it.

Sawyer stumbled and tripped into the door then fumbled with the locks without looking through the peephole. He opened the door and stared in shock. "But you…"

"Were fucking shot," Locke said tersely. He pointed to his arm in the sling just in case Sawyer needed proof. "Where the hell have you been?"

"How are you here? You're supposed to be in the hospital."

"Christ," Locke said, waving his good arm in front of him. "You fucking reek. What kind of rotgut were you drinking?"

"Jameson. Not rotgut. Why aren't you in the hospital?" Sawyer asked, swaying a little.

"You weren't there, you big idiot. I knew you were home freaking out about my 'near-death experience.'" Locke did finger quotes with his good hand. "Rigby said you were as white as a ghost when she drove you to your car last night. I didn't die, Sawyer. I'm right here."

"You should be resting. How is it possible they discharged you so soon?"

"I couldn't rest because I was worried about you. I checked myself out against doctor's orders, but I have antibiotics, pain meds, and care instructions. I also have maybe five bear claws left out of the dozen Chief brought me." Sawyer noticed the white paper bag Locke clutched in the hand sticking out of the sling. "I gotta tell you, it was almost worth getting shot. The doctor was pissed, but I assured her I have someone who could look after me and make sure I get my meds on time."

"Who the fuck is that? Stein?"

Lock smirked and shook his head. "I thought you would take care of me, but I'm not so sure now. I'm the one who got shot, but you're the one who's seconds away from falling on his face. Can I come in? My energy is starting to fade now that my worry for you has turned into irritation."

For the first time since he opened the door, Sawyer really looked at Locke and noticed his pale skin, pinched mouth, and the tiny cuts all over his face where bone fragments had pierced his flesh. Thank God he'd been wearing sunglasses or else he might've lost an eye. That was when Sawyer noticed Locke's wounded expression. God, he was such a sucker for wounded things. "I'm so sorry," Sawyer said, stepping aside so Locke could come in. "Do you want anything to eat. Is it time for your meds?"

"I just want to get cleaned up so I don't smell like a hospital. Then I want to sleep in your comfortable bed beside you. We can work this out later."

"Can we now?" Sawyer asked, a hint of humor in his voice. "I need to clean up too. My mouth tastes like I licked a toilet or something."

Following Sawyer toward the master bedroom, Locke groused, "Don't you dare kiss me with that mouth."

Once Sawyer brushed his teeth and stepped beneath the shower spray, Locke was singing a different tune. Careful to keep Locke's bandaged shoulder turned away from the water, Sawyer carefully washed Locke's hair and body before taking care of his own needs. Then he held the man he'd nearly lost the day before.

"I'm sorry I freaked out and bailed on you," Sawyer whispered before kissing him. "I just saw you go down and thought you were dead. One minute we're talking about lunch and you're looking at me with those fuck-me eyes, and the next…" Sawyer's words drifted off, the dam of emotions broke, and he started to cry. "I can't go through that kind of pain again." Sawyer straightened and started to pull away, but Locke tightened his one-armed grip, holding him close while he worked through it.

"I was going to save this chat for later, but I think we need to do it now." Locke kissed Sawyer's lips. "I know why you left the hospital, and I understand, but I came here because I'm going to fight for us. Me, the no-strings-attached guy, is standing before you and begging you not to give in to that fear." Locke took a shaky breath and said, "I never wanted the strings; I never thought I was capable of wanting strings. I want to know your favorite food, music, books, and movies." Sawyer trembled as Locke rephrased some of the things he'd said out of irritation on the first day. Locke kissed his lips and kept talking. "I want you as my friend and lover today, tomorrow, and maybe much longer. We deserve this, and I refuse to let either of us throw in the towel because it's scary. They call you relentless, but do you know what they call me?" Sawyer shook his head. "Fearless. I choose you over the fear of the unknown, Sawyer. I need you to choose me over the fear of loss. One step at a time. We can do it, baby." Locke kissed his lips again. "What are you thinking?"

Baby. God, he loved the way it sounded. Staring into Locke's eyes, Sawyer no longer saw hostility, he saw hope. There was only one thing Sawyer could say to the man who'd come to mean so much to him in so little time.

"It's about fucking time."

To be continued in *Devil's Hour*...

Want to be the first to know about my book releases and have access to extra content? You can sign up for my newsletter here: eepurl.com/dlhPYj

My favorite place to hang out and chat with my readers is my Facebook group. Would you like to be a member of Aimee's Dye Hards? We'd love to have you! Click here: www.facebook.com/groups/AimeesDyeHards

OTHER BOOKS BY
AIMEE NICOLE WALKER

Only You

The Fated Hearts Series

Chasing Mr. Wright, Book 1
Rhythm of Us, Book 2
Surrender Your Heart, Book 3
Perfect Fit, Book 4
Return to Me, Book 5
Always You, Book 6
Any Means Necessary, Book 7

Curl Up and Dye Mysteries

Dyeing to be Loved
Something to Dye For
Dyed and Gone to Heaven
I Do, or Dye Trying
A Dye Hard Holiday
Ride or Dye

ACKNOWLEDGMENTS

First, I need to thank my husband and children for their constant support and encouragement. It's not easy living with a writer who often disappears into a fictional world for long periods of time. They do so many things to help me out so that I can realize my dream. I love you guys more than words can ever express.

To my creative dream team, thanks seem hardly enough for all that you do. Miranda Turner of V8 Editing and Proofreading, thank you for your tireless work, feedback, and many laughs while editing. Jay Aheer of Simply Defined art is an incredible artist, and I love how she brings my words to life. Stacey Blake of Champagne Formats is also an amazing artist who does incredible interior formatting, illustrating, and designing for e-books and paperbacks. Judy Zweifel of Judy's' Proofreading and Jill Wexler do a great job of proofreading and polishing so my manuscripts shine.

To my lovely PA, Michelle Slagan. I'm not sure how I ever did this without you. I love you to the moon and back!

I want to thank the Brittany for being a wonderful critique partner and Rachel and Melinda for being amazing alpha readers. And to my betas, Kim, Dana, Jodie, Michael, and Laurel, I appreciate your honest feedback. I love working with you all.

ABOUT AIMEE NICOLE WALKER

Ever since she was a little girl, Aimee Nicole Walker entertained herself with stories that popped into her head. Now she gets paid to tell those stories to other people. She wears many titles—wife, mom, and animal lover are just a few of them. Her absolute favorite title is champion of the happily ever after. Love inspires everything she does, music keeps her sane, and coffee is the magic elixir that fuels her day.

I'd love to hear from you.

Want to connect with me? All my links are in one nifty location.
Click here:
linktr.ee/AimeeNicoleWalker

Made in the USA
Columbia, SC
13 December 2019